THE PEAKY BLINDERS

The Next Generation

Thomas Lewin

Grosvenor House
Publishing Limited

This book is published by
Grosvenor House Publishing Ltd
Link House
140 The Broadway, Tolworth, Surrey, KT6 7HT.
www.grosvenorhousepublishing.co.uk

A CIP record for this book
is available from the British Library

ISBN 978-1-80381-949-5

DEDICATION

To my beautiful wife, Betty Jean Lewin, you are with me every day, every hour. Bet, one day, I hope we can be together and dance across the world.

To our children, life is surely a box of chocolates, ain't it? We never know what's in front of us till we open the box. If only life, if only as parents we could go back and try again, how great that would be. When you make a mistake in class or at school, you can go back the next day and try again, "I never got that sum right; let's do it again."

Still, as a parent, you're allowed no such generosity; you fuck up, that's it. Both your mom and I, like most parents, I think, were swimming in a sea we had never swum in before. That word hindsight certainly is a wonderful thing. We had a crack. We took life by the horns and went with the ride, taking the rough with the smooth, riding it together and complaining to no one. We never let you know if we were skint or struggling like our parents before us. For that, I know we are both proud. Know that your mom and I loved you all. Whatever we did in life, we did it for all of us—not just the one. Have a nice life and know that you are all in a place we, and many of our peers, could only dream of. If you fail or fall, it is on your neck, just as it was on ours.

My parents never gave us a lot before, during and after the war; with the hardships experienced, they felt keeping us well-fed was an achievement; today, it is all about education, a career, and money, quite rightly. Back then, it was about surviving daily, and they felt they were entitled to their drink. We ate good, healthy food, such as the fruit of the barrer, nourishing and filling stews, pig trotters, cows' udder, tripe, and offal, which are now banned. But we all grew up healthy and strong without realising it. I saw how my dad worked and made his money, his little nuggets of advice. You can do anything in life if you set your mind to it. For all that alone, I am grateful. Your mom and I did the same and more for you and gave you the same advice.

To my brothers, Johnny, Reg, Billy, and Kenny and sisters Doris, Patty and Alma. Que sera, sera. I remember the indignity of having your betters come and inspect your house, lift your bedding, and sneer at your poverty. You were expected to bow your head and touch your forelocks; you knew no better, but slowly, inexorably, you got through it and could boast that you did it without gaining a criminal record or breaking the law. Still, I know many of you did—or wished you did. Many of you ended your days broken and defeated, hanging on by a mere thread without admitting it to your children. They, in turn, harked back to the good old days, not for them the suffering and hardship that you endured. There was ice on the inside windows, four to a bed, and even six, top and tailed under an army coat. Some even slept on the bare floor—the outside karzie on a freezing night. A bit of ox tail or bacon bones begged from the butcher to make a stew, dripping on a slice of stale bread, tripe and onions, if you were lucky, or maybe a pig trotter in vinegar, the rest of the time your bellies rumbling with emptiness. The good old days, indeed, were they fuck. Freezing nights in cold, empty houses built with dirt that encouraged the woodlice, rats and other creepy crawlies.

THIEVING IS A MUGS GAME

Make no mistake, from observation, I can tell you that thieving is a mug game; the problem is when you're the mug, you just don't realise you're a mug. Worse, I can tell you, the criminal underworld is a cesspit of corruption inhabited not just by the crooks and villains but the police and the judges, who are just as corrupt. The only problem is you have to be on the inside to see it. But theft is inbuilt into our psyche and has been since time immemorable, right back to the first caveman who nicked the leg of a dinosaur of the caveman two caves down, the great train robbers dropped on the biggest tickle in the country, two and a half million quid, they were heroes to much of the country. Theoretically, they were set up for life, every villain's dream, the big tickle. Yet they fucked it, and worse, they, in turn, got fucked by every friend and their uncle. Thirty years in the nick, they came out penniless, worn out, and broken.

The police in Birmingham were notoriously bent, taking backhanders in all directions whilst helping themselves to any stolen loot found when nicking the villains who had nicked it in the first place. I don't think things have changed much. They are still bent; they just changed tactics. The current bullying, rape and murder allegations are just one aspect of the widespread corruption. You need to look no further than the current post office scandal playing out now in our country, thousands of decent, honest, innocent people accused of theft and fraud and the evidence made up, making them plead guilty or/and pay monies back that they hadn't stolen. No one listened, no one gave a shit until a television drama brought it to light. Boy did the government scramble, yet the fact is, in this country, if you are accused of a crime, especially a criminal act, you are guilty before you get to court.

RICHARD VON COUDENHOV-KALERGI

Richard Nikolaou, the Count of Coudenove-Kalergi, was an Austrian-Japanese politician, philosopher, and a key figure in European integration. He was pivotal as the inaugural president of the Pan-European Union for 49 years.

The Kalergi plan is or was a far-right anti-Semitic white genocide conspiracy theory that claims that Richard von Coudenhove-Kalergi concocted a plan before and during the war years to mix white Europeans with other races via mass immigration; it was promoted in aristocratic European social circles. The conspiracy theory is most often associated with European groups and parties.

In the conspiracy theory section of Kalergis's book, he predicted that a mixed race of people of the future would arise. The man of the future will be mixed race; today's races and classes will gradually disappear, communities will be broken up, and this will leave one ruling Jewish elite. The whole idea of mixing the races would be to promote confusion and fear, ultimately leading to the destruction of the white people, leaving people more easily managed and controllable. Ludicrous as it might seem, many indigenous people in England are saying exactly that.

FOREWORD

My granddad became a peaky blinder, earning a living as best he could by becoming a bookies runner. These times were a million miles from how I live and where I live today. However, they had made a living, I would have had some sympathy; they were different times, and poverty was an everyday occurrence.

For that reason, I'm a bit surprised that Professor Carl Chinn, the well-known historian from Birmingham and an authority on Birmingham and the Peaky Blinders, expressed his contempt for his great grandfather, a slogger and Peaky Blinder from the late 1800s named Edward Derrick.

The contrast in lifestyles is evident. Although Carl's parents were from Aston and Sparkbrook, he was brought up in relative comfort, and his parents owned betting shops. From there, he studied history at Birmingham University. I know Carl and have a lot of respect for him. Still, from his life and upbringing, especially the heady heights of university, I just wonder if he has any concept of what life must have been like for his grandfather. I know because my two youngest children went to private school and university. Whether it's lefty brainwashing or liberalism, they left with a totally different outlook than when they went in.

Carl's great-great-grandfather, Edward Derek, came from a long line of a criminal family; his father and brothers were equally in constant conflict with the law, and for that reason alone, he deserves some sympathy. How hard does anyone think it must be to turn your life around from that environment? As a child aged eleven, he was placed in some form of reformatory school for boys under fourteen who had technically committed some offence like begging or stealing. In October 1894, whilst still a child, he was sentenced to seven days in prison for stealing five loaves. Five loaves, for god's sake. Why would a child want to steal five loaves?

Politicians nick computers or tablets from government offices. Well, they don't nick; they 'borrow'. That way, it salves their conscience and absolves them of guilt. I've known a few cops who have thieved before becoming cops. We all make mistakes, but let's not forget that, from an early age, I only ever saw or knew bent cops, even at 17. If the cops stopped me, they would nick something from my van, watch, etc. To me, it was the norm.

As I got older, I could feel the difference in attitude in the atmosphere. I could never put my finger on it. It was only years later I started to put the pieces together. Many of the judges in England are masons, as are most senior police. Fine, you might ask, but then why have your own lodge? What have you got to hide? The Masons boast that they are not a secretive sect, bollocks. They are very secretive. I had three friends in the masons; I only knew after they had died, and their wives told me a few things. They were mainly involved in it for their own benefit; the charity side was just the guise. These judges have regular meet-ups in Birmingham where they discuss cases over lunch. There is nothing wrong with that, you might say. Unless they decide the outcome of a case before it even reaches the court.

So, you don't believe me then? Look at the case of Kenny Noye, the gold bullion dealer accused of murdering a cop who was surveying his house in a balaclava, as you do. He was found not guilty, quite rightly. The cops were spitting blood. A few years later, the cops got him again for murder; in his first court appearance before a judge, he gave the masonic distress signal. Grasping the tie knot.

It was only years later that that same judge commented on his "Noyes" appearance and his distress signal ("there was no way I was going to help him on this one"), which begs the question: what would he have helped him on? Did Noye give that distress signal in his first murder charge against the policeman? Why is no one carrying out a serious investigation into how many masons there are in society and what positions they hold? Hmm? How many people are going before the judges and giving that same distress signal today?

My MP Andrew Mitchell was chief whip when a policeman on duty outside Downing Street accused Mitchell of calling him a pleb, quite apart from two or three police getting nicked and imprisoned for perjury, altering statements, etc, in order to help their colleague. It was still deemed acceptable for the constable to argue and fight the case in court. In his summing up, the judge turned to the jury, pointed to the cop and "said look at him. Does this policeman look intelligent enough to lie on oath?" (They lie on oath all the fucking time). The judge then brought in the balance of probabilities. Apparently, Mitchell had called a policeman on duty two years previously, a similar word (not the same word). He, therefore, guided the jury that, based on probabilities, Andrew Mitchell did or could have called the cop a pleb. Of course, the sheep, sorry, the jury, found Mitchell guilty. He had to borrow a million quid to pay his costs.

If that's not enough to make you wonder how corrupt the police and the law are, it doesn't take a lot of thought to ask why a serving MP, a member of parliament, a chief whip and a former captain in the army, brought up in a privileged upbringing, should have the sense to tape record a conversation with two police officers who arrived to take a statement from him. That statement differed from the one Andrew Mitchell taped in his office. Now, if they can do that to an MP, what can they get away with, with us poor bastards from the so-called slums?

EYES WIDE SHUT

My great granddad was the famous painter and artist Henry Lark Pratt from Derbyshire, whose works are in demand worldwide and whose paintings hang in Chatsworth house. Trained in the potteries as a porcelain artist, he branched out into painting landscapes around Derbyshire. A very well-known and respected individual and artist, he produced nine children, one of whom was a girl named Fanny who, following a good education, trained and became a teacher.

Fanny married my grandfather Frederick Charles Hipkiss, a skilled joiner, as were all the Hipkiss', going back generations and spreading throughout the black country and Birmingham. Maybe Fred was doing some carpentry work around Derbyshire, but at any rate, he wooed and courted Fanny. They got married and, for whatever reason, moved back to Birmingham, Summer Lane of all places.

After a few short years and six children, including my mom, Alma, and Ada. The eldest, then Freddie, David, Thomas Albert and John. As a teacher and the daughter of a famous artist, your life can go only two ways, in theory, either steadily along or upwards with the social flow. In the so-called slums of Summer Lane, your life can go three ways: steadily along, upwards, or you can sink.

Whatever happened, whatever went wrong, Frederick Hipkiss ran out, did a runner, disappeared off the face of the earth and was never heard from again. In those days, the late 1800s and early 1900s, no help was available. If you were destitute, you either starved or resorted to the workhouse, a fate almost as bad as death. It was no life, just an existence, working for your keep and a bed, along with the rest of the lowest of the low, the weak, beaten and downtrodden. Even a bed was a luxury; many times, when drunk, a line strung across the room to throw your arms over just enough to lift your upper body off the floor whence you tried to sleep. Hence, the expression hung over. For a few pennies more, you could have a bug-ridden mattress.

In the 1911 census, self-filled in those days, Fanny described herself as a laundress with no children and no husband. Working in a laundrette must have been one of the most soul-destroying jobs on earth at that time. To state that she had no children when she clearly had six shows that something must have been desperately wrong, either with her mind or was it more likely, the terrifying fear that her children could have been taken from her. At any rate, Fanny died at an early age in life with some illness I was never made aware of. My mom, Alma, was left to look after her siblings as best she could. We can only wonder if my grandmother Fanny, the daughter of a famous artist and a no doubt respected teacher, ended up in a pauper grave somewhere in Birmingham along with thousands of others.

THE PEAKY BLINDERS

I can't deny it, my granddad, John, was a Peaky Blinder. He was born in the bottom half of Garrison Lane in the late 1800s. This was a time when Birmingham was a small community, and it was easy for everyone to know each other. Back then, there was a boozer on every corner; you would drink in the Garrison, then maybe spend the night having a little pub crawl before finishing off at the Garrison.

The Peaky Blinders were a new and growing phenomenon around Birmingham's inner city. The Peaky's used the popular sneaky method of sewing razor blades into the peaks of their flat caps; in a confrontation, they could whip their hats off and slash their opponent across the face, taking them completely by surprise and causing blood to run into their eyes before giving them a smacking then doing a runner. That was the legend, but like everything else, the Peaky Blinders were just a trend, a fashion; much like the teddy boys of the 60s, not all were violent. Another favoured method was the belt buckle. But everyone wore heavy buckle belts; it was a requirement for their heavy work in the foundries and mines of Yorkshire, Sheffield and Birmingham. Belts were made of very heavy leather with a big and equally heavy buckle; together, they made a very fearsome and effective weapon. The streets were violent, with people prowling them looking for trouble; many carried a cutthroat razor, a favourite weapon of choice for the Glasgow Gorbals Gangsters.

A buckle belt and a cutthroat razor were quite legal and effective. Very few took the risk of carrying a knife, knowing the ultimate risk; it only needed one little mistake, one miscalculation, to be roped in on a murder charge, with hanging being the consequence of it. Violence was one thing, murder another, especially in a gang. Most sluggers and Peaky Blinders preferred to be in gangs, where you could cause damage and hide. It was a lesson learned from the many political gatherings around the country.

A constantly empty belly, little or no education, and very bleak prospects were great ingredients for violence, thuggery, and thievery. There was no such thing as a radio. It wasn't invented until the early 1900s. For entertainment at night, you played cards or board games; the middle classes had their pianos and sang along, and the lowest working classes had the streets or the boozers.

My granddad never sewed the razors into his peaked cap; having learned to box, he was quite capable of looking after himself in a fight, but being only eight stone, he carried a heavy buckle belt for protection. The streets around the bullring were notorious for their gangs, many consisting of very strong and hard lads brought together by their loyalty to their streets and each other. It was also for protection against other gangs and the police who were victimising them daily. The Irish, who had come over in the early 1800s to escape their poverty only to find themselves in another form of poverty, also formed gangs mainly to protect themselves against the English gangs and the police, who mainly preferred to side with the English gangs in any fighting. Even with the police, there was prejudice against the Irish being suspected of belonging to or having an affinity with the IRA or just generally being anti-British.

You might have a fight every Saturday night and make up over a Sunday lunchtime pint of mild or bitter. There were only three main breweries in Birmingham: Mitchell's and Butlers of Camp Hill, Ansell's of Aston Cross, and Davenports. Davenports was first established in 1829 by John Davenport. His son, also named John, moved the brewery into Bath Row in 1952. In addition to owning several public houses, the company became famous for its beer at-home service. If there were two things you had as a favourite, it was your football team or favourite beer; the villa and Ansell's brewery won by a mile, mainly because we all knew Ansell's was sited specifically over its supply of spring water, a well, deep below ground with a limitless supply. Its mild was dark and rich, its bitter clear and sharp. All because of that spring water. HP Sauce was set up directly next door using the same spring water for the same reason.

On different days of the week, when the smell from the beer making mixed with the smell from the HP sauce, it wafted across the whole of Aston and Nechells, stretching to Summer Lane and the centre of town. London had its bow bells; we had HP sauce and brewery. Cockneys would boast about being born within the sound of bow bells. If you didn't hear the bells, weren't born within the sound of the bow bells, then you weren't a true Cockney. Well, we had our HP sauce and Ansell's brewery. If you were not in between smelling distance of either, then you weren't a true Brummie; we all stood proud in that knowledge. Those outside probably boasted about its absence.

Birmingham was granted city status in 1889 by Queen Victoria following its rapid growth. Originally part of Warwickshire in the Saxon 6th century, Birmingham was one small settlement surrounded by thick forest. The home (ham) of the tribe, called after its leader, Birm or Beorma, is worth some twenty shillings. It became independent in its own right but still retained the feel of a village. Farmers brought their pigs and cattle down from the surrounding farms past the Old Crown in Digbeth and into the abattoir to be slaughtered. Sheep could be seen numbering fifty or more being herded down to the abattoir - different smells assailed the nostrils from every different angle and, according to the day, the smell of straw and cow shit. On other days, the smell of pigs. On market days, it was the fresh smell of fruit mixed with flowers. Children and grown-ups would visit the town to see the sights and be assailed by the varied smells. Flower sellers, like old ma Sutton, would shout their wares, barrow boys shouting to come and 'get yer spuds', all trying to outdo the other.

It was a time of excitement and unrest in equal measures, both political and religious; thugs roamed the streets in gangs called sluggers. They had nothing, no future, no money; all they had were their reputations built up within the community in which they lived. Bored and looking for excitement, excitement and tension hung in the air at all times, especially for idle minds on a Friday and Saturday night, for the thugs with no brains that manifested themselves in only one way: to have a fight, a scrap, to alleviate the boredom and the poverty. Or just to keep your reputation from some of the wild and many thugs that walked the streets looking to make money or just to have a fight.

Birmingham was teeming with thugs and sluggers looking to battle it out; with anybody or everybody, coppers were the main target, the enemy. They were seen as the protector of the upper and middle class, a way to establish your reputation as a hard case, but you had to hit and run, get away because if they caught you, got you down the clink, you paid a heavy price with a good belting with truncheons, canes, and/or the cat-o-nine tails. Gangs hung about in large numbers, partly out of boredom, self-protection, partly intimidation.

In Sparkhill and Bordesley, large numbers of Irish had settled seeking work as navvies, having had to escape from Ireland due to the potato famines and poverty; they were equally determined to fight for their patch, and beyond, they didn't give a fuck who they fought. Paddies loved a good fight. Even better was a good fight after they'd got a few pints of Guinness down their necks.

These acts of major violence were not just happening in Birmingham. It was happening throughout the country. Manchester, Liverpool, and London all had their gangs isolated, segregated and separated by their class, but without a doubt, Birmingham was considered the most violent. Sir Robert Peel, the then-home secretary, facing constant concerns and protests from the middle classes, formed the police force, which quickly became known as the Peelers, bobbies, or Coppers. The only problem was no one did anything to help the problem for the lower working class. There was nothing: no leisure facilities, no recreation facilities, no parks, no green fields to play in. All they had was rubble-strewn bomb pecks in which they could play a game called pitch n toss, a minor gambling game which involved a group of youths who would throw pennies to a mark. The one whose coin was the closest won the right to toss all the coins into the air; those that landed heads up won the money, and the game continued until all the money had gone. Worse, this was usually played on Sundays, as they worked six days a week. It was their only day of leisure, that and Saturday nights.

At first, the police and council turned a blind eye to these minor gambling activities by the lower riff-raff, merely showing their presence by walking the streets, usually alone on their beat and nodding hello as they passed. However, following constant complaints from the middle classes and the local clergy, who didn't work six days a week and considered Sunday a day of rest and prayer, it was felt something had to be done. Worse, these lads were causing a nuisance by swimming in the local canals, obstructing the public with their pigeon flying; others were obstructing footpaths by setting up boot blacking pitches or begging. Being young, with plenty of testosterone, it can only be wondered that these lads and even their parents felt the world and the law were against them.

Punishments were harsh. For nicking a loaf of bread, you could be sent to prison and hard labour for six months. For other crimes, you could be locked up and, without a second notice, be deported to Australia. The very thought or threat of that is surely enough to terrify anyone, with rubbish slave-type wages in filthy smoking factories and workplaces, it could only be wondered at the amount of resentment and rebelliousness amongst the lower orders. Very few could afford decent clothes. Many walked about with no shoes or ill-fitting shoes, hand-me-downs (if they were lucky), no socks, no underpants and skid marks in their pants; silver snot streaks were the norm on their sleeves due to lack of handkerchiefs. They were unknown. Food was haphazard, with many going without regular food or even days between eating.

It was within this atmosphere that the gangs formed and grew. The police were the enemy, together with those stuck-up middle classes who despised them and looked down their noses at them. Can it be any wonder that their attitude toward them prevailed, their only leisure time being a Sunday, yet they were demonised for a bit of light-hearted gambling on the bomb pecks around the area? Already denigrated as thieves, ruffians and cowards, they felt backed into a corner, victimised and alienated from the rest of society. What had once been an acceptable hobby, once ignored by the cops, now became illegal and a target for the police. There was felt to be no other way than to keep tight together and be loyal to the street and the gangs you grew into, your only defence being the bricks and brickbats in abundance on the bomb pecks.

Your street was your back garden, living room, entertainment area, home, and woe betide anyone, police or stranger who came within your domain. Your loyalties were unquestionable. We were the scum of the earth, and for reasons we knew not why, even if we did not have a criminal record, we were treated as criminals, thieves and ruffians. When one of us got nicked, we saw it as our right to defend ourselves against the enemy with whatever we could grab hold of—bricks, stones, and even mud. If any of those posh middle classes happened to be in the area, we would think nothing of brick-batting them as well.

Normal family life in many families was almost non-existent. Kids were sent out to school (if they had school) or work from twelve or to play on the bomb pecks and find their ways of passing the time. Anyone with smart or posh clothes was looked upon with suspicion, and anyone with clean fingers or fingernails was looked on as queer; normal people never had clean nails or clean hands, not in inner city Birmingham anyway. Kids with posh clothes and clean fingernails did not mix or come into these areas.

The middle classes lived in decent houses with back and front gardens and tree-lined roads in the main, away from the dank, suffocating smog of the inner city—Edgbaston to the south, Erdington and Sutton to the north. Normally, they would have one or maybe two children. By contrast, the lower working class, merely by an act of birth, were thrown into one of the thousands of back-to-backs in the city. These consisted of a front door that led straight off the street or courtyard. From one room, you had the cellar head that contained the four-ringed black stove, a marble cold slab, and a few shelves to carry even fewer plates and saucepans. Off the stairs led two bedrooms, which could be shared by as many as nine people, including mom and dad, all sleeping together top to tail; in many cases, no sheets, just army coats to keep warm as best you could.

Bed bugs and lice were rife, coming out of the plasterwork at night to feed on the little bodies as they slept, only dropping off when they were full and fat with blood, like match heads. Nits were a regular problem with nit days, where you were stuck on the chair, head over the table with the post underneath. The steel nit comb was brought out and dragged through your hair, cracking the nits as they dropped onto the paper with a fingernail. One after the other would be brought to the table and de-nitted till all was done, the paper splattered with blobs of blood. Your hair was then washed with Derbac soap—a ritual done once a week in most households.

Then there was the silverfish that came out of the bricks at night and swarmed around the grate; the problem was, these were very poor-quality houses, and that's why they were built using dirt for mortar instead of sand, all to save money. There was no electric, just gas mantles giving an eerie dull flickering glow and soot marks on the ceiling. If you were lucky, you might have your own outside karzie. More than likely, it was maybe four karzies to nine houses. God help you if you went for a shit early on a Sunday morning after some unknown drunken had been in and shit all over the seat and floor,

the uproar would follow with neighbours balling and screaming for the offender to come out and clean their shit up. Occasionally, the culprit could be found out easily enough. Most times, no one would own up, and with most of the houses being full of drunks after a Saturday night piss-up, it was anyone's guess. In this environment, people were expected to knuckle down, go to work and obey the rules. These were hovels and all you were worthy of.

It was only through the intervention of one vicar who was constantly appalled at seeing children as young as six and seven selling matches and newspapers on the streets of Birmingham in bare feet that caused him to do something about it. With the backing of one or two businessmen, he formed a club where these young boys could gather for tea and warmth; from that, he formed a football club playing on the waste ground or pecks that littered the area. With further funds, he purchased a couple of pairs of boxing gloves and formed a small boxing club, initially fighting against each other, then other clubs were formed.

Slowly but surely, the groups and clubs grew, and more and more boys were finding something to do with their lives; they had a focus, a hobby, somewhere to go, to socialise, to let off energy. The government and the council should have been responsible for this, not one individual. Instead, anything that appealed to the riff-raff, the lowest of the low, was taken away from them; no wonder that to them, the police, the council, and the middle and upper classes were the enemy. This is where John Lewin first became friends with the Kirby's, forming a bond that has carried on and passed through the generations.

The black country was so-called for good reason. With the coal mines, industrial factories chain making furnaces belching out smoke twenty-four hours a day, the whole area, including Birmingham, was one whole fog belt draped in fog and smoke that was sucked into your lungs, making you cough and spit up black phlegm, all day and night. It wasn't helped by the strong fags like Capstan full strength; you dragged into your lungs. The average lifespan was 45 years of age. Birmingham, given city status in 1889, was to become famous as the city of a thousand trades. It was famous for its jewellery quarter, stamp making, and even more for its chain making, nail making, and 1000s of manufacturing outlets around the area. But its people paid a very heavy price regarding health and poverty—cheap labour. Young children between nine and fourteen were used as cheap labour in the factories and as chimney sweeps because of their fitness, agility and ability to climb down the chimneys. Many died, and no action was taken; it was an acceptable accidental death. No one was held to account. Nail makers would work in their little quarters behind or next to their hovels, toiling all day, cutting and shaping nails to be collected by the gaffer each night. Woe betide you if you hadn't done your quota.

To earn extra money, the women would be employed on piecework, either with their husbands in the nail making, forming some fretwork into specific shapes and sizes, or sewing bags. In Birmingham, they were making the moulds for gold rings. It was mind-numbingly boring and low-paid work, slave labour, but we knew no better.

The animals of the city shared the cruelty. Horses used to pull the drays, milk carts, and coal, and passengers were worked to death, many dying where they fell, picked up immediately and taken away and sold as horse meat, suitable for dogs or shipped to France where it was eaten in soups, boiled or roasted. The bones boiled down for soaps. Deaths among adults were a regular occurrence in the factories and the mines, dismissed as a natural expectation. Many of those, paid a pittance of a wage, were given pauper funerals by their families too poor to pay for a proper funeral. Witton cemetery (known as the dead centre) would be that busy with bodies being brought in. Family attendees were scarce and far between, just a few quick words spoken over the dead by the vicar before they were hurriedly taken away for a quick mass burial. With hardship and poverty ever present.

In the winter, the sky was covered in a thick fog called a pea souper, so-called because that's what it looked like. It was thick and yellowish; as the nights set in, so would the pea souper. Drivers of the new-fangled car were forced to slow down to four miles per hour. Passengers made to walk in front, leading the way. Everywhere, the whole city was in a constant state of darkness and misery, with just one change of tattered clothing, many with no shoes on their feet. The poverty and hardship were tangible. Many went hungry for days; begging was normal; if you didn't beg, you nicked it.

The earlier French Revolution and subsequent civil conflicts caused alarm in England, where they were known as the mob, conscious of the volatile nature of the London working-class political organisations, including the earliest trade unions, were lied to and misinformed. The government acted in various ways to try to repress the people. Workers and people like weavers were threatened by the production of new machinery, threatening to put them out of work; machine-wrecking riots broke out all over the midlands and the north of England, and the rioters became known as the Luddites. The government responded by imposing severe penalties on convicted rioters whilst imposing further restrictions on the press. The official response to popular protests during these harsh periods was fear and repression, deriving partly from events in France. The people, the peasants, were slowly waking up. The answer to it was brute force by the government to keep them down and in their place.

From this environment, this atmosphere, grew the gangs, the thugs, the sluggers, the Peaky Blinders. The irony was the middle classes, more educated, would only have one or two children; the poorest, by contrast, would knock out large numbers of children, sometimes numbering ten to even twenty within the family. The city was awash with young children growing up in poverty; children were dying in their thousands of pneumonia, polio, rickets, and malnutrition. Almost subconsciously, people would carry on producing children, knowing one or more could die. It was a natural instinct. Not helped by the lack of contraception, with no money, no home life, no leisure time, except to mix and socialise with each other, in many cases, all you had was your reputation, the name you made for yourself, the only possible way to do that was by fighting.

Billy 'Nobby' Hall was a well-known slugger, only 5ft8. He was built like a brick shit house. Starting at around 14, Nobby built up his reputation quite quickly. By the time he was 21, he had established his reputation around Aston and Nechells; with his big, ruddy face and ready smile, people soon learned to get on his good side; he was widely known and respected. It only needed the odd scrap to enhance and keep his reputation. The only problem was for how long. As Nobby got older, so did his fighting abilities slow down; it's the irony of life that the harder you get, the more your reputation spreads, and the more people want to find out where you are, fight you and enhance their own reputation. If Nobby knocks ten balls of shit out of them, it's no loss to their reputation; well, I had a scrap with Nobby Hall last night. But one day, maybe one day soon, someone will come along and catch Nobby on an off day, and then they will have earned the reputation; just like the gunslingers of the old Wild West, there is always someone better around the corner.

Slowly, this started to filter into Nobby's brain. Like most of his peers, Nobby had little or no education; schools in England only started appearing from the 1870 Schools Act. Only the well-off could attend school; with little education, most people never saw or looked too far ahead. It was hard enough to think of today, next week. As one reputation began to fade, another would grow and take their place, fearful of their new vulnerability. If they were lucky and had found themselves a wife, by the time they were twenty-five, they would have started slowing down, accepting menial work in one of the local factories if they hadn't already. For a pittance of a wage, as the realisation started to sink in about the squalor and hardship they were facing, shoulders already starting to stoop, it had become a daily grind.

Up in the morning at daybreak into one of the many factories working a fifty-hour week plus Saturdays, by the time Nobby got home to his two up, one down, back to backs, usually smelling of baby shit and outside latrines, his missus worn out already he barely had time to eat his meagre dinner, sit his lazy arse down on his threadbare second-hand chair and have a nap. Before long, it was time for bed and the thought of another gruelling choking day in the factory.

For those in work, the only respite was Saturday afternoon and Sunday. Typically, Nobby, and thousands like him up and down the country, would leave work Saturday lunchtime wage packet in hand, opened, a few bob nicked before handing a few quid to the wife, then straight off down to the Garrison for a few pints and to escape the drudgery of the last six days. For a few hours, Nobby could relax with his pals, talk about old times and the adventures they had shared, the fights they had experienced, the hard cases they remembered, most now disappearing into distant memory. No one ever talked about the future because there was no future. There was tomorrow, next week, or next payday.

By closing time, Nobby would slowly stagger home, stumbling on the cobbles. Drunk and tired, he would head for bed, leaving his missus in the tip down below. Waking up for the night, if he was lucky enough to have a few coppers still in his pocket, he might head

12

off to back down the local boozer for another few pints. You just had to get your priorities right. If you smoked, like 90% of the population, you had to spread your money thinly. A packet of fags, and a drink Saturday and Sunday wasn't too much to ask. The kids would have to go without a bit of food, the missus would have to pinch what she could, and as for having a drink, well, that was a no-go, with barely enough for the husband who, after all, had worked hard all week to make money. It was only fair that he had a precious few hours in the boozer. She understood that and accepted that it was her job, like her friends, peers, and parents before her, to stay home and bring the kids up. She had a roof over her head and food in her belly; little as it may have been, she was grateful. Well, she tried to be grateful; she was expected to be. She was lucky; Nobby never hit her. Many men took their anger and bitterness out on their missus, most of the time not even realising it. Everyone accepted that.

Sunday was the traditional day of rest, a bit of Sunday breakfast maybe, maybe not, maybe a bit of dripping on toast, then off to church, well, not really. Come twelve, Nobby would be off down the boozer for a nice steady drink. If he was lucky, he might have a bit of a Sunday dinner cooked for him by his missus toiling over a little four-ring gas oven, standing over the cellar head. Sometimes, the drinking session would be livened up by the missus, frustrated and fed up, making her way down to the boozer, marching in and, to the amusement of all, throwing the dinner down all over her old man. "Eayyaa, if you like your fucking boozer so much, have yer fucking dinner in it."

Making his way home, Nobby would eat his dinner, nap on the chair, and then go to bed, thinking of another day in the factory starting tomorrow. Day in and day out, the routine was the same. Nobby was lucky. He had made his reputation as a slogger and was good at it. Wisely, once married and settled down, he kept out of the main dangerous places where his reputation would be called out; he kept his head down, drinking with his mates only and not going out at night, preferring to drink during the day and at weekends, Nobby kept a low profile.

Ginger Harris was also a major slogger with a fearful reputation and a bully. Sadly, as he got older, he found it harder and harder. Ginger 'one-punch' Harris was slowing down and finding moving more cumbersome. While refusing to admit it to anyone, Ginger knew he was vulnerable; many young guns wanted to put one on Big Ginger to gain their reputation. Through his fuddled brain, Ginger had a way out. He started laying out at the coppers. The streets were so violent that the coppers kept away from the darkened cobbled back streets, only walking the main roads, and even then, in twos, only coppers of six feet or more were accepted.

Many a reputation was made or enhanced by putting one on a copper's chin after a few pints to fire the courage up. But you had to be quite clever in using this situation to your benefit. Most sloggers found that once was enough after getting a good fucking belting on the spot or after being dragged down the nick. Back on the cobbles, your drinking mates would recall, "Did you see Ginger put that copper out?" But down the clink, it was a different story. Once in the cells, you would scream your fucking head off as half a dozen burly cops came at you with battens and truncheons.

Sobering up quickly, sharpish, black and blue, you were soon kicked out and sent on your way home, brain-dead and zombified. Jack could only hobble home, reputation made, maybe, but vowing never to make that mistake again. Some sloggers never learned at all. Ginger had clocked that the way the cops treated you was equal to the threat you greeted them with. Ginger knew the local sloggers were closing in on him. He had already lost an eye in one vicious battle. Now, they could smell the growing fear emanating from him, the underlying uncertainty he showed. Many a boxer looks for it in the ring with his opponent, the uncertainty, the glint of fear. While no one felt ready to take Ginger on, they were building up to it.

Ginger knew this, and he also knew the answer. Coming out of the White Lion one night, his mates around him, he clocked the two coppers walking towards them. With a couple of his mates giving them the usual jibes and insults, the coppers would respond, "Now, now, lads, let's get off home, ay?"

Ginger took this as his cue. "Who are you fucking talking to?" Before throwing a punch at one of the coppers. Dodging the punch, as Ginger knew full well he would do, the copper did no more than pull his truncheon out and whack Ginger across the nut and, with an "ok, ok," whip the cuffs on him, taking him down the clink. He was soon released, not having smacked the cop in the first place; no assault had taken place.

Only the odd one of Ginger's more sober mates clocked on that Ginger never hit the target; the others were too pissed to notice. All they saw was big Ginger put one on the chin of two big coppers; his reputation was enhanced. People talked about it for months; it went down into local folklore. 'Did you see Big Ginger put one on those coppers?' By the time the story had been told a few times, Ginger had knocked the two coppers out and put them in hospital for two months. 'Oh, what happened to Ginger?' After they got him down the nick, they decided it was safer to let him go. Shit scared of him, Ginger's reputation was enhanced. No one came near him for months.

John Lewin was only 5,6, strong yet wiry and inoffensive. He didn't pose a threat to anyone. John's family had originated in the Berkshire countryside and had made their living as barge people for generations. Short and wiry as they were, they were well suited to it. Barging was hard work, and much of the time, the barges were loaded up by hand, ton after ton. You had to be strong, wiry, and fit as a fiddle, delivering to all parts of the country whilst sleeping on short bunk beds in tiny cabins. A little log burner was your only comfort. The Lewin family decided that the city of a thousand trades was a better place for them. What they didn't allow for was the sheer uphill struggle of surviving in one of the 1000s of slum back-to-backs around the city. They might have got a house, a two-up, one-down, in a slum part of Birmingham, but the next step was to find a means of earning a living.

Poverty goes hand in hand with our position in society. We had been subjects for over two thousand years, most of that time serving as serfs, peasants and slaves during different periods in history;

it was ingrained into our mental psyche. In short, we were well brainwashed; the French had woken up to it, sparking the French Revolution in 1789- when the spoilt queen Marie Antoinette said, "Let them eat cake" as she sat in one of her vast chateaus eating rich venison and fresh fruit. Well, the French thought, fuck that, enough is enough; once they had got a taste of it, they have been revolting ever since. Mind, anyone who eats frogs and horses has to be a fucking odd race.

The American Revolution, which started in 1775 and ended in 1783, was about the same time as the War of Independence. New American peoples, reaching the country from all parts of Europe, didn't want the shackles of slavery held back by a fat king, George II, who sat on his throne from a distant land.

England was in political turmoil with different factions trying to get a foothold: Trotskyites, communists, and revolutionaries. Each had a different view of how to run the country; fortunately, or unfortunately, whatever side of the coin you looked at, King George, then Queen Victoria, with her vast army and devoted subjects, were just too strong for anyone to topple or want to topple. Most of us were unsure what could replace what we had. At least we were free, we lived in a democracy, and we could speak our minds. We thought we could until we said the wrong thing, and then the government found a law for it. We were not alone in the world, it seemed, communist or capitalist; the world revolved around who had the biggest punch, the biggest shout. In 1914, John D. Rockefeller ordered action against the striking coal miners in Ludlow, America, infamous for its outright murders. He sent the company guards, backed by the National Guard, to quell the strikes. Dozens of miners were out and out murdered, all accepted, all legal, simply because the miners wanted a better standard of living; they never got it. Instead, they were beaten down, murdered, and sent back down the mines, defeated. Yes, we all knew our place in the world.

THE MARKET BOYS

John Lewin had joined one of the local gangs, not for the fighting, but simply for survival. Ducking and diving to earn a living, he became a bookies runner, dodging the cops from every street corner to take illegal bets for the even dodgier bookies. Then there was always the risk of being mugged himself. Capable as he was, there was no answer to half a dozen sloggers getting hold of you and knocking the shit out of you in a dark alley for the few quid in takings. If that happened, it came out of his pocket.

With many inner-city boys working in the markets, he soon discovered that was the place to be. The market boys had a strong camaraderie, drawn together by the excitement. The markets were where it was all at. Savvy and clever, the market boys knew how to flip a coin and make a living; of course, the wages were crap, but that didn't matter. It was the perks that you gained that mattered. If you worked in one of the abattoirs, you had access to fresh cuts of meat and sides of lamb. Who was to miss the odd leg of lamb, side of lamb cutlets? You soon learned to find out, know and trust your friends and contacts. You built up a network that you could and did deal with daily. It was a little secret world all of its own. Jewellers who worked in the jewellery quarter would come into town and exchange a nice ring or other bits of jewellery for a nice leg of lamb or a couple of steaks. Little favours were the norm. Old gal Sutton, the flower seller, would pop over from her corner plot and hand you a bunch of flowers; maybe tomorrow you might pass her and hand her a couple of steaks; everyone could afford to be a bit generous and a little bit from here, or there was never missed. It was a great, friendly atmosphere where everyone felt special and unique. You looked after yourselves and each other.

Workers from the jewellery quarter making bronze or brass figurines would take rejects meant for re-smelting around the market, handing a metal knight or soldier to another trader who could make a useful ornament for them. Money or favour was never asked; that was for later; favours were built up, cemented, over months and years, everyone knowing each other, everyone trusting each other. Rejects were a common way to gain favours, whether in the jewellery quarter or surrounding factories. Working away on the benches making figurines, brass or silver cigarette cases, or gold rings, the rejects were tossed into a bin to the side to be smelted down and recast later; no one noticed what went missing from the bins. No one noticed, no one checked. Why would they? Now and again, quietly, discreetly, a perfect piece might be dropped into the reject bin and picked out later; the recipient, in most cases, didn't notice any faults being so minor. If, and once you were in the markets, you were made, all you had to do was know the rules of the game. The rules of the game were simple: you weren't stealing something, and no one nicked anything. The rejected cigarette case, figurine, or ring was not wanted; you were doing someone a favour. Those who accepted the gift in exchange for a leg of lamb or a bit of pork didn't notice or didn't care if the cigarette case had a fault; most times, it was never seen or noticed.

It went from top to bottom. Pork butchers and sausage makers found ways to increase the number of sausages by adding sawdust and other waste like offal into the mix, sometimes doubling or trebling the number of sausages made; they weren't called bangers for nothing. Why, even Typhoo tea in Digbeth cottoned on to the tea bag first invented in America in 1908, everyone knew that the bosses at Typhoo were alarmed at the number of losses, from full tea chests being tipped onto the floor and swept up as waste. Coming up with the bright idea of the tea bag, all losses were eliminated.

Nothing was wasted. Lessons were learned from every quarter. In the abattoirs, tails were cut off from bulls, udders cut off from cows and sold as offal, cheap but tasteful meat. A favourite was chitterlings, the small intestines of pigs. Tripe was another favourite; stomach lining, cooked in vinegar and onions, made a nice, cheap meal. People didn't question the exact origins of where something came from. Known as the fifth quarter, this was the profit that paid for, say, the transport. Heart lungs, ears, and pig trotters boiled and served with vinegar and onions were a staple and nourishing food. Even sheep's and pig's heads were cooked and pressed to make brawn. The brains, served on a doorstep of bread or slice of toast. No part of an animal, be it pig, lamb or cow, was wasted; everything was utilised, everything was used, blood was sold to butchers who would use it for black pudding, and even the bones were collected by the bone man, free of charge, who would then sell it to the soap manufacturers. Poverty was widespread. Everything had value.

By special licence, the pubs in the Bull Ring could open at six am, purely so the thirsty market traders could have a drink. Much of the business was done in the pubs before the markets opened to the public. The wide boys and spivs would call into the pubs, sidle up to the butcher, and order their meat before moving on to the shellfish worker and then fishmonger. Once work was finished, market traders from all walks of life would make their way into the boozers like the Bull Ring tavern carrying innocuous bags that carried various little treasures. Each would be brought out and handed over to the lucky ones chosen.

A leg of lamb from one, a few cockles and mussels from another, and a bit of cod from the monger. Everyone was happy, and everyone was earning a bit—a few quid in the pocket from one, a bit of meat for the table from another. The market was a happy, bustling place. Everybody was bustling about, happy to do the work in the knowledge that around every corner was a new deal. In one way or another, there was nothing you couldn't get if you worked or knew someone in the market. Want a gun? Someone knew someone who could get it. There had been the first and second Boer wars of 1881 and 1901. Many servicemen brought back bayonets and guns as souvenirs and, of course, just in case.

It was the dawn of a new era, and there was a sense of excitement and optimism in the city centre that didn't exist anywhere else. People walked with a spring in their step before they went to work in anticipation of what the day would bring and what they had gotten by the end of the day. Day and night, the whole Bull Ring was alive with excitement and chatter. Market workers drank all over, from the Bull Ring down to Digbeth and even along the notorious Summer Lane.

Many had nicknames to suit their trade: Jimmy the Jeweller, Billy the Fish, and Big Steak. Leg of lamb, Johnny, the Colonel, so-called because he organised a lot of the deals going on around the market, then there was Scarface Ted, so-called because of the wound inflicted on his cheek, for not delivering the leg of lamb as ordered so rumour went, but never to his face of course. Nicknames were carried with pride and honour. In the pub, someone might ask, what's your name? Kettle Jack would come the response, not because he sold kettles, but because he sold watches, the slang term. Ahhhh, everyone had heard of Kettle Jack.

The Quaker family, Cadbury, were setting up their chocolate factory in Birmingham. It was a sight to behold with fresh green lawns and cricket fields set out in fields with beautiful houses supplied to its workers who, in the main, had only been used to living in back-to-backs in the inner city. Other factory owners were doing the same in other parts of the country but not maybe with the same generosity of the Cadbury, who were true humanitarians. John Cadbury and his brother Benjamin started selling tea, coffee, and drinking chocolate from their shop in Birmingham in 1824. During his spare time and in quiet periods, the Cadbury's experimented with raw cocoa to make varieties of chocolate.

Soon, John had invented a variety of chocolates, and before long, the Cadbury chocolate factory was formed and quickly became one of the most popular chocolates in the country. Soon, his sons Richard and George took over the company, and it expanded rapidly into what became known as Bourneville village. Cadburys built nice spacious houses with a thought for the comfort of its workers; in truth, it was a revolutionary idea for the time. Gardens to front and rear, sports facilities put out for the welfare and goodness of its workers who enjoyed a good quality of life. You were encouraged to eat as much chocolate as you wanted, knowing full well you would make yourself that sick you wouldn't want another. Those Cadburys were clever, ok. Whoever caught onto the idea first was forgotten in time, but others soon caught onto it. Workers in biscuit factories were given the same privilege, and coal miners were given allowances for coal. It cost the manufacturers nothing, and the miners had to collect it from the workface, yet it ensured the loyalty and gratitude of its workforce. The workers at Cadbury's couldn't believe how privileged they felt. The environment was a million miles away from the slums and back streets where they had lived in Birmingham. For their part, Cadbury's were scrupulous in their interview and acceptance of its workers. Only the best were acceptable. In return for light work, they gained loyal and lifelong workers.

Like the coal mine and cotton mill owners of Yorkshire, Port Sunlight in Liverpool had a different outlook. Oh, they provided houses, alright. They had tight terraced little houses with a small backyard, not too much, of course, and no front garden. The houses were not there for you to enjoy your leisure time; no, you were there to work. The knockers would come around, tapping your window to ensure you were up and ready for an early start either in the factories, the mills or the pits. You earned just enough to feed yourself and your family and have a few pints on the weekend. You were there to work, not play. The backyards were just big enough for the privy, the outhouse to do the washing and enough room for a line to hang the washing out.

It took a bit for the reality of your situation to dawn on you that you were no more than slaves trapped in a situation you could not escape from. If you lost a day through illness, it made all the difference to paying your rent, going without a comforting drink on Saturday night or cutting food from the table. All those black slaves and their descendants toiling away in the cotton fields of South America have spent the last few hundred years whinging about how hard done by they have been treated; they want to try working down those mines, then they would know what slavery is.

But for those in work, with a job harsh as it was, it was still better than the gruelling treatment their parents and grandparents had received working on the land in agriculture, toiling away twelve hours a day picking potatoes or crops for a pittance of a living, in conditions far worse than the miners.

Only the most stupid or foolhardy would borrow money because then you just hocked yourself into even more misery. If you had an accident in the mines or the mills that made you unable to work, you were kicked out without a second thought, together with your wife and kids. This thought was at the forefront of your mind every working day. You became tough, bitter, and hardy but accepted your lot. The reality sunk into your very pores, slowly and inevitably, shoulders drooped, heads became bowed; you might start cocky and confident, but by the time you got to forty, you walked with a shuffle, head bowed. The wives were worn out and weary from years of fretting over watching the pennies. You knew your place in the hierarchy, the pecking order, and you were right at the bottom of the pile.

In Birmingham, it was very different. Maybe that's why the Cadbury brothers gave so much more; was it kindness or shrewd sense? Birmingham was the city of a thousand trades. Whilst the wages were always shit, you could move from one job to the next within a day. You could start a job on Monday morning, walk out by lunchtime, and start another the same afternoon. You didn't have that choice in the valleys of Wales or the pit towns and cotton mills of Yorkshire. In truth, you were in the shit. There was no competition. These poor buggers thought the mill and pit owners were being kind and generous, poor disillusioned buggers. For those who didn't want to work or could not work, there was nothing, no benefits, no social security. If you were out of work, you had to rely on family to give you a roof and look after you. If you had no family, you had no alternative but to take to the streets begging. The only problem was that there was no money around, and no one had any money spare; those who did were fully aware that they were only so far from being in the same position.

The streets were full of people begging. Many a woman would sell her body for a quickie, in some back entry, for pennies, just enough to get a loaf of bread or a bit of meat to feed themselves or their children. Others would walk the streets picking up nub ends because they couldn't afford to buy a packet of cheap fags. Another would push a little makeshift cart, picking up lumps of coal that had dropped off the various horse-drawn carts carrying coal, head bowed, worn out boots with holes in, no socks and rags on his body. Worn out and knackered like the horse drawing the cart, without realising it, waiting for his life to end and finally bring peace to his soul.

SUMMER LANE

My dad was born and lived in Summer Lane next to the barrel pub after his dad, my granddad, had moved there after his marriage. He was living in a two-up, back-to-back, outside karzie and washroom. The houses were grim, as was the area. The only escape was the corner boozer, aptly called, there was a boozer on every corner. Everyone had their favourite. When you met someone, the opening question was, where did you drink? "Where's your local?" "Who's your team, Villa?" Two opening questions that set the scene for the rest of the night. People would spend the night bonding over the comfort of supporting the same team whilst talking about their team's latest win.

You were a boxing fan if you didn't support a football team. From a very early age, it was wise to quickly learn how to box and look after yourself. Like many inner-city areas of the time, Summer Lane was an aggressive place to live. Like their grandfathers, all they had was their reputations to live by. If you had no reputation, you sidled away into the shadows. The area, like the housing, was depressing. If you were working in some shitty factory or on a building site, you came home to a small box room with only the family or games to keep you occupied. The radio was still in its infancy and not yet widespread. There was nothing more satisfying than sitting in your armchair, slippers on, sucking on your pipe whilst reading the daily post, maybe even with five or eight kids crowding into the rest of the space. Sharing five to a bed, some maybe even sleeping on the bare floors.

Yet people took pride in their houses and tried to make the best of it. First on the list was the front doorstep, woe betide anyone who didn't keep their front step nicely polished and cardinally bright red, it didn't matter how poor or bad the house was inside, as long as that front step was cleaned and polished. Then there were the rugs or carpets. If you had them, they would be hung from the bedroom windows on wash days, shaken and left to air all day of course, making sure all your neighbours could see how well you were. "Maya, have you seen that Mrs Wooten's carpets? They must have money."

If you were of school age, you were told to get out and only return when the gas streetlights were lit. You thought you had complete freedom, not realising you were being booted out to give your parents peace. It was safe; you could travel miles without fear or concern. Boxing or football allowed you to use excess energy, taking any frustration or anger out on your opponent without realising why. The football and boxing clubs had served an unexpected benefit to the area and the city; it helped to eliminate the gangs, the sloggers, and the Peaky Blinders. It rid or reduced the cowardly, though sometimes necessary, need to fight in gangs. Now, fighting in a fair, one-to-one fight or belonging to a team, not a gang, was an honour.

This is where my dad first became firm friends with Bert Kirby and the rest of the Kirby clan. The Kirby's were not only big in numbers but ferocious with it. Small in stature, not one reached more than five and a half feet. Originating from a small area of middle Ireland, their name was already on the map. It was strongly rumoured that killing anyone who got in their way was second nature to them. They had been involved in the early years of the IRA, and their hatred of the authorities was thinly disguised. If they threatened to blow your fucking kneecaps off, you knew they meant it. It didn't take long to realise that if you fell out with one, you fell out with all of them. If you fought with one, you had a pile of Jack Russell terriers swarming. If you were close to six feet tall, being beaten by such a small opponent was humiliating. You soon learned to keep away from the Kirby's. Short, stocky, aggressive, what was worse was that they all looked like clones of each other, all with the same little turned-up snout, like a badger. If half a dozen brothers stood in a room, you couldn't mistake them. If half a dozen different cousins drank in the same pub, you would still not know who was who. The image of the Celts from the Middle Ages and earlier would spring to mind, only separated by their clothes.

It didn't help much that the family was that big and spread so far and wide around Birmingham that you couldn't go into a pub without bumping into one. Worse, not one drank alone. Maybe it was due to that self-preservation borne into their very being from way back in the wild, lawless countryside of where they came from in Ireland.

My granddad John Lewin was a friend of the Kirby's, way back from before the markets, and my dad grew up, trained, sparred and drank with Bert Kirby in the boxing club. When Bert turned professional, he quickly rose the ranks to become a British flyweight champion. This was helped in no small way by his family and close friends, who would crowd out the venue and threaten any opponent as he made his way to the ring by surrounding them, jostling them whilst threatening to break their fucking legs if they dared win the fight. Surrounded by half a dozen little Rottweiler clones, all viciously threatening to do the same thing, many a flyweight felt it made more sense to lose the fight and get out with the few quid they made.

As my brothers were born and grew up, they equally forged close bonds with the Kirby's. Johnny, Reg, and Billy Lewin, with the greater number of Kirby's, Raymond, Johnny, and Rajpot Tubby. As they all went to the same Summer Lane school, they knew each other through and through. Each was tested over the years, and any weaknesses showed up over time. If there was one thing you took pride in, it was having a bottle. It was all you had in many ways. They became friends for life, the expression thick as thieves couldn't be more apt, and their loyalty unquestionable.

THE VILLAINS, CHANCERS, GANGSTERS, AND CHARACTERS

At almost a mile long, Summer Lane had many characters, some very tough and ruthless. Most, if not all, were born into poverty and desperate to get out of it. With wages so low at the time, saving money was almost impossible. Most of them, like every generation before and after, had left school with barely any education. Throughout history, there has been a war on average every twenty years. As each generation started to get in front and pull its financial socks up, it was knocked back down again. For the majority, there was no light at the end of the tunnel; for the very small few, it was debatable if there were any prospects in front of them. One great-granddad served in the Crimea War as a horse saddler, signing up for twenty years. Such was the insecurity and hardship of the time. When he eventually came out at some 45 years of age, he married my grandmother, who was only in her early twenties—a telling indication, perhaps, of her outlook.

Joseph Lucas would be seen trudging the streets pushing a cart selling paraffin oil for a few pennies; who could ever have guessed that from that small cart would grow to be Lucas Automotive Industries, one of the most successful companies in England? A few people would open a small corner shop only to earn a small income, the main purpose being it gave you a home, while the husband went out to work making better use of his wages. The whole idea of the shop was never going to make a fortune. Oh no, the shop was just a backup, run mainly by the wife. Others would use the shop or even a café as a focal point for anyone who wanted to get in touch with you, old Stan Sherrington had a café up Hockley Hill. From there, he could deal with people from all over the city, knowing where he was. Got some bent gear to get rid of; go see Stan. People far and wide knew where Stan's café was.

WHILST MANY IN THE GROUP WERE KNOWN TO ME, I CANNOT RECOLLECT THEIR NAMES, ALL WERE SUMMER LANERS, MOST WERE VILLAINS. THE SECOND FROM LEFT IS MY DAD JACK LEWIN, THE BULL RING BARROW BOY, THIRD FROM LEFT: HARRY – TWINK – DOSSITER, SAFEBREAKER, GANGSTER AND LATER RESPECTABLE BUSINESSMAN SCRAP DEALER.

Being so close to the city centre, many Summer Laners worked in or around the markets, forming even closer, tighter bonds; everyone knew everyone else. We even had our own songs:

'See those palm trees swaying way down Summer Lane.
Every night, there's a jubilation;
you can hear them sing in the salutation.
There ain't no snow on Snow Hill no need to catch a train,
To a sunnier climb where the weathers fine.
Coz' it's summer in Summer Lane.'

This was sung with great gusto every Friday and Saturday night in the pubs up and down Summer Lane, the Trees, the Barrel, The Stag. Loud and with a fighting pride, it was our song. No one else had such a personal song, and everyone was proud of it. There was a sense of speciality about it, a uniqueness. Only Londoners, cockneys, had their own song.

Diamond-Lilly Hawkins's family had built up the chain of fresh seafood and jellied eels, flaunting their wealth on a Friday or Saturday night with diamond rings and jewellery. Far from it, there was never a show or a hint of jealousy. If anything, it incentivised any friends or locals to open their minds to the possibilities and prospects within their grasp; why, Diamond Lil, an early girlfriend of my dad, for all her diamonds, still lived in a council house, just like they did. As much as you might like a nice private house with a front and back garden and grass, that was an impossible dream. Once you had a council house, you had a house for life; giving up your council house would be like sliding down a razor blade using your balls for brakes. Oh no, a council house was for life.

One or two did break the mould. When they did, they didn't look back. The only barrier to getting on the ladder and making your fortune was getting the few quid you needed in the first place, your pot, with wages so low that it was almost impossible. With the average wage of only a couple of quid a week, by the time you woke up to the possibility of earning more money working for yourself, you were married, got a couple of kids and the rent to pay, in short, like those coal miners and cotton mill workers, you were fixed. With just a few bob left to buy a couple of pints on a Saturday night, it was even more of a bind. With the average wage being some two pounds ten shillings, if you saved the ten bob a week for a year, you only had twenty-five quid, nothing. There was only one alternative, and that was a bit of larceny. If you couldn't get the start-up pot legally, it left only one way: you had to nick it.

But to nick it, you had to do so in an honourable way, which allowed you to keep face with your peers. Only the lowest of the low would consider breaking into someone's house and stealing personal possessions. Robbing a church was the very lowest of the low, no matter how many valuables were in the place. Shoplifting was seen as petty; how humiliating it was to get nicked and up before the court for nicking a joint of beef. Mind, it was ok to buy it from those who nicked it. Consequently, a thriving little black market was built up, with people buying goods off the back of the lorry. Not many people were bothered about where something came from.

It was the norm to be in the pub at any time of the day or night and be offered a side of beef at a knockdown price, a watch, or maybe even a suit or jacket; everything was on offer. The only rule was that you had to keep your gob shut. In any walk of life, squealing or grassing was a definite no-no. Anyone caught doing so was ostracised from the mainstream. Mainly, this was only done by the spiteful rat who had never been offered the side of beef in the first place; there is nothing more guaranteed to arouse jealousy in your fellow man than him missing out on a nice bargain.

No one asked questions; It would be a soft mumble here and a slight cough there. Big Nose Billy's had a tickle, of course. Big Nose Billy's had a tickle. He was buying everybody in the boozer a fucking drink last night. Of course, not everyone assumed the money made was nicked. Most times, everyone would assume you were a clever, wide boy who always seemed to be making money.

Graham was slim, good-looking, well-spoken, and could spin a line. He always wore a nice business suit, hair smart and slicked back, and always had a ready smile. Most people didn't even know Graham's last name till he got nicked. No one would have the bottle or audacity to ask anyone what they did or how they got their money; that was considered bad form. People would ruminate all night in The Stag, muttering to each other, "I'd like to know what he's fucking up to; he's at it somewhere, hmm." Sometimes, after weeks of scratching their brains and becoming increasingly frustrated, one might rustle up the courage to sidle up to Graham and put the feelers out, "Err, alright, son, want a drink?"

By accepting your offer of a drink, Graham was somewhat obligated to you, but still, you couldn't ask outright. You had to ask in a roundabout way, "How's things, Gra?"

"Alright. Mate."

Wrong answer.

"Any tickles going?"

"I dunno, mate, not that I know of."

Wrong fucking answer again. You've just wasted the price of a pint and an hour trying to winkle out of him what he's up to and learned nothing.

Only when a small article appeared in the Birmingham Mail did everyone catch on to what Graham was up to. Graham made a very nice living bouncing cheques, always with a small overnight suitcase. He would book into a nice four-star hotel, say on a Thursday night, and come Friday night and with the banks closed, he would confidently walk up to reception, point out that he had a very important business meeting that evening and needed some cash to pay for the meal in the expensive restaurant in town. No one could refuse the gentleman. In most cases, the hotel would take the loss of being far more troublesome and expensive to report and pursue the matter, plus what did they have to go on? A nondescript description and an empty small suitcase left in the hotel room. Graham would walk down to breakfast, eat up, and then walk out, leaving a nice heavy bill for accommodation, meals, and drinks. Crafty bloody sod. If he did, by chance, get nicked, the fine was invariably quite small; well, in the scheme of things, it wasn't a lot.

"Well, what do you know? That Graham is a crafty bastard? That's what he's been up to." A collective nod of approval and respect would travel around the bar. There was always kudos for how someone cleverly made their living.

Such was the reputation of Summer Lane that the cops tried to keep well clear of it, only going down in twos, many a night, a copper had found himself thrown or pushed into a shop window. In reprisal, they would go steaming in mob-handed, throw you in the paddy wagon, and you wouldn't leave the cell till you had had the shit knocked well and truly out of you. It took some people a long time to learn.

Life was hard enough before the war. There were no benefits or social security to fall back on. To live, you had to work. If you didn't work, you starved; simple. My great-granddad, Frederick Hipkiss, had disappeared from the face of the earth, and rumours abounded that he had killed someone he had had a fight with at one of the bars around Summer Lane. My mom's mom never heard from him again. No information exists about him or where his final resting place is; that's it, gone, never to be mentioned or brought up again. That's how life was, the harsh reality of it.

My grandmother, beautiful as she was, was forced to bring up her five sons, and my mom was forced into the workhouse. My mom brought up the kids as best as possible; eventually, unable to cope, they were placed in Erdington orphanage, except for Albert and Fred, the two eldest, who were old enough to work. Yes, life was certainly harsh. Many a person, a face, a character of the city, a wide boy, would quietly disappear off the face of the earth. One minute, the life and soul of the boozers. The next, sudden whispers would slowly circulate that the poor bastard had hit hard times and died. With no one to pay for his funeral, he would be quietly given a pauper burial, all hush, hush. Sometimes, life jumps up and takes you by surprise, smacking you hard in the face and causing you to sink to a place you never thought you would ever sink to.

You can live life as a wolf or go along in life like the sheep. Many a character around Summer Lane didn't like being one of the sheep. Many had no choice but to. My dad decided from an early age that he didn't want to spend the rest of his life working his balls off in dead-end jobs in one of the many factories around the area. For a pittance, a barely liveable wage. After WWI, there was no improvement. Things were just as bad, if not even worse. With more than a million dead from fighting in an unnecessary war, all started after the assassination of Austrian Archduke Franz Ferdinand. Millions more came home to a land supposedly fit for heroes. In truth, they came home to a broken country, barely on its knees, with houses bombed to bits. This was a common theme throughout history; we, the peasants, are brought in like cannon fodder to be used as pawns to fight in wars started by some arrogant bastard at the top who is unrelated to us. But we are expected to be grateful and sing 'God Save the Queen', bowing and scraping as we go. The sheer ludicrousness of it makes you want to weep; worse, we are treated like shit by the authorities and by the council. Who feels they have an automatic right to come unannounced to your home, demand entry, inspect your bedding, cleanliness and sanitation? Everything was made to humble and humiliate you; worse, the options were limited.

A lot of companies didn't want ex-soldiers working for them. Many of them had no skills or training, and many were mentally or physically damaged. One option was the police or the prison service. It was an easy way out for someone with little ability or skill. The wages were not too good, but there was a promise of a guaranteed wage, plenty of overtime, plus a decent pension. They could carry on wearing a uniform but without the fear of bombs dropping on top of them. Better still, they didn't have to work for a living or get their hands dirty. It was a job only a very few would want.

After a short stint in some of the factories, many decided that life wasn't for them; with big ambitions but limited abilities, their options were reduced even further unless they thought bent. My dad, Jack Lewin, was never a villain; he lived off his wits, ducking and diving to earn a coin. Having worked in the market like his granddad and seeing the potential, he got a hawker licence and a barrer and set up a stall in the Bull Ring selling fruit and veg. In between school, mom would take over the barrer whilst dad would go ducking and diving around the pubs, selling anything he could get his hands on. The barrer provided a living, not a lot, but it also supplied the food my mom would take home to cook a meal for her growing family, not only her eight kids but also a couple of her brothers who she kept from going into homes. A turkey frame from Lewis's deli counter for a shilling finished the stew off. After, of course, Mom cut off a few slices of turkey for Dad's sandwiches.

For the time they lived, they lived a good life, unlike many in the lane. Mom would make a stew on Monday, stocking it up throughout the week to keep us well-fed. On Sunday, she would make a good English breakfast followed by a full-blown Sunday roast with a leg of lamb and a bit of roast beef, with plenty left over. A late supper would be a nice fry up of bubble and squeak with a doorstep of bread and butter. No lard on a slice of bread for us, alright, or an empty belly to go to bed on. If we ran out of stew, Mom would get us a nice pig trotter, cooked and smothered in vinegar. Another day, it might be a sheep's head, the brains scraped out and spread on a slice of toast; that was Dad's little treat. Chitterlings and cow udder were other treats my mom would serve, cooked in milk to a nice colour. No doubt, for the time we lived in, we lived quite well. Not many people lived as well as we did. Indeed, many thought my dad was rich. Such was the lifestyle they lived for the area.

Mom and Dad never sought to impress or rely on clothes to look smart; they knew the realities of hardship and going without. Only a mug would spend money on fancy clothes just to impress, though quite a few did that knowing that it could lead to better things. Mom and Dad never had to. Through hard work and cleverness, they had the ability to make money. Some companies, like Blundell's, made their living off the backs of the poor, either lending money or giving tokens to buy school wear, even supplying kids clothes themselves at extortionate prices paid back weekly on the never, never. So-called because you never paid it back. Once caught in the trap, by the time you had paid the first lot off, you were forced to buy a new uniform, and so the cycle continued whilst we walked around with spuds in our socks, holes in our boots and arses hanging out thinking our peers were rich we never realised that in reality, they were eating lard on stale bread to survive.

It was a time of hardship and poverty. The Second World War, whilst not of our making, was a just war. Almost no doubt, everyone was fully aware that Hitler was a monster, a dictator who wanted to rule the world. He wanted the Reich to last 1000 years, but Hitler would not have risen to power if the Western nations hadn't clamped down so hard after WWI, that again, a war not of our making. Now, here were all these men, soldiers returning from the war only to face even more hardship and poverty, their wives and parents struggling to put food on the table in run-down, rat-infested houses. They saw the few men who had avoided the war for various reasons, earning a good living while dealing on the black market. It didn't take a lot of brains or thought to know how to improve their lives.

Not for them the prison service or becoming a copper, a screw? Locking up your fellow man merely for nicking food to put on the table was far worse than being in the war; no, growing up in and around Summer Lane, they had made good, lifelong friends; the war had only tested and strengthened those friendships. It was a natural progression to form small gangs and teams, operating on their own terms, living on their wits and making a living, thieving and robbery. Even better, or worse, whichever way you looked at it, these men, who were already ruthless enough, knew how to kill a man and knew how to shoot and use a gun.

These men were solid, reliable, and trustworthy. They knew the merits of keeping their mouths shut and acting as a team; the army had taught them well. Each team was formed on their friendship and knowledge of each other; each team was solid and prepared to stand. Harry Twink-Dossiter was a skilled safebreaker. If he was put on to a number but didn't like the job, or he didn't feel there was enough in it for him or his team, he would pass it on to someone else. There was loyalty and care built up on those streets, and it was carried on from the army to look after number one first whilst also looking out for your fellow man. Look after your fellow man, and you are looking after yourself.

If Twink saw a good deal whilst weighing up a safe-breaking job, he might put it to big Jock McCloy or my brother Johnny Lewin together with the Kirby's. Their speciality was warehouse or factory robberies, sometimes safe breaking, but that was more specialised. Sometimes, they would diversify into something else if nothing was in the picture. Georgie Crow would nick or look out for haulage companies, nicking loads of valuable goods in transit. The drivers often would approach someone they knew in the boozer and put them onto a valuable load, all the same people mixed and drank in the same boozers around Summer Lane. On a Saturday night, it was quite the norm for a driver or factory worker to casually sidle up to one of the known villains and ask if they were interested in a little warehouse or factory job, maybe a lorry laden with toys or cigarettes, nothing was turned down, if Johnny, ray Kirby or George were not interested they knew someone who would be., the worker concerned was also in the same boat financially, working to feed his wife and kids, pay the rent on shit or low wages, for doing very little except pass on a bit of useful information, he knew he was going to earn a couple of hundred quid, far more than he could earn in his job over six months. It was as simple as nicking apples off a tree, a steady progression from scrumping. All the driver had to do was be in the boozer when the lorry was nicked. Sometimes, all they had to do was break into the empty haulage yard, jump into the pinpointed lorry, and go off, knowing full well they were safe till the next morning. By then, the load was off and sold. The London gangs were well bang at it. As soon as one little enterprise was discovered, it didn't take long for word to spread around.

No one considered they were doing anything wrong or bad; it was just a way of getting in front, making a living, and lifting yourself out of the gutter. Everyone felt they were honourable and acting with honour. The rich were nicking of us all the time.

The only difference was they would do it blatantly, it's called business, but in reality, it's just an excuse to suck us dry. At least when we did the nicking, we did it honestly.

Each or every villain had their speciality. Each relished in their uniqueness' or individual skill. My brother Billy was not a villain, considering himself a businessman who specialised in company setups. Firstly, he would rent a decent-sized shop around the area, kit it out, sign it up, and then start putting stock in as it started coming into him. In the meantime, he would start ordering small amounts of goods from salesmen coming into his shop, desperate to sell him stock. Reluctantly, he might order fifty quid's worth, on credit, of course. He was making 60% on the dodgy stuff and 10% on the legal gear. The dodgy stuff would subsidise the legal stuff while he built his credit.

If someone bought him a lorry load of shirts, the simple trick was to go out and buy a couple of dozen shirts, legally. Shoes, the same, if the police called into the shop making enquiries, he would politely bring out receipts. It would end up taking him a few months to get rid of all the shirts at nicely discounted profits. In the meantime, he was building up a nice little credit limit with all the traders bringing him in new stock with the credit limit rising to, say, circa 1000 quid, with two or three dozen firms giving him credit, it added up to a very nice pile of stock. After twelve or eighteen months and earning a nice little wage, he would close the shop down, remove the sign, disappear, and find another shop on the other side of town, putting his wife, Doreen, in as the face for a few weeks. A new sign would go up over the shop, and a new business started with a shop load of stock paid for in cash. Billy had every reason to stand all cocky and arrogant on his shop doorstep, a big smile on his face. One or two others had similar little scams.

Tommy and his partner had done the same over a few years, eventually building up to a warehouse around Summer Lane. With a shop full of buckshee stock, they would start the mace up slowly but steadily. They would build up their stock, earning a little profit as they went along, maybe a little too slowly. One night, the warehouse went up in flames, the stock was replaced in bigger amounts, and some would end up in Billy's shop. In the meantime, he made sure he was well-insured. If he got broken into, he was very grateful to the thieves who did it.

You see, this is where the misunderstanding comes in about being robbed. If you're in business, of course, whether it be a shopkeeper or a warehouse owner, when they get robbed, they cry crocodile tears and mourn the loss of their stock, but most people in business are grateful for a little break-in. It allows them to bang in a right few quid on top, which enables them to build their stock up and put them right in front. Many shopkeepers or factory owners would drop it out on a Saturday night down The Bull or The Stag, that they were open to a little break-in. A deal would be made so that certain stock could be lifted and the promise of a further drink on top if all went well. Invariably, things went well; the only ones losing out were the insurance people, and that was the risk they took.

There was a hierarchy amongst the teams; each thought they were superior to another, specialising in a different scam. Whilst Harry the safebreaker was not a snob, he sure thought he was a cut above the lowly shoplifter. Our kid Billy would strut around fucking Summer Lane for all the world like the bee's knees. You could always tell the ones who were at it by their fancy pinstripe suits with hand-stitched lapels; everyone who was anyone had to have their hand-stitched lapels. Except Jack Lewin, of course, my old man, he was happy with his suit and cravat. Never thinking he had to impress anyone, he would sit in the boozer, twiddling his thumbs, watching all the moves, not saying a word, clocking with a little smile.

The wide boys standing up and around the bar, strutting about, pulling a roll out of their bins and buying a round, "Get them in again, landlord, my shout." Little Peggy, the kite bouncer, stood to the side. Peggy was a bit of a dark horse, short in stature at circa 5ft 6. No one was quite sure what he did half the time. If a nice little job was happening and someone needed another man, and Peggy was on the side, he was invited to join in or participate. But then he would disappear for weeks at a time. No one knew if he was in the nick or not. But Peggy was another one into bouncing kites.

Dapper and smart with it, Peggy would drive around the country, hitting smart hotels like the Savoy or Grosvenor. Not for him, a little guest house. Oh no. It had to be a top hotel. He would either ring ahead or book in as a worldly traveller carrying a small posh suitcase and a bulging briefcase for three or four nights, spending freely at the bar and naturally putting it all on the tab. If he happened to pick up the odd bird, who couldn't fail to be impressed, especially with the amount of booze and champagne he bought them?

A night or two before leaving, he would pull the night manager and mention that he had an important meeting, missed the bank, and needed some cash to entertain his guests. Naturally, the manager would give him the money he needed and signed for. He would leave the hotel, leaving his empty suitcase in the room and briefcase under his arm. A little bonus would be if he clocked a wealthy guest, leaving a load of jewellery or expensive watches in their room. He would have that as well. Peggy lived off the Hogg alright for years, with no one knowing what he was up to. It was only after he got nicked the one time that it all spewed out. Half a dozen hotels put two and two together and hit him; well, the cops hit him, of course. The other hotels didn't bother, too much hassle. Peggy got a two-stretch; he was out in eighteen months to start again, and such a shrewd move enhanced his reputation.

That was the nice part about it. Of course, that was Summer Lane for you. The golden rule was keeping your gob shut and things close to your chest. You only knew what your closest pal did if you were both in the same team or passed a little tickle onto someone else, and the place was done a short while later. Then you would just give a little nod, and right then? That was enough. If a bung came your way, it would be handed over separately and away from prying eyes. You knew who you were dealing with, and you knew who you could trust to get your bung as agreed if you got nicked. Well, that was all in the run of it; a couple of stretches in the clink freshened you up for the next time.

No one said a word, least of all the working pecks sitting in the seats or on the benches around the boozer. They were content to earn their wages legitimately in the local shops or factories without the risk of getting nicked. They were more than happy to buy something from the back of the lorry; of course, that was only natural. If it was off the back of a lorry, then it wasn't nicked, was it? Taking a bit from work was different. That was just one of the perks. Everybody had a perk of one kind or another. The only ones that were avoided were the snides and the grasses. These were the ones who didn't have the balls to nick something and resented having to clock into work doing a job they hated for the shit wage they were paid. We all knew or had a good idea who they were and avoided them at all costs. Sadly, they missed out altogether, adding to their resentment and bitterness.

The publicans were not slow off the mark either. All pubs were managed only. The breweries made sure of that. They had a stranglehold on the beer they sold in their pubs run by their handpicked management team. Their beer and spirits were all delivered to order, allowing for a pint or two of wastage, every pint, every bottle was accounted for, and the breweries had it all locked down tight, except for one little chink. The publicans were not slow to jump on it.

There was always someone with a few crates or a few hundred boxes of spirits, knowing they could be trusted. The publicans had no worries about buying a few cases of whiskey or other spirits from them. At half price or less, these bottles would go up on the shelves next to the other optics or were discreetly placed. Coming up to closing time, time would be called on the dot. With most people leaving, only the handpicked stragglers would be left behind for the overs. Retiring to the back smoke room, they could drink and discuss business to their heart's content. From the landlord's position, he only served top shelf on overs. By the night's end, everything in the till was his own, including tips from the grateful client.

"Have one yourself, Landlord."

He did.

In any pub, any night over the weekend down Summer Lane, you can be offered anything from a side of lamb or a joint of beef, a nice suit or a pair of trousers, to a diamond ring or nice watch. Between all this, you had the penny wink man coming around with a pint glass of penny winks and a free pin to pick them. Hawkins jellied eels and fresh seafood straight from the market. If it were a darts night or the landlord felt generous, a buffet of sandwiches and cheese, pickled onions, and black pudding would be laid out on the bar. After the war, it was a good time to be alive, but only if you were on the right side of the fence. There was a great deal of hardship; people lived hand to mouth, just about. Many barely lived or survived. Those who would have begged didn't bother, knowing no one would give them a penny. If anyone had any change, it was kept tight in their pockets. If you wanted something, you had to go out and get it according to your abilities. By the same token, we all knew we could go to Aunty Beryl or Aunty Doris for a bit of sugar, maybe a slice of lard or a few slices of bread. This is always spoken about as a typical kindness of the people in the back streets. Our neighbours Would give you their last shilling, and we would all like to boast. The reality was a bit more cynical. Oh, Aunty Beryl would give you her last shilling, of course. Common sense told Aunty Beryl that she might need to borrow something next week. Our needs and friendship were born out of necessity.

In the good old days, people boasted that it was all different then. Them was the good old days when neighbours would give you their last penny. Course they fucking would because they had fuck all else to give, and if they didn't give you their last penny, they knew they could never come to you when they needed a penny, mind, a few tried.

Another proud boast was that you would never walk into a boozer without someone shouting up and buying you a pint. Well, this was true, up to a point, and it was according to who you were. The working pecks never brought you a pint or had a pint bought back simply because they never had enough money to afford to. If someone bought them a pint, it was because they liked them or could afford to take the loss. In the main, people would dip into their bins and buy a drink because they knew the kindness would be reciprocated. It was an unspoken gesture; you just did it. But woe betide you if you never brought a drink back after the third or fourth time. It would have sunk in, and you would be dismissed, "He's a tight bastard, harrumph." Unless you had the skin of a rhino, you made sure you returned the favour.

Historically, the reputation of Summer Lane was built on its hardship and suffering by the multitudes of decent, hardworking people and families who struggled daily to survive from one day to the next. This is true, but the real reputation was enhanced by the rogues, villains and chancers who lived in or around the lane, worked in the markets, and around the Bull Ring, the thieves, and the characters. Without them, Summer Lane would have been like any other street. London's respectable, hardworking people didn't make the reputation of the East End; it was the villains, crooks, and gangsters like Jack Spot. The working people just jumped onto it and made it their own. In Carl's case, his father and grandfather were illegal bookies, in itself a cache to being one of the faces or characters around the lane. I'm not taking it away from those people, oh no, but before and after the war, when people were being rehoused in Kitts Green and Kingstanding, with nice front and back gardens, no one or not many would admit to having moved from Summer Lane, its reputation was known far and wide. Only after historians started writing about Summer Lane was a different slant put on it.

Everyone, according to their abilities, would try to find an edge. If you were a working peck trying to survive on the low wages, you would be up like a shot if you felt there was a spare bit of meat going to be put on the table. Many people didn't eat from one day to the next, and you didn't see too many fat bellies around Summer Lane. It was so devoid of greenery that no one could grow even a few vegetables.

Firstly, you had to learn to stand up for yourself. To stand shoulder to shoulder, you had to learn to fight. Once you could have a scrap, you could stand equal to your peers. Four years in the army fighting Hitler, soon sorted you out. When you came home from the war, reality hit you. The very shrewd ones buckled down and looked for opportunities that could lift them up. Lou Baxter was a bookies runner taking bets whilst hiding in side entries to avoid getting nicked by the old bill. Learning his trade, Lou took to it like a duck to water. With his mustard Crombie and black velvet collar, smart, polished shoes and suit, he certainly looked the part; without a doubt, Lou was smart. Within a few years, Lou had got himself a pitch on the Perry Barr dog track. Starting small, he grew to take some of the biggest bets on the track. Good as gold, he never forgot his mates back in the lane; all bets kept trickling back. Lou had it well sussed out and was a great networker. Like horse racing, the dogs were as bent as you could get. Lou knew every bent trainer and every lame dog. True to form, the best dogs were built up only to lose at the odd race.

Only a few were privy to the knowledge and the potentially winning dog. Strict instructions were laid down that you couldn't just walk into the local bookies in or around Summer Lane. In all possibility, they were known to you and were friends who drank with you on a Saturday night. Oh no, you couldn't take the piss like that. To do so, you would be ostracised from any future dealings, or if you got a good belting, too big a stroke or a stroke too many, you would get your kneecaps blown off. Many soldiers coming back from the front brought back guns or pistols. Many brought back a bayonet that was taken off a dead German, willingly or not. They also brought back a brutality that could only be picked up from the battlefields.

There was discipline and respect that everyone understood. If you were privy to the information, you would take a tram ride out of town, maybe mix it with a day out somewhere, the unspoken understanding to head out to different areas, like star tips. With the average wage at thirty bob a week and odds of five to one, a five-pound bet was not wholly unheard of, so it didn't raise any suspicions. The bookie took the hit without realising he had been suckered. The punter could live nicely for a week or two, being generous with a few drinks in the stag. Lou would get his bung in the form of a fiver for his kindness, and everyone was happy except the losing bookie. Fuck him. He would make it back, of course.

Most of the time, Lou could pass the bets without any real fixing, such as his knowledge of the track, the owners, and the dogs. You could often turn up at the track, sidle up to Lou, and he would give you a dog to lay a bet on. It might only be at three to one, but a quid bet, placed at the opposite side of the track, would return you three quid, with a two quid profit over a week's wages, not bad for a night out.

In the meantime, my uncle Jimmy-Pussyfoot-Littleford would be setting up his little scam on the car park of the dog track. Pussyfoot, so called because he always seemed to be Pussyfooting about, was, in fact, a very serious and methodical thinker, admired far and wide for his little scams, known only to a very few but spoken about in awe by many more. Fucking hell, he did that? It was so simple, yet no one would or had thought about it themselves.

Upon his return from the South Americas, Sir Walter Raleigh, having brought with him tobacco and the potato in the late 1500s and whilst addressing Queen Elizabeth I and the court, one lord had the temerity to point out that, "well, I could have done that?" Standing up and flinging his cloak aside, Sir Walter Raleigh picked up an egg and invited the gentleman to stand it on its head. Having tried and failed, the gentleman gave up, saying it was impossible. Sir Walter then picked up the egg, cracked the end and stood it on its end. Flustered and blustering, the gentleman protested, "Why, I could have done that."

"But I did it first, sir," replied Sir Walter.

Well, that was my uncle Jimmy, Pussyfoot. It was only afterwards when told, people would stand in awe, "Well fuck me with a bargepole; I would never have thought of that." Jimmy wasn't a thief. He didn't fancy that way through in life; firstly, the odds of getting nicked were too favourable. Secondly, he didn't like the humiliation of ending up in the nick. No, Jimmy, like my dad, preferred to use his wits.

On race days, he would push his little pram across to the car park. His pram was made up of four wheels upon which sat a box. On top of the box was a roulette wheel, with a little button to the side that he could push to slow or stop the wheel with his belly at will, all surrounded by a posh velvet skirting. With a couple of lookouts, he would set up his wheel, with his lookouts having a bet whilst keeping a lookout for the cops. A crowd would soon start creeping over to have a nose, and, seeing the lookouts winning, they were soon drawn into the net. He had a captive audience; by their very nature, people who came out to the dogs were gamblers. On alternate days, he would bring out his three pots and the pea trick on top of the covered-up roulette wheel. Pussyfoot earned a nice living for months before it slowly dawned on the crowds that no one was winning; slowly, inevitably, the muttering would go around the crowds, "Don't go on that, you're on a loser." Eventually, Pussyfoot threw the towel in and found something else. There was always something else.

One nice little tickle would be to take a short-term rent on a factory unit, then a cheap poster with a made-up company name above the gates. With a phone installed, Pussyfoot would start ringing around out-of-town companies ordering various items or goods. When salesmen called in, as they inevitably would, he would negotiate a price on a bulk order. If he was refused credit on the order, he would send them away, not interested. They would soon be back the next day, agreeing to the big order. Only first, having checked out buyers, he would order anything sellable. Toys from Chad Valley, drainpipes or garden furniture from some manufacturers. He didn't care what it was; if it were sellable, he would negotiate a price and order it. Upon delivery, the driver would be met by Pussyfoot, all dressed up and looking the part in a pin-striped suit and a nice smile, either to sign the receipt, invoice to follow, or if it were on insistence, a cheque would be signed, filled out and passed over.

Ideally, Pussyfoot would try to get all deliveries for Thursday, Friday, or Saturday morning. With his own lorry pulling in Sunday, loading up and taking them to his pre-arranged drop-offs at half price. Everyone happy, well, almost everyone. Sometimes, if he managed to meet the driver at the security gates, he could have the load taken to an empty unit and dropped on the front, "It's alright, driver, my lads will be out shortly to take it in, thank you, and off you go. A pound tip in your bin." Pussyfoot could then deny receiving the goods.

Many people were jumping onto the Insurance scams, either through robberies, break-ins, or fires. Pussyfoot wasn't slow in catching on, but he thought of a less suspicious way: finding a little factory unit down by the house that Jack built by the Barton Arms. He had got himself a little contract producing pressings for a local factory. Setting up a dozen presses, he got the local housewives in part-time pressing out metal badges or plates.

Pussyfoot could have earned a nice living legally and built up on it if he had just stuck it out and worked at it, but typically, he started to get a bit bored with the work and dismayed at the low wage he was taking. Anyway, it all might end next week. Making sure he'd got very good insurance and a good accountant for his books, Pussyfoot turned up one day to find his factory burned down. Laying off his staff with a few kind and grateful words, he put a claim into the insurance for close to twenty grand, an awful lot of money, with the average wage being so low. The insurance assessors couldn't tell what was what, and the fire was so fierce, just as well as the metal pressings were indistinguishable. Pussyfoot had searched a few scrap yards to find as close as possible, and with his insurance pay-off, Pussyfoot brought a nice little restaurant with a pleasant flat above it, which became a meeting point for many years.

Being crooked was a completely acceptable profession so long as you were honourably crooked. The more ruthless you were, the more determined you were to get in front and climb up the slippery ladder. Before and immediately after the war, poverty and hardship ensured everyone started playing on a level playing field. One or two would manage to take on a little corner shop. This was fine, but it was hard work and only provided a little income, the main benefit being the accommodation above, the husband having to go out to work in one of the local factories to ensure a decent living.

Joey Wragg had set himself up with a nice little shop down by HP Sauce. Not for him, a little factory job. He had gotten a nice little job in a bakery delivering bread and cakes. Last on his van was a pile of cakes and loaves, which he delivered to his shop first. Joe was onto a nice little earner, without a doubt. With other little deals he got for his shop, he earned a good reputation for selling anything at a good price, whether a loaf of bread or a nice shirt. Joe and his missus were living very well indeed. But squirrelling it all away, Joe was savvy, eventually buying himself a nice big, detached house in Great Barr.

Mom was ambitious, determined, and a climber. She would beg the old man to get a little hardware shop so they could earn a better living than the fruit and veg and be respectable, but he would have none of it. The simple fact was the old man was earning just too much money. The barrer was making a living, not a lot, just enough to keep the wolf from the door. Plus, the fruit and veg gained off the barrer, sometimes it might just be the specks, damaged fruit or veg, but we ate well with the damage cut out. In the meantime, Dad was earning well selling his wares in the pubs. The bonus was he could drink and enjoy a nice social life with his pals. If he sold one watch, the profit would buy him his drinks. At closing time, nicely pissed, he would head off back to the barrer where mom had been working away, take over and head for the lock-up to put it away.

Meanwhile, Mom would head off home to get dinner for us kids. Fruit and veg all bagged up, all she had to do was call into the delicatessen of Lewis's department store, pick up a turkey frame for a bob or so, and that was it, in a three-gallon aluminium pot that was our dinner for the week. We might live in the so-called slums, but we ate well. Dad was in his oil tot. Popular and well-liked, he led a nice lifestyle. Why change something that worked so well?

Some people worked in gangs or teams, while others preferred to work alone. The advantage of this was twofold: first, no one knew what you were up to, and second, whatever money you made went into your own bin. At worst, if you only found a hundred quid in the safe, you didn't have to split it. Harry Twink Dossiter worked alone.

Known for always having a twinkle in his eye and a ready smile, his nickname was well-earned. As with everyone else, only a select few knew what Twink did, and even less guessed what jobs he was pulling or where, and the only way anyone got their information was from the Birmingham evening mail. Summer Lane would hit the headlines twice or thrice weekly, at least once on the front pages. A surge of excitement would whip up and down the lane as the lads entered the local boozers, mail under their arm, a pint of mild ordered, paper laid on the bar, open to the latest crime, *nudge, nudge*, a little whisper through tight lips, "Looks like Twinks pulled off a little blinder, Billy?"

"Hmmm, yeah, what a nice little tickle." No one knew for sure, but it was a good guess.

Another factory was broken into, along with the safe and a nice chunk of money.

Sometimes, if it was a team job, and because there were so many teams, it was difficult to tell who had done what. All anyone could do would be to guess. "Did you see that little number last night?" An artic lorry, with fifteen tons of brass, had been nicked out of the haulage yard. Disappeared off the face of the earth, or burnt out, on some bomb peck on the edge of town, well away from Summer Lane. The only way anyone had any inkling of who it could be, which one of the teams had pulled the job, is when the culprit walked into the boozer buying everyone a drink. There was a sigh of relief for those struggling without a tickle. Not only would they get their beer or whiskey bought for the night, but there would most likely be a chance of a bung to carry you through for a few days.

"Any chance of a few quid, John?"

"Ahhhrrr heaaa, how much do you want?"

"A tenner will do, John." The roll would be pulled out, a tenner peeled off and handed over. "Oh, well done, John; I'll have it back for you as soon as I get a tickle."

"It's ok, son." Johnny may or may not get his tenner back, but it didn't matter; there didn't seem any end to the good times, and Johnny knew that next time, it might well be him being skint and needing a bung. That's how it was. Capitalism was the name of the game, but deep down, they were all socialists at heart. It had been drummed into them for generations. All for one, one for all, help your friends or neighbours out today because you might be in the karzie next week. If nothing else, a few of the Summers Laners were only too happy to tell everyone that they might be from the two ups and downs, but they were far from skint.

The same attitude and mentality was adopted in the east end of London by cockney friends, working people or villains alike. Frank Chopper Carson was mad with it. He had moved up from London after finding it too hot for comfort in the east end. Frank was known for always using the chopper, carrying one stuck down his trousers. He was very quick to bring it out if someone upset him. The only problem was he fell out with the gangster Jack Spot, who had George Walker, the boxer, working for him as his minder. Jack Spot was someone you didn't fuck about with. With his minder George, Frank decided it was wiser to get out of London, and through contacts, he ended up down Summer Lane. Accepted as the villain he was and being sound, he had no real problem settling in. The only problem was Frank was a bit of a loose cannon. You could be having a drink with him one night in The Stag, all nice and crusty when he'd lose his temper, bring out his chopper, whack you across the bonce, and you'd lose a fucking ear-ole.

One night, as all was going well, the songs were being pushed out, and the usual crowd were in the barrel. Mad Frank was having a nice tot with George Crow and some of the Marnie's. One of Timmy Marnie's pals took a bit of a dislike to Frank. Some people just didn't like Cockney's, and to be fair, Frank had a bit of a gob on him, that typical cockney gob. Copping umbrage at the guy's snide remark, Frank did no more than whip his chopper out and whack the guy across the bonce. His ear flew off across the barrel floor, claret spewing all over the place. Everyone went sober, quick, sharpish. The problem was no one knew what to do, everyone was pissed, and what Frank did was out of order. Well, it was out of order, but when someone's got a chopper, it makes sense to sit back and not do anything rash. Timmy Marnie's mate was not a Summer Laner, and in all fairness, he did speak out of school. I mean, you might not like cockneys, but you just don't tell them at 10 pm when you've all had a drink, no matter how strong you think your backup is. As everyone was sobering up, and Frank was still holding the chopper, it was decided that whilst Frank wasn't totally clear, Timmy's mate was in the wrong. The problem resolved itself with the amount of claret still gushing from the guy's head. A tea towel was grabbed off the bar, the ear picked up and placed where it should have been, and he was bustled out and up to the general.

No one saw Timmy's mate again, and the Marnies kept out of the barrel for a couple of weeks, letting it all naturally quieten down. The problem is Frank made people nervous; some tough cookies lived in the lane. More than a few could and would have a proper fight. Dennis Sully Sullivan was rock-hard and big with it. He didn't need tools; his two weapons were his fists. No one in the lane argued with Sully. They had all grown up with him. Worse, he had a head and body like fucking granite. Even those who could fight often carried a tool as backup, not from fear; oh no, it was just in case someone came at them mob-handed. Mob-handed or single-handed, it was a matter of pride and self-respect. With Frankie Carson, it was a different ball game. Quite bluntly, Frank was fucking unhinged. Most carried a tool for self-defence. One favourite was a heavy buckle belt, some so heavy it could be over half a pound. There was nothing illegal in wearing a belt, but if you got a belt with it, you knew you had been belted, alright, hence the term, 'give him a good belting son.' None carried a knife, mainly through pride, mostly through fear of the death penalty. Using a knife was considered the most cowardly of acts, un-manly. Plus, there was no bigger shame than the shame of being up in court on a knife charge, even worse, murder.

But mad Frankie? That was a bit different. Maybe it was his upbringing. Sometimes, the system sends them over the edge. Approved schools, borstals, prisons, and many villains who had undergone the system were somehow damaged. Couple that with a harsh interwar family life, and you have all the ingredients for a loose cannon. Mad Frank was a loose cannon, alright. Only the most desperate would take him on a job, and only specific jobs. Frank had worked with some heavy teams in London. It was the norm to go into a bank raid with guns and machetes, even shooting a member of staff if need be. You had to be as threatening and menacing as possible. Up here, in Birmingham, it was a bit different. The threat itself was enough.

Someone had put a little earner onto George Crow, a bookie known to leave his shop on a Saturday afternoon with a briefcase full of winnings, plus he was inclined to flash and boast about his four-carat diamond ring and expensive watch. A few people were aware of them, but no one ever knew for sure how much was in the briefcase. It was a bit of a risky blag just to come away with a few quid. This time around, George and Frank were both skint and desperate. Plus, as mad Frank said in his broad, east-end cockney accent, "We'll have his fucking groin (ring) and kettle (watch)." Well, they got hold of the bookie alright; knowing where he lived, they waited outside his house in Handsworth. Confronting him, mad Frank went in without hesitation at the heavy. George was a big, heavy bloke, an ex-boxer with his nose spread across his face; his size and demeanour were enough to menace the bookie. But Frank wanted to make sure. Grabbing the briefcase, he shouted, "Give us the fucking ring." Grabbing the watch, he wrenched it off the bookie's arm, but the ring wouldn't come off. Screaming to George to hold his fucking arm out, mad Frank brought out his chopper. George, thinking Frank was joking, held out the bookie's arm, thinking it was all a ploy to make the bookie take his groin off. Frank brought the chopper down without further ado, chopping off the ring finger and the one next to it. Tough as he was, George's bottle completely fell out. Spluttering, he could only watch as Frank grabbed the groin and pulled it off the finger before both were doing a runner. The bookie was screaming in pain and terror, "My fucking fingers."

"Fuck me, Frank. Was there any need for that?" George was shitting himself; a bit of threatening was one thing, maybe the odd, menacing smack that would be his word against yours, but this? This was well over the top, a ten stretch of hard labour staring them in the face. Mad Frank had nothing to lose, but George had a wife and two kids. The kettle and groin went down to London to be sold, the briefcase opened up, and the contents divvied between the two; decent as the amount was, it didn't lessen the horror of what they had done. Hitting the front page of the evening mail, it was the talk of Summer Lane for weeks, worse, the whole of Birmingham. The whispering was at full pitch in the boozers. The very fact that Frank had disappeared only confirmed that he was involved, "that's Frank, all right, the mad bastard," the murmurs spread around.

From that moment on, the villains kept their distance from Frank. Oh, they drank with him, okay? They didn't have much choice, but Frank was kept at a distance when it came to tickles. Everyone had plenty of bottle. Those at the blagging and robberies weighed up the risks and, knowing that the odds were with them, accepted full well the jobs on offer. A simple factory or warehouse robbery would warrant a few years in the nick, a bank robbery a ten stretch. Life in prison was very, very harsh; sewing mailbags during the day or locked up in a grim cell, you were only let out for half an hour of fresh air. Then, you were only allowed to walk around the prison yard in twos, talking being forbidden.

The rules were worldwide; whether " in Europe, America or London, talking was met with heavy punishment. You could always tell anyone who had been to prison as they talked out the side of their mouth in a whisper; it was gangster talk, but it was instilled in prison.

Ex-cons would talk about the good times they had had or experienced in Clink, but you started to realise it was all bravado. Not many wanted to go back there except the odd ones who had spent that much time, they had become institutionalised. No family, no roots. Prison was a harsh place to be, especially before and after WWII. The prison guards were picked from the very working-class population that produced the prisoners themselves, which has been the case for centuries. Ironically, the rich upper classes chose and paid a barely living wage to the lowest classes to lock up, guard, and beat up their fellow men, and they did it with gusto. It was the one profession, next to the police, that you could take all your hate, vengeance and bitterness and focus it onto your fellow man and be rewarded for doing so. You could use the birch, the whip, or baton. You could even get away literally with murder. Many a prisoner was murdered in prison or down the local nick, the body seen by a prison doctor and a death certificate issued with the cause of death being accidental. The slate was wiped clean, no charges, and everything was buried. A win, win all around, well, for the cops or prison officers involved.

Many prisoners entered prison, giving a guard or prison officer a smack. The screws, as they were known, would wait till all the cons were locked up. Mob-handed, they would head for the cell with the prisoner in, shields and batons at the ready, and knock ten balls of shit out of the con, sometimes breaking arms and legs. Deliberately, that will shut the fucker up. The governors turned a blind eye, accepting it as self-defence; sometimes, the cons were segregated, put on rule 43, and locked up twenty-four hours a day. Under rule 43, the screws could go in at will with no witnesses, no one seeing them from one day to the next, and meals delivered to their cells. Those who were more aggressive would sometimes cover themselves with their own excrement to put the screws off, determined not to be beaten. The screws themselves were mainly drawn from veteran soldiers returning from the war, most unskilled, most with low education and no training and all from the lower working class. The ideal people to be given the job. With the anger and bitterness that they brought back from the war. They were only too willing to take it out on the cons; in fact, it was a prerequisite for getting the job in the first place. They had to agree verbally to use the cat or the birch if ordered. Those who refused walked out of the job. It takes a certain type to do that kind of job.

GELIGNITE AND SAFEBREAKING

Prison was the cons university. It was almost like your badge of honour to get your first nicking. You weren't a man if you hadn't been nicked and served a bit of porridge. In fact, you weren't fully trusted till you had been tested. In America, the mafia would smile, slap you on the back and congratulate you on losing your cherry, taking your punishment without squealing. More than one crook or villain aspiring to join a gang would give it all the tough talk and bravado. Many talked out the side of their mouths to fit in and impress their peers, yet it was a habit you only picked up in prison. Only to find when they were first confronted by three vicious coppers in the nick, their bottles would go, and they would end up screaming to high heaven. You had to serve your apprenticeship. The climb up the ladder from a small fine in the magistrates court, maybe another fine. Probation, followed by more probation, approved school, before borstal.

These were destined to mark and test you out and prove your soundness and ability to keep your mouth shut under pressure. By the time you were twenty, you were almost a fully-fledged villain and were well on your way to becoming a gangster. Now, all it needed was a bit of rounding off. Prison was the ideal place. By now, you were quite well-known within the prison fraternity. Your reputation known, and your position is established. There were three or four tiers in prison. First, you had the nonce, the perverts, child molesters and rapists. Sometimes, it was difficult to know who was who or recognise them. If there was one thing the prison service didn't do, it was discriminate. Not for them to be concerned about who was mixed in with whom. No, the whole idea was to humiliate and degrade you. What it did was harden you, focus your mind, and make you more determined.

Then you had the petty thieves, shoplifters and general low life, most of whom shouldn't have been there in the first place. But then you had the serious villains, the professionals or wannabe professionals. Not that they liked prison, of course, but they might as well make full use of the benefits whilst in it. Those benefits included getting to know each other better. Learn more little tricks of the trade and any potential jobs worth considering. Twink had learned his safe-breaking skills from some kindly London gangsters, who taught him how much gelignite to use, where to use it, and how. Twink became very skilled at it. In return, the favour was called in. Twink was asked to blow up the car of a well-known grass in London with him in it. It was well deserved. He had put a lot of good men in prison.

Twink, in turn, taught his trusted good friends Johnny Lewin and Ray Kirby how to break the safes. The only problem was getting the gelignite or dynamite. This turned out to be a nice little touch for Raymond when he happened to get on friendly terms with a sheep rustler from Yorkshire who happened to be doing a three-stretch for rustling a truckload of sheep. Normally, a serious villain like Johnny or Ray Kirby wouldn't have anything in common with sheep rustlers, but this was one of the great levellers about prison when you've got nothing to do all day except sew mailbags, get to know each other and talk.

At dinner time one day, Ray and Johnny find themselves opposite the rustler, who turns out to be a nice guy. Ray and Johnnie's reputation was already known in prison, but they were quite surprised to find out there was much more to rustling than they thought. This guy was part of a rife team around the north of England and Wales. They had butchers lined up all over the place. Many with their own slaughtering facilities. With rationing in place, no butcher refused the offer of a couple of nice fat sheep at half price even after rationing. This also extended to cattle and young bullocks. Johnny and Ray were almost tempted to consider a bit of sheep smuggling.

These guys were very well-organised and professional. They would spend their days going to markets, watching farmers buying and selling stock, visiting their farms, and seeing where their sheep and cattle were grazing in relation to the farmer's house. Most of the time, the sheep left out to graze miles away in the mountains. The rustlers could go out at will with a couple of big stock lorries, back up to a field and herd the sheep on in total confidence, driving away even less suspicion would be aroused as sheep and cattle were being delivered all day and night. It was just a matter of driving to and delivering the stock to the list of butchers they had to hand. Even better, seeing a copper in the country was almost an impossibility.

But this wasn't the best bit, although that was nice enough on its own; it then transpired that the sheep rustlers were also well adept at safe breaking. The little earholes of Ray and Johnny pricked up. Following sales of hundreds of sheep, livestock and cattle, large amounts of cash were kept in the safe overnight or until the next market day. The rustlers were also well into safe breaking, usually from auction houses well away from the towns or built-up areas. "Yes," said Ray, "that's all very good, but it's getting the bloody nitro or dynamite."

The rustler then dropped the bombshell. The north of England, with its mines and quarries, was awash with nitro glycerine, dynamite and gelignite. It was used almost daily to clear the mines and quarries. They were kept normally in boxes, and there was so much used daily that no one kept a check on anything. Who would travel so far out into the country to find a mine or quarry, hoping to nick some gelignite? In sheds with flimsy locks. So flimsy were the locks that the rustlers didn't break into the sheds, arousing suspicion. They would pick the lock, nick a few supplies, and then replace the padlock. It was as sweet as a nut, and Ray and Johnny couldn't believe their ears. Sorted. Contact details were exchanged when they got out. Visits would be made. Friendships would be cemented. Sometimes, you had to be careful.

One Saturday afternoon, The Stag was chock-a-block, with everyone having a drink. Two burly guys walked in, smartly dressed and sat down. The atmosphere went from cheerful and relaxed to deathly silence, with no one uttering a word. The minutes ticked away when, after half an hour, the two guys, feeling uncomfortable, said hello to a couple of the villains and introduced themselves as a couple of cons who had been in the nick with them. This was how they had been extended an invite when they got out, with the meet being one of the pubs in the lane. Immediately, the atmosphere relaxed, and laughing broke out with the fear being mentioned that everyone thought they were old bill. No one in prison clothes and smart suits. They looked quite different. Normally, when people walk into a social group or pub, they would introduce themselves as the old friends they think they are. These two just walked in, sat down and never said a word. Bright sparks.

The years after WWII were fruitful and productive for any self-respecting villain. Factories were built in between and amongst housing estates in the slum dwellings, many with barely any security. You could almost go up to the back gates, which would fall apart with the slightest nudge. The flimsy peters (safes) could be easily manhandled onto a trolley, wheeled out to a van and carted off somewhere quiet where it could be blown open. Of course, a few mistakes were made. Once, they put that much jelly in it, blowing the safe to smithereens and the hundreds of pounds in notes. That's the problem with gelignite, which is soft and brown. It didn't look dangerous. It was only when you put the fuse in and set it off that you knew its capabilities; many Irishmen had lost their life or a limb if they got lucky. Every time Johnny or Raymond did one, it was squeaky bum time.

Once, they took young Lenny Kirby, who wanted some of the action, not to mention some of the easy money that could be made. Sadly, on his second trip out, someone made a cock up, and young Lenny blew his fucking hand off. Screaming like a man possessed, they had to drag him out of the factory, through the double gates and into the car. Not knowing what to do, Lenny, still screaming in pain, decided they could only drop him off at the general in town, telling him to say he had fallen under the train at Snow Hill Station. The doctors didn't believe him but sedated him as best they could, amputated his arm to the elbow and stitched it. The next morning, before lights up, Lenny was up, dressed and out of the hospital before the cops arrived. From that moment on, he became known as One Arm Lenny and never participated in another raid again.

Thieving and robbing were not always as easy as some people made out. It had its risks.

The other big problem that arose was the attention of the government and the police. Normally, the cops were not too bothered about a lot of robberies, factory break-ins, nicked lorries, etc. They often suspected it was an inside job, either the factory owners pulling an insurance scam or one of the lorry drivers setting the load up to be nicked. Either way, the load was covered by insurance, and no one was getting hurt. The cops would write in the report, give a knowing smirk and throw the file to the back of the draw. The old bill would often take a backhander along the way to turn a blind eye. After all, most of them had only taken the job to earn a living, so precarious were the times they were living in. Once nicked, the cops had an expression, *there but for the grace of god go I*, because they knew they were only a step away from doing the same things themselves. In fact, many did, but they did it differently.

If they happened to nick someone who had pulled a job off, most likely through being squealed on, a big chunk of the money would go missing again, this time into the cops' pockets. If a bank job was pulled with two grand nicked, a grand would go into the senior detective's pockets in charge of the case. If anyone was stupid enough to accuse the cops of nicking the money, the judge would pile on an extra couple of years for the cheek of defaming the police. Not many villains were stupid enough to try that little scream once it shot around the grapevine. Not many solicitors wanted to be part of it either. Oh no, no, no. The judges also kept that in the top pocket. You had to play by the rules. The cops and the legal profession have a perverted way of looking at justice, which might surprise most people. If a chunk of money went missing from a robbery or break-in after the robbers were nicked, it was down to the robbers. No one blinked. The robbers got the hate and blame. If you had committed violence, then don't expect justice; if you had violence committed against you, the law turned a blind eye.

The cops were pulling it in all ways, from the lowly beat Bobby getting his free fish n chips from the local chippy to the odd pint from the local landlord for turning a blind eye to the afters, for the major detectives in charge of serious crime. If they weren't taking backhanders from various sources, they were nicking from the pile once the thieves or villains were nicked. If they raided your house and found a few hundred quid, they would take that as well, handing it into the court as unexplained dishonest money after taking a skim off the top. Trying to scream about that was a complete no, no as well. Either way, you were bolloxed, you knew it, the cops knew it, and you gained a criminal record. If someone had robbed a shop but never admitted where or when the cops had no proof but just put it in storage as unexplained. Over time, little items would go missing till, eventually, nothing was left. Nothing was ever said; it just disappeared into the heather.

Another little result would be if they picked some little low-life Herbert up for robbing a shop, a warehouse, or a factory to butter him up and put him on a promise. He knows he's going down for a three-stretch anyway, but if he throws his hands up to a few more little jobs, the cops would let his girlfriend visit him so he could have a little fuck in his cell. Sometimes, if the rewards were big enough, the cops might give him a night in a hotel. Nice free meals for him and his bird. The idiot was so thick he never realised or gave it a thought. In the meantime, the cops were clearing a workload of hundreds of jobs in the town. The judges never gave a fuck. As far as they were concerned, someone was being nicked for something. All was good for the newspapers. Everyone was doing their job and showing results. Course, this was happening all over the country. It only attracted attention when the cops were a little bit too overconfident. The judge would note that it would be impossible for the thief to have committed twenty factory break-ins on the same night, sometimes carrying lorry loads of gear. Or twenty houses so far apart it would have been impossible for one person to get around to them all. Whether the judges turned a blind eye or were just stupid was immaterial. They had to be seen to be scrupulously correct, with all boxes ticked. To those who coughed up, so hard was their lifestyle, their home life, twelve months in nick with three good meals a day was seen as a welcome break. If it wasn't seen as a punishment, quite a few would volunteer for a stretch.

After the war, the other very lucrative money maker was, of course, the scrap yards. They were springing up on every street corner, the bigger ones handling the scrap war machinery left over like tanks, aeroplanes and trucks to the smaller scrap yards handling the smaller stuff, brass, copper, and aluminium, 70% of it nicked from the local building sites or factories being demolished around Birmingham. As the laws were being implemented, the scrap yard owner had to record all his transactions in a book. With many petty crooks walking in, they could only take a name. There were lots of Joe blogs and Mickey Mouse's.

For a time, this worked a treat with no one any the wiser, but then the cops caught on, as did the scrap dealers. Which came first, the chicken or the egg? At any rate, it was considered prudent to leave a bung in the book by way of a few quid, but the size of the bung depended on how busy you were in the scrap yard. Two detectives were assigned full-time to visit the yards around Birmingham and check the books. It was that lucrative many detectives like Wilco kept deliberately failing their exams to avoid promotion. You could always tell the cops who were at it by the nice houses they bought in areas like Sutton Coldfield.

Starting off as a beat copper in rented accommodation, the wages were so poor you had very little chance of affording to save for a deposit, so never mind paying the mortgage on a house. By the time they reached detective rank, they would be married with kids and houses even more expensive. It was a never-ending mill wheel. Yet these detectives always managed to buy a nice house, the wife's working chief. A good and clever detective could go all week without hardly spending a shilling of his own money. If he walked into the pub, the landlord would offer a free drink, or if not, the landlord would be one of the local scrap dealers or other dodgy characters. It always paid to hedge your bets with the cops, especially the influential detectives, you never knew when you might need them, either for a driving offence or a bit of criminality.

Soon, just giving a bung wasn't enough. All the senior cops knew that serious amounts of metal were being nicked. It was alright for the cops on the case to take the bung, but the senior chiefs needed some nicking's. Soon the word went out to the scrap dealers, a little whisper in the old cake hole. It wasn't enough to bung a few quid in the book. Those upstairs needed results. Everybody's lucrative livelihood was on the line. The dicks didn't want to lose their lucrative little backhanders. The scrap dealer didn't want to end up in nick for handling stolen metal, an odds-on certainty knowing most of the metal in his yard was nicked in the first place.

A compromise was soon reached. The scrap dealer would throw the odd body in, usually a mug, a working peck nicking the odd bit of copper or brass off the factory floor. No one in the factory gave a thought to old Alf picking up the sweepings from the floor. It was just rubbish, but when the cops nicked him and then went to his factory, the foreman and boss had no alternative but to accept that poor Alf had nicked the metal. Theft was theft, right? The scrap dealer would console himself in the knowledge that Alf had been earning a nice few quid over the last few months. Alf would get a small fine and a bit of probation, and he would soon get another job, maybe a similar one where he could nick a bit of metal. After all, he had to get his fine money back; other than that, he took it on the chin. Well, he had no fucking choice. As for the cops? Well, they didn't give a shit. A thief is a thief, except if you're a cop. Fuck him.

For the more professional thieves, it was a slightly different matter. They didn't know any better way to earn a living or as easy. Nine times out of ten, they didn't have to break in anywhere. Climbing up onto a church roof and nicking the lead was easy enough. The weight caused the problem with lead. It was common, heavy, and didn't fetch as much money as copper. Whichever way they nicked it was the easy bit, well, almost, in desperation, they would resort to nicking grate and gully coverings from out of the roads. Either way, nicking metal gave them a fairly easy way of making money. The only problem now was being thrown in by the scrap dealer. As the cops tightened the leash, more and more scrap dealers felt they had no choice but to throw the odd body in.

This led to the problem of who to trust. No scrap dealer will ever admit to throwing you in or grassing on you. But you were placing your life in your hands at all times. Sometimes, admittedly, you could just be unlucky enough to find a couple of cops just doing a routine inspection, but this was very rare. At any rate, it always gave the scrap dealer his get-out.

The shrewd villains knew that time was against them. Most had done army service on conscription call-ups, but many had attended approved schools. It was a doddle that was even better than being at home. Harsh and brutal as it was, it was still better than the alternative, with a nice warm bed, decent clothes and four meals a day. Plenty of activities and even an education.

From there, the next progression was borstal. That was a bit of a different ball game where the place was full of testosterone-filled kids looking to prove themselves and make their reputation. Worse, some of them came from seriously damaged backgrounds and were mentally really fucked up. Having come through that, a bit of probation or/and fines, the next prospect was a bit of porridge; sounds simple, doesn't it?

A bit of porridge wasn't so bad. Three months could be a doddle. For some villains, it was a bit of a sabbatical. It kept them off the booze, and they ate four square meals a day. Even being locked up in the Peter wasn't so bad. You could most likely be in with your best pal where you could go over old mistakes, vow to learn not to make them again, and discuss future jobs and blags. The world was their oyster, and they were nothing if not optimistic. The problem was, by now, they were married, had a couple of kids, and blocked their minds to birthdays, but when it came to Christmas, many would be shed under the blanket at night.

Time inside was eighteen months, the previous time twelve months. Deep down, they knew the next time would be a three-stretch, maybe even more. Some took it in their stride, giving it the big bravado. Others just tried giving it the big bravado. Deep down, their bottles were going, and each new job had to be preceded by a few drinks first to build themselves up to it. In the main, they never even realised.

By now, major teams were being formed around the city, and they were becoming more skilled and professional. They had learned from their parents and the Peaky Blinders, who, in the main, were just amateur thugs and sluggers. Many had served in the forces they were used to discipline, skilled in keeping their mouths shut, following orders and accepting one leadership. They were also trained in explosives. That's where Twink had got his experience. Gangs who interreacted and built up from each other learned from each other and used each other for specific jobs. Some specialised in factory break-ins, warehouse robberies or insurance frauds. But not many wanted to get into the really big stuff, robbing banks with guns. It was easy enough, alright. The only problem was that no one could figure out exactly how much was in the banks. It was all guesswork.

In London, the heavy boys had it more sewn up. They would know if there were twenty or thirty grand in; they had good contacts and were more professional. Here in Birmingham, it was more hit-and-miss. One post office reportedly had ten grand in, a lot of money at the time. Between four of them, that was two and a half grand each, nice money, steaming in with a sawn-off and pickaxe handles, firing a round into the ceiling and battering the counter whilst making lots of noise was bad enough as it was. To then walk out with only fifteen hundred quid was a bit of a piss take to say the least. I mean, it was fucking demoralising, all that and the risk of a ten stretch for three hundred and fifty quid each.

No, quite sensibly, the men would stick to the smaller, more lucrative jobs of which there was an abundance. A factory loaded with drinks, clothes, or other goods could raise three or four grand without breaking a sweat, often instigated by the factory or warehouse owners themselves. Everyone was making money, everyone was happy. For a bit, the cops couldn't get their heads around it. Oh, they were picking out and finding out who the villains were, of course. But it became even harder to pinpoint them because they were so spread out around the city. With that confidence came even more daring. Someone had grassed on one of the gangs; it maybe wouldn't have mattered if it had been anyone else, but three of the gang were part of the Kirby clan. Raymond was fucking furious, and so was Johnny Lewin. Clearly, whoever had put them in had done so inadvertently. The Kirby's involved got eight to ten years each and were fucked. They wanted revenge.

THE FIRST ONE IS
ALWAYS THE HARDEST

It took a bit of time to find out who it was. It was a process of elimination, but the one name kept coming up time and time again: he wasn't a Summer Laner. He came from outside the centre over Northfield Way. Knowing the tickles and reputation of the Summer Lane gangs, he eventually ingratiated himself into their company and quickly became one of the gang. This was starting to become a regular problem with the gangs who had grown up with each other, knew each other and trusted each other from Summer Lane school days. They were starting to take each other for granted and accepted each other at face value, "Oh, this is Charlie. He's a good friend of Reg."

"Oh, that's alright then."

Only he wasn't a good friend of Reg at all. Reg hardly knew the geezer.

In America, the mafia would only allow true Italians into their ranks, most of them having to go back three or four generations. In Sicily, you were accepted on the basis that if you squealed, the whole of your family would be wiped out. Not many squealed. In London, the gangsters had the threat of fear. Many a grass was shot and buried in the footing of some motorway or high-rise building and never heard from again. The cockneys were also very good at getting the jocks to do their dirty business for them. Hired killers were brought in from Manchester. Once Ray Coombe had been locked up with Mad Frank Fraser, the London gangster and henchman of the Richardson brothers, Fraser's reputation was known throughout the country, mainly built up from in the nick, the prison grapevine, the Richardson were utterly fucking ruthless.

It was known that they would kill you or have you killed without much of a separate thought, much of it carried out by Fraser, who would manage to invite someone or get someone to con his victim into visiting the Richardson's scrap yard. From there, he would be tortured, killed, and then crushed in one of the cars, the body disappearing forever; without a body, there was no proof of murder. Who would ever think of something like that? Mad Frank had a couple of party tricks that started to spread about. Known also as Mad Frank, the dentist, he would pull his victim's teeth out one by one until he squealed. The first tooth usually did the trick. Another little party piece was the shock treatment. Many reckoned Frank had learned this little trick in Broadmoor, where he himself had been the recipient. First, Frank would tell his victim to take his trousers off. With the Richardson's mustered around looking menacing, it was difficult to refuse.

Once the trousers were off, Frank would attach a pair of jump leads to his balls, attached to a heavy-duty 12-volt battery via a switch. For the first twenty minutes, it was explained to the victim how painful it was. It was fucking painful. Some people had died from it, if not from the shock, then from a heart attack. Frank's reputation was widespread; everyone who was anyone around London had heard about some of the things that Frank had done. A few turns on the nob, and people soon opened up and started screaming, telling Frank what he wanted to know.

In the nick, most of the screws were terrified of Frank, and a fair few of the cons were as well, but mostly it was the cops or the screws who were the focus of attention. It wasn't Mad Frank's size; after all, he was only five foot six in his socks. It's just that he had no fucking boundaries. Once he started, he never stopped. He was remorseless. Once, the screws, frightened of his constant threats and violence, decided to go steaming into his cell one night after everyone was banged up. They forced him over the bed and broke both his legs. Frank couldn't walk for months. It put Frank out of action for a bit and gave the screws some peace. This incident alone spread throughout the prisons and beyond, enhancing Mad Frank's reputation even further, "don't fuck with Frank." The violence committed by the screws was acceptable, just as it was by the police. The other bonus, of course, was the salutary lesson it gave for the other cons. Listening to the ruckus, the screaming, balling and shouting, it wasn't hard to figure out what was happening. Seeing Mad Frank subdued and hobbling along on sticks a few days later, it didn't take a lot of brains, "Good on ya, Frank, ya sorted those bastards out, nice one." Back in the cells, it was a little different. Fuck that for a lark; not many went too far with giving the screws some verbal gyp.

Ray was on his way out of the nick with only a few more weeks of his seven-year stretch to do. Mad Frank wanted a little favour. He wanted some grass in London shot. Ray didn't fancy this too much at all, but he had his reputation to think of. He had spent seven years in the nick, much of it in Broadmoor, building up his reputation. If he refused, he knew his reputation would be in tatters. On his release, he was instructed to go down to London, meet up with the Richardson's, pick the gun up along with the instructions, where the grass lived, his name and description and kill him.

Ray didn't fancy this at all. Belting someone was one thing. It was almost acceptable. But to kill someone? A stranger, in cold blood? This was a fucking hanging offence. The cops and the judges didn't give a monkeys; they had hung many people, even in the most extenuating circumstances. Oh, it was alright when the powers that be wanted you to kill someone. You were called up and told to kill the enemy. Their enemy. But when you got back from the war and wanted to kill your enemy, that was a no-no. But he couldn't see a way out. After a lot of soul searching and bottling it a few times, Ray built himself up to shoot the grass but deliberately shot him in the legs. The shooting was reported in all the local papers, an assassination attempt without mentioning exactly where the grass was shot, the Richardson's accepted Rays story. Honour was restored, and Ray was given a thank you and a bung of a few grand for his trouble. Thank fuck for that.

But it gave the Kirby's an idea of how to deal with their little grass. The bodies in the scrap rumour had been known and circulating in Birmingham for some time, but that's all it was considered to be a rumour. Initially, it had been an old tramp who fell asleep in one of the scrap cars. The poor bastard had died whilst asleep in the car from the harsh winter cold, well, at least that's what they thought. By the time they realised it was too late, he was being crushed. It was only through being in the back seat that he was seen. If he had been put in the boot, no one would have been any the wiser. There was so much dirt, shit and oil spewing out of the car that the blood was lost in it. From there, the scrap, now reduced to a two-foot square cube, was taken to the foundries in South Wales with dozens of other little cubes, melted down in the vast furnaces and turned into new metal. Any bodies in the original car were now incinerated. Rather than report it to the cops, which could bring all kinds of problems down on the scrap dealer, it was considered prudent to keep their mouths shut. No one was ever the wiser.

Apparently, this was a regular method used by the mafia in America. Owing to omerta, the mafia code of silence, it took some time before it started leaking out. It was only through the contacts built up between the mafia and the London gangsters that the secret leaked. Until this book is published, chances are, no one else knew about it at all. Any gossip, fuelled by rumour, was just that, gossip. That is, of course, until someone did speak out of school. The method used in the James Bond film Goldfinger is exactly how it was done. But by now, half the mafia were screaming like canaries.

The cars were stripped bare to the carcass. Once enough cars were built up to make a load, they were shipped off to the foundries in South Wales. Once there, they joined the queue straight up to the furnaces themselves. Within one hour, they were off the lorry and melted down. No graves, no burials, no chopping up of bodies to get rid of them, simply put them in the furnace, no one would dream of it. Even better, you got paid for the extra weight of the body. It was a win, win all round. Up until then, bodies were usually dumped in the footings of newly built flats or multi-story office blocks, guaranteed never to be discovered for generations. In America, the favoured method was to take them out into the vast Nevada desert, where they were buried, never to be found again. But scrap cars and foundries were the latest phenomena.

But first, it was finding the right scrap yard. Only two or three of Birmingham's crushing plants were in use. Most of the little tat yards just stripped the carcasses bare before taking them whole to one of the main crushers. Their income came from the spares and the nonferrous, and they were paid accordingly. So that wiped any of them out for getting rid of the body. Putting a body in the boot at that point could be very dodgy. But who else?

None of the three top crushing plants in Birmingham were known to the gangs. Well, one or two were, of course, but only from a distance. A couple had come from Summer Lane or around themselves but were too far apart to be trusted. Oh, ok, a couple of tons of brass or copper fine; after all, everyone wants to earn, "Yes, no problem, Ray, drop it in late Monday afternoon," and by Tuesday morning, it was mingled in with all the rest of the scrap, unidentifiable. But a body? Leave it out. As for the rest of the scrap dealers around town, fuck that, it was too much of a risk. Oh, it was all bravado in the boozer, "Yes, no problem, drop it around," but you took your life in your fucking hands. It was self-preservation. Most had already done a bit of porridge trying to get their money to buy the scrap yard in the first place. The three words were tied in with each other. Murder? Death penalty?

There was only one way for it. A couple of Ray's brothers owned scrap yards, including his old man Bert, the ex-British champion. A good couple of days were spent skirting around the subject before getting to the real nitty gritty. Then, the subject was only touched on. The upshot was the body had to be taken to the yard after it had closed on a given night. The last person working on that car, usually a young kid, would be responsible for a final check of the vehicle, doors and boot, opened and emptied of anything that shouldn't be there. He was the last witness. Bert would also make sure someone else was in the yard to make the last-minute checks and lock up; that way, Bert was none the wiser and was also out of the yard.

All Ray, Johnny and the others had to do was get the grassing bastard set up and kill him. The easiest way to do that was a bang over the head, a quick grab, and bundled into the boot of a car. From there, the body was taken down to Bert's scrap yard, carried in and dumped in the boot of the car, waiting to go to the crushers the next day. The doors were unlocked and locked with a spare key, with no one being none the wiser. A tense few hours were spent the next day till word came through that the car had gone through the foundry with no one knowing. That was the first one.

Another favoured method of getting rid of someone, and probably the best of all, was to throw them on the tracks of a busy rail line. This worked a treat, but the problem was getting the victim to the railway tracks in the first place. You can hardly go up to your victim and say, "Can we have a word, Charlie?"

"Yeah, of course, down the boozer?"

"Oh no, Charlie, let's take a walk down the railway line." No, first of all, you had to innocently suggest going for a drink, down to some out-of-the-way boozer with a handy couple of bomb pecks around the area—there were plenty of them.

After getting a few pints down their neck, it was easy enough to walk them past the bomb peck and put a bar over their bonce. From there, it was just a matter of lugging the body to some out-of-the-way mainline and throwing it over the bridge. The bang on the bonce would have been eradicated in the mess the train would have done to him. The only problem with that method was that it became quite popular in London and the rest of the country. Manchester and Liverpool were two favoured locations, but the cops soon started to smell a rat; just too many bodies were jumping off bridges after a few drinks, and surely not that many people were committing suicide. Once the cops twigged on, it became a simple matter of elimination. Of suspects, of course. Digging deeper, the dead body was found to have recently grassed on a couple of major villains; once caught, they were found guilty and banged up for life, and bodies stopped going over bridges overnight.

Not many people did any grassing. Only the lowest of the low would throw their mates in; the army had taught them that. Even the cops had a certain sympathy, if not a grudging understanding, of the villains themselves. The years before and after the war were desperate; people were starving, and if you didn't work, you starved. Perverse as it might sound to some people, there was an honour about the villains and an honourable way of doing things.

Not for them, some petty shoplifting or robbing of churches, mugging old people who had no money anyway. These villains held their heads up among their peers. What they did was admired and respected, even amongst decent working people who would have had a go themselves if they had got the bottle. Robbing a warehouse of a few grands worth of gear was considered a harmless crime. The warehouse owner was more than likely behind the robbery in the first place. If he wasn't, he was grateful to be able to load his insurance up and make a few extra grand for himself. Most of the villains were well-known around town in Birmingham, but that was not necessarily a good thing because the cops all knew who they were anyway. But it didn't matter. Sometimes, the lines were so blurred between buying a bit of fiddled meat from the market or a nice gold bracelet nicked from the jewellery quarter no one gave it any thought. Everyone was at it in some form or another. It was just a simple progression from buying some meat to asking one of the villains if he knew someone willing to rob his shop or factory.

Poverty was still widespread around the slums of Birmingham, Manchester, London, and other major cities. In Birmingham, the back-to-backs, slum terraces, two ups and one down, with eight or more people in a family, were the norm. It even brought the well-to-do middle classes to explore and visit these so-called poorest of the poor. It was like a day out for those from such classes; they didn't know or understand poverty. One or two did, though, and soon learned to ingratiate and mingle with the villains, wide boys and wheeler dealers that made their living around the town and Summer Lane. Amongst the poverty, actors, singers, and other well-to-do personalities would often call in for a tot or two before walking out with a nice deal tucked under their belts.

You could walk into one of the ground floor rooms off the cobbled courtyard of six houses, three outside toilets and a wash house, not knowing what you were walking on, so black was the floor. Great granddad huddled up close to a fire barely lit, with no coal left, skin discoloured by the intense heat contrasted with no heat, shivering in worn-out threadbare clothes. What spare teeth he had in his head chattering with the cold. His granddaughter, worn out and knackered, and four of their kids huddled around were all threadbare and cold. This was early autumn, and the running fear was how they would get through the winter. No one knew what a pair of underpants were. If they had underpants or socks, they would have been lucky. Handkerchiefs were unknown and unheard of, your ragged-arsed pants were full of skid marks, and your sleeve was full of silver snot that you wore like a badge of honour. For the odd few that did use a handkerchief, usually the master of the house, these would be washed on the gas cooker in one of the saucepans. Once washed, the snot dissolved by boiling, the saucepan would be washed out under the tap and returned to the gas ring to cook the evening meal. If you were lucky, the meal was cooked first. If you were even luckier, you were never privy to see the hankies being boiled. It was quite normal to walk into someone's house and see the snot rags being boiled on the gas ring.

On the cellar head, stood the four-ring gas cooker next to the Belfast sink. Above this, shelves held the few plates to be shared within the family. To the side, the marble cold slab that kept the margarine or milk cold for the short time it was around, in between the shelves, the distempered flaking plaster or cold bare bricks stood gloomily staring back. There was no such thing as fridges or freezers. Some of them would turn a gas ring on to give some heat to the room, not too much as the meter had to be fed by a coin, and very few had any coins to spare. Only a very few people had the brains, know-how, or even the bottle to realise how simple it was to fiddle with the gas by turning the meter around or even putting another meter in taken from one of the recently vacated slum houses awaiting demolition.

With many houses still with gas lighting via mantles on the walls, the poor bastards never realised how much better their quality of life would be if only they had had the brains to know. Heating and light are free throughout the year. Instead, they lived in cold and damp, shivering and waiting to die without even realising it. For the lucky or unlucky few who had electricity, none knew how easy the meters were to fiddle. Stop the wheel going around, and you stop the built-in clock recording the electricity used. After all, the utilities are not going to give a fuck about you, are they? You are their profit. Whether you die is irrelevant to them, the same with the government; they were overwhelmed as it was with the amount of poverty that existed throughout the country. If you did, or do, someone else will simply take on the bills. Life was harsh, alright.

The utilities (gas and electricity) are not a charity; let's face it: whilst oil and gas are formed underground over several millions of years from prehistoric decomposing organisms, you might well feel entitled to believe that you, the people, all of us, own it. No, no, no, you silly Billy, well. We may think we own it, except for that one per cent at the top who say they own it. You only have to look at the Middle East, the billions lining the pockets of those few who run the countries. Someone has to make a profit, but not us plebs. Whilst you might be forgiven for thinking gas and electricity should be a non-profit utility, in reality, we have to pay in the hot regions, we have to pay to keep cool; in the cold extremities, we have to pay to keep warm.

The lack of money is like a ticking time bomb. If thirty per cent of your income goes on heating and you can avoid that, then in one simple swipe, you have increased your quality of life and food spending consumption. The difference between life and death. Those very few who did know and fiddle with the meters just couldn't afford to share that knowledge with the next-door neighbour. You couldn't afford the risk of the whole courtyard being at it and the meter bills going through the floor. Besides, it's odds that if caught, they would squeal. Besides that, again, many were so worn down and out both physically and mentally. They were at great risk of being caught out on days the meter readers came to visit.

Many a time, the rent man would call. If he didn't open the door himself, little Johnny would answer only to say, "Mommy says to tell you she's not in, mister." The rent man replied, "Son when your mom comes from under the table, tell her I'll call next week."

For those right on the bottom rung, it was all they could do to survive. There was nothing the government liked more than a subservient population.

Old man Clark would go out with his pram every day, seven days a week, pushing the little baby pram he had found somewhere. If Clarky had ever walked proud and upright, it would have been in the distant past. Maybe he had served his time in the army if he had no one knew. Clarky would shuffle out head down, sweeping the floor with his eyes, a scruffy moth-ridden pair of trousers and coat, shivering under a threadbare jumper as he scanned the floor for nub ends, a bit of wood or a piece of coal that had fallen off the wagon as it turned a corner. There were always a few prize lumps around Joe Taroni's little bit of bomb peck.

The nub ends would go in his pocket, the bits of coal and wood into his pram. After a day of scavenging, he would return home, stoke the fire up, the rest in the hearth before turning to the table, tipping his nubs out, breaking off the burnt ends and tipping the baccy into his little tin. His wife sitting there on a threadbare chair that he had managed to scavenge from some empty house, worn out and with eyes dead. After he had finished his rituals, old man Clarky would then settle down in front of the now built-up fire, roll a few fags before settling down with a weariness that was constant, smoking his fags and maybe visiting some distant past. It was a ritual that had been carried out since early man. It was an occupation some animals carried out daily. Bears hunted and ate all summer, storing fat for their winter hibernation. Clarky was doing it all year round. Hunting, searching, scavenging.

No one looked down on Clarky. If they did, they didn't shout too much about it. He was that far down in the gutter, and people didn't want to see it. None of them were too far up the rung of the ladder themselves, and it was difficult to retain any dignity when you couldn't even wash your clothes or body properly. To have a bath, you had to bring the bathtub in that was hanging off the wall outside your house. For that, you had to heat saucepan after saucepan on the four gas rings of the oven, that's if you had four saucepans and could afford the gas. Mostly, you would wait the week till everyone was either filthy or smelling. Then it would normally be dad or granddad first, followed by the oldest to the youngest, with the water being at its dirtiest. The saying 'Don't throw the baby out with the bathwater' was often no truer because of the confines and lack of privacy. Any older female or mom would have to wait till everyone was out before having a strip wash in the Belfast sink. The expression tide marks was aptly applied to more than the odd one or two. This was the line that people washed themselves to, mainly the arms and neck.

In these conditions, you were either young or old. There was no in-between. If you were a pretty girl before getting married, that soon disappeared after you were married and became pregnant. Month after month of grinding, poverty quickly wore you down. By the time you were 30 and with at least six kids, living with the in-laws, and at least two of your kids sharing your bed, you were worn out. Incest was rife amongst some families and known about due to the close sharing, but it was buried as a taboo subject. Something never to be admitted or even accepted as known about, you heard the rumours, but that was it, rumours. The only social welfare checks were by the council for pissed beds, mattresses and bed lice. When they came, they didn't see you; they just marched in, noses in the air, eyes looking straight ahead. It wouldn't have been so bad, but these were only jobsworths themselves, two steps away from being in the same position. Lo, behold, if they lifted your bedding up and found maggots, lice or piss.

For the sons of the Peaky Blinders, things were picking up and looking better by the day. They had learned their lessons from the Peaky Blinders. The sloggers, those who had built their reputations on the fights they had and how hard they were, some were lucky, like John Lewin, and many ended their lives with dignity and respect but very little else. Their sons wanted better, and there were only two ways of doing that. Either get a job, work hard and scrimp and save or nick it. It wasn't a hard choice; nicking it became the obvious solution.

A lot joined the forces, the army, the more educated the air force. The pay wasn't brilliant, but you had a roof over your head, four square meals a day and an income, a wage. For two years or more, you could square bash, try and save a few quid, and with a bit of luck, come out and get a house. Buying a house was unheard of. We were peasants. Peasants could not afford to buy a house. Anyone who even considered buying a house was considered a pure and simple mug.

If anyone was stupid enough to consider buying a house, they faced years of uphill struggle, remorselessly having to find the money to pay the mortgage every month on a house that never rose in value, year in, year out. It was never-ending, but so again was renting a shit hole slum council house, if you were lucky enough to get on the housing ladder. First, you had to get on the list. Once on the list, you had to build points up. To build points up, you had to satisfy certain criteria. First, you had to have children from pregnancy. The more children you had, the more you built your points up. It was a debilitating, wearisome process. Four kids in a slum house in a one down two up, you were already old and not too far from the knacker's yard.

If you had a skill, it wasn't so bad. All the Hipkisses were skilled joiners/carpenters, low paid as it was skilled workers could always get a job. The unskilled, uneducated at the bottom of the ladder were on the losing wicket. If they were unfortunate enough to get a job, it was shit work in the foundries, on the building sites, or in the factories doing the lowest of the dirtiest jobs, most times you were that thick you didn't realise you were in a job in which you were dying, slowly, month by month. Those fresh out of the army, the sons of the Peaky Blinders, the Summer Laners, knew this. They had listened to the speeches by Sir Winston Churchill and others. They would come home to a land fit for heroes. Did they fuck. They came home to a wife and a couple of kids worn down by rationing, having to survive on a day-to-day basis in a back-to-back, two up, one down. Very quickly, they found employers didn't want ex-army service personnel except for the lowest of the low menial work.

Soldiers were untrained, unskilled, and, in many cases, damaged. Many a soldier came back from the war suffering some mental damage like shell shock, etc.

Meeting up in the boozers, it quickly became obvious what the future held for them: did they go down that route or adopt a different attitude? Looking around at the elderly generation. The ones who had served in the First World War barely twenty-five years before. That was the great war, the war to end all wars, so it was said due to the suffering and death inflicted on so many millions, there will never be another war. Yet throughout history, there has been a war on average every twenty years. Every twenty years, 100s of 1000s were killed, murdered, mothers left widowed and penniless. WWI was not of our making; that was initiated by some duke in some far European country being assassinated. WWII was caused as a direct result of the incompetent way WWI ended, with the Germans being strangled both financially and otherwise, again, not of our making.

Now, sitting here in the boozers, deflated and looking around at that generation who had served in the First World War, old men, worn out, some with no legs at all, some without an arm, most damaged in some way or another, putting a smile on things but knowing it was too late to do anything. Once, they had been proud young men, just like the ones sitting opposite them, handsome, full of confidence, cocksure, happy and brainwashed enough to volunteer to fight in a war not of their making. Now here they were, some not even into their fifties, worn out and knackered, grateful for the dead-end job in the factories that gave them a roof over their head, food in their bellies and a few pints down the boozer, well fuck that for a lark.

Some of them hadn't served in battle but had been called up for national service by conscription. Fighting was one thing. Brainwashing was another. You were bound by duty to your country and your fellow man, oh yes, that's all fine and fucking dandy, but looking around and seeing how their fathers had been treated, how their older siblings were being treated was a whole different ball game.

No, this generation was not as stupid, forgiving or accepting as the older generations. They were trained, they were skilled, they knew their friends, they had a loyal friendship base, and each was determined to set out in the world on their own terms. Not for them a menial factory job grinding them down five and a half days a week, for a petty two pound ten shilling wage, not when they could rob a factory and make two hundred quid in less than two hours. No one got hurt, only the factory owner who would soon make it back up through his workers, and they deserved robbing anyway; they were robbing bastards themselves. Once the ideas took root, the roots didn't take long to spread.

Perverse thinking? Maybe it's all according to which side of the fence you're sitting on. If I was sitting in a twenty-bedroom mansion, surrounded by lush acres of land, receiving a phone call from my manager who is looking after the twenty thousand workers of mine down in the pits for pennies and a few bags of coal, then you will no doubt think I'm perverse.

Or maybe you're a lord who bought his title in one way or another, either by paying for it or simply choosing the right side to stand with during some major battle, together with a title given a castle or manor, a few thousand acres and all the serfs and peasants that go with it to provide your income, your only obligation being to pay some taxes each half year or yearly. For that, you got a title for life that you could pass on to your children simply for being your children. If your serfs or peasants got out of line, tried to nick a spare chicken, or poached a salmon from the local river, you could do what you wanted with them. Maybe hang them or chop a hand off, anything to serve as a warning for the little bastards not to do it again. Better still, get one of the other peasants to carry out the punishment; that way, the message becomes even clearer for them. Quite rightly, for us? We say fuck you.

The majority of the population knew no better. We had been serfs for centuries, doffing our caps to our superiors. We were used to doing as we were told or suffering the consequences. Our grandparents started to fight back and tried to rebel blindly without knowing exactly how to fight back. As a result, we mainly fought amongst our own cousins, cousins fighting amongst cousins, and brothers amongst brothers. Some fought politically, trying to change the system from within by forming a political party, but they had little chance. The Tories had been in power for centuries, a natural progression from the royal families. Until the last century, they had been the only party till the liberals came along, weak, spineless and inefficient. Anyone else was either communist, Nazi, too far right, or too far left to the extreme. Either way, how could you possibly beat a party headed by the biggest Tory family in the country? The royal family. They even had their own queen council to keep us in our place.

The top lawyers in the country, the top ten per cent, look after the top one per cent. Fucking great ay. No chance against the powerful land-owning Tories. How can you possibly beat them? Even the new Labour Party were on a knife edge, coming in the main from the middle classes, none of whom knew what it was like to be at the bottom of the ladder. No, now we have started to think of a different way. Slavery might have ended officially hundreds of years earlier, but we were still slaves. We just thought those niggers in the South American plantations were slaves, but we were treated exactly the same except for the whippings. The government prints the money. We have to get up in the morning, go to a shit job and slave all day for a shit wage which just about pays for your rent and barely enough food to fill your bellies. And we were free?

No. The only way was to look after and fend for yourself and your own, of course, fuck everyone else. At first, it was just the odd few jobs you kept between one or two of you; some acted alone, others in groups of twos or more, the only criteria being secrecy and the ability to keep your gob shut, oh, and of course the savvy ness to pick out and choose a likely target to hit or rob. After the war, there were abundant opportunities for people to take advantage of. There were literally hundreds of ex-army veterans unemployed or disabled trying to earn money on the streets, children of ten or younger, forced out to earn money, some selling matches, others the evening paper, yet others shoelaces, many blackened and barefoot- then you had the shysters, the charlatans, the medical men trying to sell anything from a cure for arthritis to a growing toenail, they would set up stall from a standing platform to a horse and cart. Pikey s travelled the land selling hand-cut pegs, whittled down dollies or would tell your fortune if you crossed their palms with silver. Woe betide you if you didn't because as sure as night followed day, you would be cursed. The easy way was the local factories or warehouses; often, you would find money in the weak, easily broken into safes.

Once in the factory, it was a simple case of grabbing and stealing as much clothing or other goods as you could carry. Very quickly, it became obvious that a car or van was essential to carry out your business. Having made enough money to purchase a cheap van, it was a simple matter of breaking into a factory, nicking a load of gear, and then selling it. Half the time, you didn't even have to work at selling it. You simply let it be known that you had a load of swag, be it jumpers, trousers or suits. Anything essential. You could walk into The Stag in Summer Lane at 7 pm, and by 9 pm, you would have sold everything you owned.

One of your neighbours would walk in, "What ya got, John?" Grab it off you, run out, tell their neighbours, and within minutes, half of Summer Lane would buy something off you in The Stag. They weren't stupid. While they didn't have the bottle to go out and nick something, they knew a good deal about it when they saw it. The landlord of the boozer knew when he was onto a good thing. Not only did he get a special discount, but he also got the benefit of the extra trade. On a nightly basis, the pubs in Summer Lane were brimming with people excitedly looking for a deal or just turning up with the expectation of getting a deal.

Not only were the traders from the bull ring markets calling in each afternoon or early evening with their little goodies, a few chops, a leg of lamb or pork, maybe a nice ornament. But there were also the villains with their little treats. Only guesswork made you wonder what was fiddled or what was nicked or really, really nicked. To everyone, it was just of the back of the wagon, and that was good enough.

The Birmingham evening mail was a great help in advertising. Every night, there would be front-page headlines of a major factory robbery in Birmingham, a major break-in at a clothing factory, and one hundred turkeys stolen from a big butcher shop. Upon reading the news, the locals would make sure they were up early and in the boozers, ready to grab a cheap bargain turkey for Christmas. Everyone was happy, well, most of them. If it wasn't a turkey, it would be something else. Publicising the amount of stock stolen from a warehouse or the sum of money nicked from a post office was common. This served two purposes and two benefits. For the locals around Summer Lane, it let us all know that plenty of clobbers would be coming around, or maybe turkeys, giving everyone a chance to build up a few quid. It also lets the other villains know what had been made by a specific little team. "Eyaa. Did you see that little tickle last night? I reckon that was Ronnie Evans and his team, fuck me with a bargepole. What a nice touch." Not only did Ronnie set the bar for the others, but it also let those who were not having a good run know that they might be in for a touch. Sure enough, when Ronnie turned up at The Stag Friday night, it became clear he'd had a touch. When he modestly started buying a few drinks, it was an opportunity to shuffle over and accept a drink.

"Alright, Ron, had a touch?"

"Yeah, Jim, not too bad. How are things with you?"

"Not too good, Ron. We ain't had a tickle for over a week." At that, Ron would draw a few quid out of his bin and bung Jimmy a drink. This was all part of the good socialist mentality that existed in and around Summer Lane, all for one, one for all. Besides, Ronnie knew full well that he might struggle in a couple of weeks. It was a mindset that sat well with most who were at it, drink and be merry today; tomorrow, we might be skint. Course, one or two thought very differently. What is mine is my own, fuck the others. Life had taught them to be a bit heartless. Not everyone was or thought like Robin of the Hood. Your stature or reputation was built on the jobs you carried out; the bigger the job, the more daring, and the higher your stature or standing within the community.

A courtyard off High Park Street, Nechells, 25th April 1966.

Summer Lane was almost three-quarters of a mile long, made up of block after block of terraced houses and back-to-backs leading off little entries to communal cobbled or blue brick courtyards. Thrown in amongst the mix would be a factory or builder's yard, shared toilets kept rigorously clean even after someone had shit in them or spewed up over them after a drunken Saturday night. No one would admit to it, of course. Quietly or discreetly, they or the missus would sneak over as furtively as possible and clean it out, hopefully before anyone else went over to use it. Woe betide you if they did because all hell would break loose, "which dirty bastard shit all over the karzie?" In shame, someone might come over, shoulders huddled in embarrassment. "It was our Lenny. Sorry, he reckons that bitter in the barrel was orf last night." Quickly, she'd clean the offending karzie. No one made too big a fuss because they knew it could just as well be their old man next week or even her. It was a regular occurrence. On a Monday, there would be line after line of washing hanging out. Mondays were wash day, and the lines were hung as a badge of honour, wearisome as it was. If there were two ways the neighbours held their heads up and their dignity, it was in their clean washing on washdays and the polished front step. These would be rigorously scrubbed each week, polished and buffed up daily. Woe betide those who had a dirty doorstep, "Eearr our Doris. Can't yow afford a bit of polish then?"

"Fuck off," Doris would reply.

The factories, woodworkers, joinery factories, nail makers, and brass polishers were between the back-to-backs. It was as though someone had said, some bright spark in the council, of course, don't forget to plop a few factories in between so the labour won't be too far away from them, and of course, it wasn't, you could literally leave school, call into next door, or the furniture manufacturer across the road ask for a job and start that very afternoon or the next day, with a bit of luck, or not as it seemed, you might get a job as an apprentice. Of course, you were trained for about a third of the average wage. Most, with no education, no hope, and no visibility of any future, chose labour with more money.

The one advantage, of course, was that you could simply roll out of bed, walk twenty paces, and you were in work. The disadvantage was if you'd had a piss-up on a Friday night and couldn't get up Saturday morning, the boss would simply send someone knocking on your door.

Everyone knew everyone. You got married, finally, after years of building up points, living in the attic or front room of your parent's house, knocking out kids, you would be given your house, and that's where you stayed till the day you died, as your kids grew up, they got married, built there points up and as was council policy they would be given a house next door or a few houses away, in Summer Lane you could have four or five brothers or sisters, straddled from one end to the other, cousins, uncles, aunties. Only the stupidest fools would put one on someone's chin on a Saturday night without knowing who they were related to. "Don't touch him. that's Big Ronnie's son for fucks sake." You didn't put one on Ronnie's chin. Everyone was an auntie or uncle. "Go and ask Auntie Doris for a bit of marg or a slab of dripping." It was only years later you actually wondered who was actually auntie and who was uncle. It didn't matter.

Course, then you had the uncle, uncle. After your real dad died in the war, your mom might bring in Uncle Jimmy. If Jimmy didn't last too long, your mom might bring in Uncle Tommy. It never occurred to you that your uncle wasn't really your uncle. It didn't matter. Every bloke with a pair of trousers in the road was your uncle. Most times, it brought in extra kudos. Uncles were much better for the nip than Auntie Mary. Sometimes, it could be quite lucrative, "Gis a tanner, Uncle Bob!" Bob had the choice of telling you to fuck off or giving you the tanner. It wouldn't look good, uncle telling you to piss off.

Many a time, you might see someone smart in a nice suit, Trilby on his bonce, calling up the entry carrying a little bag or parcel, scratching their heads with curiosity. The neighbours would be bursting to know what was happening, and something was always going on, from debt collectors calling around. Rent men on a Monday morning, coal men on a Friday payday. To the bloke in the smart suit and titfer on his bonce. "Alright, Ethel? Ay, was that your new boyfriend I saw calling at your door this afternoon?" You knew it wasn't because we all knew Ethel was married. Still, we had to find some way of opening the conversation to find out. With a negative no, it was, "Well, he was a good-looking bloke, wasn't he? Hmmmm, Ethel wasn't going to bite. Sometimes you might get a bit of joy, but it "was our Billy's mate who brought him a bit of lamb across from work, for Sunday dinner." Ohhh, curiosity satisfied. Yes, there was always something going on down the lane. It broke the boredom up.

You would have the little terrace shops between the factories and the tenements. Again, you could see some bright spark from the council who had sat at his dark oak-stained desk and worked out how many shops to put between the houses and factories. No one needed to walk too far. Food had to be bought daily due to lack of storage and keeping it chilled. Every block of terraces had at least one corner shop, and each shop varied only slightly. Metal signs all over the front outer wall advertising Will's Whiff Cigarettes or Hovis bread. On the floor inside sacks of flour or wheat. Next to a huge block of cheese and a block of margarine that you could cut off as you needed. Inside the dark but cheerful shop were shelves holding all kinds of goods and food, the tantalising smells pervading the room, maybe a radio shop. Along the way, Diamond Lily Hawkins ran the jellied eels shop selling penny winks, cockles and whelks for a few pennies. The sweet shop selling penny bags of sherbet, blackjacks, and bottled pop miraculously made up around the back of the shop and brought to you for a penny. It never occurred to us that she had to sell twelve bottles to make a shilling, twenty shillings worth to make a pound. We just trusted and never gave it a thought that however she produced it, her hygiene was up to standard. If you wanted anything more exotic, you had to walk a mile up the road to the Bull Ring. If you could afford it, you got the tram and made a day out of it. "See you Saturday, Jean, by the rag market," where you met up having done half your shopping and have a cup of tea, maybe a bag of chips or a bag of whelks according to what pennies you had in your purse, and a fag of course.

Meeting up in the Bull Ring, the rag market, or Lewis's was a major part of Saturday life for most Brummies". It was a day to relax, forget the pressures and stress of daily living and enjoy the hustle and bustle of the markets.

Thieving, or buying bent gear, was part and parcel of everyday life in the lane. You either swam with it or starved. If you didn't starve, you struggled daily to survive. The cops, slow as they were, were taking their time trying to figure out, catch on and understand exactly what and how much was going on. Very few neighbours or people squealed. Woe betide them if they did and were caught, there was no escape for them.

GETTING ORGANISED AND FORMING THE GANGS

You could place a bet that if you called into any boozer on a Saturday afternoon or night or any cobbled backyard with a few dozen chickens, you'd hear, "Okay ladies, come and get your bargains, buy yourself a nice chicken for tomorrow's dinner" all of the back of a lorry and all half price. Everyone would be out like a shot. Only the very odd one would refrain. Maybe with a sniff. For the coppers casually walking along, usually in twos, it was simply a case of keeping an eye out for a friendly face and being coppers, the enemy. There weren't too many of them. But there was always the odd one. "Morning, officers, nice day, ain't it."

"Morning, missus," they said, pulling themselves to a stop. "How's things today, then?" Most, if not all, the coppers knew what was happening almost daily and why. They were not impartial in buying or accepting a bit of meat or something themselves. After all, a copper's pay wasn't brilliant.

After the pleasantries had been carried out and a few, "How's your lads then? Still keeping out of trouble?"

A subtle, "how's things going then? All quiet, is it?" The question deliberately pointed at a tangent. Looking around, all innocent to see no one was looking, the missus would blurt it out with built-up excitement, trying to sound casual. "Oh yes, you know what it's like around here. Mind, it was busy yesterday. One of those Lewin's came around selling fresh chickens. Of course, I don't know where they came from." Of course, she didn't know where they came from, but she knew full well that they were bent. "I didn't buy one mind."

The coppers would give each other a knowing look. Oh yes, sometimes, if a butcher had been broken into and a hundred fresh chickens nicked, the cops would give each other another knowing look. "Ahhh, the Lewins ay? Which one would that be, missus?" If there hadn't been a robbery, they would guess it was a bit of fiddling down in the market that was happening all the time. At any rate, they would mentally jot it down in their heads. After thanking the missus, maybe giving her a half crown for her trouble and kindness, they would saunter on, "Hmmmm, those Lewins, ay?" Reporting it to the Sergeant when they got back. Bit by bit, slowly but steadily, they built up their little files of information.

Their main informants were some of the men who had their own scores to settle for one reason or another. Old Harry had done his stint in the first world war, coming home minus one leg and a miserly pension. Harry was not a happy bunny. Struggling to survive on a daily basis, all he had was his missus for company. Neither one could afford to go out for a drink or wanted to. Their only company, the radio to listen to by the coal and slack fire. One or two would feel sorry for him and, knowing he had done service, would drop him in the odd chicken or bit of mutton. He would never squeal on those and could turn a blind eye to them, but he hated people who thieved or broke into factories. It was all wrong that these people could make big money whilst he had to walk on crutches, having done his duty for his country.

No one gave a thought when they saw Harry talking to a couple of the coppers as they stood on the corner. Everyone knew Harry was lonely. After all, his missus never spoke from one day to the next, poor old bastard. No one saw either when the copper slipped Harry. It was a rolled-up ten-bob note. "Thanks, Harry. Keep it up."

A police informant was few and far between around the lane for all that. Too many people knew each other, and people of all walks kept things close to their chests. There were that many deals going on in and around the markets and businesses, and no one knew what was a little deal, a bit of larceny, or a major blag.

While everyone admired the cockneys and what they got up to, not many in Birmingham had the bottle or inclination to go that far regularly. Of course, the rewards were far higher, but so was the porridge. You would pick the national paper up to hear six had gone in heavy-handed with shotguns, pickaxe handles and clubs and got away with a huge sum of money. Thousands of pounds in cash made you drool until you did the sums. Split between six, backhanders paid out, and bungs to bent cops didn't mount up that high. Here, you could pull three jobs between the three of you for the same amount without very little risk.

Using guns brought in stiffer sentences. Many times, they would have to shoot, trying to hit the ceiling or the legs for less damage, but that in itself brought in the risk of an attempted murder charge. If some died as a result, it brought in an automatic murder charge. Guilty, it was a hanging offence. More than one London gangster did that and was topped without hesitation.

Without a murder, and if caught, it was a straight of ten-fifteen or twenty stretch. The cockneys seemed to take that in their strides, such was the poverty and hardships suffered in London. But prison was hard, gruelling. There were no niceties here. In contrast, you could get a two stretch for robbing a factory according to the barrister who acted for you and what you could bung. Course that built up the more you got nicked.

The first bang-up was taken in your stride. You can't expect the gain without getting a bit of pain. Besides, when you got into Winson Green, which was daunting and abysmal as it was, you knew everyone. Six months was a break. Twelve months was a bit of a holiday that gave you a break from all the boozing and eating that was knocking your body about. As soon as you hit the ground after the usual check-ins, being issued with the thin striped uniform, you were inundated with shouts of, "Alright Billy, come for a fucking holiday, have you?" Followed by lots of laughter. The Barron would be the first to sidle over with a pack of baccy, then Dicky Dalton or big nose Billy Henry would shout you over or up onto the third floor and join him in his peter.

OK, it wasn't a holiday camp, but you could make the most of it with a bit of laughter amongst good friends. If you were lucky enough to get on an outside work party, you could take your top off and get yourself a tan. Once out, you were refreshed, cleansed out and fit. With bravado, you could walk out and boast of doing it "On my fucking head, son," and return to normal. In the meantime, your friends and family were looking after your wife and kids, giving them a bung regularly. Things weren't too bad at all, mind, you resolved not to get nicked again, oh no. Fuck that. That's the last time I'm going down, till the next time.

Ray Camber had found a nice little tickle at the Dudley co-op. Putting it to Dicky Dalton, they both went over to have a recce. The co-op took all their money in on a Friday and Saturday, which was too late to put into the bank, so they locked it in the peter in the office, and the key was hung in a safe place. Stupid as it may sound, this was quite the norm; the management just didn't want to be responsible for taking the keys home and forgetting about them. Being so lackadaisical, it was very easy to adopt the attitude that some of these companies deserved to be fucking robbed. So you could be employing some 200, 300 people from all over the town, and you let them know you've got large sums of money in the safe?

In the safe, it was estimated that there was a right few grand, probably forty or fifty grand. Plenty enough for Ray to bring his brother in on the tickle, who was suffering a bit of hardship.. in turn, Dick felt it was a good idea to bring in Billy Henry, who had a little van which would be handy to carry the cash, much of which was in coins.

With all in agreement, they decided to do the break-in on the quietest night of the weekend, Sunday. It went as sweet as a nut. Pulling up in the van at ten pm, they cracked a window at the back. Once in, they found the keys, opened the safe and eureka all the money tumbled onto their feet. All their Christmases had come at once. They had the money in bags within minutes and were away from Dudley by midnight. Divvying up the proceeds at Ray's house, they all split up and headed home. They had just made one mistake. Well, silly prat Billy Henry had. Breaking into the window, he had left a thumbprint. It took four days for the cops to find out who it was and where Billy lived.

Raiding Billy's house at 6 am the next morning, Billy was taken completely by surprise. Bouncing him down into the back of the squad car, he was soon whipped off to Dudley nick. Out of Billy's share of the cash, which was mostly untouched, half disappeared by the time it ended up in court. Dicky Dalton, Ray and his brother were shitting themselves for a few days till it was clear that Billy had kept his gob shut and they hadn't left any dabs. Returning the loyalty, it was decided to bung an extra few quid to his missus. Billy got a two-stretch for that, plus an extra year for not cooperating with the police. From that moment on, Billy was forever known in a jovial way as Silly Billy. It was a salutary reminder to everyone to remember to wear the mitts. Billy bitterly regretted not doing so. Not only did he get a three stretch, all his fucking money went, much of it in the cop's pockets.

Even worse, which would have given Ray pause, this was the big tickle they all dreamed about, the one to set them up for life. A nice detached house in Sutton at the time would fetch five grand. They had enough for ten such houses with just him and his brother. Still, by bringing in others (to do them a favour), they had not only deprived themselves in more ways than one, but they had come very close to getting nicked, all of them. Dear, oh, dear.

With each job pulled, lessons were learned. Each prison sentence was seen as a shake-up and wake-up call, and friends and acquaintances were gathered, made, and stored for their usefulness and future reference. Most kept to their regular known acquaintances. Known and trusted over a lifetime in most cases. Most had specific methods and known sources or targets. Now, the Kirbys and the Lewins had discovered the gelignite and dynamite, which were in demand all over Birmingham. Knowing how sound they were and trusted, other gang members would travel from one side of the city to another to seek their advice or help, but they knew their worth. They also knew the higher risks they were taking simply for what they were dealing with.

Their experiences were often simply called on for a bit of safe breaking. Much as anyone tried to find out the source of their jelly or dynamite, there was no way they would let them in on the secret. Even Harry Twink Dossiter never let anyone know his source. Mind, Twink never let anyone know anything. Twink was a bit too shrewd for that, and Johnny and Ray thought they were sitting on top of the pile. Meeting up at one of the many pubs, they would be approached regularly. We've got a factory over Digbeth with a peter in. It's too big to break out and carry away. Would you be interested in doing a number on it for us? The first concern was who was involved. Doing a blag was the easy part. Knowing the company you were dealing with was the most important. There were two or three major teams in or around Northfield. But they were a different entity altogether, and many grasses kept cropping up from there.

Northfield was an overspill, built mainly to provide houses and service the Austin car factory. The villains and crooks were just wannabes with no collective history of loyalty or family soundness. Dealing with them, it paid to be careful. Once any concerns were put at ease, it became a straightforward matter of negotiation. Straight away, before even getting into the boozer for the first meet, they knew their weak position; they had an idea of how much money was in the peter. Their only problem was they couldn't fucking open it. Johnny and Ray didn't hesitate after everything was put on the table. "Ok, yes, we can do it, but we'll want 50%." 50 fucking %, and they'd done all the leg work, but fair enough, the deal was done. They all went on the due date, let themselves into the factory, blew the safe, took their cut and drove home. It was as easy as taking cake. It was easy to become complacent. And they were starting to.

Twink preferred to work on his own, never talking to anyone, and keeping things very close to his chest. No doubt, Twink was shrewd, alright. Smartly dressed and looking the part at all times, Twink would spend his days mooching and popping into different contacts around Birmingham and beyond, preferably out of the way and beyond. Twink would do his homework, whereas Ray and Johnny would let others do the work. Twink made a point of doing it all himself. He would find the offices or factory, figure out how big the workforce was, and then simply work out when they did the banking. Most companies did their banking on a Friday afternoon or Monday, according to which twink would get all his gear together, set out for the night, break in, set the safe up, blow it, get the cashout, then saunter off, all alone, safe in the knowledge that everything he did was in his own hands. Till the one and only night, Twink got nicked, and it all came on top.

The problem was it was all becoming too easy. Burglar alarms were unheard of. Lots of old buildings were literally falling apart. Butchers kept their stock in a back room with nine times out of ten a weak pair of gates leading onto a backyard. They may as well have left the fucking front door open and put a note up saying help yourselves, folks. On a normal weekday leading up to the weekend, they would have at least fifty or so chickens, rabbits, ducks and a few full lamb and beef carcasses. Christmas was even more lucrative, with the butchers putting a big sign up outside the shop. 'Orders are being taken now for turkeys, ducks, etc.' It was simply a matter of sending the wife in to ask the right questions upon which the butcher would actually boast, "No need to worry, missus, as long as you've got yer order in, in time, we've got a hundred turkeys on order up to yet."

"Really?"

"Hmmmmm. And it's only October, so we can double that number, then there will be all the ducks, etc." Someone will have a field day, and that's a fact for those eyeing the place up. It's just a matter of asking a few questions and finding trustworthy buyers; there were plenty of those about it. Then, it was deciding when to do the break-in. If they left it too late, they could have been beaten by some other thieving bastard.

It will be a sickener for the butcher, but it won't put him out of business. He just won't make a profit or very little over Christmas. It was the same with the hauliers. Many drivers enjoyed a pint or two in the pub and weren't averse to sidling up to one of the teams or gangs. They were the only ones at the bar in hand-made smart suits. After a polite conversation, "How do you think Villa will do Saturday, Jim?" Before casually dropping it out, there will be a ten-ton load of brass in the yard over the weekend. Jim's ears pricked up dead sharpish and his brain was working overtime. Nicking it was easy. It was just a case of getting a buyer lined up for delivery. That wasn't too hard, either. Within the week, the lorry had been nicked, the load taken to the dealer, a short wait for his money, then a visit to the boozer, a couple of drinks for the lorry driver before a discreet visit to the toilets where a thick little envelope would be passed over, shoved in his pocket, a smile of thanks and a walk back to the bar. Sorted. It was a nice Christmas all around. Well, not all around, of course.

Sometimes, it felt like we owned the city. Such was the buzz that emanated around Summer Lane and the town itself. Even the cops were respectful. For themselves, they knew they were only a few steps away from poverty, some of them even closer. The only thing keeping them above water was the uniform and the shared police accommodation they were given. We knew everyone, and everyone knew us. We could walk along Summer Lane from one pub to the next, and we knew everyone in them. We could walk up Constitution Hill, down into Digbeth and know everyone there as well. Walking into Yates Wine Lodge, sawdust on the floor, you would be talking to your mates in one corner of the bar with different teams huddled into groups around the huge bar and floors. Barrel upon barrel lined the walls behind the bar with wines from around the world. Even here, there was a sense of excitement, vibrancy, and a worldly experience. Very few drank alone. With a nod, you could walk over to the group in the far corner or the team in the middle of the bar and be introduced. "This is Jack; he's sound." that was your introduction. By the night's end, you knew them well, and they knew you. It was this relaxed, but by the same token, a serious sense of belonging, accepted.

You could never walk into a pub and just introduce yourself. You would be completely blanked or even (and it did happen) told to fuck off. No, Summer Laners and townies stuck together. We had all been through too much, from our grandparents through the

First and Second World Wars. We knew that we could only rely on and trust each other. This loyalty and generosity of spirit only came about from hardship and poverty. Each and every one of us grew up knowing we could call next door or down the entry to Auntie Lily for a bit of food, dripping or lard, to get us through the day. Likewise, in the boozers, someone would always buy you a pint if you were on the floor.

Indeed, many a time, you had no choice but to walk into the boozer because you had piss all. The smart ones would always ensure you had enough in your bin for that first half, but someone would jump up and buy you a pint as soon as you walked in. It was the norm. Before the night was out, you could either walk out pissed, having had your drink bought all night, or brought your own, having been bunged a few quid. Very few of us locked our doors. And then only in case Fred from next door in the terrace courtyard might walk in pissed one night by mistake. It happened regularly. OK, the cynical might say it was because we had fuck all to nick in the first place. That was very true. But it was the principle. Any would-be petty thief would not know that, but woe betide the little bastard if he did.

A friend of Jack Lewin's walked into The Stag one night, skint and desperate for money, sidling up to Jack, who was in his usual little crowd. After the usual pleasantries, he asked Jack if he knew anyone who might be interested in his Austin car. He had to sell it as he was skint. Jack wasn't very interested in a car, having got the barrer selling fruit and vegetables down the market. He didn't need a car. It was a short walk to the Bull Ring to pick up his barrer, set it up and start selling. There were plenty of trams to get around from one part of the city to another. Besides, Jack did most of his business around Summer Lane, and his business was buying or selling. Jack would buy or sell anything if there was a coin in it. "How much do you want?" He asked his pal. "£15, quid." Now, being friends and being business-like are two separate entities. Jack would have lent it to him if the pal wanted to borrow a fiver, but this was different. After a bit of haggling, his mate accepted a fiver for the car, passing the log book and keys over to Jack's mate, got up and walked out of the pub.

Within fifteen minutes, another pal came over. What was all that about Jack, "I've just bought Fred's Austin, wannit?" By the end of the night, the car had passed from Jack's hands another two times before being sold for twenty-five quid. Only then did the final buyer in the pub go out to check what he had bought and paid for. Starting it up, he walked back in the boozer, smiling and declaring himself happy with the deal. That made four people happy. A fiver was equivalent to a week's wages. Not bad for a night's work. Yes, there was dire poverty, and it would continue. The majority of people in Summer Lane, in the slums in or around the town, Hockley, Aston, and Nechells, Duddeston, were struggling to survive. Some were incapable of even helping themselves. But if you had your head screwed on and were willing to take the risk, opportunities and money were to be made.

No one was the slightest bit interested in what the other bloke had made or how much he had made. He had made a deal on his own merits. That was enough. No jealousy or resentment, each man resided in his ability and trusted his judgment. If he had discovered or known how much the car had originally sold for and then complained, he would have been looked on as a proper mug. Jealousy was either very rare or didn't exist. That was to come later. Envy yes. There was nothing wrong with admiring or even envying what one of your fellow peers had. It was common knowledge that Jimmy was a very clever thief. Some people were natural earners. My dad, Jack Lewin, was a natural earner and always had a few quid in his bin. My brother Johnny hadn't got that ability.

Within even the small communities of Summer Lane and its surroundings, there was a hierarchy; those at the very, very bottom of the ladder were resigned to their fate, too tired and worn down to even worry or be concerned about anyone else or what they were earning except to express a tinge of envy that they were working and they couldn't.

Those in work with 2 kids survived by the skin of their teeth, happy to buy a bit of meat at half price whilst keeping themselves to themselves. They held no resentment or jealousy towards the wide boys, chancers and villains, preferring the guaranteed but steady wage they were earning, low as it was. If they budgeted carefully and lived within their limits, they could survive. Besides, knowing what the villains were up to, they saw a constant stream getting nicked and going down. They preferred working.

For the chancers and villains, if truth be told, most of them knew no better, having left school with no education and being forced to serve in the war, not of their making or compulsory national service. All they were good for was a low-paid labouring job in some gruesome factory or the building site, fuck that for a lark. Better to take your chances on the street, on your own wits, living day by day. For the up-to-yet-successful but hardened villain? Well, it was never going to come to an end; they were leading great lives and making money hand over fist. Life was good. If they did occasionally get nicked, well, so what? It was part and parcel of the life they had chosen. Besides, a bit of porridge never hurt anyone. There was no shame because everyone was in the same boat. No one was innocent. For having a go, you were treated like a hero and a mini-celebrity in most cases.

If anything, when you came out, you were greeted with a cheery, "All alright, Jack, it's been a bit quiet around here. We've missed you and getting some nice deals." The first six months were no problem. The next eighteen months were harder, especially if you had kids. Still, all in all, it was worth it for the lifestyle you led until the porridge started getting a little bit longer.

DREAMING OF THE BIG TICKLE

The shrewd villains knew that the odds were against them. As lucrative as it was, getting away with and from a robbery meant a one in 100 chance of getting nicked, but those odds were reduced the more you participated. Once nicked, you were observed constantly, not just you but all your associates and friends, your movements, your spending, your habits.

Twink got caught bang to rights one night doing the factory safe down Digbeth. He had paid due diligence and done his homework. He had sussed out how many workers were employed in the factory. He had spent hour after hour sitting in his van, a hole drilled in the side panel, observing the comings and goings of staff, how many staff, and when the wages were delivered. Twink just made one elementary mistake. He forgot about the security guard.

Well, he didn't forget about the security guard exactly. He had spent hours observing that the guard came around every two hours, walking around the factory itself before a quick stroll around the offices. After that, he would casually walk back to his office at the far end of the factory, where he poured himself a cup of tea before reading the daily paper. Twink had plenty of time. His only mistake was changing his times slightly on that particular night. This time coincided with the guard looking up and seeing a light in the main office. A torchlight.

Without further ado, the guard scrambled off to the local call point and rang Steelhouse Lane police station. The cops came steaming around mob-handed. Having blown the safe and thrown all the money into a heavy-duty carry bag, Twink calmly started making his way out. This was the most crucial period; just a few yards more, and Twink would be in his car and away with the loot.

The cops had found where he had broken in, clocked his car hidden on the side street, and just hid around in different little spots. Twink fell apart in shock as the cops jumped out on him. Without a doubt, he was caught completely bang to rights; the safe had been blown, and he was carrying his tools and the contents of the peter. Twink was fucked.

Most times, the odds of getting caught and getting bang to rights were hundreds to one; whatever you did, as long as you got away, you had a bigger than average chance of still getting away with the job. Twink had no such luck. Twink pleaded guilty to safe breaking six months later and got a full seven stretch. Whilst the cops couldn't prove it, Twink's modus operandi was the same; they knew he was responsible for a few high-end safe break-ins. Twink wasn't happy at all. His one consolation was that after a fairly successful career as a safebreaker, he had got a few quid stashed away and bought himself a modest house in Erdington. After seven long years behind bars, Twink had plenty of time to think. When he came out, he got a little scrap yard over Hockley and followed the usual route to respectability—his own little business.

All but the odd few villains did their thieving with the main goal: to get enough, then open and set up their own business. The hardened few saw themselves as professionals, with the main goal being the big tickle. Having had a little tickle, they would sit in the boozer at night lamenting their little reward. They had broken into a warehouse a few nights earlier and nicked a lorry load of electric fires, but they were not expensive fires at all. By the time they sold them off to the local fence and divvied them up, they had only given them a few hundred quid each.

The average wage was only five or six quid a week, so a few hundred quid is a lot of money, but not when you're celebrating, buying all and sundry a drink, paying your debts and lending your mates on the floor a few quid. Night after night, they would sit there, puffing away on an extra strong capstan, warming their little bodies with the fire. "What we want is that fucking big tickle, one big tickle, and we can fucking retire." Each would nod in assent, drifting off into some far of space. If they weren't so serious, you could almost find it funny. After each tickle, they would repeat the same mantra, divvy up, and then chew the fat over that elusive fucking big one. It was like the pools or the horses. One big win, and that was it; one big win, and they were set up for life, the big dream.

In between, they would get a nicking, first of six months sewing mail bags. Then, twelve months of hard labour and then a two-week stretch; slowly but surely, the drinks became a necessity, a habit that they didn't realise had become habitual. Slowly, the tickles started becoming less and less; subconsciously, they were shying away more and more from those big tickles, the smaller ones becoming less and less. Sadly, like the old Peaky Blinders and sloggers of their parent's days, they couldn't see that there was a full stop sign staring them in the face, and they were coming to the end of their prime. The good old days were receding, slowly but surely. Slowly, it dawned on them that they were missing their now growing-up children, their wives struggling to survive. Whilst they were looked after by their peers with the odd bungs now and again, the bungs were getting smaller as the tickles were getting smaller and far between. From major banks, warehouses and factory robberies, they subconsciously resorted to petty deals or even shoplifting to get a few quid to buy a drink. At twenty, you had that much bottle you felt you could take on the world. When the cops gave you a baton over the bonce, you knew it was only their uniform that stopped you from giving them a smack. At twenty, you didn't see that in ten years; having done a bit of porridge, you would see things differently.

The shrewd ones had set out on a different path with a different agenda. We all knew that the only way to get in front was to nick it; it was just different ways they chose to nick it. Many skimmed it off the deals they were doing around the town and the Bull Ring. Squirrelling little bits away day after day, deal after deal, not for them pissing it up every night in The Stag or The Barrell. Oh no, they would pop in alright, have a quick half, a little mooch here, a word there, to show their face, all the time keeping their ears open and alert for any deals, then off again to the next boozer, something or nothing learned but very little spent. Some would buy a whiskey, which gave the air of them being flusher; no one noticed that they only drank one whiskey before leaving. "He's a dark horse that Billy, ain't he? Always running around doing some business." Undoubtedly, that Billy, a shrewd fucker. Everyone assumed he had plenty of money, but no one knew where it came from.

For sure, sometimes Summer Lane was like the fucking wild west. Fighting on a Friday night was the norm; the only things missing were the Colt 45s. Robberies and break-ins were regular weekly news headlines. Everyone would buy the evening mail and read avidly to see who was at it and what had been done. From there, it was a case of working out who had done it. It was so tempting and lucrative that even the women were not shy about participating.

Jean 'The Redhead' Kirby was a stunning-looking woman, slim and statuesque with lengthy bright red hair; she would walk into a factory or decent-sized retailer, and with her looks alone, she would get the job. Within the day, she would suss out its security and how much, on average, the shop was taking, which would give her a rough estimate for the week. She would clock how much stock was in the shop plus store in the back if there was somewhere to park and load up. Sometimes, she worked at the job for a few weeks or months. Her contact and partner just drove up every week, pulling up at the back, key supplied by Jean, who had quietly made a copy without anyone knowing, took a small load of selected items, then drove away. She could have two or three little jobs like that, which became pensions, only coming to a stop when management raised the alarm. Until then, they would put it down to shoplifters. If that happened, Jean would simply move on to another target, going through the whole process again; if anyone in the business sussed anything, no one said anything. If a factory had to be investigated, Jean would get a job and do the same. All the time, she was earning a wage, so when she got a very big drink, it was squirrelled away into her little money box, her little *big* money box. Jean was a very shrewd girl. Of course, no one except her small group of very close contacts knew what she was up to, and even then, only those who participated in the latest little scam, the rule being gob shut at all times. The redhead went on to own her own home and retire without a hint of a criminal record.

With so many opportunities, Reg, Johnny and Pussyfoot decided it made sense to buy or rent a barn in the country. It was not too far out but not too near either; country property was cheap, with old semi-derelict barns being almost given away. Finding a barn with hardly any roof beside the Clent Hills, the farmer thought he had seen Jimmy coming, taking his money with a smile. From Jimmy's point of view, he knew he had a bargain; legitimately, he could store goods out of the way without raising any suspicions. Secretly, they could store artic lorry loads of bent goods without any pressure to get rid of them as quickly as possible; this was a very lucrative little market with anyone trusted within the teams allowed to store their nicked lorries for a percentage of the goods. They were even allowed to have a bung. Once the goods were sold the lorry would be taken to some industrial estate and dumped, no one any the wiser.

Diamond Lilly Hawkins and her family had worked for years in the Bull Ring markets on the fresh fish stalls, slowly building up until they could rent a little shop. Diamond Lilly had worked for years scrimping and saving. An ex-girlfriend of Jack Lewin, she knew the value and importance of money. Many people didn't. She tried to impart this knowledge to Jack and anyone else who would listen, but not many listened.

Once Lily and her family had got the one shop up and running, they bought another one above the Barton Arms pub. Not only did they have the guaranteed custom from the boozer, but from the hippodrome theatre as well. They had a little diamond mine, and soon, they had a chain of shops around the inner city in big letters above the shop window. HAWKINS JELLIED EELS. With each shop, Lilly would buy another diamond ring, no doubt at the right price, from one of the many contacts she had around. Lily never forgot her roots; she still drank in the lane, walking in The Stag with her fur coat and fingers smothered in diamonds.

That didn't apply to all, of course. Jack Brown was born and brought up in Summer Lane along with his relatives, cousins, etc, spread out around the area. Jack's main aim and goal was to own a scrap yard like many others. Jack typically was friendly enough but ruthless in his methods and dealings. Following WWII, the country was awash with scrap. Scrap tanks, aeroplanes, shell casings, etc. Ward scrap metal yard up Bordsley Green had a contract with the government to buy all their military equipment. Then there were the thousands of houses, deserted and bombed out during the war, and the many bomb pecks in the surrounding areas.

Scrap metal was abundant everywhere, and the government and businesses cried out for it as it rebuilt the country. Few people had much of an idea of its worth or value; bronze fetched more than brass, copper fetched more than lead or iron, and nickel was sky-high. Whilst the scrap yards had to be licenced, the police found it difficult to know how to police it. The difficulty was knowing what was stolen and what wasn't. It was legal if a homeowner brought in a bit of copper from his garden or house. If he took it from a bomb peck or a bombed-out house, it was technically stolen. Stolen from who or what was the mystery? Someone had to clear it away, but at any rate, it was nicked.

The police soon learned to take it as the better of two evils. They just decided to take the bung, and the scrap yard owners soon realised that the best option was to put a bung in the books. The size of the bung was commensurate with how busy they were. Most of them were very busy. Then there were the licenced rag 'n' bone men or tatters. They brought in brass beds galore as homeowners replaced the noisy squeaking and uncomfortable mattresses with the new cheap modern divans. The homeowners were just glad to get rid of them for the price of a goldfish. The tatters could be seen every day several times a day; people were throwing out beds left, right and centre. Any scrap, any rags? Come and get your goldfish.

Soon, Jack's yard was doing very well, which was fair play to him. Up with the lark, he would toil all day buying scrap metal, learning how to study the markets. If copper was low, he would store it as long as he could, surviving on what he was making on his other metals, bought at the right price and held, he knew it was better than money in the bank. Like other scrap dealers, he quickly learned how to stretch the profits; a small magnet on the scales placed strategically could reduce a hundred-weight bag of copper to three-quarters of a hundred weights. In effect, for every hundred pounds of copper he was buying, he was only paying the price of a half hundred. Multiply that with the rest of the metals, and you could soon be on the road to making a lot of money. If you played it straight with your fellow man, you only made a percentage and nothing on the scales. There was only one simple answer. Fuck your fellow man. It was quite simple. If it was bent and you knew it was bent, you reduced your price yet again. It was a win, win, all the way.

With nickel and other precious metals, it was even easier. Nine times out of ten, the bloke bringing it in had no idea of its true value, except it was worth more than copper and brass. Most scrap yards didn't advertise their prices. Oh no, you sussed out the punters as they walked in. Sometimes, he hadn't even got a clue to its value. With the right mindset and ruthlessness, a scrap yard could be a very lucrative business. Later in life, it was used as the business model to follow in years to come. Buy a major company at a given price, showing the banks and shareholders projected figures, that's a figure put forward that you anticipate achieving. Gradually, and within months, start putting the prices up by ten per cent, whilst putting the weights on the scales to reduce the stock. Be it a bar of chocolate or a packet of biscuits, put a bar of chocolate up by ten per cent, then reduce the weight of the chocolate by three or even five per cent, which saw your profit margins rise by fifteen per cent or more. This not only made the companies millions, but it also ensured shareholders invested in the company. Morally bankrupt but totally legal. In the scrap yard, it was known as thieving and illegal. But no scrap metal merchant ever got nicked for it. Years later, when it became known as a normally accepted business practice, it was perfectly acceptable. It is morally wrong and frowned upon, but good business practice. These scrap metal merchants were the entrepreneurs of their day.

Other people sought different ways to make a living. Before, in between, and after the First and Second World Wars, the country had been in turmoil with political unrest, a lack of work, and different political parties that were only too ready to stoke the fires of rebellion and uncertainty. Joseph Lucas was born in Carver Street Hockley, a modest man with a local school education followed by an apprenticeship; setting out in business for himself, Joe started out selling buckets, shovels and paraffin from a little trolley he had made himself and roamed the streets of Hockley and Aston selling his wares. Working twelve-hour days, he walked the streets shouting out his wares, building up his customers in and around Summer Lane. By 1860, he had established himself with a small shop, and from that shop, he progressed very rapidly to establish Lucas Industries manufacturing parts for the automotive manufacturers. In doing so, he established his factories and provided work for hundreds of local people. Like the Cadburys, he was known as a hardworking humanitarian. An example to many, including Jack Lewin, who set out to sell fruit and veg from a barrer in the Bull Ring. If you had a bit of initiative, there would be opportunities galore.

Others struggled with little means to set up, buy or rent a shop selling to the local community where they were born. A shop was hard work, most times barely making a living. Shop owners quickly realised that the shop alone was not enough; the sensible saw it as giving enough to pay the rent, the heating and lighting. This allowed the husband to go out and get a job, making his income stretch further. With hard work, they could save to buy their own home.

Another would buy a little café. Not only did this provide an income, but it also became a meeting point which could lead to other little deals. One such was Stan Sherrington, who set up a café in Hockley. Stan, also born in Summer Lane, was well known as a wheeler and dealer, sometimes sailing close to the wind with his dealings. Stan had come to realise that he needed something else to provide a comfortable living, an edge. A café was the ideal solution. Friends could come in for coffee, chew the fat, and discuss deals, potential deals, or other regional opportunities, all above board, without arousing suspicion; it was an ideal setup.

Jack Lewin had the barrer. The only problem was that it could be hard work for little return. In good weather, it was fine; in winter, in heavy snow or rain, it was harsh. But shoppers came out expecting to be able to buy their fruit and vegetables. They had low betide; if you let them down, your customers would just go to another hawker. Jack's answer was to use the barrer as the main provider, and he went on buying, selling, and wheeler-dealing in other areas. Whilst Alma looked after the barrer, trundling along after she had got the kids off to school, Jack would set off. First, to buy his stock, kettles and groins that he could carry. Having spent all his spare cash, sitting around the boozers, Jack would roll up his arms and show his kettles. "Does anyone want to buy a nice watch?" Before lifting his fingers and showing a nice sovereign or diamond ring. Jack was very popular around Summer Lane, having been born and brought up there. Well-known around Aston and the city centre, it was accepted that Jack Lewin would be a millionaire.

Alma would also add to the pot by coming out on Saturday and Sunday carrying her dolly basket filled with goods of the day. In summer, sweets and socks, and in the winter, coming up to Christmas toys, teddy bears and sweets. Knowing them as all the locals did, there was no doubt that not only were Jack and Alma going to be millionaires, but they were shrewd as well. We had all seen others go the same route: a barrer, a shop, then a factory.

Unfortunately, no one knew that Jack and Alma had no choice but to have a half of mild as they sat or stood in the boozers they worked in and got quite attached to a drink or two. From a half or two, it spread to five or six. Without even realising it, whilst everyone thought they were very well off, they were running into a habit of spending their profits behind bars. It was the downfall of more than one or two people with the right idea and the right product.

Joe Lucas had to do all his selling on the road; the last thing he could do was pop into the boozer. By the time he got home, he was just about capable of doing his books, checking his money and the profit made before making his way to bed. After a six-day week of church on a Sunday, there was barely enough time to relax.

Ruthless as he was, Jack Brown soon started on the up. With his scrap yard making nice money, he soon found himself in a good enough position to buy himself and his family a nice detached house on Eachelhurst Road. Almost everyone dreamed of getting away from the slums of Summer Lane. Some loved the camaraderie and friendship. For those like Jack Brown, the goal was to find a nice house in Sutton Coldfield—even Great Barr. For most of the working pecks, it was a nice council house in the newly developed Kingstanding or Kitts Green. Both huge housing estates on the edge of the countryside are very posh indeed. Many, like Jack Lewin and big Dennis Sullivan, were never bothered either way; born and brought up in Summer Lane, it was home. Many of those who left never looked back. Most would never mention or even admit to ever having lived in Summer Lane or around the area, ashamed as they were of it. If you came from Summer Lane, you were bent or close to it, such as the reputation the lane had made for itself. Others would ensure they returned every Friday or Saturday night for a good knees-up. Those who stayed just never saw the changes.

Every Sunday afternoon, Jack would drive from his nice house in EachelHurst in his posh second-hand Mercedes, pull up outside The Barrell, get himself a pint and sit in his car with the window down, a permanent little smile on his face, saying hello to everyone who passed or walked across to him. Many thought Jack was returning, having not forgotten his roots, my old man included. Others saw it differently. At any rate, having slowly finished his pint of mild, Jack would slowly start the engine and set off, savouring every moment of seeing Summer Lane and its people disappear in his rear view mirror. Many couldn't blame him.

The reputation of Summer Lane was now reaching the upper echelons of the various government and police departments. It was bad enough that we had had the devastation and killing of the war, a major housing rebuilding programme was being carried out in all the major cities, and the last thing they needed was the organising and forming of major crime gangs in London, Birmingham and other major cities. Worse, with the knowledge of gelignite and access to dynamite, bombings were seen as a major solution to doing away and killing grasses and others who created problems. Another favoured method was arson. If someone upset you or tried to gip you on one of the jobs, the easy solution was to put them away.

Initially, the normal solution would be to give the person concerned a good going over, scaring him and/or breaking a few bones. Now, this wasn't providing the solution needed. If people were desperate, they would try any means to rob another thief of his load of scrap or goods. If there had ever been any honour amongst thieves, it was disappearing at a steady pace. It was dog-eat-dog. If you nicked it, you were considered fair game to be robbed. There were only so many you could blow up. Another favourite method gaining popularity was to burn the fuckers out, but first, you had to check no kids were in the house.

To many of the villains, the robbers, the blaggards, and the chancers, they didn't see an end to the good times. The chancers just drifted with the times and the opportunities. Those who had set up in business, many in little shops, and others who may have been doing a bit of tatting were finding it hard, slow work getting in front. Having rented a house down Aston with a small yard and stables, my brother Billy Lewin got himself a pony and cart. After a few months, he threw the towel in, finding it too hard and ruthless whilst making pennies. Slowly, inevitably, the police started making inroads, which affected the villains and the robbers.

Many of the police were getting pissed off by their superiors, and pressure was being put on them to reduce the robberies, reduce the violence. The only obvious answer to that was to meet violence with more violence. Initially, the police, mainly drawn from the armed forces returning from WWII, were not too interested in creating big waves. They were already finding out, to their misfortune, that with too much interference, they were open to a good belting. For the low-paid crap wages they were getting, they didn't want or need the hassle that went with the job—especially the lowest of the low-beat Bobbie.

They got the odd little perk of a free baked spud, maybe the odd bag of fish n' chips wrapped up in the daily mail, but the real perks, the bungs, enjoyed by the sergeants up, were unknown to them. It was left to the plain clothes CID to start making inroads. The CID had been taking bungs for years, but not of the villains who were doing the actual break-ins, robberies and safe braking. To them, the cops were the enemy. They had every reason to look at them as filth, among other nicknames. They knew from experience that the police were not only taking bungs but were also nicking money off the top from those they legally nicked in the first place. It was against the grain. With the natural hatred building up against the cops coupled with the gradual building up of the hatred of the cops themselves, it made all the ingredients for a continuous clash of opposing sides. Nicking is one thing. Robbing someone is all fair in love and war, but a copper is supposed to uphold the law, yet they were nicking as much of it as they could get.

From being first nicked, many a villain would boast about giving the cops some strong verbal assaults. If there was no evidence against them, this would result in the cops giving them a belting, all legal, of course, and if it wasn't, who could they complain to? The cops? No, they just had to learn to take it as par for the course. Whips, batons and even the cat o' nine tails were used without discrimination. The villains would often leave the police station black and blue but without divulging any information to incriminate themselves. Most slowly started to find other ways to make a living, from twelve months in prison, which was increasing to three years and five years; prison was hard enough as it was. Coupled with the constant harassment, they were getting from the police; it was now beginning to look more and more unappealing. Coupled with that was that the old Summer Lane, the Summer Lane they had been born and bred into, was starting to disappear. Blocks of houses were being demolished from Lozells down.

Where Summer Lane had once been a thriving hub of activity, now it was starting to look and sound different. Only the odd medicine man now stood on the corners selling his remedies for all ailments, little bottles with a strange, murky-looking liquid guaranteed to cure all ills. "Arthritis, my love, this will cure it. Toe fungal? Just bathe it every night with a bit of my medicine.

Bad back, sir? Just get the wife to rub this in every night for over two weeks, and I guarantee it will disappear." After two weeks, it most likely fucking had. If not, you were persuaded to buy another bottle. Quite a few stood for it. Many started to wise up. The baked potato man only came down the lane at weekends, as did the penny-wink man. Only at weekends did the cockles and mussels man visit the pubs selling his wares. Where once the boozers were a hive of activity during opening hours day or night, seven days a week with people bringing in a bit of gear, a couple of suits, a radio, whatever you wanted, you could guarantee on getting something and making a few quid. Now, it was slowly disappearing along with the chancers.

Friends were starting to disappear from the lane more frequently, either to prison or after much urging from the wives. "Come on, Jack, we need to get away from this lot. Let's take that nice council house over Kingstanding. They've even got inside bathrooms; it's posh." For many, it was a dream come true.

Many started to realise and see the benefits and advantages after making the move. The children flourished in a pleasant and fresh environment where the roads were lined with trees and even more magical grass verges. Within a short walk were the countryside and green fields, and the newly built schools were also a million times better. The teachers treated you with consideration and respect. In the schools in or around Summer Lane, it was made clear that you were nothing more than factory fodder destined for the post-war building sites or foundries around the area.

Teaching and getting a good education were secondary; the attitude of the teachers was universal. What was the point of teaching children, especially these scruffy urchins, knowing they would only end up in a factory or even prison at some point? It was often felt that even the parents only shunted them off to school to get them out of the house; in most cases, that was true. The only problem was this filtered down and across to the kids, leaving some who rebelled by not wanting to learn. Where most just shrugged and kept their head down, the hardened few chose otherwise.

THE NEXT GENERATION.

I was born the second youngest of the next generation after the war, the second youngest of a family of eight. Three sisters and four brothers, not for me the hardship and poverty of my grandad's generation, the struggles of my dad's generation. Thankfully, by making the efforts my mom and dad made in getting a hawker license and becoming a barrow boy, my mom backed him 100%. They made a living in the hardest times and ensured we eight kids were well fed with good healthy food off the barrer. Some days, it might be the specks left over a bit of damaged fruit, but together with the potatoes and veg, it all made for healthy, nutritious food. On the way home from the Bull Ring, my mom would call into the delicatessen floor of Lewis's, call up to the meat counter, and order a turkey frame.

Turkey and chicken were served and cut fresh off the bone. The assistants didn't mess about. With plenty of meat still left on the frame, they would toss it aside and start on a fresh new frame; for a sixpence, my mom would walk out with the frame, get on the bus, turkey in one hand, me in the other. Once home, the turkey would be set on the table, and more meat would be cut off and made into sandwiches for my dad's lunch the following day. The frame would then go into the two-gallon pot along with the fruit and veg to make a stew that fed us all for a few days, topped up and served with a doorstep of bread.

Sunday would be a proper roast dinner with all the trimmings. One Sunday, a nice fat chicken, another a bit of pork or beef. Without a doubt, we ate well. It might be a bit of ox tail, chitterlings', or cow's udder in the week. Maybe even a pig's trotter cooked perfectly and served in vinegar. Hmm, delicious, all the while backed up by one of mom's stews.

As with hundreds of others, our mom and dad had taken the offer of a nice new council house in Kingstanding, hot water and an inside bath, a small garden to the front and a long one to the back where we kept chickens, ducks and rabbits, not as pets, but together with the veg to go into a pot and make a meal of stew. Strangely, many people were given the opportunity to get a nice new house in a posh newly built area, and people started to change. Back in the slums, people had always tried to maintain dignity, but now they felt it was only right to present a better appearance. Down the lane, you would polish your front doorstep. How you lived behind the door was another matter; people went without decent food for days, eating scraps, but no one would know. On a Monday, many neighbours would have to take their only suit into the pawn shop to raise a few shillings until Friday. They would skulk into the shop, hoping no one would notice or brazenly front it out like most of them did, knowing there was no alternative. "Here we go again; I'm just taking Fred's suit in till Friday." "Oh, and me with our Harold's." But in Kingstanding, they could hide it more.

In Kingstanding, they had few pawn shops. They had to get the bus down to the old end to pawn Fred's suit discreetly. Luckily for them, Blundell's, the high-interest money lender, recognised an opportunity when they saw it. Blundells took all the hard work out of borrowing at extortionate interest rates. Not only would they call on you at your convenience, but you could also buy school uniforms and shoes off them, household items, or borrow money. Even better, they would call around every week on payday on the dot and collect their monthly payment, never having any worries about not getting it. Once caught in the net, there was no escape. Before they had even paid off one loan, another was needed for yet another school uniform. It was a never-ending treadmill of debt that people didn't even realise they were treading.

Whether Dad would allow it was another matter, but neither he nor Mom would stand for the idea of borrowing money. If there was one thing they were sure of, it was the value of it. There was no way they would work hard all week just to give it away to some extortionate money lender—oh no, not when it could be spent in the pub. With the turnabout in circumstances came another, more subtle change in people's attitudes. Down Summer Lane, people had no choice but to be natural and show their true characters and personalities. After all, many of them had lived in Summer Lane for most, if not all, of their lives.

But here in Kingstanding, they could be different; they could put an act on, and no one knew any better. People even stopped admitting they came from Summer Lane or thereabout. The reputation of Summer Lane had taken its toll. To admit to coming from Summer Lane was to admit to being from the slums or even being crooked; God forbid, no one wanted that around their necks.

Mom and Dad thought very differently. For their own reasons, neither of them felt inclined or the need to put an act on. Dad had served his time in the army, paid his dues, worked hard and got himself a barrow. Mom had known hardship yet must also have known her mother's circumstances as a teacher and the granddaughter of such a famous artist. Either way, she felt no need to put an act on or, indeed, try to impress anyone. They were both down-to-earth, salt-of-the-earth people, and that's how they saw themselves. To put an act on would be a betrayal of who they were.

Each Saturday night, they would sing the songs of Summer Lane with gusto in the College Arms or Kinsgstanding with those Summer Laners who also felt the same. While in the army, Mom had made ends meet as best she could. This involved buying ration books from other neighbours who couldn't make enough money or manage their finances just as well. This also didn't go down well with the same neighbours either. While they felt they had no choice but to accept Mom's money, they weren't happy having to do so, knowing that she was stockpiling sugar and making money out of it. Inevitably, whilst unexpected, the odd one or two did squeal on her, resulting in the cops calling around to search the house and question her. Thankfully, whilst she had a wardrobe full of sugar in the bedroom, the police only saw what she showed them in the kitchen. They accepted her explanation.

Sadly, genuine as she was, she and Dad still never saw the potential pitfalls in front of them. Shrugging her shoulders, she would just give her usual response of fuck 'em' all. Life was too short, and there were far more important things to worry about than some clearly jealous neighbour who had got it in for her. Sadly, that was one of Mom and Dad's big mistakes. They never recognised the signals.

As the times changed, very slowly, so did the people's attitudes. Before, during and after the war, it was all about survival. As things started to improve, so did people's expectations and perceptions. Now, as people had nice houses and gardens, more emphasis was placed on appearances. A nice house required a reasonably nice dress or a suit. My mom and dad were still stuck down the old end. Not for them, fancy clothes did not make the man. Their main concern was first making a living so they could pay the bills and keep us kids well-fed with good, nourishing food.

Consequently, we kids grew up with our arses hanging out, not knowing what a handkerchief or a pair of underpants were. If we had a runny nose, we would just wipe it on our jumper or coat sleeve, a sliver of snot as our badge of honour. Neither Mom nor Dad was bothered about appearances. Dad wore the same old suit week in and week out, with a jumper and a cravat, Mom an ankle-length dress. If we felt any difference, we never noticed it or commented on it.

Our childhood in Kingstanding was a time of happy memories and growing up with the ducks, rabbits, and chickens running around our feet, till the unexpected reared its ugly head in the form of the council evicting us for running a business from a council property, strictly against the rules in case you never realised it. Poor mom and dad never gave it a thought. All the while, they were going blithely along, happy with their lot and the nice living they were making, whilst all the time, some of the neighbours were simmering with resentment.

Hindsight is a wonderful thing. Who would have believed that your neighbours, most of whom were friendly towards you, grateful for the odd pound of butter or lard you loaned them or gave them, even the odd pound to help pay the rent, would always be scheming to get rid of you? This time, it was the smell of rotten fruit kept in the air raid shelter. With the proof of this, and after warnings, the council gave them notice. My mom and dad took it on the chin without digging deeper. If they had, they would have realised that this is a factor only amongst the lower working classes; maybe it's ingrained in our psyche over hundreds of years. You never see it in the upper classes; they know how to protect each other. The middle classes, the backbone of the country, are just too busy making a living and getting on with their lives to wonder what their next-door neighbour is getting up to.

It's a strange quirk of human nature that If the middle or upper class buy a nice fancy car, a nice house, or a castle, the next-door neighbour will only look with aspirations of having the same thing. They will boast, my neighbour has a nice Rolls Royce or Jaguar." Their success reflects on you." Next year, that could be me. The lower working class, by contrast, will look on with envy and resentment. It's a fact of life that few people realise, particularly those amongst the working classes. Being born amongst them, we assume everyone is the same. Go up Roman Road, the posh area in Four Oaks, and you might see a concrete mixer on the drive, but that's ok because the house owner owns the company. We, down in the bottom tier, will boast about how our neighbours would give us their last shilling, their last loaf of bread or share a meal. What differentiates us from those in the upper classes is that we boast, and it's true. I grew up on this mantra: we boast about it. We revel in it. It was only when I moved away and bought our first house in Sutton Coldfield that I saw the real truth of it. All my lifelong neighbours and friends stopped talking to me. If I ever went down "the old end," former friends and neighbours would whisper and nudge behind my back. Without realising it, we had become "one of them," then I realised how it works. Yes, your working-class next-door neighbour will give you his last shilling simply because he knows he might need a shilling from you next week or a bit of offal or lard. But by God, you earn 20 quid more than him, and the knives will come out with an increasing vengeance. It's something you don't see when you're in it; sadly, my parents never saw it at all. Salt of the earth indeed.

When the eviction van turned up, it was small consolation when one of the removal men, upon seeing the circumstances, turned to Mom, sneered at the neighbours and said, "Don't worry, love, one day you will come back and walk down this road with a fur coat on." For the old man, well, he kept out of the way, running his barrer up by Latham's on the Dyas road; he had a living to make.

Without further ado, we were brought down to Nechells. If Summer Lane was bad enough, Nechells Green was just as bad, if not worse.

To me and my kid brother Kenny, it was one big playground, well, except for one thing, of course, and that was the fucking school. Starting with the infants, we went to Cromwell Street School, named after the street it was built into. Typically built in the Victorian period, its appearance was just as daunting on the outside as on the inside. Being so young, it didn't dawn on me for years that the teachers hated us. I just assumed we were doing something wrong to get the cane across my arse every day, what for I don't know, but together with my newfound friends Johnny, Bee, Bee, Beards, David Parry, and Robert Turl Turley, it soon became a regular occurrence.

Were my parents treated like this at Summer Lane School? If they were, they never said anything. My mom, being left-handed, a Hipkiss trait, was smacked repeatedly for writing with the devil's hand. Such was the prejudice she was forced to write with her right hand. Most times, it would be before the lunch break, before the dreaded voice would shout, Lewin, Turley, Beards, Parry, get outside and wait for the headmaster, Mr Onions. Sometimes, one of us might escape the beating, but it never stopped. Mr Onions was a fucking tyrant, a terrifying bully. First, we would wait in line outside the classroom, like obedient little chimps, till Mr Onions was ready for us, and then we would be ordered to go and wait outside his office. Knowing what was to come, we would just stand there shitting ourselves until we were called in, whack, whack, whack. After six of the best, we would be made again to wait outside crying in fucking agony whilst rubbing our arses to try and lessen the pain. As the pain died down, our cries of agony would turn into cries of laughter as we each looked at the other's faces, trying to find fun in the adversity. None of us learned anything the whole time we were at that school. Alphabet, what alphabet, tables? What are they? Whatever we had done wrong, none of us knew. Each time we were called out, the other kids buried their little heads in their books, thankful it wasn't their names being shouted out. It never was, of course, but they never learned fuck all anyway.

Our distraction from it all was the bomb pecks around us. Nechells and Duddeston was one big bomb peck, either of houses bombed during the war or being demolished for house clearance. Our routine quickly became established and repeated five days a week, with Saturday and Sunday being treated as a holiday without the misery of school. Stopping in bed as long as possible, knowing what was looming in front of us, we would finally get up, get dressed, and have a quick swill of freezing cold water in the Belfast sink before making our way to school across the bomb peck. Shoulders slumped faces as long as Livery Street, dreading the day ahead.

Where our house in Kingstanding had been posh, with an inside toilet, upstairs bathroom, hot water, light and airy, our house in Rocky Lane, Nechells, was dark, gloomy and forbidding. Very Victorian, two steps straight off the street leading into the parlour, the hallway that led to the living room at the back, past the front parlour room, past the cellar head and the stairs to the three bedrooms above, well, in fact, two bedrooms and a gloomy attic in the loft. These were temporary homes for my older brothers and sister, Doris, after they had married and needed somewhere before getting a council house. It is yet another normal practice for all of us, with no one knowing better. First, we would get married, then move into whichever parent had a room they could spare, humped into the spare bedroom or backroom. The slow process began. First, it was a must to get pregnant, then points for having no home in the first place. Then maybe another child before you had enough points, maybe even more. It was humiliating and degrading, but we knew no better. It was the way of life for the majority. If there was anyone smarter who knew better, they kept it to themselves.

Bugs in the wall were a regular occurrence. No one explained that when the houses were being built, and to save money, the soil was used instead of sand. It didn't take the bugs long to start nesting in the walls, and silverfish would monopolise the hearth during the night after the fires had died down, only disappearing once the fires were either built back up or a new fire made. The kitchen or scullery, dreary as it was, was made up of distempered walls on bare brick; this led out to the small back garden where never a blade of grass grew, which led to the outside karzie. All that was without the fucking nits', lice and other body feeders, and we were lucky. At least we had our parlour house with front and back doors and a covered-in side entry.

Behind us and divided by a rickety fence was another back-to-back consisting of a two-up, one down. They put an old man in there who never smiled or spoke to anyone. The rumour was that he had had a shop once before retiring. One day, Kenny and I were having a little nose around the place when he came out like a bull in a China shop shouting, balling, and carrying a machete. Running down the entry, we were shitting ourselves. I was eight, and Kenny was six. He was fucking ranting and raving. Kenny got in the house and bolted upstairs. I bolted into the karzie and hid behind the door; thankfully, I was that skinny. He never saw me when he pushed the door open. We were grateful when he died a short time later. Mom noticed something oddly quiet and went up to peek behind the curtains. When the men in white came to collect him, they had to put pegs on their noses, blood pouring from them. He had exploded and been lying in his bed for weeks.

Most of the others, like my mate Johnny Beards, lived in little back-to-backs down Scofield Street. His front room led straight off the front two steps that led off the pavement straight into his living room. Well, I say living room; it was the only room, except for the cellar head that contained the white Belfast sink next to the cooker. A cold marble slab next to it for the butter, meat, and cheese, a few shelves above it to hold the pitiful few plates and saucepans you owned. One or two bedrooms above, hence known as a two up, one down, or a one up one down, that was your fucking lot in life. When the rent man called for his weekly payment or some other debtor, you were unfortunate enough to have borrowed money; there was nowhere to hide, try as you might.

One day, Mrs Beards clocked the rent man coming down Schofield Street. Panicking, she shouted at Bee. "Bee, here's the rent man. Tell him I ain't in. I will pay him next week." Unfortunately, Bee Bee's mom never shut the front door before diving under the table to hide. With Bee Bee dutifully telling the rent man, "Mom ain't in, Mister." He could do no more than stare through the gap between the door and say, "Oh, hello, Mrs Beards. What are you doing under the table then?" Flustered, Mrs Beards could only scrabble from under the table whilst explaining that she was looking for a shoe. "But, anyway, I've got no money this week. You'll have to wait till next." The rent men and debtors were used to it. If they didn't appreciate how hard life was for the people, they tried to keep good humour about it. In their embarrassment at having no money, many would just simply try to hide rather than explain that they were simply skint. Even for the ones who had a job and went out six days a week working on the building sites or factories, it was a constant struggle to make ends meet.

But that was the parents. As kids, we never had that worry, except for getting some food in our bellies or a few pennies from wherever we could to buy some sweets. Nechells and Duddeston was one big playground of empty houses and factories or scarred empty wasteland where we could spend hour after hour having fun and whiling away the hours without even realising it, the only downside being having to go to school. We would try various ways to skive off to no avail. Mom was used to it. Our only option was to build a thick skin without realising it. In class one day, the teacher came striding over to look at my work, teaching us the times tables. She could see I was doing nothing. The numbers in front of me just blurred into one another. Grabbing my hair, she started bouncing my bonce off the fucking desk, rhythmically to the chant of her voice, "1 and 1 is 2. 2 and 2 is 4." Well, all I could see were blurred numbers which meant sweet fuck all. From that very moment on, as an eight-year-old kid, I made my mind up to resolutely ignore the lot and learn fuck all.

There were only two ways you could go as far as I was concerned: cower down, try your best and keep your head down. Even if you did sweet fuck, all the teachers would leave you alone because they could see you were at least trying, or you could say, "fuck you." From that moment when my head started banging on my desk, that became my mantra in life in all things. "Fuck you." Course, there was a third option: to become a teacher's pet; one or two tried that way—bringing in an apple on a Monday morning. It was only the odd one, though, and we all knew who it was. It was a Little Miss Squeaky Clean in the smart uniform bought on credit from Blundells. There was nothing that made us spit blood more than the contempt we had for these little creeps. Worse, it served no purpose; oh, of course, the teacher smiled and said thank you, but behind the smile, you knew they didn't like us.

If they weren't fresh out of university and knew nothing, they were old, coming up to retirement, and just ticking the boxes until they could retire and get away. We were factory fodder. They knew it. We didn't. Worse, they let us know it at every opportunity. For us, the select few who did know it, we just rebelled. It took the smarter ones years to find those little nuggets, but it was too late by then. The boys ended up in the proverbial factory or building site, and the girls in Woolworths were on the shop or factory floors. For the odd one or two who got an apprenticeship or a job in the office? Well, they thought they were the elite, the bee's knees. You would see them coming home on the bus or from the bus stop, squeaky clean but with no money.

DAYS OF YOUTH AND INNOCENCE

We were grateful for what we had received without realising it. "Get up them wooden hills, or you won't know what day it is."

"Yes, Mom."

"Stop yer fucking snivelling, or you'll get a sharp crack around the ear ole. If you don't like it, there's the door, fuck off and don't come back." One day, I decided to do just that. I filled my little nap sac with bread and biscuits, tied it to the end of the stick like I saw them do in the pictures, and set off. I got to the park at the bottom of Scofield Street before I realised that was as far as I knew. Where the fuck do I go next? When the panic set in, I made my way back home via the bomb pecks, taking my time, so I didn't get in till after my mom and Dad were in the boozer. I snuck in straight for bed, thankful for my home and bed. I kept my mouth shut and never said another word again. If Mom or Dad had any thoughts, they never expressed them; what more could I ask for or expect? I had clothes on me, a pair of pants, food in my belly and a roof over my head, and I never complained again. It was a paradox that here we were, the lowest of the low living in the so-called slums of Birmingham, living hand to mouth, yet we were grateful for what little we received, what crumbs were thrown at us.

Some of my mates weren't so lucky. Jacky, down Scofield Street, lived with his brother Danny and their mom in a two-up one down in a courtyard of six other houses. Six houses with their own outside karzie, walking into Jackie's house after school was always a bit of a revelation, as poor as she was. Jack's mom was bedbound, the bed being by the fireplace in the corner of the room, her legs patterned with chilblains from the only heat in the house, the fire. Jackie's Dad had left home years ago, apparently never to look back. No one knew where he was; it was the great unmentionable. How they survived, god knows, but both Jackie and Danny forever walked around with happy faces bent over and stomachs that seemed to be stuck to their spines. His mom would always find us a word to test our spelling on. "How do you spell the word diesel?" We were flummoxed, leaving her to spell it for us proudly.

Roger the Dodger Hardiman was one of nineteen. Fucking nineteen. Dodger lived opposite us, and his mom was forever sending him over to borrow a bit of lard or half a loaf. We never got it back, but that's how Dodger and I became friends. How they lived, we don't know. How they slept, the mind could only boggle, yet still, they had room for Pat, the lodger. We assumed Pat was a long-standing friend of the family who was helping towards the rent. He was so much of a fixture in the house that even one or two kids started to look like him. However, everyone called him Uncle Pat.

Whenever you spoke to the Dodger, he seemed a bit hyped up. We assumed this was part and parcel of his personality. His brother, deaf and dumb Johnny, was the same. When he spoke, in sign language, of course, he was always animated, swinging his arms and shouting like a fucking dervish. He couldn't speak, but that didn't stop him shouting. Because we were so used to it, none of us gave it any further thought. There were lots of kids like that around Nechells. It was the hunger within them because they were always so constantly fucking hungry that it made them hyper. Hyperactive. According to legend, Johnny wasn't born deaf and dumb but caught a disease when he was a child that made him deaf and dumb.

My mate Jim was a bit different. He always walked around with a face as long as Livery Street, head bowed and belly sucked in like it was sticking to his spine, but he never moaned, never complained. If he was hungry or starving, he never let us know. The only outside sign as he bit his nails to the quick, but so did I. When I called around his house. It was always spic n span but bare, with no bed bugs, silverfish, or lice in their house. There was fuck all for them to feed on, and the house was bare and cold; how they lived behind closed doors, no one knew; certainly, I never had a clue. As soon as

I was old enough to realise I knew his mom, Maud, would walk the few yards to the beehive, stand outside, offering a fuck to anyone who would give her the price of half a mild.

She obviously wasn't doing it to put food on the table or return it to her husband. As soon as some bloke was prepared to put up with it or take the risk, she would take him round the corner to the outside toilet and do the business, which, in fairness, didn't take too long before reappearing, a bob or two in her pocket entering through the side entrance into the boozer, the punter entering through the opposite door as far away as possible. Maud was only a short woman of just barely five feet, chubby with it and no teeth. She had a husband at home, so what must their life be like to lead that kind of existence? Maud's husband was a lovely, quiet, timid bloke, but why didn't he try to stop it? Who knows. Even more interesting, no one said a word.

I suppose my mom knew that Jim was my mate but never heard her run his mom down. It was like it was no big deal—almost acceptable. Everyone has to earn a few bob to the best of their abilities. So what.

My mate Jerry lived down a long acre just above Frank Grounds haulage yard. His sister was a nice-looking girl who always hung around the yard at the end of a shift on a Friday night. As a kid, I assumed she had a boyfriend who worked there. Till one day, my mate said, "Boyfriend, you stupid prat, she's always down there on a Friday night to get some money." It still took me a few years longer to catch on. Jerry had a great singing voice, strong and powerful, often singing in the boozers he was once invited to sing on Noel Gardon's lunchtime show at the ATV studios in Aston. When I questioned why he never turned up, his shoulders slumped, and "My bottle went, Tom." Looking at him, surprised, I could only wonder. Jerry was a big, strong lad, afraid of no one, but that's what Nechells and the back streets of Birmingham do to you. Your confidence is knocked out of you slowly before you leave primary school by teachers, only one rung up the ladder from us. By the time you reach 15, you know your destiny.

Maybe it was the contrast, the move from Kingstanding to Rocky Lane, where the ice grew inside the window, but it wasn't too long before I caught double pneumonia. Up to the general, I was taken and placed in isolation in my own partitioned glass unit, with other kids the same kind of age on either side of me. Unbeknown to me, I came very close to kicking the proverbial bucket, the weight just dropping off me. I remember one day looking up and seeing this vision in front of me: a bloke dressed all in black, quiet, holding his hands together as though in prayer. All the family spread on either side of him and around the bed. I was just puzzled, wondering who it was.

I must have got better because the next thing I knew, I was being carried on the old man's back from Steel House Lane on the bus. Once in the house, a big fuss was made of me, "Get him in front of that fire." I could feel the heat from the roaring fire on my body. "Get these eggs down him," and I was fed boiled eggs till I was going to pop. I'd never had so much fuss. Nor since. As I got better, I could see and notice people wince if they looked at my bare body; I was skin and bone. I had no stomach; my belly button touched my spine, and I stuck my stomach in my ribs. I would stand out like a concentration camp victim. My brother-in-law George, a Charles Atlas devotee, would look in disgust at my bare body. My party trick was that I could bend over and suck my toes without bending my legs; I was quite proud of that.

It didn't take long for things to settle down to normal. Before long, it was fuck off or get out, and my younger brother Kenny took over as the family favourite, the little brat. The days rolled into weeks, the weeks into months, the months into years without you even realising, the school days being the only bug bare. I never heard anyone say, "Oh, I'm so looking forward to going to school," with a big smile. Everyone walked like they'd got a hundredweight sack of coal on their backs, another one on their chin, pulling their faces down. Our only respite, our only break being the bomb pecks to play on after school and at weekends, apart from the flicks, the Saturday matinee, we lived for the Saturday matinee.

It didn't come easy, though. We had to earn the tanner entrance fee. If it wasn't fetching a hundredweight of coal from Powell's yard in a long acre, it was a hundredweight of coke from down the fucking gasworks in Saltley. It was difficult to know what was worse. Powell's was only around the corner in Thimblemill Lane. First, we had to queue up with dozens of other kids doing the same thing. Old man Powell would load our barrow, which was his barrow, made of solid block wood and a set of four cast iron wheels. Loaded up, we had to push the barrow around to the house, tip it in the cellar, and then return it to the yard, all the time barely able to hear anything above the loud clattering of the cast iron wheels along the cobbles. Dozens of barrows going off in all different directions, screaming in pain and agony. Me pulling, Kenny pushing, well, pretending to.

It was just as bad if it was the coke yard, even though we had a lighter pram to push it in. First, we had to push the pram down to and past the beehive, the brit, and down Nechells place, then downhill to the gas works where dozens of us would be queuing up in lines to fetch the coke and be loaded up. Then it would be pushing the fucking thing back up the hill, which I swear by now had grown as big as Mount Everest. Stopping every few yards, we silently prayed for someone to see us and give us a hand, but no one ever did. By the time we eventually got home, we had to spend an hour recuperating before finding the energy to make our way to the flicks with our well-earned tanner. Sometimes, we might get another couple of coppers for an ice cream, though those times were few and far between.

Once sat in the Aston cross flicks, we were soon drawn into the excitement of the all-pervading atmosphere, chattering, laughing, and gaiety as we all found our seats and jostled with each other, lights blaring. Even the nits got excited as they jumped from head-to-head of the kids in front of us as they had a feeding frenzy. Then the lights would go down, the curtains drawn wide, and everyone went silent in unison.

It could be Davey Crocket and the Wild Frontier, the Sisco Kid, or Roy Rogers and his horse, Trigger. Worse, aliens from out of space invading Earth, normally from Mars. Green, slimy and terrifying. One minute, we would be urging our heroes on; the next, screaming and shouting in terror. We didn't realise it then, but we were trapped in a never-ending world where we had to attend every week and not miss a series. If we did, we would lose the plot, but we never did. On our way home, we would gallop up Rocky Lane, our horse between our legs, the reins in our left hand, whipping our little arses with our right. My Davey Crocket bearskin was on my nut, and I was Davey Crocket. For that one moment, that short ten or fifteen minutes, we were in a different world and a million miles from Rocky Lane and Nechells.

Once a year, we collected our daily mail boots and socks from some local pick-up point, be it Digbeth Police Station, Saltley gasworks, or some other designated place. We knew they were free, but everyone was given a pair. I never thought about it then; it was like the free school dinners. Most of us in school had free school dinners. I don't know because I knew my mom and Dad could afford to pay for the school dinners; it just came automatically. If it's free, grab it. No one looks a gift horse in the mouth. These daily mail boots were like big hob-nailed army boots, with steel caps on the toes and heels to make them last longer. You couldn't go very long without hearing the clattering of metal boots on the cobbles.

I don't know whether these boots were meant to last the year, but they rarely did, except for my mate Keith Broadfield. Keith lived in a two-up one down in Aston. His single mom had to work. The one room was threadbare, but the one thing standing on a cupboard in the corner was a shoe. Baffled, Keith explained that once worn out, his mom would get a strip of leather, put the boot on the last and make a new sole for his boot, nailing and trimming to suit. Only after that did I notice that Keith's boots were always ragged around the sole, where his mom had rough-cut the leather. Poor fucker, they must have been hard up. Other families disguised the big letters DM, cut into the sides of the boots, and deliberately burnt in to avoid people profiteering. Then, they were sold, and the kids were made to go to school in ragged footwear, hand-me-downs, or even bare feet.

Poverty was all around us, but we never saw it. I thought we were rich. Even my friends used to think we were well off. Many with young children and babies were on prescription issue multivitamin Orange. No one would deny it because everyone had it; it was the norm. In our innocence, no one thought anything else; it was like school dinners. I felt slightly embarrassed as I handed over my dinner ticket, knowing it was a different colour. Still, I felt no different once that tray was in my hands and away from the table. I was eating the same food as those who paid, and when we were offered seconds, I was up like a shot.

My Dad had to throw in the fruit and veg. Kingstanding, he would use the air raid shelter to store his stock. Buying in bulk meant he could buy cheaper and make more profit. For a while, he rented a small yard up Potters Hill, but with the cost of the lorry, fuel and rent, he found it difficult to continue. By evicting him, the council had, in effect, robbed him of his livelihood. Not to be outdone, my Dad went into general dealing full-time. He used fruit and vegetables as the bread and butter of his earnings, supplementing it with general dealing and selling around the pubs. Now, it was to become his main means of income.

Our front room in Rocky Lane became his shop; it was an Aladdin's cave of goodies which varied according to the year. In winter, electric fires, toys of all sorts, fancy goods, soft toys, dolls, and teddy bears galore. In summer, mirrors, ornaments, and bagged sweets. Both mom and Dad would work at selling the stock. Mom would fill up her dolly basket at lunchtime and head down to the beehive or brit, the dolly placed between her legs in her regular chair. She would settle down with a half of mild, waiting for the punters to sidle over, "Giss a bag of them sweets, Alma. Ay, how much are those stockings? I'll have a pair of them." By the end of a good night, Mom had earned enough to pay for her own booze for the night and for tomorrow's dinner. OK, it might only have been tripe and onions or pig trotters, but we always ate well with the backup of the stew. Well, most times.

Mom and Dad were entrepreneurs, without a doubt. As they grew up, they felt a natural pride in their abilities, not a lowly job in one of the local factories. Fuck that for a living. Working for someone else for peanuts, then paying thirty per cent in tax, no thank you. Both were well respected and known for miles around Birmingham, stretching from Summer Lane to Kingstanding, from Nechells to the Bull Ring and Digbeth. Even further than that, as people moved from Summer Lane to Kitts Green and beyond, so did my Dad's contacts. Whilst I never felt big-headed about it, I always felt a certain confidence or cockiness within myself. Maybe that was just me, but without realising it, any of us. The storm clouds were gathering, and I was too young to see them. My mom and Dad were too blithely happy with their lot to see it. Hindsight is wonderful, and I could never understand why my mom and Dad never bought a shop or ran a proper set-up business. For now, he was doing far better without the responsibility around his or mom's neck. In truth, they thought the good times would never end.

Within Nechells, most were working pecks on the ladder's bottom rung, either in the factories or building sites. My mate Johnny lived opposite, and his Dad worked on a building site; many a night, I would be sitting on my front doorstep watching the world go by, seeing Johnny's Dad get off the number 8 bus by Hughes's paper shop, walk the hundred yards or so to his house, knapsack on his back, shoulders slumped. Weary looking with a face as long as fucking Livery Street, knackered. He wouldn't be seen again till 6.30 the next morning when he would emerge from the house, full knapsack on his back containing sandwiches and a flask of tea and make his way down to the number 8 bus. This was a regular sight to behold around Nechells as various men set off to work and then back at night. The look was always the same. In the morning, they were gloomy, looking at the day ahead and what was in store for them. At night, coming home, worn out and knackered. Shuffling along the road, tired and worn out, barely able to lift one foot in front of the other. They go into their little two ups and downs to eat a meagre dinner and slump in front of the radio before going to bed. Never a smile to be seen from Monday to Saturday from any of them. Not many people laughed with joy around Nechells. Laughter like the sparrow was a rarity. Even the birds never sang; around the back streets of Birmingham, people spoke with a growl or a cynical sneer. Laughter was seen as a weakness. To be tough, you had to look tough. The only time your guard dropped was just before closing time in the boozer after ten pints, and you started singing Roll Out the Barrell with gusto.

The routine was the same week in and week out, but only observed over many months and years. A passer-by walking past would never see it. Walking into the pub on an occasional night, you wouldn't see it. The same people were now dressed up with a bit of a smile on their faces, not much of a smile, just a flicker; behind the smile, the observer would notice the tightness in the jaw, the hint of depression behind the eyes in the knowledge of what's in store for tomorrow. You had to observe it over some time for it to sink in. The casual passer-by might say he's a cheerful soul. From an early age, I knew enough to be grateful my mom and Dad made their own living. It was a goal I aspired to without even realising it.

The same people I saw going to work at twenty, I also saw at thirty. Fifty. Then sixty, worn out and knackered, looking forward to retirement without realising they would be just passing the time before dying. A few did work for themselves, but only a few. The Taronis down Scofield Street were a big, rough family of coal merchants. Old Joe, the head of the family, was at the bottom. Having worked in coal all his life, he was to die of the coal lung disease. Son number one, Joe, lived a bit further up on the corner of Weston Street. From a very early age, he learned that it was the talk of Nechells that Joe would be a millionaire. He had three lorries on the go parked up on the bomb peck opposite his two up one down corner house and employed four to six people. Joe was a loud and gregarious bloke. It would be all serious in the mornings as he came out of his house and instructed his men before setting off to the coal yards to load up.

The work was dirty but rewarding. First, all three lorries would load up under Joe's supervision. Sixty-plus-one hundred weight bags would be filled and weighed on the scales, then put over the weighbridge and weighed again, with Joe going in to pay for his orders. From there, he would give his final instructions to his men, who then went off in different directions around the city. Joe's preference was the posh quarter, Sutton Coldfield.

As I got older and stronger, Joe would give me a Saturday job, which involved carrying coal to the houses. First, on hitting the road, the lorry would slow down, then in turns shouting out of either side of the lorry, *ANY COAL*, repeating along the road till someone came out. "Six bags, please, coalman." I learned quickly in life that everyone has to have an edge. That made all the difference between survival and failure. On the coal, it was the drops. When loading up at the yard, there was no finesse. The bags would be shovel-filled, whipped onto the scales, then flung into position, a couple of lumps jumping out of the bag onto the lorry. Once a customer placed an order, the sacks were delivered to the back entry, and the customers would only be concerned with counting that six bags were brought in. No thought was given to the two or more lumps that had dropped on the lorry or the footpath. Certainly not by the customer. Another puzzle that took some working out was two men huddled in the well of the lorry going over the scales but then walking out separately after the bags were filled and put back on the scales. Each man equalled one bag of coal.

Sometimes, the customer never even counted the bags going up the entry and into the cellar. It became a natural habit to watch out of the corner of your eye as you stumbled up the yard to see if the customer was looking out of the window and if she wasn't. She wasn't standing outside as you dropped the sack down the entry. It was only natural to drop a bag short. No one will know the difference between five hundred weight and six in the cellar, especially when it's on top of another bag of coal. With the bits picked up off the road and what had dropped out of the bags, it didn't take long to make another hundredweight sack up. Out of sixty bags, filling an extra three or four sacks wasn't too much trouble. That was the extra perk of the job. Why didn't old man Coleman, who invented the mustard, say that his fortune was made from the surplus left on people's plates? Yet another perk was what was about in the gardens of the houses. A skilled eye could spot the difference immediately if no one was in and the back gates were left open. A nice pedigree dog or a line full of clothing could easily disappear.

Saturday was always the bust-up day. Working on Saturday gave me first-hand access. Only one delivery was made on Saturday so everyone could be back down Scofield Street by lunchtime to get paid. Then, the arguments would start. Effing and blinding all over the dispute would be who was paid enough and who was not. Sometimes, it was only settled with a sharp smack to bring the argument to an end. After that, sorted, all would trot off to The Eagle at the top of Scofield Street to sing and drink merrily away. Sadly, that was Joe's downfall. Just as my Dad liked his drop of mild. Joe liked his glass of wine. Joe's fortune went down the karzie and pissed up the wall. From being the budding millionaire, Joe ended up in a council house over Falcon Lodge doing odd jobs for his brother Henry.

Next to Joe lived the Indian with his brood of kids. I would see him take a couple of live chickens across the pecks and chop their heads off next to Joe's lorries. Heads chopped off. They would scatter all over the peck, flapping their wings. It was a sight to behold, legs going everywhere in frantic desperation. Eventually, they dropped lifeless to the ground. Having waited, the Indian would pick them up and take them to his house, making them into a big curry. That would last his family the week. We had our stews, and the Indian had his curries. Scofield Street was a hive of activity. If there weren't fights going on, the Indian chopping his chicken's heads off, it was something else. Black African/Caribbean would turn up to make drums out of 45-gallon steel barrels, cutting them in half and knocking the tops into different shapes to produce different sounds. Why did they come here? No one knew. But they would spend all day hammering away until they got the exact sound.

At the top of Scofield Street and opposite Anthony's, the corner shop lived the second oldest Taroni, Henry. Henry kept to himself, having nothing to do with anyone, even much with his family. Henry was on a mission. In his yard, Henry kept pigs and his scrap wagon, not for him the coal. He saw more prospects in the scrap metal, but to get the metal, Henry needed more diesel. To get more diesel, Henry kept the pigs, which allowed him special dispensation vouchers that allowed him extra diesel. Rationing was ongoing, and it was hard to see any way forward. Making money in the scrap required a lot of hard work, a lot of cutting corners, and a determination to succeed, among others. Whilst Joe would enjoy his rewards and have a good piss up in the pub, Henry would be beavering away day after day making his money, at night counting it like a little sheeny, even the pig swill was free, and bread collected from the big bins scattered about the area. Henry would often ask me to go with him, picking up stale bread from the many bins around the town. Henry had a pot on the go in his yard, full of the heaving, stinking mess he fed to the pigs who were always escaping and running around Scofield Street. The next brother along was George. George was equally ambitious, but he didn't have that extra drive that Joe or Henry had. I think the other thing about George was that he liked his home comforts. He was married to a woman who demanded the best, and Henry's wife Kitty was just grateful.

Walk into George's house, and the first thing that hit you was the thick shag pile carpet on the floor, fucking white of all things. No one knew whether it was his missus doing the demanding or George himself wanting a better standard of living. Still, considering he only lived in a mid-terrace in Saltley, he dressed it like a mansion. Very few people realise the effort required to make money and save it. Joe knew how to make money, just as my old Dad did. They both made it easy, but they both pissed it up the wall. If I worked for George down his yard on a Saturday, he would watch me all morning as I fed tin cans into a crusher, all for ten bob. Just before I'd finished, George would find an excuse to piss off, "I'll be back in a minute, or I'll see you later, Tommy." I'd spend the rest of the bloody day, probably Sunday as well, chasing all over the green for my ten bob. I don't think George was too good with money. Or maybe that's how he was making it. I don't think the youngest, Stanley, knew what he wanted. Slouching around the green, he seemed to be in his own little world. I don't think Stanley was the full shilling.

I never thought to ask about my Dad's attitude to making money. He carried his bankroll in his pocket and at least 500 quid in one big roll. The average wage for the time was about eight quid a week, so I knew my Dad was rich. Everyone else in Nechells thought so, too. Mom's pleas to him to buy the little hardware shop for sale up in Nechells Park Road fell on deaf ears. Mom wanted to be respectable, to have a little business, something with her name across the front. Dad just saw a burden weighing down on his shoulders. It was utterly stupid. Why lumber yourself with an immediate debt of rent, rates, and taxes, all on the prospect of making money when he was already making money with his own shop in his own front room, no rates, no taxes. No rent. There was a lot of sense in his logic. It never occurred to me to question his wisdom or logic. As young as I was, I could see the sense in my Dad's thinking. I could already see people who had shops around Nechells. The Anthony's on the corner had a nice little shop, but they weren't rich. Mrs Anthony ran the shop, and her husband worked in a factory, and from this, he could buy a nice Ford Zodiac. Everyone was pleased for him; certainly, he was the only one in Nechells with a posh new car, but no one was jealous.

You had three choices around Nechells, Aston, and Duddeston: throw the towel in and give up on anything. Many did. You could see it daily as people struggled to survive without realising it. By the time you were forty, you were counting down and yearning for retirement when you could stop working and collect your pension. Or, you could go to work, be the factory fodder, work in the factories or building sites, and be grounded down on low peasant wages. Or, take a chance, live by your own abilities and wits and work for yourself. I was proud of my Dad and brother Billy for choosing the latter. Better to die a free man than a slave to the yoke of poverty.

But again, in the innocence of my youth, I didn't see the storm clouds gathering. The robberies, safe braking, and bank robberies were still a major problem in Birmingham, as in all major cities. The difference is that they decided to handle it in a majorly bigger way in Birmingham. Stories were growing stronger by the month that London cops were fitting people up to try and reduce the spate of robberies hitting the capital, many involved shotguns and heavy weapons. Orders were sent from above to put the perpetrators away at any cost, by whatever means necessary. The first method was the beltings. We knew from the talk that they would get the hardened villains in and torture them into confessing. It was the only way to get them to talk. Playing by the Queensbury rules was a complete waste of time. It still hardly worked. Hardened villains are used to a good hiding, which is part and parcel of their lives. As it was in Birmingham. The torture and belting just made the villains harder. It also justified the villains' attitudes to corruption. Corruption breeds corruption. The cops were pulling their hair out with frustration.

My Dad wasn't a villain or a crook; he was clever enough to make a living based on his abilities, but my eldest brother Johnny was. Along with the Kirby's and other well-known villains, their reputations preceded them worse. With their aversions to grassing, they formed an impenetrable wall of silence. To the cops, they could only wonder and exaggerate anything going on. With everyone doing well, there would invariably be a party every Friday or Saturday night at our house down Rocky Lane. Mostly spontaneous, it would follow on from a regular little sing-song in one of the pubs. Towards closing time, someone would suggest returning to one of the houses for a party.

A crate or two of beer would be brought from the landlord, maybe a bottle of whiskey, and everyone would head back to the house where Jacky Willis would get on the piano and start banging away at the keys. The cops could only wonder at what was going on, add two and two together and come up with seven, a veritable haven of crooks and gangsters whooping it up on ill-gotten gains whilst planning more jobs. Nothing could be further from the truth. Yes, I had witnessed gelignite being passed around and examined. It was a natural occurrence, but that's as far as it went. This was a party, and everyone was having a good time. There was plenty of singing and bowls of Mom's famous chicken stew passed around. Mom and Dad, in their innocence, never gave it any other thought. Till one night, Dad got nicked.

This is when I first came face to face with Percy Postins, Pip the Planter, a play on his initials. Everyone was becoming aware of Pip the Planter, an evil, pasty-faced bastard with a pudgy round face like a football under his standard detective hat and plain clothes. It was midnight when the door went. The cops walked in and arrested my old man, Pip the Planter, giving his by now regular knowing little smirks as they took him down to the nick.

My Dad was a regular wheeler dealer who bought and sold goods at a profit. He was good at it. The two things he never allowed for was that the cops, in their wisdom, must have been imagining our house to be a veritable cesspit of stolen goods from all over Birmingham. The second most obvious thing that neither my mom nor Dad gave a thought to was that we lived in a council house. A council house is government property. There is an unwritten understanding that the police can, at will, come to your house, kick the door off its hinges, and you can't do fuck all about it. Worse, far worse, was that my Mom and Dad were running a business from a council house, a clear breach of the tenancy rules, albeit a blind eye was being turned to it. So, whilst my Dad thought he was being shrewd and clever, he also left himself wide open to any charges the bent police laid against him. So, appearing in court charged with receiving stolen jewellery whilst effectively being unemployed, the poor fucker never had a leg to stand on. He was sent down for two years with no evidence against him except what was manufactured by Pip the Planter and no mention of his entrepreneurial skills as a businessman. He should have bought that hardware shop. Another factor that is highlighted but rarely brought up is the general vulnerability of a council house tenant. It's only brought up on the rarest of occasions, but when it does, you're made to realise you are a lower, second-class human being. Obey the rules and doff your cap when required. Everything will be fine. Make one mistake, transgress, and you are reminded of your position in the pecking order. Worse, it's often caused by people who are no better off or only slightly better off than you.

This was yet another factor that none of us took into account. A lesson that my family never learned from the Kingstanding eviction was the jealousy motivation. Where my mom and Dad, quite rightly, thought they were harming no one, they didn't think that drawing off a note from a thick bundle in their pockets was enough to piss one or two people off for the pettiest of reasons. Grasses like Charlie Hinze in hock to the cops with the threat of prison themselves unless they threw a body in. Their neighbours, many of whom were barely surviving on the wages they were getting, saw these people drinking and living well whilst throwing money about in the pubs like there was no tomorrow. On the bottom rung of the ladder, not much motivation was needed to stab you without the need of a knife.

This was my first fully-fledged experience of proper police corruption. I was never privy to private conversations in our house, but neither did my Mom and Dad hide stuff from us. We were taught from a very early age that grassing. Police informing was the most disgusting thing of all to do to your fellow human being. What purpose does it serve? OK, your neighbours letting a couple of rooms without permission, so you ring the council and inform them? Another neighbour drives his car with no tax. Do you squeal on him? No one likes to be accused of being a police informer. It is world-renowned as the lowest of the low. No one will admit to being a police informer. Yet plenty actually do. Some little scroat will get nicked for thieving. Looking at two years in the clink, he will squeal his head to inform on all his mates to get his sentence reduced to eighteen months.

Young as I was, it soon became clear to me that the police were corrupt, but to blatantly fit people up seemed beyond my comprehension. An acquaintance of the family named Dennis Woodall was arrested on suspicion of some robbery or other. Pip the Planter approached his cell bars in the cells, holding a screwdriver towards him, innocently asking, "Do you recognise this?" Dennis almost grabbed it as he went to examine it before screaming in panic and jumping backwards, "No, no, I don't." The next morning, they had to let Dennis go through a lack of evidence, but the cops were learning daily. Pip the Planter was soon joined by other equally bent cops, who were given permission and carte blanche to use any methods required to fit people up and put them away. If they weren't guilty of one, then they were obviously guilty of something. Just fit them up where possible. You have to ask what kind of mindset can do that without any feelings of guilt towards the family. Some even took advantage of it to pay a visit to the girlfriend or wife of the villain they had just put away for a shagging session.

Rumours were strong that the police were being aided and abetted, even if it was unconsciously by the judges and solicitors. In many cases, it was all subtle, nothing concrete, just a nod and a knowing look. Hard as you might try to deny it, if you were fitted up, you were going down. Try screaming fit up. Your own legally funded solicitor would tell you to keep quiet. Nothing upsets a judge more than to hear of the police fitting someone up. Your solicitor will not work too hard on legal aid, and the judge will only top you up an extra couple of years on your sentence. It was a no-win situation learned the hard way. Hundreds of people were being fitted up every year in Birmingham, ignored by solicitors, barristers and judges alike. Enforce the law, yes, of course, carry out the rule of law, and when caught, shoot them. Lock them up. But the very act of fitting people up makes the upholders of the law no better than the criminals they are supposed to be setting an example to, worse in fact. The country takes pride in the fact that all men get a fair and unbiased trial, no matter how much money they earn. Bollocks.

When my Dad came out of prison, he just carried on as before, restocked the front room and carried on dealing. Our house was a hive of activity, with Saturdays busier than New Street Station. People would come from all over the town to buy stock off Dad, sheets, clothes, and toys. They would place orders, then resell them at a profit in far-flung pubs or factories. One contact, George Stevens, worked for the Rover car company. He made such a nice living that he bought a little house in Great Barr, as did Joe Wragg, who had a shop in Aston. Dad's prison service and fit-up were soon forgotten as he busied himself to make money.

GROWING PAINS

Slowly, the time passed, and it was time to leave Cromwell Street and head across the road to the seniors. Charles Arthur Street, like Cromwell Street, was built back in the dark Victorian ages and was as dismal inside as outside. I was walking out of a miserable dark and cold Victorian parlour house only to walk into a miserable dark and cold Victorian school. The teachers split into two groups, most uninterested in us as kids and just clocking in to mark time and get their pay cheque, the other few making it quite clear that they hated us. If not hated, they despised us, looking down their noses as they spoke to us.

This was brought home to me on the first day of woodwork class. The woodwork teacher, Mr Lloyd, quickly christened Lloyd the bastard and introduced himself by lecturing us. It was obvious he had practised it. Now he said, "This is Whispering Willy," as he picked up this terrifying-looking cane and started bending it back and forth. Extolling the reputation of his Whispering Willy, he spat the words out, eyes darting from one to the other, lips glistening wet with excitement and relish. It was world-renowned and spoken of in fear by boys who had left school and spread its reputation far and wide. I believed him. Giving it a loud, sharp smack on the desk, he frightened the fucking life out of me. Looking around, I could see I wasn't the only one.

One night, someone climbed the fence and burnt the woodwork shed down. I never learned a thing except to make a little teapot stand out of three pieces of wood. Lloyd was a coward and a bully. Worse, he was a failed ex-copper. From what I gather, he'd had some bad experiences and didn't much like any one of us. I couldn't figure out why he automatically didn't like me. One day, talking to my desk mate across the big workbench, I saw his eyes open in fear, and instinctively, I ducked. The wooden block plane flying across the room hit him square on the bonce, knocking him out. Lloyd shit himself. None of us thought to say anything. If any of us went crying to our parents, it was likely we would get another smack and be told not to whine.

Along with about another third of the class of thirty or so, I had left Cromwell Street without any knowledge of the times tables or of the English alphabet. My education, along with my pals Bee Bee and Robert Turley, was about zero. It set the bar for the next four years.

We had to go to school; it was enforced. If we didn't go to school, we would be chased up by the school boardman, who would threaten our parents. With what felt like a hundredweight sack on our backs, we would turn up, faces as long as Livery Street, attend the assembly, sit on our little arses, legs crossed, trying our very best not to let a loud fart escape knowing how fucking loud it would be in the quite assembly room as we said prayers. It always happened during prayers. If we weren't terrified of dropping a fart, we were mesmerised by the nits jumping from head-to-head, the little bastards looking for new fresh blood. Then, it was into one of the classrooms that led to the assembly room.

The teacher would stand before us in class, put chalk on the board, and tell us what to do. The only fucking problem was I didn't know what she meant, so I just sat there for the lesson with a blank face, uninterested. Historically, all my family on my Mom's Side were carpenters and joiners. Only after the woodwork shed was burnt down and Lloyd was shunted off that we were sent to another school to learn woodwork did I discover I enjoyed it. The two teachers spoke to us and showed us what to do like humans. But it was too late; we only had another couple of months left. Apart from PT or physical education, I only enjoyed geography because we could learn visually. The teachers never seemed to catch on; instead, they resorted to the normal practice of getting outside Lewin and waiting outside the headmaster's office. From there, I would get six of the best across my arse, most times not knowing what I or we had done.

The next four years were a slow process of no learning. I have never heard of things like O levels or general leaving certificates. A fucking nightmare. One day in Mr. Hughes's class, yet another ignorant, disinterested teacher. Welsh at that. One of the pupils, a girl. Had the audacity to ask him honestly what kind of work we could expect to get on leaving school? Pausing slowly, turning for effect and looking down at us through his pinzness glasses, he slowly delivered the killer blow. Looking at the girls, I suspect most of them will get a job at one of the local shops like Woolworths for a couple of years before getting married. The boys will mainly go into the local factories or building sites. One or maybe two of you. If you're really lucky and work hard, you may get an apprenticeship with a possible city and guilds at the end of five years.

Looking at the girl, I could see her crestfallen face dropping to her desk. The others looked equally stunned or dumb as the significance of what he said sank in. Pushing his glasses back up on his nose, pleased with his pronouncement and its effect on the class, he turned and started chalking on the board, dead pleased with himself. The bastard.

Most of the kids in the school would dutifully file in, as smartly dressed as possible under the circumstances, knuckle down and obediently learn their lessons. Sitting there, looking at them individually, I did not know if their knowledge of learning was as bad as mine or better. We seemed to be all attending under duress, even the teachers, passing the hours and days to break time and 4pm.

My mate, Robert Turl Turley, would turn up in class and immediately be sent out to wash his hands again. Turl's hands were ingrained with spirits and sap in the wood, and he used them in his dad's wood yard. Turl's dad owned a wood company on Cheston Street, and his wood yard adjoined his house. Turl had to work a couple of hours each morning in the woodshed. After school, another couple of hours. He had to work for his keep. In truth, Turl was learning more out of school than in it. If the teachers had just once sat and considered that, it might have been different, but no, they just didn't care about us. No one spoke to us on a human level. We were there to be spoken down to. Every morning, without fail, Turley was sent out to wash his hands. He was sent to the headmasters for the cane if he didn't get them cleaned the second time. Most times, we went together.

Modest in nature, Turl was a dutiful son. When I went around his house, I noticed that the family sat on orange boxes covered in sheets; the table was made up of boxes in a big square, again with a sheet spread across the top. Turley's dad got his wood from all over the place and, amongst other things, made his living chopping it up and selling it as firewood; if there was any embarrassment at living on orange and apple boxes, I never noticed it. We were all in the same position of survival. None of us realised that the teachers were only a couple of pay cheques away from sleeping on a park bench themselves; I was to find this out later in life. For all his treatment at school, Turley became a millionaire, having taken over the yard and built it into a profitable used car parts business.

In my class, in truth, in the two schools I attended, well, suffered, and there were no bad kids. We were all just trying to get through daily and weekly. Most knuckled down, did as they were told and learned as much as possible, for that third of a class left to stagnate and rot, including me. The pity is that for the want of a bit of extra time spent on a one-to-one basis, maybe even a one-to-two basis could have made all the difference.

I would never be an academic; I didn't want to be, but I couldn't understand numbers. Looking at numbers on paper, they would all just become a blur. Shown properly, with some sympathy and consideration, we could all have learned the basics of tables and education. Instead, we were made to leave school with no education and knowing fuck all.

My one saving grace was   Miss Smith, a music teacher who was drafted into the school to teach us English and, of all things, music, fucking music! Miss Smith was a pianist and had high hopes of playing for the philharmonic orchestra. Instead, she became a teacher; maybe they thought a bit of culture would benefit us; yes, I could just see myself playing for the philharmonic. The turnover of teachers at Charles Arthur Street was quite regular; no one gave it any thought, but maybe those who came saw it as a dead-end job with no future, just like us. Miss Smith was ancient, at least sixty-five, so I guessed that she must have been shipped in out of sympathy and to see out her pension.

Following a little altercation in the classroom, Miss Smith made me kneel behind her on the floor while she taught the rest of the class. Having an arse as big as a barn door and in protest, I wrote fuck off on it in big chalk letters. Walking through the school during the break with fuck of visible to everyone, she was quickly ushered into the headmaster's office, where it was cleaned off. It was obvious who the culprit was: me. Initially expelled, no other school would have me; Upper Thomas Street in Aston gave me a complete blank. Mr troop felt he had no other choice but to keep me on at Charles Arthur Street, where I saw out the final few months of my prison term. The final score was when someone wrote fuck off, in big white chalk letters on the blackboard, with Mr Collie's comment, well, we all know who did that, don't we? Obviously, I was deemed the culprit. Unmanageable as we were. Well, from their viewpoint. Me, Turley and David Parry were taken to a storeroom at the far end of the playground and asked if we would like to tidy it up; of course, we agreed; it was heaven, no school, well, no stuffy learning. We were told to take our time till the end of term, and we were conned, but it suited us. In the meantime, Miss Smith, for some reason, kept inviting me to her home on the pretext of doing various little jobs in her garden; it became a regular occurrence, and Miss Smith came to have a soft spot for me.

Thankfully, my last day at Charlie inexorably came with no big fanfare. I wasn't overly excited, having been working in the shed. It was just another day that I wanted to get over. Mr. Troop called me into his office and asked me to write my resume to describe myself as he thought it was more appropriate. Thinking it was strange, I didn't realise he was only trying to be fair. He didn't know what to write about me, probably just as well.

There were no big speeches by any of the teachers, no congratulations, no big farewell, best of luck goodbye speech from Mr Troop. Shoulders slumped, I felt he held an air of resignation; we were just one little bunch of hundreds he had seen go through the door. None of us as pupils congratulated nor wished each other well. There were no smiles, just a relief to escape those school gates. We were going out into the big wide world, not knowing what was in front of us; from what Hughes had told us, our expectations were not high. The school report was in hand, and I wrote it myself. Most of the teachers were hiding somewhere, and we left the school behind before three p.m., well before normal leaving time. Yet, another indicator of how quickly the school wanted us out and off the premises, having fallen between dates I was not yet fifteen, we walked out the gates with a feeling of fear, excitement and expectation.

Full of hope and excitement, I soon got a job as an apprentice bricklayer for a small company called Emlyn Williams. Having taken up boxing at the Morris commercial club under the trainer Wally Cox, I cycled the ten miles to the job over Solihull with gusto. The job was great, the wages were crap, and I know I left school with zero education and no knowledge of maths or the timetables. Still, it didn't take me long to figure out my sums. The labourer Colin was on eight quid a week, the skilled bricklayers were on ten quid a week, and I was on three quid a week, soon rising to three pounds ten bob because I was a good worker. This was my first fucking wake-up call. It was bad enough the labourer was getting eight quid a week, but then he had to get the bus from Kingstanding every morning and back at night; how much was that costing him? The skilled bricklayers had their own cars, so how much was that costing them? Out of my three pounds fifty, I was giving my Mom two quid a week. Initially, I was dead chuffed to do so, but leaving me one pound fifty to spend didn't seem great. What about if I had had to pay for the bus fair? I would be left fuck all at the end of the week; thankfully, I didn't drink or smoke.

When the tutor at Brooklyn Technical College told me I was wasting my time learning bricklaying as I didn't have a clue about maths, I guess that was all I needed to throw the towel in. I must have had a stamp on my fucking head saying thicko. At three pounds fifty, I had to know my tables as well. Within days, my mate had put me onto a plumber's mate job down Aston. This company had contracts all over the country and paid me nine quid a week plus expenses for being away; this was more like it; I was getting almost as much as the skilled bricky at Emlyn Williams and more than the labourer.

Like bricklaying, plumbing was a job I could enjoy, but it left me unsatisfied and with no great hopes for the future. Maybe it was me; of course, it was me. Most people settle down to a job, collect their wages, and are happy with their lot. I used to see things around the corner that just used to frighten the fucking crap out of me. My mate Johnny Roberts was a few years older than me and someone I admired. Smart and snazzy, he would be tip-toeing around the town dressed up to the nines in his best teddy boy suit, blue velvet collar, hand-stitched lapels and big boppers for all the world as he owned it. When he danced up the Locarno, he glided around the floor like a film star, throwing the birds around. He swivelled his hips and feet, going in all directions. Then, one day, he got married. She was a nice little bird with a nice figure and tidy. Soon after, I called around his house in Long Acre, knocking on the back door, and his Mom pointed me through to the front; as was common, the newly married took a room or a bed in one of the parents' houses.

Walking into the front room gave me the shock of my life. Johnny had just come in from work; he was sitting on the chair in big, muddied boots and jeans, knackered and worn out, frazzled. His missus was sitting there, tit out trying to feed the baby that didn't want to be fed and was screaming its fucking head off, a shitty napkin lying on the floor, baby sick running down her blouse. It frightened the fucking life out of me. Is this what marriage does. Is this the end goal? Looking at Johnny, I couldn't believe it. This was not the hero I had admired for so long. In one fell swoop, my whole life flashed in front of me, I saw the innocent kid I was at nine, and then I looked at myself now as I looked at Johnny Roberts;

he wasn't all that much older than me, not really, then I looked at his Mom, an old lady, like my Mom and dad. One minute, we are the bee's knees, thinking we know it all, and within a flash, we are old and done for. Worn out like all my mate's parents.

I wanted more out of life than my life to end by age thirty. Was boxing the way forward. I was good. I had won the abas, and there was talk of my turning professional, but that was a long way off, and I wasn't overly optimistic. I loved boxing, but the only ones making money were the heavyweights. My hero was Johnny Prescott, who lived just down the road on William Henry Street with his uncle Tommy. Johnny was only a cruiserweight but had built himself up to make heavy. To make up for that, he had the heart of a lion, fighting some of the best around, Henry Cooper, Brian London, the blonde bomber from London, and the next big thing, Billy Walker. His brother was George Walker, the former light heavyweight champion who had fought Dennis – the Welsh lion—Powell for the British title. Dennis had me in his gym over in West Bromwich and was showing interest in me as a boxer. I first met Dennis while working on a farm in Wales, looking for a boxing club. Dennis came over to see me and set me up with a bag in the barn to do some training. Now, he wanted me to turn professional.

My only continuing and growing fear was my weight. Stupidly, I thought I would grow into a heavyweight. I was light welterweight, ten stone two. It slowly dawned on me that I would just about make middleweight, not where the money was. As Nechells kids, we would watch Johnny drive down Rocky Lane in his open-top white convertible, two blondes next to him on the seat, Christine Keeler another week with Mandy Rice Davis; he was bringing home world models every week, banging them in his aunt and uncles little mid-terrace bedroom. But that was the dream. Billy Monaghan, Johnny's stable mate on the Biddles team, wasn't too happy that Johnny was getting all the money and the glory. Brian Cartwright, the British and European flyweight champion in the same stable, was getting peanuts. When he got out of the game, what had he got, sweet eff all, to boot he was trawling the streets tatting with a thirty hundredweight pickup; bloody hell, that was one of the first things my brother Billy had tried. It was hard work for pennies. Yet he strutted around like a world champion.

I also knew I wasn't a scientific boxer; some boxers were clever and used their skills to win fights, Cartwright was a skilled boxer, as was Pat Cowdell, Ray Corbet was a good British welterweight, but he was punchy; Ray didn't talk, he fucking grunted. On his retirement, Ray just about had enough money to set up a little scrap yard; his house was a little mid-terrace in the small heath of Coventry Road; for all that, he had to sell his soul to the devil, throw the odd body in and bung the cops as well, well, he didn't actually throw any bodies in, his yard manager Roy Bravington did that.

I wasn't overly optimistic. It was very clear the big money was in the heavyweight division. Billy Monaghan was only cruiserweight; he had fought some of the best in the country, yet he was still working for the GPO. Worse, if I did start to get somewhere, even at middleweight, which seemed a bit more realistic, who would look after me? Who would watch my back? I don't think I had much confidence in my old man, a good man but too easy going, and Billy, my brother? Cunning as he was in many ways, I'd already realised he liked being the centre of attention, buying drinks all around. I was a fighter, not a boxer; for every ten punches I laid, I would take ten back. Most boxers I knew were punchy, Corbet grunted, as did many of them; I could see myself going the same way, forty years of age, maybe a title or two, a little council house up Kitts green, and a scrap yard maybe, everyone shouting hello Tommy. Maybe even one or two trying it on. Flat nose, cauliflower ears giving a Neanderthal grunt every now and again. There were more than a few in the pubs.

Billy Walker was lucky. He had his brother George look after him. George had been heavy for Jack Spot, the London gangster, and knew his way around; he'd also served time in prison for stealing a load of swag, par for the course for anyone who wanted to get on, in fairness. Having won the British title, he set up a little garage in London, where he made a modest living. When Billy came into the heavyweight division, the blonde bombshell, they both hit the Jackpot. Billy made the money, George managed him and the money.

Going from a garage to a chain of baked potato outlets to the famous Brent Walker conglomerate that owns cinemas, betting shops, and racing courses, money makes money. Sadly, not many people really appreciate that.

It was more than a coincidence that two other factors came within the sphere of my little world around the same time. Number one was the bullies; I was never bullied at Cromwell Street or Charles Arthur. Though I gathered there were bullies about, once I reached my teens and started strutting my stuff on the social scene of Nechells Green, it became a different matter. Some of my mates, knowing I was a bit handy, would somehow expect me to look after them if they got into trouble. Once expecting me to help them out with a bit of bother they were having with some blacks up Summer Lane. It was rather a few more than some.

Now, I was only five foot nine and slight with it. Slim is the word. But herberts would come along, spotting me as a ripe little target. I could never figure it out. What was I doing to upset so many people? Was it just a coincidence? Would I have just turned a blind eye before? Walked away. On the green one day, my mates Robert Turley, Dave Parry, Malcolm Bellerby and a couple of others and I were sitting on the bench watching the world go by, minding our own business, when this copper walked past with his girlfriend in plain clothes, with his uniform trousers on, and big shiny boots it wasn't hard to spot he was a copper, to impress his bird he comes charging over, grabs Turley by the collar and starts threatening him.

Well, I never heard Turl say anything. He ain't that kind of kid. But the tosspot obviously wanted to be the big shit, jumping up and to Turls defence. I started giving the idiot a boxing lesson all around the green. Eventually, Tony Williams and Nobby Hall came to my defence. Seeing I was whacking the copper, they urged me to walk away. "He's a copper tom, a fucking copper." This wasn't the first time I had had altercations with coppers, the fact is, and I was only just starting to find out. Coppers love that uniform. They also see us young slum kids as sitting targets. If it's not us, it's a Pakistani. The blacks get it even worse.

147

I wasn't the first. It had been the case since time immemorial. I put a uniform on some of these picks and a target in front, and we become sitting ducks for them. In this instance, like others, my mate disappeared into the background, and my pretty face was the only one he saw. Even though Malcolm jumped off the bench onto his back and started smacking him like a good un, he didn't forget it. It wasn't the first time, either. Each time, I never got charged. I couldn't understand it. The Canadian mounted police boast that they always get there, man; well, they're fucking bound to ain't they? The country is covered in snow for most of the year. But the British cops like to boast they do too, but what they do is keep little books, and in their books go the names of all their sworn enemies. Building up over time. It must be laid down and cut in stone in every nick in the country; patience is a virtue; we have time on our side, and they do. The police word for a villain is bastard, and they like using it, sharing police digs or sitting in the canteen locker room. You can only imagine them dissecting this little bastard or that little bastard. Winding each other up with the smell of the hunt, don't you worry, we'll have that little bastard Lewin one day.

If they can't get them the normal way, through honesty and patience, they realise there is an easier way to fit the bastards up. Fitting up was becoming the norm and widespread once the cops realised how easy it was to get away with it.

I was already seeing how corrupt the cops were; we, like the blacks and Asians, were easy targets; who do we go to? Once, with my brother Billy, we stopped outside the Cromwell pub in Nechells. Now Billy always had vans, 5cwt, and transits. They were his work tools; he carried stock in them, and he had also had a drink; now, the cops at that time were never too hot on drunk drivers; as long as you drove sensibly, the cops would always turn a blind eye. They liked a drink or two themselves, but it didn't stop being a leverage tool if the opportunity arose. On this occasion, the cop wanted to look into the back of the van, where Billy had some of his stock, including some watches.

Well, having asked what he'd got and dropped a hint, Billy explained, then offered him a gents watch as a little bribe, seeing a weakness; the cop then got greedy, dropping a strong hint for a woman's watch. Obviously, for his wife. In disgust, Billy gave him a woman's watch, strongly suggesting that that was enough. The cop walked away with two nice watches. You can't do fuck all; it's their word against yours, and who do you believe?

Sid Hobday ran a scrap yard down Gopsal Street. At the back of town, now Sid was quite ruthless in his dealings; apart from the magnet on the scales, Sid also paid accordingly, so by the time you had walked out of the yard, you were only paid about half of the value of the metal you had taken in. Sid was doing excellently out of the scrap, mainly because everyone knew he was sound and would not throw them in. Tailor-made pinstripe suits, a nice big detached house in Sutton Coldfield, and a Rolls Royce Sid were coining it. The only problem was that the cops could see it, and he was flaunting it in front of them. Sid hated cops with a vengeance. Number one, he would not give them the obligatory bung; now that's a definite no, no, worse, he would not throw a body in. Another definite no-no is that if there are two things you cannot do in scrap metal, it is not throwing a body in and not giving a bung. The cops don't like that at all. Worse, they were fucking terrified of Sid, who was like a twenty-stone rottweiler on steroids.

He would pay young kids to wreck the cop's cars when they saw them walking Into his yard; they would shut themselves as they had to go through his books to check his metal purchases. He slags them off all the while. Up to 70% or more of scrap metal is bent. You know it. The cops know it. Proving it is a different matter, but for all their fear of Sid, they persevered. First, he got a two-stretch, full of bitterness and even more hatred. He just came out and carried on. Eventually, they steamed in one day, took his books away, and went to town on them. When punters call into the yard, you must enter their name, address and vehicle number into the book. Well, Sid did; the only problem was he thought he was being wise enough; now, if he had given suitable bungs in the book and been nice with it, it probably would have been enough. But without the bungs, the cops felt Sid was well and truly taking the piss; it was not on.

Going through the book with a tooth comb, the cops found all kinds of false numbers, one a police car, another a tractor, and yet another a motorbike. How can a motorbike possibly bring in half a ton of metal? Well, factually, Sid had fulfilled his obligations; by the time the cops got through with them, the prosecution had tied it up, and Sid didn't have much chance in court. Sid was found guilty and got a seven stretch. By the time he finally came out, Sid was fucked. He was spitting blood, trying to find ways to get his revenge. "I'd like to put a fucking hidden camera in the office and catch the filthy bastards." He had to sell his nice house in Sutton, the Rolls Royce went, and so did the good times. Sid knew he was buying bent metal; he deserved what he got. But he had fulfilled his obligations according to the law. The cops exemplified Sid because he wasn't playing the game. He wasn't bunging, he wasn't throwing bodies in, Sid was just greedy, he wanted it all for himself. We can't have that, can we?

Before we know it, all the scrap dealers countrywide will catch on and stop bunging. We all know the metal was bent because I have put it in writing. The cops knew it was bent, but Hobday had filled in his books correctly. It would be normal to assume that the villains, bringing in bent metal, would put false number plates on the vehicles. Knowing it and proving it are two very different things. But it's proof enough that the cops can do anything they want if they choose to do so, especially once you already have a criminal record. This type of thing intrigued me for years. How many people borrow? Which is stealing, a pen or something else from work? Before you know it, most people in the country would be in nick. But oh, that's different.

Only a few knew that to survive, make money and avoid being nicked, you just had to know how to play the system, use the police and keep them on your side. Once you knew that little secret, you could get away with virtually anything. If you refused to play the games, you were a mug, which is another lesson we learned.

My new friend, Miss Smith, the ex-schoolteacher, would argue and chastise me. Talking to her one day after I had mowed her lawn and done a bit of weeding, I tried to explain how bent and corrupt the police actually were. "Oh, Thomas, don't talk rubbish; the police are not dishonest. They cannot possibly be." Her face was set in stone. There was no way I was going to change her mind. As far as she was concerned, the police were the guardians of law and order. She soon changed her mind a few years later when she started seeing a few things.

NO EDUCATION, NO FUTURE

For the first few years of my teenage life, I was happily getting out there and experimenting with the world. Thick as two planks, with no education, I was flitting from job to job, trying to find something to settle into. My little niche in life. The problem is, with very little or no education, the thing that starts hitting you in the face is that your prospects are almost zilch, if not zilch. If your old man's rich, owns a major company or is titled, you've cracked it. You're either given an allowance which enables you to piss off and waste it or your life. For a better example, think of Paul Getty, the oil tycoon. Even with his kids still wasting it and stuffing it up their noses, they are treated with the utmost respect simply because they have the money. If they lived in Castle Vale, it would be a different story. As has always been the case, it's not what you know but who you know.

As the years go on, you see countless examples of children, the sons or daughters of businesspeople or celebrities, having been given a golden opportunity on a silver platter, and what do they do, waste it. I was fortunate, without even realising it at the time, that I had the savviness of my dad to earn a living, or at least want to, and I had the underlying ambition of my mother. Two factors that I wasn't fully aware of at the time. The simple fact is I was from the slums. I had no education to speak of. According to the job itself, if my employer was unaware of it, he soon sussed me out after a few weeks. From apprentice bricklayer to plumbers' mate, even doing a night shift down Lucas industries of all places, the very birthplace of Joseph Lucas. But if this was the be-all and end-all of my life, this was no part of it.

Working on a press on piecework is one of the most depressingly mind-numbing jobs anyone could do. The blacks have been moaning for the last few hundred years about how they were abused as slaves in the cotton fields of Georgia. Watching them here at Lucas's, along with the white older blokes, made me want to cut my throat. This is what slavery was about. I tried to stick it out for a bit, thinking it was me. For fucks sake, just do the job and try it. Well, I tried it, kept trying it, and looked around at all the other blokes. Twist, turn and stamp, twist, turn and stamp. In between twisting, turning and stamping, I looked across at all my fellow workmates, mainly a lot older than me, in their forties or even fifties, brain-dead from the neck up. OK, it was the night shift, but no one smiled, no one said hello. They just walked in, their shoulders slumped, did their stint, and walked out the next morning, their shoulders even more slumped. No, no, no, fuck this for a lark. I'm not dying here. I must have been on the same money and didn't think it was enough. The only difference between those black slaves and us is the black slaves got whipped. It couldn't have been that bad because they still smiled. We never.

It was made worse because Birmingham was opening up to the world. We'd got Bill Hailey and his rockets. Elvis Presley from America, Tommy Steel and Cliff Richards from England. After the austerity of WWII, it was amazing. Course, to our parents, who had been brought up in the Victorian era, it was absolutely shocking. Television stations banned showing Elvis Presley dancing from the hips down. It was outrageous, shouted Middle America. Well, it was, but not to us.

Drinking had been strictly rationed during the war to keep us plebs in order. Twelve till two and ten minutes drink up time in the boozer, 10pm on the dot with ten minutes drinking up. A good landlord was judged by how well-organised he was in getting the boozers out of the boozer. They were monitored closely by the police. What it did was turn the British people into a load of gulping drinkers, and then there were the Indian and Chinese curry houses. There was an abundance of them shooting up all over the city. The whole country was opening up to them. It was brilliant, and my first experience was, of course, courtesy of some of the major villains of the time who would take me under their wing. First, taking me out drinking with them to the many and varied boozers around the town. Before heading for the big one, the Indian, greeted by dim lights and flock wallpaper and Indian music playing quietly in the background, I was mesmerised. Course, the villains with their pin-striped suits, blazers and grey slacks would immediately be treated with the utmost respect before sitting down to a chicken curry that most often could have been a dog. A new and exotic experience driven by our own knowledge of how food was served in our country. We thought they didn't call sausage bangers for nothing; we just assumed that we were actually getting chicken when we ordered a chicken curry. It took a few years before it filtered through that we were eating dog or cat. Big Harry Walker took me under his wing and, one night, whilst out drinking, decided to take me with his mates to his favourite restaurant in town. Walking in, dim exotic romantic lights and flock wallpaper on the walls, Harry ordered me a chicken curry along with the other six, except for Desperate Dan, who ordered the vindaloo, the hottest curry in the place.

When the meal arrived, along with two bottles of wine, I couldn't believe how big the chicken leg was. It took up most of the plate. "Jeez, that's a big chicken,"

"I told ya, didn't I," said Harry, puffing his chest out. "They give good value here. Now get it down, ya." Well, the rice and curry made a lovely meal. Though the leg did look a bit bluish. But was drunk, like the others. Getting back to Harry's, where we slept the night, Desperate Dan shit the bed. A week later, public health raided a group of curry houses in town, Indian and Chinese and closed them down immediately for serving dogs and cats (God knows what else) in the curry. Harry's favourite restaurant was one of them. The Chinese did it differently and had been getting away with it for years. They had chopped the meat into little bits, making it difficult to know the difference. One day, the dustmen went to empty the bins at the Chinese opposite St Martin Church when they noticed the dog pelts not quite hidden under the lids. They were closed down and remained closed for years, never reopening as a restaurant again, such was the publicity. Still, it didn't put people off having a curry. You can't beat a good curry after a skin full of booze, the only problem being your arse burnt for 48 hours after.

THE GANGS

Birmingham was the second biggest city next to London, yet it felt comfortable to be a part of it. Never feeling overwhelmed, we felt that we knew everyone, and everyone knew us. Venturing out, we would start from the green, having a pint in The Brit or The Beehive, up to The Turks Head, and then into town, buzzing with life. From The Crown to the Yates's Wine Lodge, it was yet another amazing experience as part of our growing up. Yates's was massive, with a bar stretching around three sides of the room, sawdust on the floor and barrels lined up against the back wall from which you would order the wine of choice. Never having tasted wine before, I drank it eagerly. The red wine was lovely till I got outside and hit the fresh air, zonk, out I went like a light, shitting the bed during the night.

As great as the experience was, it put me off wine for years. Wine knocked me out. Cider made me sick and knocked me out. The beer was disgusting. "Ooh, I had a heavy night last night. Ten pints, I drunk?"

"Ten fucking pints? Oh, I could only manage eight." Then another would jump in, "I had twelve." It was like it was some kind of competition. Walking into Yates's, you would be bumping into all the townies, wide boys and duckers and divers, each huddled in their little groups around the bar. From first walking in, you would be standing next to one group you would be introduced to through a short "Tommy Lewin." This would be repeated throughout the night as people from each group would pop over and say hello. That was your introduction. Once you knew and were accepted by one of the groups, the next time you went in, you were automatically accepted by the rest of the group. Those new friends and gangs were then known to you for life. Years later, it would be commandeered as a new experience called networking. We networked automatically, and it was called making friends. The only criteria were that you were sound and could keep your mouth shut.

There was no nastiness, no bitching, backbiting or even much petty fighting. It was a new era in Birmingham. After WWII, things were looking good. There was an air of optimism around the city and the country, where my mom and dad had grown up in the era of the horse and cart, silent movies, new-fangled trams and not even a radio, suffering through two world wars, seeing family and friends killed in wars not of their making, dying from many and various causes, rickets, pneumonia, polio, malnutrition and more. We grew up in a completely different era, with cars, buses, the television, and plenty of work for all, no matter how low it was. OK, we'd had army coats on the bed, suffered the misery of ice on the inside of our single pane rattling windows, no hot water, bathing in the tin bath, but things were looking up.

There was a vibrancy and excitement wherever you went. Well, around the town, in the local boozers on a nightly basis, you still had the doom and gloom of the local factory workers, sitting in the boozers moaning about their lot and the lack of money. Course, they didn't think to realise if they didn't spend so much in the fucking boozer and on fags, they would have a bit more in their pocket. Still, you couldn't tell them; it was the only life they knew. In the services, they were given packets of fags for free to help them get through the week. They were the older generation. They were of the generation that had seen the hardships of WWII. Now, the world belonged to us, the younger, post-war generation. We were quick to forget what had gone on before, the millions who had died or been killed. In truth, we didn't care.

The uplift in optimism was only followed by the reality hitting some of us in the face; having left school with little or no education, we drifted into dead-end, low-paid jobs. It was not only me but also my peers who saw those zombies in the car factories, on the night shift at Lucas's, or at the building sites. OK, you're as fit as a fiddle when you are fifteen. I could throw a shovel all day. Then you look across at the sixty-year-old boy fetching bricks for the bricky or digging a trench. You see the deadness in his eyes, the weariness in his body. Most times, the foreman, out of pity or kindness, will put him on an easy job, like directing the traffic if it's a roadside job or making the tea. However, it still doesn't hide that weariness or deadness in the eyes. By the time he's woken up to it, he's sixty and working towards retirement.

He's fucked, and he knows it. With five years to go and counting, he starts to become aware that after a lifetime of working, he's got sweet fuck all to show for it except a half-tidy rented house that doesn't belong to him. His kids have all grown up and fled the nest, and now it's just him and his wife left to enjoy their retirement. Great. But then he looks ahead to what his pensions would be and realises that he will only be able to survive maybe a charabanc trip to Weston Super Mare a couple of times a year, but that would be about it. Every week, he would be lucky enough for a couple of nights a week in the boozer while putting a little bit aside for his funeral. With retirement at sixty-five, many kicked the bucket soon after or by the time they were seventy, some fucking life. If I saw this, how many others saw it? That was me, my future.

My best pal, Rudy the German, was one of them. I had known Rudy for some time and knew him as a savvy guy with plenty of bottle. One of two brothers, Rudy, lived up Nechells Park Road behind the Army and Navy stores. I could never figure out whether Rudy was born in Germany or England. No one wanted to ask. Likewise, his mother was a stern, indomitable-looking woman who could stop you dead in your tracks with a look in her eye. Rudy reckoned she frightened the crap out of him, tough as he was. To the rest of us, we used to speculate about what she used to do in Germany. Had she been in the Gestapo? Maybe the SS. Maybe, even worse, in one of the camps in Germany, no one wanted to ask; no one had the balls to ask. Certainly, Rudy and his brother Hans were German in appearance and name.

One day, Rudy pulled me on the green with Billy Lovell. As he called it, they had been earning a lucrative little wage doing security work. In truth, it was protection money from some local shopkeepers. Now Billy Lovell was fucking dangerous, very quiet, disturbingly quiet, it was a job getting a sentence out of him, but he oozed fear. "Now look, Tommy. Billy and I have a few shops on the go, but we want to expand. We know you can look after yourself, so we thought you might like to come with us; that way, we can cover more shops."

Feigning interest, I asked what it involved and how much was in it for me. Rudy even personified the German, with short blonde cropped hair and a square jaw. He looked like he had just stepped out of a German war film, the Gestapo ones. In his clipped, staccato way of talking, he said, "Well, you see, Tommy, at the moment, we're making a tidy hundred quid a week. But if you throw in with us, we could treble that, easy." How they had it tidied up was that Rudy would just pop into the shop on a quiet Monday or mid-week morning, introduce himself, and ask the shopkeeper if he had insurance. The shopkeeper would reply that he was on high alert from the very question itself. It didn't matter because then the

German would just point out how his insurance would go through the roof if he started making claims. After all, look what the little local toe rags did to the hardware shop down Bloomsbury Street. The shopkeeper was aware of the window being smashed in Bloomsbury Street and some of the nicked stuff. It didn't take a lot of brains for the shopkeeper to realise it made more sense to pay Rudy the fiver a week he was asking. If the shopkeeper didn't pay, Rudy would just disappear out of town for the day with a strong alibi, leaving Billy Lovell to call in and lean on the shopkeeper a bit heavier. Not many people refused after Billy's visit.

The big advantage Rudy and Billy had was that they didn't drink. Their plan was quite simple: to put the lolly away till they had enough to put it into some business, like transport, or in the longer term, a nice little boozer. The plans sounded great and well thought out, but somehow, I felt it wasn't for me. Putting the heavy on someone was not something I thought of as a way to make money. Thanking Rudy and Billy Lovell, I politely declined their offer.

I was now stepping out into the real world. It was a world most people didn't see. If you work nine to five, it's a completely different lifestyle. You get up in the morning, go to work with like-minded fellow human beings, and from the 8 am start. All you want to do is clock in, get through the day, clock off, go home, watch the telly, and then go to bed, repeating the routine the next day and the next until Friday night or Saturday lunchtime. Then, it may be a couple of hours shopping up the town, paying off your slate at the local corner shop, and maybe a night out drinking. It was the norm, and 95% of us led that lifestyle. Great and fine, and I'm not knocking it. But I had seen far too much of it. I knew where it led but didn't want to be a part of it. Those old pensioners huddled around the coal fire or sitting in the boozers nursing a pint wrapped up to keep warm and grateful for the little company they had of like-minded cronies. Eyes dead, bodies worn out, they were in God's waiting room and didn't even realise it. I wanted a life, and I wanted to live it. The trick was in finding the right niche that was right for you. I wasn't sure what I wanted; none of us did, but we all knew we wanted more money.

My dad had shown me the way forward in his dealings. Having been a barrow boy for much of his life, he was forced to stop by the neighbours squealing on him for running a business from our home in Kingstanding. It was a fruit and veg business, and without somewhere to store the fruit, he was onto a loser, and we were evicted. When we moved down to Nechells, he had found earning a living from the barrow impossible. He had decided to set himself up as a general dealer. To the uninitiated, a general dealer is a dealer in general goods. Dad would buy his stock from whenever and wherever. Summer would be toys, fancy goods, mirrors, clothes, etc. In the winter, with fancy goods, electric fires, and kid's toys, he would buy and sell anything, but he wouldn't knowingly deal in bent stuff; it wasn't worth it. Saturday morning, small businessmen and shopkeepers like Joey Wragg would be calling around the house down Rocky Lane, where our front room was his shop. This time, he could operate with impunity and without the council harassing him.

But it was a double-edged sword. Anyone in business will know how hard it is to succeed in business. You might envy the corner shopkeeper, but that shop will never make his fortune. It was only by the husband going out to work. The wife, running the shop, said it was possible to make a decent living. One friend down Saltley had a little factory making electric fires. He and his wife toiled six days a week just to earn a living, hoping eventually they could increase the turnover and their income. My dad's little fallback was that he was classed as unemployed. Times were uncertain, and selling was far from guaranteed every week, shrewd as my dad was. He had no choice but to use the system. So be it if the council insisted he did not work from home. The downside was that the cops would imagine all kinds of chicanery behind closed doors. As my older brothers Johnny and Reg were professional villains and well-known villains like the Marnies and the Kirbys, all had an instinctive dislike for grasses and police informers.

This must have really been pissing the cops off, whose brains would be running riot with all these villains' doing robberies around the town and then bringing the stuff to the old man who was then selling it at vast profits enabling him to drink every night in

The Beehive or The Brit, far from it. The old man was shrewd enough to buy his stuff at the right price and sell it at a profit. But it didn't help if some little grass did get nicked, then threw my dad in as the one he had sold the gear to, with no evidence. The only way to do the old man was to fit him up. This is where Pip the Planter came in.

Pip. Or Percy. A play on his name, Percy Postons, was brought in to quell the rising tide of criminality that was going on and building up in Birmingham. To fight fire with fire, you might say. Now, Pip was indiscriminate. He didn't give a fuck who he fitted up, innocent or not. If you were suspected in any way of being a part of any criminal activity that brought you to the attention of the cops, then they would fit you up without any qualms at all. Worse, Pip was not alone. Several CIDs around Birmingham had been given carte blanche to bring the villains in by hook or crook. Most times, it was by crook. Worse still, the solicitors and the judges knew all about it. They were a party to it. Not knowingly, of course. Oh no, one couldn't be seen condoning police corruption, but who polices the police? The police, of course. It's an interesting aspect of life that when we look at an American gangster movie, we think it's only normal when the governor tells his police force to get the gangsters by hook or by crook, in effect, to be crooked themselves. So, how do you reconcile fitting people up by any means? Who are the crooks?

Thankfully, and coincidentally, but not fully, they fucked up when they blatantly fitted up the so-called Birmingham Six. These six paddies were playing cards on the night train to Dublin when someone heard their Irish accents, called the old bill, and like bulls in a China shop, they gone steaming in, convinced they've got their men. It was known that they had been fundraising for the IRA around Birmingham. It didn't help that one or two had a criminal record—more power to the cops. You see, you have to understand the mentality of the police. They don't give a fuck if you were innocent or guilty of that crime. If you have a criminal record, you are guilty anyway. If it's not one thing, it's another. Worse, the cops are under orders from the politicians to get results. Now that gives them a secondary double reason to fit someone up, and they don't give a fuck who. Rumours circulated the town of people doing time for murder, break-ins, and bank robberies that they hadn't a clue about. The cops had complete carte blanche. It was staggering and unbelievable that the police could act and behave like this with complete impunity, and worse, and slowly, it pervaded all ranks.

Normally, when you get in front of a judge, if you start to shout fit up, your brief will tell you to shut up immediately. "Oh no, no, we can't have that old son, can we?" Once you accuse the cops of fitting up, that gives them the right to go through your life with a tooth comb, including bringing your criminal record out in court. And trust me, when the prosecution has detailed every aspect of your criminality, there won't be a rock for you to climb under. Why do you think they won't allow cameras into the courtroom? Mind, America does, and they still manage to fit people up, mainly by hiding evidence that could scupper the trial or help prove the accused's innocence, as is done here, of course, in case after case. Sometimes, many years later, it is discovered that evidence that could have cleared a convicted criminal was mislaid or deliberately hidden by the prosecution. Why would people representing truth and justice, resort to such criminal activity?

Another big factor in your fit-up is your defence. Like a proper mug, you can choose legal aid or funding your defence when you go into court, considering a simple driving offence will cost you circa two grand and upwards. If you're on a major criminal charge, you can be talking twenty grand plus, and that's a big plus. You ain't got the money if you didn't do the crime. If you have the money, the question is, where did you get it? So, you're between a rock and a hard place. Then, you must find your solicitor, who will recommend a barrister or QC. That's a queen's council. The clue is in the initials QC. In medieval times, the sheriffs protected the king's lands and chattels. Today, it is the police.

The cops will furnish your criminal record to your defence, putting them in the picture immediately. Now, if you robbed a shop or a post office three years ago, and you're now being charged with robbing a bank, then unless you've got a 100% alibi, you're fixed again because now your solicitor will be sceptical. Either way, he will get his money, and the QC will get his money. However, there is a ceiling to the amount they can claim from legal aid, so they will simply pull back. In contrast, the public prosecution office has unlimited funds. Imagine, if you will, a heavyweight boxer being pitted against a light welterweight. Legal Aid is a little private bank for the legal profession. I tell you, the legal profession is as corrupt as any. Sadly, people don't realise how corrupt the legal profession is. Fair trial? Of course, you're getting a fair trial. You're getting legal aid, ain't ya?

We each see what we want to see in life, usually from our own viewpoint. Go out and rob a factory. That's theft, quite clearly. If a cop takes bungs, backhanders or helps themselves to stolen money brought into the nick, it's considered fair game; after all, they didn't nick it in the first place, did they? It was already nicked, and someone is paying for the crime. With solicitors, barristers, or the Queen's Council, it is looked at differently again. So, you're up in court on charges with a three-day window; low and behold, with the fit-up and lack of effort by your defence, you are found guilty within a day and a half; what do your defence team do? Why, they put in for costs totalling three days, a set fee, you see, it's justified. I once bought a business that suffered with a bit of subsidence; the seller's solicitors didn't notify me about it. It was buyer beware, fair enough, but when I sold it, it mysteriously popped up in the documents of my solicitor, who had no choice but to tell me. Shocked, I insisted he remove it. Grudgingly, he did. He deducted one thousand pounds in costs from the proceeds, from a clear quote of five hundred pounds. It was my punishment. He felt justified in ripping me off if I was making money. He wanted some of it. I tell you, bent.

Regardless of what you may feel or think, the police have no conscience in their dealings; it is part of their training. Innocent or guilty, you are just a number. If you have a criminal record, you are guilty. All it needs is a nudge to help it along. If you have no criminal record, that is completely different; the police don't know you or who you are. That is why when you read about a case in the newspapers where the defendant is so blatantly guilty but is declared innocent, it's because the police and judges have nothing to show or prove otherwise. That's to show us all how fair the justice system is.

The Birmingham six were found guilty, of course, and spent twenty years in nick before it was found that they were innocent after all. In those twenty years, they were spat at, belted, and God knows what else. During their sentence, one died, and Paddy Hill came out bitter, of course, and then lost his family. The police? Did they get done for verballing the six up? Not at all. The worst that happened was, finally, Lloyd House, the epicentre of all the fit-ups, was disbanded. Most of the CIDs either retired, went sick, or were fired in a few cases; that's justice for you. As for any admittance of guilt, well, if you're a convicted criminal sent to prison yet still protest your innocence, you're simply in denial and dismissed; well, it applies to the cops as well. See, if you were to ask a cop if he has any feelings of guilt, if he can sleep with himself for fitting six innocent men up, and no one would, they simply deny it, and they live in denial also. Such is the reputation of our police. Even the public feels the same. Ask the average member of the public how they feel about police officers being corrupt or fitting people up, and they will harrumph, fold their arms and refuse to accept that the six innocent men were innocent.

It took several years and the Good Friday peace process for everyone to realise that the Irish had a justified argument in fighting for a country they felt belonged to them. The Americans believed them. Why, half of America is Irish after they fled following the great potato famine? That's colonialism for you.

Most police do not want to carry guns, quite rightly so. We are not America. But for the police who do, we have to accept they are a different breed altogether. They consider themselves the elite. It doesn't take a lot of imagination to think of them biting at the bit to get their first kill under their belt. All is well and good, but what about the many innocent victims shot dead, like the Brazilian Jean Charles Menezes, rushing to catch the train to work? The police picked him out as a suspected terrorist. With no thought of catching him in the open, they wait till he's on the train itself before rushing in and shooting him dead, an innocent kid. Waiting for orders from a distant head office all excited, the opportunity to catch him beforehand was lost. No one was found guilty of anything, just a million or so of taxpayers' money paid to the kid's family to shut them up. The officer in charge of the operation? She went on to become chief constable.

The Birmingham girl who was pregnant was shot in the stomach and killed mistakenly by the police, who thought it was her boyfriend holding her hostage in the stairwell of the block of flats. It was a dispute between lovers, an argument, and stupidly, to make his point, the boyfriend took a shotgun. Panicking, the cops buttered her mother up for months till the trial of her boyfriend. It was only years later that it dawned on her mother that she had been suckered by a bunch of cops who had needlessly killed her daughter. It was never established or disclosed if there were cartridges in the gun, and the boyfriend concerned ended up in a mental hospital. His life was destroyed as well. The Irishman was walking in London with a table leg wrapped in brown paper, which he was carrying home. Foolishly, the guy was drunk. Being drunk and Irish whilst carrying a table leg wrapped in brown paper was a definite no. Rushing to the scene, the cops shot him dead. If they shouted, "Police, drop your weapon," the poor bugger in his sozzled state probably didn't realise his predicament. Did he lift "the leg" up before they shot him? No common sense, see. There are more and more cases regularly, yet we, the public, turn a blind eye to it. The police know this and bank on it.

So again, you're fucked. If anyone in this country feels we have a fair justice system in the world, think again. No, there is a way to be bent in England. And that's to be legal and legally bent; if you're legally bent, you can get away with anything. Look at the government. They are screwing us to the ground at every turn, it's called daylight robbery. But not big business; big business is useful, and only banks rob them. Look at the banks, another institution backed by the government and big business that screws us to the ground at every opportunity. Again, daylight robbery, see? Because it's done in broad daylight. Not in the dark.

So, if you have a scrap yard, you could buy bent metal all day long, so long as you throw the odd body in, that's a customer. More importantly, put the weekly bung in the book, a bit extra, and a crate of spirits for Christmas. If you have any kind of business with just a whiff of bentness about it, the easiest solution is to give a bung. A bung smooths all ills. If not a bung, throw a body in. Unfortunately, fitting up criminals or those suspected of being criminals doesn't work. You only have to look around to see this. It spreads the crimes around. I saw this and observed it as I was growing up; a clear example was Charlie Hinze. Charlie was a likeable villain from Aston. He grew up with all the local and known villains, chancers and spivs of the time. Now, like most villains, you progress from the petty nicking to the big stuff. You progress because that's where the big money is. Why work your nuts off all year round for a wage that just about enables you to live after the government has taken three-quarters of it off you when you can rob a post office or bank in twenty minutes and make two years' wages and enough of a stake to put into a business?

The odds of getting away with the crime are some 99 to 1. That reduces if you've got loose lips and someone grasses on you. In Charlie's case, after getting nicked a few times and not liking the porridge he was forced to eat for a couple of years, Charlie turned to grass, informer. It didn't stop him from thieving, but Charlie would throw a body in whenever Pip, the Planter, was brought in and started sniffing around, ready to nick him and fit him up. It was something I was finding out as I went along in life. Charlie wasn't the only one. There were dozens more. These were the next generation of the Peaky Blinders. What no one else realised was that they were crafting their skills even further by throwing bodies in before they were even nicked themselves. Most cops have their little informers in the back pocket. Like Pip the Planter, the corrupt ones would have a small team of informers. Grasses like Charlie were willing to call their cop and throw someone in. This saved their skins and gave them free rein to continue their little jobs without hindrance. Don't go on that film characterisation of the weedy little rat sucking on a roll-up, shifty-eyed, whilst giving his cop friend the latest info before being thrown a fiver.

Eventually, it catches up with them, but most of the time, it's too late. Whilst on remand in Winson Green Prison, Charlie was talking to Reg Baldwin when someone walked past the cell and called Charlie a grass. In the nick, you just can't let that pass, especially in front of witnesses like Reg. Muttering, I'm not standing for that. Charlie got up to sort the bloke out; he was back shortly afterwards with some nice cuts and damage to his face. Unfortunately for Charlie, the bloke who called him a grass was Billy Lovell, someone you didn't mess with.

Birmingham was an exciting place after the war years. The city was thriving with jobs galore; you could leave a job you had started at noon and start another at one pm. But the wages were low. There was also an abundance of other opportunities. It was simply finding your niche. I had tried various jobs but found them lacking in opportunities or financial rewards, such as apprentice bricklayer and apprentice plumber, with no education, which was very limiting. No, there was only one way forward: to be self-employed, take your chances in life, living on your wits and abilities, like my dad and my older brother Billy, who was one of the smartest men around. Billy would open up a shop and get it stocked with goods, selling it as he went along. If it didn't do too well, he would simply close the business and start again.

Billy and Johnny had a network of friends who all worked together. Still, as the occasion arose, they mostly worked alone, finding it more beneficial to be independent of my Uncle Jimmy. Pussyfoot would spend weeks or months planning or working out little scams that made him thousands of pounds without any great risk and away from the eyes of the cops. Jimmy would simply rent a factory unit as cheaply as possible and order lorry loads of goods on a month's credit if he could get it or payment on collection. Once the lorry was unloaded or delivered, it would then be discovered that the managing director was not available to pay the driver, unable to reach his company and facing the prospect of reloading a lorry load of goods, the driver agreed that he would return empty-handed, with a signed delivery note, goods to be paid for within four weeks.

This was one of many scams Jimmy pulled regularly, having built up a few lorry loads of goods and sold them to known buyers.

He would simply close the unit up and disappear as he went along. Because of its complexity, the police were either never called in the first place or simply threw the towel in after the first knock on the empty premises. This could just be a civil matter. Another of his little scams was when he managed to get a nice little contract with a car manufacturing company. It was a potentially lucrative little business pressing badges. Pussyfoot had to get himself a little factory unit down by the Barton Arms, Aston, half a dozen pressing machines and a bunch of women working part-time on the presses. Still, it was a slow process to make his fortune. With a good accountant and solicitor on board, his little factory went up in flames, and all his badges and pressing machines were utterly destroyed in the fire. Jimmy put in a claim for twenty grand and got it. The only problem was that Jimmy liked his whiskey and had the ladies around. Twenty grand minus backhanders and expenses was a lot of money, more than twenty years of average wages. Or three nice houses, Jimmy blew the lot on a failed restaurant and a lady friend.

The opportunities were endless, but so was the minefield of discovering them. Forming into groups, gangs, or teams was a natural progression, mainly hoping to be more financially beneficial. It could sometimes take years before you realise it was a complete waste of time, but the problem was so many people were so secretive. The two guys who had the car repair pitch in Hockley were right bang at it, ringing and doctoring cars. They had done their training and homework. One was an expert in mechanics, the other in bodywork. If a van came in with crappy bodywork, they would give it a big rub down, any bad spots cut out and, if need be, replaced with a cardboard sheet. The cardboard was stiff and had a smooth face for spraying. From there, it was put through the auctions, sold as seen, and the price bumped up.

If it were a mechanical problem, they would just get one of their little contacts to nick them a similar model. It would be put in the adjoining workshop/garage that no one knew about, stripped right down, and all usable parts put to one side for future use and used as required. The parts would then be stripped of any numbers, put into a new body and sold for top bat. A few of us knew they were at it somewhere, but none knew the facts. As far as we were concerned, they were just scratching a living, starting cars up. Good job, because then no one could squeal. All the time, they looked at the rest of us with smug little smiles like we were a bunch of mugs. There was no teamwork there then. In most cases, this is how it operated, a big difference from how my dad said it worked in his day back in Summer Lane and the city.

Then you were picked on your soundness, ability to keep your mouth shut, and discreetness. Nothing was worse than a grass or someone who spoke out of school. My big advantage was that being born in Summer Lane but growing up in Nechells meant I had two feet in both camps. My dad and his dad were born and grew up in Summer Lane. My older brothers all grew up in Summer Lane, so our reputation for being sound stood us in good stead, or so we thought. Forming gangs or teams was a natural progression. There was no motive behind it other than friendship, loyalty and any other benefits that might come from it. The only problem with being in a gang was that it was a distraction and removed the ability to focus on your goals and aims. There were various gangs dotted around Nechells Aston and the city centre. I knew most of them, and most of them knew me.

Most of my friends, peers, and I grew up and naturally started jobs working predictably in one of the many factories, shops or building companies dotted around the city, as did I. This was fine. Still, your life then was not only spread out in front of you but also restricted you in many ways; ten quid a week for the next twenty-five years and a council house was not a great incentive. No, I wanted more out of life, and I couldn't see myself getting it working for someone else on low wages. I worked for my dad as a driver for a time, delivering goods to various shops. George 'Fruity Tuit' Fewtrell was my dad's semi-business partner and drinking pal. Fruity Tuit's son Eddie had a nice tickle just as the Bermuda Club was sold for two grand. There were various stories about how he made the two grand, but no one knew the truth. Eddie was shrewd, alright. My brother Johnny had also had a nice tickle and, with Billy Henry and Ray Kirby, had also been offered the club but turned it down. Two grand was a lot of money at the time, and they felt it was too risky to take on something they knew nothing about except on the opposite side of the bar. When they saw how well the Fewtrells did, they came to regret it, but they would have drunk all the profits.

With the city booming, restrictions were being eased on licencing drinking establishments, allowing nightclubs to open up and prosper. From a member's drinking club, Eddie was able to extend his licence, allowing late-night drinking. It also had a roulette table allowing gambling, which was a big money maker. Within two years, Eddie had made that much money. He then bought the Cedar Club on Constitution Hill. Ringing his brother Don, who worked on wages in a Coventry car factory, Eddie offered him a job running the Cedar Club. Don left Coventry like a shot. Within a few short years, Eddie had most of the clubs in the town employing all his brothers in prestigious positions. He had hit upon the boom time in club land; young people had money to spend, and the villains were only too happy to flash the cash they had made so easily. It was the start of the rock n roll era. After the austerity of the war years, the vibrancy and excitement in the country became tangible.

Fruity Tuit didn't like or get on with any of his kids for some reason. I think the feeling was mutual. All except Kenny, his older son, who was a bit simple; he equally didn't like his brothers and spoke disparagingly of them. They likewise kept him at a distance, never mentioning his name. Kenny supplemented his dole money by selling a few items that he could blag cheaply off his or my old man. Fruity Tuit lived in a flat up the top of Cromwell Street and Bradburn Way and would walk down to our house in Rocky Lane at nine am, where they would pick out fancy goods from the front room. Gilt mirrors would be loaded onto my little 5CWT Austin A55 van together with other items of goods, and by ten o'clock, we would be off around the shops. Fruity Tuit would most times have sold his stock by noon, and we'd be back to The Beehive pub, where my dad was already on his first half. I was paid a day's wages, and off I went. I just assumed Fruity Tuit, and the old man liked a drink. Eddie complained that his old man was an alcoholic.

To many, Fruity Tuit was considered one of the best salesmen in the country, but my dad reckons he was the best conman, certainly in Birmingham. Certainly, Eddie owed some of his entrepreneurial skills to his dad, even if it was only genetic. With three dozen guilt-framed mirrors on my van, the shopkeeper ordering two dozen, fruit would somehow get him to buy the other dozen. I agreed with my dad.

THE GANGSTERS

As I was feeling my feet, I started spreading my wings more and more around the city. Big as it was, Birmingham was a small community where most people knew one another, if not directly, then it was by friends of friends. We were comfortable with our fellow Brummies even though we fell out and fought each other a lot. The Asians and other immigrants were few and mainly integrated if not wholly accepted. At the very least, they kept to themselves and just got on with their lives. It was only in areas like Handsworth that the blacks and Caribbean congregated and ganged up and created ghettos. It didn't bother the rest of us in the city. They kept to themselves, opening their shops in the community, taking jobs that none of us wanted in the foundries or train depots, so they remained, in the main, unseen. It suited the rest of us. Later, as more Asians came into the country, they formed growing communities or ghettos of their own. Handsworth, a once thriving "posh area, became overcrowded and run down through multi-occupation because of its big, detached houses and villas. The cultural differences were quite clear, with houses being decorated with Christmas trees in the height of summer. They loved bright colours. Beds were shared, with one getting up to work while the night shift worker got into his warm bed. Well, they slept on the floor back home. This was a luxury.

When I walked up Rupert Street, I knew the Asian twins and where they lived, but it didn't detract from knowing everyone else. It was a great time to grow up in Birmingham, to be a part of it, and to experience the atmosphere. The Asian twins introduced me to my first curry with eggs in it. Who puts boiled eggs in a stew? The air was full of excitement and optimism. The Second World War was now becoming a distant memory, poverty was disappearing, the army coat was gone, replaced by blankets, even better by a million miles, and we now had beds with no top and tailing. The gangs were well established in Birmingham, and we all knew who we were and where we came from.

Back in my grandad's days in the mid to late 1800s, the city grew from a small village-type community with Aston at its core. Still, there was a slight change in attitude and direction. In contrast, the gangs of my dad's day had been tight-knit and loyal to one another. These new gangs of my brother's generation and those slightly older than me were a different breed. They were all wide boys, smart arses who thought they were god's gift to the criminal underworld. Yes, like me, they had known hardship, but not of that generation that had come home from the war. These had not done national service even though they thought they knew it all and carried themselves like the gangsters they thought they were. The buckle belts and baggy trousers had now disappeared. In their place came the Hepworth, Burton or Colliers, handmade suits, and stitched lapels, if you don't mind, the one sure way to tell or let everyone know your suit was handmade. Many of us would fiddle or finger the lapels to draw attention to the stitching. The days of the teddy boy suits had or were disappearing fast. The long sky-blue coats, black velvet collars, tight trousers and beetle crushers were just a fad disappearing as quickly as it had appeared. Now it was the three-piece suit, handmade.

From a fight at school, our prowess developed and extended to the outer areas where we established our positions alongside our peers. If you had nothing to offer in the way of talent and couldn't fight, you were out of the picture except for the odd hello in passing or in the bar. But for all that, it also came with a sense of arrogance. Each little group thought they were the cream of other groups.

Elvis Presley, Bill Haley, Fats Domino, followed by the Beatles, Adam Faith, Marty Wild and the Wild Cats, were ushering in a new era. This all coincided with Eddie Fewtrell jumping on the bandwagon with his clubs. Sharp as he was, Eddie wasn't slow to miss a trick. A half-page advert would go in The Mail or Mercury announcing the up-and-coming band of the Beatles or Tom Jones, the Welsh crooner. Many clubs hit the jackpot by signing these acts for a few quid just before they hit the big time. Fewtrell was one of the first. He was getting these acts for as little as twenty quid, charging the young, eager punters two quid to get in the door. Of course, they would hardly spend anything once in the club because the price of drinks was too expensive, but that didn't matter. Eddie had covered the cost of the band and bouncers over the door at two quid entrances. The big money came in from the gangsters, the wide boys, the businesspeople, the big spenders who had money to burn. They had to be seen to be spending money. They didn't care about the expensive drinks. They were welcomed and feted as the big shits they thought they were. By midnight everyone was pissed. It was slowly passed around that Tom Jones or the Beatles had got stuck in a traffic jam or were delayed leaving the last venue. At any rate, they were not going to make it. The gangsters and businesspeople didn't give a toss. They weren't there to hear the band, and most times, they never knew who was turning up. As for the average punter, they were either too pissed to care or didn't quite know what to say or do anyway.

If one or two of them had the nerve to go and complain to the doormen or one of the Fewtrells, they would be fobbed off. "Don't worry, he will be here later. He's been held up on the motorway," or "he's had a breakdown on the motorway." It worked a treat every time. If there was anyone persistent enough and sober enough to carry on complaining, they would either give them their two quid back or, if they were troublesome, give them a clip around the ear, a boot up the arse and told to get out. Sobered up the next morning, they would shake themselves off, get over it and turn up at the club the following week. No one could afford to miss out on a night in the clubs. They were the city hot spots, the places to be seen and to see. 10-30, they were the only places.

By chance or design, Eddie had hit the jackpot. He might well slag his old man for being an alcoholic and abandoning the family, but if he didn't learn anything from old Fruity Tuit, he certainly picked his genes up. I only briefly knew and worked for Fruity Tuit, and he taught me plenty. For that alone, the Fewtrells should be grateful. It's not the time spent with someone. It's having the door opened and showing you the way. My dad tried to teach my older brothers the business of making money. Except for Billy, they were not interested. It's either in you or it's not.

Another great advantage Eddie had was his brothers, all seven or eight of them. None were what you would call hard in the sense of being hard, but there were plenty of hard cases around Aston, Nechells, etc. Each could look after themselves, but together, they were quite formidable. Backed up by half a dozen bouncers if you caused trouble, you didn't have a fucking chance. Worse, most of the punters were three parts pissed by the time they got to the club at ten or eleven o'clock. With a couple of bevvies down their necks, they were fucked before they started. If they were stupid enough to be a bit gobby, a quick smack on the chin would sort them out. When you are drunk, it only takes a slight tap to knock you out. Most boxers know that. Coming round as you sat on your arse outside, few would recollect exactly what happened. The next day, it would be completely forgotten. For many, it was considered a bit of a badge of honour, "Cor' fucking blimey, I had a good night up Fewtrels last night, got kicked out."

The Fewtrell's reputation was enhanced even further. The bouncers were big guys. Big Smithy was an ex-boxer, and Kelly was just a brute thug. Mark Bennet, the scouser, just liked hitting people. If it went off, he would wait to the side, bring a leaded truncheon out and smack you over the bonce, bang, game over. Most times, if not every time, the punter was that drunk he never knew what hit him. He would just be tossed aside or into the gutter, and waking up later, he would just toddle off, still drunk and fuddled. This was all normal and accepted behaviour. The cops just never gave a fuck thinking the bouncers were doing their job. There were some hard troublemakers about. Then there were the pros. The shortage of bouncers was so acute that Eddie would take on the boxers. My pals and former boxing club teammates, the Murry brothers, Johnny Burns and even Lloyd Hibbert, the British welterweight champion, were at the doors. The punters were very quick to recognise them. When they came to the club, three parts pissed the bouncers were stone sober. One clip off them, and it was lights out. They had the pick of the girls and earned more than from boxing.

Yet another big advantage he had was that many of his customers, his punters, the gangsters like the Avery's, the Brown's, the grass and police informer Charlie Hinze was that they all grew up knowing each other down Aston. Apart from being mates, no one would rock the boat and risk losing membership to such a prestigious group. If you were in the *Click*, you were welcomed with open arms in all the clubs in town. I was in the *Click*. You were known by all the bouncers and club owners and welcomed with a call out to your name as you entered the door. If you were minor, it was, "All right, Tom? In you go." If you were a bit higher in the pecking order, it was, "Hello Johnny, old son, how are you? Nice to see you. Have a good night." If you were a tatter, car dealer, or steel stockholder, the welcome mat jumped up a few notches, and it furthered a little personal chat before being ushered into the inner sanctum. All this helped and added to your feelings of being someone special, part of the elite. Your very presence would also have a knock-on effect on others in the club. "Behave, that's David over there with his team." It was only the mugs who misbehaved, generally or those from further out who didn't know the score.

Another favourite trick Eddie had, if someone called him out, was not to go outside. Oh no, that could be dangerous. He would invite them to a fair fight inside the club. Usually, this would be after midnight and early in the morning, the punter pissed and Eddie stone-cold sober. He would form a circle on the dance floor made up of punters and his bouncers strategically placed around the circle. Each gave the odd dig to help Eddie, but no one ever won a fight. To be fair, there are a lot of troublesome nutters out there looking for trouble who think they can fight. Most people who can look after themselves know they can't drink.

Johnny Prescott was a different kettle of fish. Not only was Johnny the Midlands heavyweight boxing champion, but he was also one of the top boxers in the country, only losing the British title by a narrow margin. He was also one of the nicest and friendliest guys you could ever meet. But Chrissy Fewtrell, one of Eddies younger brothers, was dead set against him, most likely out of jealousy. Johnny was strutting about the town with some top models in his arms, Miss World, if you don't mind. Most of us loved and respected Prescott. The more popular he became, the more Chrissie seethed, till one night, it all boiled over. Chrissy invited Johnny to a fight outside the club.

Eventually, having tried all the ways to avoid trouble, Johnny felt he had no choice but to go outside with Chris. With Eddie asking Johnny to take it steady, he felt he had no choice but to play with him in a little boxing match. Chrissy knew it. After a few minutes, it was all over, and they went back into the club. Chrissy never tried it on again. But it enhanced the Fewtrell's reputation even further, with most bystanders being the bouncers and none wishing to lose favour. It was soon put about that Chris beat Johnny Prescott. None but the most stupid would believe it, but there are a lot of stupid people about. From Johnny's point of view, it wasn't a matter of any of the bouncers sorting him out. Rather, he knew if it would be a fallout with Eddie, the knock-on effect being banned from all his clubs, and owning most of the best clubs in Birmingham, it would have left him out in the cold a bit. Chris never realised this. In his own mind, he was the top hard case. Most of the bouncers let him think that. With eight or more clubs around Birmingham and some five or six bouncers in each, it gave a total of forty or fifty bouncers or more to call on, if needed, a small army.

I had the misfortune to find this out in the Balalaika Club just below the Cedar Club, owned by my Uncle Jack Hale. It was a nice place for a quiet drink till one night, the new owner of the Fleur de Leas popped in. He had bought the club off another Uncle Geoff Elliot. The guy apologised for giving my mate Ernie Trainer the sack a few nights earlier. I took umbrage at this and decided to stick one on his chin out of misguided loyalty. Down he went, got up and walked out. Five minutes later, Dinky, the black gambler, asked if I could give him a lift home to get some more gambling money. He was having a bad night, so we went. Coming back twenty minutes later, we were confronted by a mob of about twenty bouncers queuing and jostling to get into the Balalaika. Getting out of the car to have a nose, Dinky shouted, "Get the fuck in, Tom." It dawned on me quickly that the owner had gone and brought a team back. They were tooled up with shooters and pickaxe handles, the lot.

Thankfully, over the next few days, it was calmed down with the help and pacifying of a few friends.

It was this kind of situation that enhanced the Fewtrell's reputation, as well as the other club owners. If one guy can muster that number of bouncers up from one club, what could the Fewtrells put together from nigh on ten clubs, and all the time, the cops were given fair notice and the suitable bung to keep well out of the way.

There were gangs in my dad's day, in the Peaky Blinders day, but with each generation, the gangs evolved. In my granddad's day, they were mainly thick, uneducated thugs acting in mass gangs stalking the streets or alone, very few of them having the brains or the inclination to go out robbing. The penalties were harsh: either hard time in prison or the risk of deportation to Australia. No education suited the government, with only one per cent at the top benefiting from that, followed by the middle classes. Our lot in life right at the bottom end of society was seen as cheap fodder for the factories, the mines and the fields. Housing was dire, with no proper sanitation, money, and only the lowest-paid jobs. It was the beginning of the Industrial Revolution, with many peasants coming in from the country where they had worked on farms for little or no wages, only to find that they were no better off in the industrial heartland of the big cities.

With no education and no brains, it was a deliberate policy designed to keep you in your place, controlled, as the slave traders did in the cotton fields of South America, like in my granddad's day. Those black slaves never knew any better. In my dad's day and after the war years, a small minority started to question traditional thinking. I found working in teams, not gangs, teams of two or three, better and more beneficial. Too many in the team and it reduced the spoils, but it also led to loose tongues or the risk of loose tongues. Having served in the army or having done conscription, they knew the benefits of teamwork and keeping the old gob shut. Now, in my brother's day, the generation above me was made up of gangsters. As the clubs started to open up, so did the gangsters start to blossom. They weren't really gangsters, of course. They were just the next generation of the sons of the Peaky Blinders, but with the accessibility to guns, sawn and handguns, they started to think they were gangsters. And there were quite a few of them.

Johnny Avery was one of the leading gangsters, short, stocky, and with a serious face, thinning a bit on top. Roy Brady was another, slim, medium height with a constant smirk on his face. Roy was a well-known and respected villain and a clever thief who rarely got caught. To those in the know, his nickname was Little Big Head, given to him by his dad, Vince. In his mind, Roy was a legend in the town, if not the country. Roy's big payday came when he married Mae Brown. Then, there was no stopping him. His head hit the stratosphere.

The only problem was they were all legends in their own minds. They strutted the stage for a time, each to their preferred field, each superior to the other. There were the car ringers. These were dotted around the town, with only a few odd people privy to their little scams. This was getting the little petty criminals to nick specific cars and deliver them to a specific address from where they were quickly and secretly moved to another address where they were stripped for parts that were put in another car, which was then sold, or simply rung, the number plates transferred over, and all engine and chassis numbers filed off. Either method was highly profitable, with the owners enjoying the benefits in the pubs and clubs. The coppers were not even looking in their direction. Then you had the fraudsters and con artists who made their living in a host of different ways.

Some, like my Uncle Pussyfoot, were into all kinds of scams. One cousin, Billy, would be opening up shops and warehouses, making up anything from fancy goods to televisions before selling them on. At one stage, he had almost all the lorry drivers in Rupert Street bringing him gear that had disappeared off the backs of the lorries. If it was spirits, it would go to one of the many club owners around the city. Eddie had not long bought the Bermuda Club, and bent fags and spirits were a great help, as it was to Brendan with his Irish clubs. In turn, they would water it down and serve it late at night or early morning to the punters who were too pissed to notice. To get pissed, you had to drink from dusk to dawn. No one gave a thought to the fact we walked out at 6 am more sober than when we walked in. No one drank whiskey or spirits neat. Even the barmaids were at it, serving half-shots.

Then you had those slightly higher up in the pecking order like Tonks, the car dealer. Tonks had a big car pitch on the Stratford Road selling cars from the cheap bangers to high-end saloons, some rung, some cannibalised, but that was only a rumour amongst those in the know. Tonks was very clever and kept things very close to his chest. What was known was that he strutted around the clubs at weekends, throwing money about like confetti. For him and others like the scrap merchants, the greetings were of the top order, and the gambling rooms opened specifically for them to spend their money. What did they spend? If they had to bung the old bill, they still had plenty to throw about, mainly through not worrying about the tax man. The problem was, well, it certainly wasn't a problem for us; the various government departments just couldn't keep up. They were all stuck in the dusty cobweb offices of the pre-war years. It was the same with the coppers. The plain clothes coppers were still walking around in the same government issue overcoat, trousers and trilby hats they wore pre-war. When one walked into a pub or club, they stood out like a sore thumb. However, that was soon to change as well.

Those were the respectable big spenders, the so-called white-collar fraudsters, and the type of club owners like Fewtrell's who were happy to openly welcome into the clubs as honoured guests and friends. The villains and gangsters were also welcome, of course. They also had a lot of money to spend but with reservations. The bouncers warmly welcomed them, just in case they got nicked mind. One had to be careful under the circumstances. It was alright to buy the booze off you or a bit of bent gear, but as Billy found out when he went into those same clubs, the owners kept their distance. They were now respectable club owners above all that.

The gangsters would strut into the club team handed, acknowledging the welcome by the bouncers with due deference, wearing their Hepworth tailor-made suits with hand-stitched lapels and waistcoats. They looked and felt the part. With money burning in their pockets, they had plenty to spend. Some would walk in with a smile and a jaunty sprint like Larry Wills or Caesar, so-called because of his big nose. Both nice, friendly guys, then you would have Roy 'Little Big Head' Brady, strutting in with an arrogance that suited him, his head swelling with his own self-importance that made him appear a lot taller than his 5 feet, 8 inches. Usually, he would lead the way with his pals behind him in pecking order. Charlie Hinze led to the front, his shoulders slumped to make him seem more unassuming and invisible. He was not nicknamed 'the hump' for nothing. With all his guilt, it must have been hard to stand upright. The thing with Charlie, as with many of the gangsters, was that they had to be seen to act in a certain way. Like Tonks and the scrap dealers, the car dealers strutted into the clubs with a swagger and openness that befitted their station. Except for the tax man, they had nothing to hide. You were judged on how you looked and what you spent, no one knew whether you lived in a mansion or a cheap bedsit in Aston, most times it was that or a council flat, it didn't matter, for those few hours, you could be whoever you wanted to be.

With the gangsters, it was a different kettle of fish. They had to be seen to be acting like gangsters, serious, scowling, shoulders hunched. When they spoke, it was out of the sides of their mouths like gangsters do. When I asked my brother Johnny why they spoke out the sides of their mouths, he reluctantly explained. In prisons in the old days, the regime was very strict. You were in there for punishment and only allowed out for work, which was sewing mailbags or being locked in your cell twenty-three hours a day. When you were allowed out for that one-hour-a-day exercise around a two-man pathway that snaked around the prison yard, you were not allowed to speak as part of your prison punishment. You soon learned how to whisper or talk out of the side of your mouth. Well, for fucks sake, that was it, so to be a gangster, you had to talk out the side of your mouth. You had only broken your cherry when you did a bit of porridge. It was no wonder that some people who had never seen the inside of a cell would start talking out the side of their mouth. It even extended into the pubs and clubs where they would stand by the bar talking to each other from the sides of their mouths, first to the left, then to their companion on the right. Once you realised what it was all about, watching their eyes flitting from left to right became hilarious.

Be it the Cedar or The Rum Runner, Edwards No. 8 or Barbarella's, the modus operandi would be the same. David Brown would be standing at one end of the bar surrounded by big Benjy and a dozen or so of his favoured workers, gangsters, or unpaid minders. David would be standing there in his velvet-collared Crombie for all the world, the biggest gangster in Birmingham. David had earned his stripes and made his name by shooting a competitor in the legs. Following a major fallout, the guy steamed into David's office at his steel stockholding company to have words. David was waiting for him with a double barrel shotgun, Benjy and Roy Brady. Without further ado, he shot the guy in both legs and his arse, not enough to cripple him but enough to put the shits up him and send him packing. Only after the guy had left did David's and Brady's bottles go with the enormity of what they had done. In gangster folklore around Birmingham, David's reputation was enhanced by this fearful action. In truth, as told by his manager Gerald Avery, David shit himself. With his contacts in the police built up over the years in business from scrap to steel, David did no more than ring his local contact, who advised him what to do. It's good to have pals in Steelhouse Lane.

Without further ado, he dialled 999 to report the incident. He was brought in and met by his local contact, who took his statement. In his panic, David assumed that the guy would squeal his head at having left his office. He didn't. Too late, David made his statement, clearing himself with a simple self-defence story. With a hefty bung to the old bill, his case was put before the court where, with mitigating circumstances put forward and a sympathetic version put over by the cops, David got a measly two years in the nick where he was treated with the utmost respect. His business was run for him by Gerald. After serving eighteen months in the nick, he was released, his reputation hitting the stratosphere, "Don't fuck with David. He'll blow you away."

It didn't stop him either. One time after, he had a fallout with a guy who nicked one of his chequebooks and bounced them all over town. When they caught him, they decided to teach him a lesson. David had had a vat installed in his factory unit filled with acid. It was a legitimate business asset. Not only was it a great way to do away with people, but it was also a great frightener. Bringing the bloke in, they tied him up, hooked him to the crane and swung him over the vat of acid, Brady shouting, "Tip the fucking mongrel in Dave." Larry Wills was on the crane, deliberately juddering the controls. The guy was truly and literally shitting himself. With the lesson learned, they felt they dropped the guy to the ground, tarred and feathered him, bunged him a few quid and told him to fuck off out of town and not come back. But he didn't. One or two others actually did disappear into the acid.

Being a young kid, I couldn't get my head around it. To me, I had always been brought up to recognise the police as bent and corrupt, not to be trusted and not to be liked. What a silly billy I was. No wonder all those gangsters looked down their little noses at me, the mug. No, you had to play the cops and use them. If David had kept schtum and the bloke had squealed, David would have got a ten stretch, but being the shrewdy he was, by squealing first, he cooperated with the police by cooperating. The cops will do their bit to help you. Eddie Fewtrell and his brothers used the same tactic in his clubs. If one of the bouncers went a bit too far and knocked seven bells out of a couple or group of clubbers and it went too far, he would simply ring the old bill. A visit would be made, an explanation would be made, and a suitable bung would be put forward. If one of the clubbers had the temerity to scream to the coppers that he had suffered a broken leg, arm and various bruises, the cops would just listen half-heartedly and then walk away.

The Fewtrells were just doing their work for them, clearing the streets of all the drunken brawlers, so that was alright then. If Eddie knew there was a major problem brewing with someone, he would ring his top man at Steelhouse Lane and explain the situation. His contact would order all his men to stay well away from that area around that time that night. Eddie would get all his brothers in, all his bouncers knowing they had carte blanche to do what they wanted without getting nicked. Shrewd ay? Solicitors and hospitals never gave it a thought. No one questioned the actions of the police. Who else would you go to? All the while, the Fewtrell's reputation was growing.

In a lesser way, it's a bit like the scrap metal dealers. You will never hear a metal merchant admit to being a grass or bunging the old bill. Oh no, it's against the moral code, see? So, we all put them in this exalted position, "Oh, he's shrewd that Stan." Well, there's fuck all shrewd against throwing a body in or giving a bung. In the case of the nightclub owner, it's slightly different. Eddie was sharp enough to realise the strength was in numbers. On the door of the Cedar would be a minimum of three bouncers, all very capable lads capable of using their fists or a stick. You would have the backup of Don or his brother Chris at the first point of entry. No one in a group of more than five would be allowed into the club. Of those that were, most had had a few drinks anyway. Any problems at this stage would mean a straight ban from being allowed in. Once in the club, you were outnumbered five to one, which is not very good odds, especially when drunk. As a further addition, if a bit of information was dropped out in unguarded moments whilst drunk, it was seen as cooperating with the police to pass it on, which wasn't a bad thing at all. If some gobby villain got nicked a week or so later, he would spend forever wondering who the grass was who dubbed him in. It was a win-win all around. The cops are having their work done for them whilst the club owners' reputation is enhanced, and the backup of the police is there if required.

Now back out, David was propping the bar up at the nightclubs, enhancing his minder reputation. David never got on with his father, Jack, being kicked out and told to do it alone. Still, he did and eventually set up his own steel company. Meanwhile, when old Jack died, he left the bulk of the steal business to his eldest daughter Jean, a real chip off the old block, built like a fucking Sherman tank and with a ruthless streak running the entire length of her body, Jean was as hard as nails and without an ounce of sympathy or compassion in her.

Jean would be at the opposite side of the bar with her little favoured minions, little Caesar and Larry Wills and others. Caesar and Larry were her two go-to boys whom she trusted implicitly. Standing there, it was a sight to behold. Jean was standing by the bar, a glass in her hand or on the bar, surveying the room with those cold, empty eyes like a shark. None of her expensive clothes could detract from that. One night, a clubber dropped dead of a heart attack feet away from her. Normally, most people would show some concern, but Jean just looked across, blinked those cold eyes, turned away, and picked up her glass. Her boys followed suit, "Fucking nuisance, spoiling my night by dropping dead." Her minders, conscious of the moment and feeling the prestige flowing over them, would look equally serious, glass-in-hand faces set in that serious expression, tailor-made pin-striped suits on with hand-stitched lapels from Hepworth's the tailor, eyes darting from left to right, scanning the room for potential trouble or threats, or just to note how many other people were looking at them. Whilst at the same time looking at the blokes down their noses or with utter indifference, the same went if they saw any bird they fancied, only deigning to talk to them with some effort, it was the same with David's little gang of minders or friends as they thought they were.

Everybody was at it. Even the girls behind the bar were coining it. My bird, Carolyn, worked behind the bar. One night, the club was heaving and roasting hot. Donald glimpsed across the bar and noticed all the girls had knee-high boots. In disbelief, he shouted, "Bloody hell, girls, what are you doing in those high boots? Your feet must be sweating." In exasperation, Carolyn shouted back, we've got no bloody choice. "Look at this," pointing to the floor. "Our feet are swimming in drink." Looking across, Donald could see that the floor was awash with booze, so rushed were they. Thankfully, he never twigged that the girls were milking the club and the punters, shoving upwards of a hundred quid a night down their boots. It was a great time with everyone looking for or making an edge.

My little team consisted of me, Micky Avery, his brother-in-law Sunna, David and Frank Harris, Joe McGrail, and Mick. Mick stood at six feet, had an open face and a tendency to be quiet.

The fact his brother Gerald worked for David was an asset in his favour. However, still, we were looked on and dismissed as young pups trying to get a foothold into the higher echelons. The problem was they didn't want us. We had to earn our stripes and didn't know how. Sunna was a little snide who would nick the milk out of his mom's tit without a thought. He was only in the company due to his position with Avo.

David and Frank were just happy-go-lucky mates looking for a nice night out, a chance to blag a bird and get their end away, and the opportunity of a little tickle if it came along. On the other hand, Joey was a different kettle of fish altogether. Bright red hair of Irish descent, standing almost six feet, he had a brooding air of menace. If he said two words all night, that was what you would get out of him. Thankfully, Joey was a good mate, but I knew he could be utterly ruthless if you upset him or got on the wrong side of him. He was very loyal to Avo, and many a time, if Avo had any trouble, he would drop a hint to Joey, who would go out to sort them out without hesitating and without a second thought. He would stab or carve someone up within the blink of an eye. I was just glad to be on Joey's fucking good side.

It wasn't that Micky was afraid to have a knock. He was a big man, and he was more than happy to give you a slash across the face with a razor if he felt he had to and could get away with it, as many a man found out to his cost. One is Johnny Cole, another hard case who ended up with a road map of Britain on his face for trying to put one on Avo. Coley was a decent enough mate, but he was a bit thick. You could put one on his chin, and two hours later, he would walk back up to you and say you only beat me with a lucky punch, lucky punched him three times, and he still came back. He never went back to Avo. But if one of the others was willing to sort the problem out for him, he was more than happy to let them do so, and he took the credit. Most times, Joey was more than willing. Somehow, I got the impression that Joey liked hurting people if he was in the mood. Maybe it was that red hair, or maybe it was his Irish heritage. While the others, the older ones, had the guns, we had to make do with what we had.

However, it worked, everyone had to behave in a certain way. Only the punters who came into the clubs or actors in the films went swirling and laughing as they made their way in and around the nightclubs. Life was very serious to us, whether up-and-coming or those at the top bar; you didn't know who was watching or ready to pounce. It only took one unguarded moment, a spilt drink, or a step on the wrong person's toes, to cause upset, resulting in a bottle being stuck in your face or a knife put in your gut before disappearing into the crowd. It was easily done and happened with regularity. So, at all times, it pays to keep your gob shut, observe, listen and learn. Like the three wise monkeys, shoulders hunched, ready to adopt the boxer's stance within a minute's notice.

Reg Baldwin was another heavy gangster, quiet and brooding. Reg came from a big family of Baldwins, his dad a major boxer back in the day, even working on the fairground booths. Reg was a quiet, brooding, stocky bloke built like a brick shit house. He knew all the London gangsters and was a mate of mad Frankie Fraser. No one knew exactly what Reg got up to because he kept to himself, rarely speaking to anyone except to say hello or ta'ra. Reg was another mystery bloke who frequented the clubs, coming and going like a silent ghost. It was only when he got nicked and got his first ten stretches that we all discovered it was for armed robbery.

Reg didn't fuck about. He would go in for the Full Monty with a small, hand-picked team of no more than one or two. Robbing banks and security vans, thinking nothing of shooting one of the guards to put the shits up him and the others. It worked a treat every time, his favourite weapons being a sawn-off or a small calibre browning. Reg had hit the jackpot a few times, but this one time, an ex-partner had put him in. Reg was very specific. Many a would-be villain wanted to be a gangster. The problem was when it came to the real heavy stuff, not many had the bottle to go through with it. This was one of those times, having done a couple of decent hoists with Reg whilst planning the next one, the guy started to realise he hadn't got the bottle for it. Once, having decided to do the security van at Parks Factory in Bordesly Green, he did one final recce the week before on the allotted day. Turning up well before the security van, Reg was gobsmacked to see five hooded guys jump out of a van and go storming into the security guards, waving pickaxe handles and sawn offs. Reg and his pal were gobsmacked. This was their number, and someone had jumped in before them. Worse, by their actions and manner, Reg recognised who they were: another group of Aston boys, the cheeky bastards, nicking their job. You can't trust no fucker.

By now, instead of admitting it and losing face, Reg's pal found another excuse not to be on the job and squealed at Reg and his mate, throwing them in, claiming a big reward. Whilst inside, the squealer got his just deserts and disappeared off the face of the earth, quite rightly so.

One night Ray Kirby, Johnny Lewin, Big Jock and George Crow were in a dingy nightclub on Soho Road. It had gone off big time with the owner and one of the black bouncers on the door who didn't want to pay for their protection, or insurance as they preferred to call it. By now they were well into the safe, breaking using the nitro. Two nights after the row a bomb was put on the doorstep aiming to blow the whole fucking club up. The owner and bouncers were inside. Unfortunately, only the front door and reception were destroyed. With the front page spread in the Birmingham Mail, the message was sent and understood, and an apology was made and sent. Not many clubs could afford the insurance, especially the smaller ones. Apart from the damage, it was the loss of income whilst closed. Worse, it was the reputational damage. Not many people wanted to go to a nightclub where you stood the risk of getting blown up. Fuck that for a lark.

Big Dennis Sullivan, Sully, had bought the continental opposite, employing Big Danny McCausland on the door. Sully had got his scrap yard down Cheston Street but thought the clubs were where the big money was, but Sully was no Eddie Fewtrell. One night, Reg, Billy, and Ray Kirby were in the club when Billy started to get a bit loud. McCausland, hard as he was and unaware of the strength, told Billy to shut it. Well, not one of them was over five foot six, so McCausland didn't think he would have a problem. It was a big mistake. One of them walked out to his car, came back with a machete and put it straight across McCausland's dumpling. McCausland, sensing something or seeing the shock on Billy's face, moved his head just in time. The machete sliced off big McCausland's ear and half his cheek with it, claret throwing all over the place big Sullies bottle completely fell out. Grabbing a towel off the bar, he wrapped it around McCausland's head whilst telling the team to piss off. Hard as Sully was, he decided the club scene was not for him, put it up for sale, sold it to Johnny Prescott and got out.

Yet another unusual character in the clubs was Colin Lawler, who was a bit of an enigma to all of us. Colin was the son of Wallace Lawler, the respected and well-known liberal MP. It was only later that Colin told me the full story. Wallace was a hardworking councillor in Birmingham when his wife Catherine first set her sights on him. She was an office clerk born and bred in Aston next to the Cross cinema. She recognised Wallace was ambitious and going places. To boot, he had a small but growing manufacturing business in Sparkhill. Having set her sights on him, she went all out to pull him in, first courting, helping him in his ambitions, then getting married.

Backing him all the way, Wallace, unfortunately/fortunately, had a massive fire at his small factory. After rebuilding the factory, he found he had a little bit left over which he put aside to help promote himself to becoming a liberal MP for Birmingham Ladywood. To us at the bottom of the ladder, he was a great humanitarian genuinely concerned about fighting to get the slum houses demolished around Birmingham. Aston was soon forgotten as Catherine lifted herself up, with Wallace becoming a little bit of a snob, quite rightly so and all.

Their eldest son, Colin, my mate, was followed by Terry and a sister, and they all were accepted into and went on to grammar school. The only problem was Colin rebelled and joined the navy. When he came out, he rebelled even further, buying a small, terraced house down Aston for £500, the houses his father was trying to demolish, and the houses where his mother was born and grew up.

Colin was enamoured with the colourful people and gangsters around Birmingham, falling in love and marrying Anne Boyle. With his education and knowledge, he rented a little yard in Grosvenor Road and set up a transport business.

In addition to the transport business, the yard was turning over a tidy sum dealing in scrap metal. Colin, with his brother-in-law, the Beef, nicknamed because he was built like a big fat heifer, was coining it in. Being the son of a now very prominent MP, the cops had no choice but to keep well clear of him. They were coining it in, hand over fist. Unfortunately, Colin liked his bit of hash, marihuana even with a bit of coke tinkled over it.

Colin and the Beef liked nothing better than to stand posing at the bar of one of the nightclubs or social clubs around the town with their followers. Both big blokes made a striking pair, immaculately and expensively dressed in tailor-made hand-stitched suits. The only difference was that Beef kept himself sober, was ambitious and didn't do the drugs. The Beef wanted and bought a big house in Penns Lane, Sutton, putting himself across as a respected businessman. The problem was Colin was a bit naïve. With the help of the drugs addling to his brain, Colin thought he was amongst family and friends. Sadly, they were all fucking him left, right and centre at every opportunity. Too late, he only woke up when he found he was broke and skinned out, having to go to Jeanie Brown for a job in her steel business in Nechells. To his dying day, I don't think Colin fully understood why his mother was so desperate to escape Aston. If he did, he kept it to himself.

One day, a couple of lads who worked for Lawler called on me and asked me if I was interested in buying a lorry load of wallets. Seeing the potential to make a right nice few quid, I dived in until they told me they had nicked the load from Lawler, along with the lawyer's brother-in-law, the Beef. This didn't sit well with me at all. What kind of scum bags nick off their own? I saw too much of this from people who earned a living from the guy and his family. Grassing is not something I'm a party to, but this was different. Although Lawler wasn't a close mate, being a different generation,

I felt obliged to tell him. What happened after that? I don't know whether Colin got his customers' wallets back. Still, after expressing his gratitude, he went bust shortly afterwards, having to lower his pride by asking Jean for a job.

I don't know what would have happened if that hadn't opened his eyes to why his mother was keen to escape Aston. To the present day, I don't know if I had done the right thing. Perverse as it may seem, I grew up thinking there was an honour amongst crooks. Robbing off your own seemed the easiest way out, and it seemed to be growing more and more prevalent within the community I was mixing with. You'd invite your pals into your house and then have to check that nothing had been nicked. This was the next generation of the Peaky Blinders, the sons and grandsons of those proud groups. I was becoming more and more disillusioned. The widespread grassing was next.

Another of the gangsters from Aston frequenting the clubs were the members of the Pepper Pot Gang, so-called because, whilst using real shotguns, they would empty the cartridges and fill them with pepper. It had a devastating effect on the banks and post offices that they robbed without actually hurting anyone. It also ensured that if and when they got nicked, they would only get a light sentence due to their deliberate intent not to hurt anyone. It didn't work too well for them. While they revelled in the headlines, they got in the newspapers. When they got their collar felt, they still got a heavy eight-and-ten stretch. With each stretch, the shoulders slumped even more, the utter misery of shuffling about the exercise yard slowly, head down, shoulders slumped like Neanderthal men, talking out the sides of their mouths. Ten years of waking up every morning to a dishful of porridge ain't very pleasant. Coming out after his final ten stretch, one even collaborated with one of the coppers to write a book. Would you fucking believe it? This is another nail in the coffin of what used to be deemed honour. Once, they were men of honour, of standing in their community, so they thought, shoulders back, head held high. As they came out after their latest stretch, their shoulders slumped more and more.

THE FILTH

Call them what you will: coppers, filth, rozzers, pigs, the police deserve every label put on them. I'm not talking about your everyday copper on the beat, the bobby. They, in all genuineness, join the police to do good. Well, in the main, I truly believe they do. Maybe the job itself corrupts them, the people they have to deal with. Many join because they ain't got the brains to earn a living in the real world. As a cop, they get a decent wage plus a guaranteed pension. Tim was a cop down Bloomsbury Street Station when I first met him. I was fifteen when he ran past me on the green chasing a bunch of my mates. When I told him to leave them alone, having done nothing wrong, he had the audacity to call me a bastard, a regular insult used by cops to anyone from a criminal or undesirable background. Not being a bastard, I put one on his chin quick sharpish. Down he went, but unfortunately for me, one of his plain clothes mates lurked nearby. Although I got nicked and trundled down to Bloomsbury Street nick, I was never charged. They would have looked right prats if they did, and I am a fifteen-year-old kid. But the cops have an attitude that says sit back and put it all in the little book they keep. Worse, this was multiplied five times by my brothers, who equally hated the police and let them know it, oh, for want of a few brains, ay?

I was to find this out as I went along in life, but years later, moving into my new house in Sutton Coldfield, I was gobsmacked to find Tim six doors up. Tim had been a qualified carpenter before joining the force, but the wages were so bad he joined the police. He could only afford the house because his inspector helped him with the deposit. Of course, it doesn't harm their ego either. More than one copper told me they grow ten feet tall when wearing that uniform.

No, when they go into plain clothes, the change comes, the corruption creeps in, and the uniformed boys become noddies whilst they are the elite. When they go into a pub or club, it's in twos and never alone. They are quickly recognised by their attitude, stance and demeanour, which they are trained to adopt. They are special, and they know it. The more they progress up the CID ladder, the more special and powerful they become. Previously, the CID stood out like a sore thumb. Now, they could and were dressing to suit their situation. They were learning and evolving with the times. You could be sitting in a pub shouting your gob off without realising that the scruffy, nondescript, long-haired little low life sitting in the corner was an experienced copper or even a delicious-looking blond with a nice body and long legs, picking up every word you uttered as you bragged, trying to impress.

The villains and the gangsters were getting far too arrogant, outrageous and cocky, as with the London gangsters, the death penalty had been dropped, resulting in an upsurge of killings. Word went out from the top. Put a stop to this. The easiest and simplest way is via the grass. But it's getting the fuckers first. For years, the cops of all persuasions relied on the good old method of belting. If they had a strong suspicion that you were responsible for a job, they would put in a plan to steam in heavy-handed at six in the morning together with all your mates at the same time, taken to different police stations and interrogated, if you felt brave enough to give them a load of lip you would be beaten black and blue, whipped till you cried and left to suffer in the cells. With no access to a solicitor and no one knowing where you were to call a solicitor, you were fucked unless you had strong nerves, lots of bottle and certainty that nothing incriminating would be found in your house. There was a good chance you would be released. If one of your mates bottled it, you were in shit street.

The cops had all the time in the world to watch, plan and scheme. The clubs were a great breeding ground for the villains, many unaware that the cops were watching them, seeing the money they were spending. It helped that the club owners or immediate staff were more than willing to help with a pointer or two. "Oh yes. Reg is a good spender here, and so are the Kirby's. They spent about three hundred quid Friday night." Donald or Chris would be seen helping the cops. Still, the real reason was to divert any unwanted attention from themselves. Yes, they weren't averse to buying a bit of bent jewellery. The spending habits of the Browns or Bradys were never questioned. They had businesses. Only the suspected villains known to be not working were targeted. The shrewd ones would open and run a little business like a café or shop.

It was still hard work for the cops, who found it an uphill struggle. These were hardened villains, crooks, and gangsters. It wouldn't be easy. No one wanted to be accused of being a grass for their reputation or the repercussions. It would need all the brains, cunning, and corruption of the cops to gain any inroads.

Slowly, the cops started working more closely with the prosecution and the judges. One subtle and sure way was via the masons, the only masonic lodge set up in Birmingham solely for the police and the judiciary. A private group? A private sect? How convenient! It's not hard to imagine how easy it could be at any meeting to have a private chat in utter confidence about certain individuals. Hmmm?? John Palmer, later known as Goldfinger, caught on quickly and got out of Birmingham sharpish. The rest of us thick divs never imagined the cops could stoop to such levels as fitting up and planting. They were the police, after all, but they stooped, together with the masonic lodge, and the judicial system was considered and known as utterly corrupt.

First, they worked on the chink in the window whilst the villain was sweating in his twelve by six peter. For hours on end, the cops would be sitting with a cup of coffee, looking at graphs on the wall, pins stuck in strategic places. In the meantime, they would be liaising with their colleagues at other nicks, keeping tabs on what they were up to and how they were progressing. If they got one chink of light through the curtain, they would go in for the kill. Now it was really squeaky bottle time. The sweating villain would by now have sweat bouncing off his fucking bonce. One way of finding a way out was to squeal without squealing. This was an early and simple way to get results. First, you had to agree to help without helping. This means without putting anything in writing or signing anything. (You were still a grass).

By this time, you had become friends with the cop leading the team. He was no longer the enemy. He was your pal trying to help you. "OK, Charlie, this is what we will do. Give us something to nick those other bastards, and as we have no proof or evidence against you, we'll either let you go or do you for some minor charge. This will take the suspicion away from you, and we get all the others." Phew, Charlie would heave a sigh of relief, telling them where most or all of the gear was stashed in a garage, and the old bill would go steaming in. All that was needed was one chink of evidence, a name casually mentioned. If that name had no alibi, he was fucked. Confident as he may have initially felt, he soon discovered that his wife or pals were no alibi. Charlie would have the bulk of the jewellery hidden away, the recipient of his information never having a clue that Charlie had thrown him in. With an item of jewellery as evidence, an unsigned verbal statement and no alibi, a sympathetic judge he would be sent down before even realising that he had been well stitched up.

With the evidence in front of them, the rest of the team spread over different nicks and either felt obliged to cough up or just keep their gobs shut. Either way, it didn't help that by the time the verbals had been put in, they were fucked. If they coughed, they got a lighter sentence. If they coughed too late, it made no difference. It was becoming more and more of a dilemma as time passed. If you are one of half a dozen nicked, do you cough immediately or try to bluff it out until it becomes too late to do a deal? For the next five or eight years, they would be pulling their hair out, wondering who the fuck had put them in. It couldn't be Charlie. He got done as well. The trick worked a treat. Charlie was out and about to have another crack. He just got off lightly on a minor charge because he was a shrewd villain. Yes, that's it. He's shrewd.

These were early days, but the cops, slowly but surely, were making inroads. It left everyone uncertain, paranoid and suspicious of everyone else. The doubts were settling in. The more doubts that seeped in, the better it got for the cops and the worse for the villains. It didn't help that the London gangsters were being grassed on, brought up before the judges and sentenced to heavy terms in prison:

the Kray's thirty stretch, the Richardson brothers twenty years. Charlie Richardson reckoned he didn't even know what was fucking going on. He was a businessman, and unfortunately, he employed mad Frankie Frazer. Between them, they had a few enemies who were more than willing to fit them up for a reward or a favour. Rich as he was, Charlie was fucked. The very same thing was going on in London. The word had gone out, "By hook or crook, bring them in, put them away. It looks like they are starting to run the country," and in truth, they were. Many were getting away with blue murder.

The problem was that it was getting increasingly difficult to distinguish who the crooks were and out of those crooks who were the biggest. From the age of 14, I only ever saw bent cops. If a team of bent cops raid a house and plant stuff that the guy's children know was not there in the first place, then that is proof to those kids that the cops are crooked. I had had stuff nicked off me by different cops over different parts of the country. You can't complain because who will believe you? Every villain knew that if they had four or five grand in cash in their house, half would have disappeared by the time it got to court. Lo and behold, if you try to scream fit up or money stolen, your mouthpiece will tell you to shut up. The judges don't like it. Whether the judges suspect anything, we never know, but if you have a criminal record which most do, then you're fucked. All you risk is more added to your sentence by an angry judge.

Corruption breeds corruption. If you've had the good fortune to have been brought up in a respectable area, sent to a nice school, private or state, been to university, then got a nice plum job with prospects you can only look down with disdain and contempt at those being sentenced to prison for robbing a bank or just stealing. When you're on that bottom rung of the ladder, as many of us were after the war, treated as factory fodder by the schools that were not in the slightest bit interested, living in shit-hole houses with no visible future on the horizon, then you see things differently. My parents did not ask to fight in a war, not of their making. Coming home from that war, if they were lucky. They did not ask to be put into slum housing. I have friends I was at school with who are still in council housing, have no money, just a basic state pension, and have never even had a holiday.

Anyone from my background will tell you that I am confident I would bet anyone good money if ten cops were in a room with a known crook and there was cash available stolen or not, then they would nick it. If it was uniform cops, five out of ten would nick it. If it was plain clothes, the whole ten would nick it, that's a fact. Somehow, and for some perverse reason, they feel they are fully justified. Put half the neighbours in the area into such a tempting position, and they would nick it, too. No one is innocent.

The cops were finding the normal methods of knocking the shit out of the villains, giving them the biggest beltings under the sun. Even verballing up was still not working with the hardest of the villains. The cops, by now, were acting with impunity; they knew they had the government and the judge's blessings, but the defence lawyers were too intimidated to do anything about it. In Birmingham, there were deep, unspoken rules. The IRA were a menace to the country. When the Mulberry Bush was blown up, the cops were determined to do something about it. They picked up six potential paddies on a train heading for Ireland and guessed they had the right men. First, they knocked seven bells of shit out of them, and then they found traces of nitro on their fingers that actually came from the cards they were playing with.

It was clear very quickly that the cops had made a mistake, but for years, they knew the public was behind them, so they didn't care. Another major criminal act had been ticked off, but that's where they made their mistake, yet no one got punished, and no one felt any guilt. As far as the cops are concerned, every sentence is justified. If the bastards didn't do this one, then they are guilty of something else, fucking great ay. It's like justifying the justification. It's like bringing a dog in on suspicion of biting a child, "but he does look like the dog officer."

"OK, that's good enough. Put the little mutt down. If he's not guilty of biting this child, he's bound to have bit some other child."

We are all god's children, but not all the time. Then again, you wouldn't treat a dog like that.

The cops were getting more and more brazen. In truth, they were invincible, and they knew it. If you had a criminal record, no matter how minor, and were seen associating with known criminals, you were putting your life on the line. If you happened to be visiting a friend in all innocence at the same time as the cops raided the house, you stood the risk of being nicked along with him. That is fine and understandable, but you also stood the risk of being fitted up alongside him. Many men are still in prison for doing exactly that.

If planting had never been a part of policing before, it had become a major weapon in the fight against crime. Boy, did those villains start fucking scattering. Whether he was the first is unknown, but Percy' Pip the Planter' was the most notorious. If there was a major act of villainy, a robbery that had been carried out, someone suspected but with no proof or evidence to be seen, then the call went out, "Bring Pip in." Pip was only too happy to oblige, at close to six feet, big and bulky with a football-shaped white pasty face and a constant smirk. Pip was a sickening, make-your-skin-crawl individual, but he was a terrifying sight to behold. If you had been arrested, were locked up in the holding cell, and Pip walked in, you knew you were fucked or close to it.

One such person was Dennis Aziz, who was in on a suspected break-in. With no evidence against him, Dennis knew he had no worries till Pip the Planter approached him with a small jemmy. Pip asked, "Is this yours, Dennis?" before handing it over through the bars. Dennis almost went to take it to examine it before realising his mistake and jumping back in horror. He was lucky that time; many others were not after being caught out with the same little trick. Pip had many aces up his sleeve. You almost had the impression he never came out in the sun, only to nick people, then go back to the nick or his house, sitting up all night plotting and scheming how to fit someone up. Worse, his colleagues throughout the force knew about him and revelled in the fear he spread. Not one, it seems, had the integrity or thought to report on it over generations. No one dropped hints to any solicitor friend who, in turn, might drop it out to some friendly judge whilst sipping a gin and tonic in one of the local bars. Everyone feigned ignorance and a lack of knowledge of any corruption. In effect, no legal professional was aware of any wrongdoing.

Every police officer, every cop in Birmingham of every rank, knew and boasted about Pip the Planter. He was notorious, and villains trembled at the mere mention of his name. Such was his reputation that if ever things started to get too hot for him, by whom no one knew, his superiors would transfer him to another force for a few months or a year until it died down. If all the cops in Birmingham knew about his reputation, you had to ask why no one thought or felt the need to stop him and his other bent colleagues.

Although I had heard of Pip, it was a distance away. My first experience with him was around 1961, when I was about fourteen. Pip came around our house in Rocky Lane and nicked my dad. It was 1 am, and due to my age, I was an inadequate witness, but Pip fitted my dad up, and he got two years. My dad was a hardworking dealer, but that cut no ice with the cops or Pip the Planter. The second time I came across Pip was when he called to the back of our house in Rocky Lane one morning just before mid-day. This time, he had no need to fit us up. I had had the day off from Pilkington Glass, where I was working with Rudy Swarm. Two hours earlier, Charlie Hinze had called round to see the old man.

Not being in, Charlie handed me a bundle of jewellery and told me to give it to Dad when he came back. For safekeeping, and in front of Charlie, I put the jewellery in the middle drawer of a three-draw cabinet that one of my uncles had made as a wedding present. Now, here was Pip, with a warrant asking whose house it was, walking in through the kitchen, into the lounge, hallway, and front room. He then went straight to the middle drawer of the three-draw cabinet. I was gobsmacked. It was obvious Charlie had fitted us up, intending to fit my dad up. Exactly what went down, I don't know. I will never know how it worked, but somehow, Charlie, the grass, had been caught by Pip or pulled in by Pip and told he wanted a body. This was to become a new and tried method by the cops and Pip. If caught in dodgy circumstances, the pressure would be put on to throw another body in to protect their necks. My dad was a dealer, not a crook. His only crime was that he was not a police informer, and neither was any of my family. As far as the cops were concerned, our house was a den full of thieves, including me.

Just as my dad came through the door, we were whisked off without preamble straight to Blackpool, not to any Birmingham nick but to Blackpool. It was clearly well-planned and organised. The cops would have known before they got to the house. From there, we were sent and held in Risley Prison. Apparently, a major robbery had been carried out at some Blackpool jewellers. My dad was in ill health, old and incapable of robbing any kind of shop. My mom had only recently died, and we were still mourning her loss. Anyone looking at me would question my participation. It didn't matter. The cops don't give a fuck. The same mantra applies; if we didn't do this, we would be guilty of something. In my case, it was probably let him rot as well. I had never been to Blackpool, and I don't think my dad had either. I couldn't tell the truth because that would be squealing. Besides, no one would believe any family friend could pull such a stroke at this stage. The solicitors acting on legal aid don't give a shit, thinking you're half guilty anyway. All they want is an easy payday. One day, someone might realise how many millions are completely wasted on legal aid in this country.

To the day I die, I still don't know what I had to plead guilty to, robbing a jewellery shop or receiving stolen goods. If we both tried to plead innocent, it took the risk of both of us getting done. Being so young, I was sentenced to borstal.

When I came out, my dad presented me with his fifty per cent share of the press club with Jack Hale, a drinking club opposite the law courts of all places. No one ever believed that Charlie Hinze had fitted us up or put us in. Quite the opposite, in fact. We were looked on as the mugs for being stupid enough to get nicked in the first place. Charlie? A grass? Never, he's our mate. He's a nice bloke; I would happily have shot him. He deserved shooting, but I had to be satisfied by knocking him out as he stood close to Pip the Planter in the Cedar Club. Charlie continued to be friends with the Averys, Browns and Bradys, who wouldn't have a word said about him, and no wonder indeed as I was to find out. As Pip the Planter continued his fitting up, more and more of them started throwing bodies into the suit. It seemed like the criminal underworld had settled into panic mode, looking around like rats in a trap, furtive and on edge, eyes darting left and right, one by one, like Skittles lined up in an alley. The old, sound, trustworthy villains were now lining up to get in first and throw their pals in before they were fitted up. The old bill was laughing their nuts off. Jean Brown only saved herself by getting a private consultation, a diagnosis of incurable cancer and admittance to a private hospital. It must have cost her thousands. But she was by then one of the richest women in England. More and more, I was becoming aware of the total absence of morals amongst the people I had been brought up to believe were sound. Principled people, "But he's a nice bloke is Charlie, and if he's useful, then all the better." Charlie was a chameleon. Fitting in with anyone for his own ends. As it was getting harder to make a living and make easy money, principles went down the drainpipe. Seeing Hinze walking out of Ray Kirby's house, Ray just shrugged his shoulders and grunted when I pulled him up. These were your friends, no loyalty, no integrity.

Pip, together with more than a few dozen bent cops, was flying through the criminal underworld like a torpedo in a force ten gale. Picking and fitting villains up left, right and centre, but Pip was the best and the worst. The mere mention of his name was enough to frighten the shit out of you. I had opened a warehouse in Victoria Road, Aston. My plan was to build up a credit line and sell toys and fancy goods. I had taken the shop over from Sid Hobday, the scrap metal dealer, who was now languishing in nick doing a seven-stretch. It never occurred to me that the shop/warehouse had previously traded as a fancy goods shop years ago and had gone bankrupt—my chances of getting credit sunk to almost zero.

In the meantime, Ernie Trainer, having nowhere to live, had moved in with me. I bought a nice Jaguar from a dealer with a car pitch opposite. Unbeknown to me, the guy was at it, too. Taking in cars from people offering to sell whilst taking a commission, he was selling the cars, putting the money in his pocket, and then disappearing. Fortunately, I had a signed receipt. But when caught out, it didn't stop him screaming to the cops that I had diddled him out of the car money. Calling into my warehouse, the cops asked to see the receipt and, if possible, take a copy. As my bottle started to go at the thought, the one dick pointed out, "It's OK, Tom, you don't have to worry. We've not got Pip the Planter here." That's how well-known and notorious Pip was. Every villain in Birmingham knew him. Every cop knew him. They would even use him as a threat, like a hidden Rottweiler kept in the background. I followed them over to Victoria Road nick, receipt tightly held. As we walked out, the one dick pointed at a few soft toys I had on the shelves and said, "If you had looked after us, none of this need have happened." He meant I would have been left alone if I had given him a bung. Most of the villains in and around Birmingham had no such luck. They were being rounded, fitted and locked up. If a robbery had been committed and the cops knew who it was or suspected who it was, they would simply take items from the scene, bank notes or jewellery, and fit them somewhere in a drawer in the victim's house. Sitting as cocky as you like and knowing he had nothing in the house, he would scream blue murder at the find.

In court, his solicitor, barrister, or QC would advise him strongly not to make any accusations against the police. If he did, he would get an extra couple of years added on. No matter how innocent he pleaded, he didn't have a chance, for one thing, and it's the main thing: the only people who didn't know you had a criminal record was the jury. The cops knew, the barristers knew, even the judge knew, so you're fucked before you even get in the dock. They could manoeuvre the evidence in whichever way they wanted with impunity.

Whatever the cops thought about my receipt for the Jag, they decided to jump on me at every opportunity. I would be driving along and pulled over. My documents checked boot and looked into it. It became so ridiculous that I was pulled four or five times a week. Clearly, the car had been put on the national list. I was even pulled over in Boston by ten different cops—each time for no reason. So, when Gerald Avery asked if I wanted to swap his smaller engine Jag, plus a bung of a few quid, I had some difficulty keeping calm as I agreed to the deal. Working for Brown, David had to poke his nose in looking for the scam.

Course, they never gave the obvious reason a thought, and I couldn't tell them, could I? I wasn't pulling any scam, but a week later had to let out a chuckle when Gerald pulled me up the Cedar, "Fucking hell, Tom. What have you been up to? I got stopped three times in one day last week." Chuckling, I apologised to Gerald whilst explaining the facts to him. "Oh, that's OK, Tom. I just wondered what the fuck was going on. It was only one day, and then it stopped." Thank you, Gerald.

Soon, the accusations of grassing were being flown around the town like confetti. Now, every other villain was being accused of being a grass. It was almost funny. If you were outside of it, it was funny, hilariously funny. But if you were on the inside, it was a fucking nightmare. Everyone was growing paranoid. The cops were in a win-win situation, laughing their nuts off. When you went to court, you had to rely on memory. If you made one simple mistake, the prosecution would jump on you like a terrier. When the cops got in the dock, they read facts from their notebooks and conversations from the arrest. "So, Officer, you say Mr Collins admitted stealing the safe and said, I throw my hands up, guv?"

"Yes, sir." Then, the next cop gets up, reading from his notes. "Mr Collins admitted the offence saying, 'I throw my hands up guv.'" With a hint of a smirk on his face, word for word, the same as his colleagues. It was fucking unbelievable, and they were allowed to get away with it. You think you see British justice with your own solicitor on legal aid. Don't be fucking silly, it's simple maths. To defend you, he wants ten grand. The court allocates him two grand, so he does two grand's worth of work. He doesn't give a fuck about you.

The villains, crooks and gangsters were running around like fucking rats with bangers up their arses. Eyes darted all over the place, arms and legs twitching. If you approached them cheerfully and openly, they would look at you with suspicion, eyes darting all over the place, looking to see if you were fitting them up. One day, I rang my pal Micky up, well, I thought he was my pal, for some advice. He came over to my house, eyes darting everywhere, hopping on burnt coals. I'm sure he wondered if we had a mic hidden around the place. He had gotten away with a murder, then got a twenty stretch for drug dealing. Now living in Spain, he thought everyone was on top. Thinking about it, he wasn't far off. He was utterly paranoid, thinking everyone was trying to set him up.

Another pal, Ray, got a seven stretch for robbing the Walsall Co-op. Now, this was a lovely little touch. Ray's brother had a pal whose wife worked in the Co-op as a cleaner. He knew where the keys to the safe were kept, which held circa forty grand at the time (about 250 grand today). All they had to do was break in, enter by a side window, and empty the peter. It was as sweet as a nut, but Ray's brother wanted to bring his pal Colin, who was on the floor, in. Fine, but Ray wanted to bring his pal in, who he had served time with in Broadmoor, because he felt sorry for him. The spoils were split five ways, with equal amounts going to the cleaner's husband. It gets better. On the weekend, with all the money in, they go to the Co-op. Getting in and finding the key was a piece of piss. Opening the safe, the money gushed out all over them. They couldn't get their second wind. Bagging up the notes, they decided they had enough not to bother about the twenty grand in silver. "Why not?"

"Well, we thought we had enough with the notes, Tom." Fuck me, and this was Ray, the hard gangster.

Once home, they excitedly counted up the money. Twenty grand, divvying it up, it worked out at four grand each, giving Colin four grand for the cleaner's hubby. Colin set off with four grand in one pocket and four grand in the other. Colin couldn't help but finger the two piles and weigh up his options. He had a nice big, chunky eight grand in his bin. Who's going to do anything? He decided to say nowt and keep the eight grand. The cleaner's hubby kept quiet for a week, then one more week before going to the cops. What was he going to get? A fine? His wife was innocent. By the following week, the cops had rounded the lot up. One by one, whoever they nicked first grassed on the others. Ray accused Colin of being the grass. Colin accused Ray of being the grass. But it was Ray's brother who knew the cleaner's husband? It was fucking funny. If there was anything to put you off robbing, then this was it: Ray got a seven, and Colin got a three, probably for squealing in the first place. In this case, no fitting up was needed. They got themselves nicked with their greed and stupidity.

So now, not only had you got the old bill fitting you up willy-nilly and at will, you then had to take the risks of your mates fucking you at the first opportunity. If you were lucky enough not to be fucked by the one, you stood the risk of being squealed on by the other. It was a bleeding minefield, alright. The great train robbers had a lovely touch. Over two and a half million pounds between fifteen or so of them, even allowing for backhanders, left them with a lot of money. A nice house in Sutton costs circa six grand, which is a lot of houses.

These weren't kids; they were grown men, and they did everything professionally. What happened? They left their dabs all over the farmhouse, and worse, all the sharks came out and started robbing them blind. OK, I suppose it's to be expected and straightforward. Your good mate asks you to look after 150 grand while he goes on the run and then gets nicked. Facing a thirty stretch, you've got enough to buy 50 houses. What do you do? Fuck him, haha. One of the saddest stories had to be Bruce Welch. Now, Bruce wasn't stupid. He had had various businesses, from car sales to nightclubs, but his weakness was gambling. Bruce was put onto the train robbery because of his knowledge of nicking money from the trains on the South Coast Line. His dabs were found at Leatherslade farm, but his first mistake was trusting his best mate with his stash hidden in a forest in north Devon. His mate not only nicked his money but grassed on him so he could get away with nicking the money in the first place. What a stroke-puller. If that wasn't bad enough, the doctors bodged an operation on his leg whilst he was in the nick, which resulted in Bruce eventually losing his leg and ending his days in a wheelchair. Talk about bad luck, with misfortune still smiling on him. He lived into his 90s to give him more time to think about his cock ups.

With the cops fitting anyone up that so much as blinked, everyone started looking out for themselves. It wasn't just a case of keeping your gob shut and hoping for the best. Now, if you got your collar felt first, it was deciding whether to grass straight away and throw the others in or wait. If you waited, there was the risk the next one might grass, leaving you with nowhere to go and no deals to be made. Bodies were being thrown in, and people were being grassed on, but was it stopping crime or the criminals? They did this with the metal merchants. First, you had to give a bung when they came to check your books. Then you had to throw a body in every now and again to satisfy the cop's little books. It was favours for favours. You could buy bent metal all day for the rest of the week, no worries.

My uncle Jeff Elliot wasn't a crook. He was a professional gambler and ex-nightclub owner who owned the Fleur De Leys, a beautiful downtown cabaret club. He was also one of the most decent guys you could wish to meet, but he swore that Johnny, the gangster, fitted him up. I don't know. Johnny and his brother were friends of mine. You don't like to think of your friends as grasses. At any rate, Johnny sold and asked Jeff to sell a pile of jewellery. On the night, a bird with a cockney voice rang Jeff and told him not to take the gear to London the next day. Maybe Jeff had had a drink, maybe it was just age, but he told me that being a cockney accent, he assumed someone was winding him up. But at any rate, as planned, he set off the next morning for London. He was stopped at Spaghetti Junction by Pip the Planter, got nicked and got two years.

Now, I didn't know what to think or do. This is the thing with grasses, you see, it's like Chinese whispers. Johnny was a mate, but I also had my suspicions about him. Only many years later, when I bumped into my old girlfriend, a lovely, savvy bird named Carolyn, did some of the truth come out well. She had been married to Keith Miller, a snide but clever thief I suspected of being a bit of a grass himself. He had a brother named Peter who worked around the town with different guys at different times and places. Some of these guys kept getting nicked for no obvious reason. Before going out with and marrying Miller, Carolyn had been going out with this cockney guy named Jim, who was a handy villain. They lived that well in the Savoy for much of the time. Peter and Jim got together and started doing a few jobs before it came on top. Jim was sure Miller had grassed on him. Carolyn was truthful and said she didn't know but wouldn't be surprised.

Then she dropped the googly on me without even realising it. Before meeting up with Carolyn, Jim had been going with this cockney bird, who Johnny the gangster had nicked off him. The dates fitted. Was this the same cockney bird who rang up Jeff Elliot the night before he set off for London? Now, what a coincidence is that? Johnny, the gangster, brings a pile of jewellery to Jeff. A bird with a cockney voice rings on the night, warning him not to go to London; how many cockney birds are there in Birmingham? Who would have Jeff's number? Johnny knows Jeff's going to London. He's got a cockney bird. To me, this has a ring to it. The same ring that brought Charlie Hinze to our house on that day years earlier, who dropped a pile of jewellery off with me only for the cops to appear within the next two hours. Pip the Planter, at that. I never knew for sure if it was Pip who nicked Uncle Jeff.

What a coincidence. I wonder how many times this was happening around Brum. This was more than coincidental and speaks volumes about the accepted corruption within our country's judicial system. All the while, I know Johnny, the gangster, has committed far more crimes before and since. By giving the cops a body for a few items of jewellery, Johnny the gangster, along with Charlie Hinze, was given free rein to commit many more robberies, including armoured car hold-ups. That was very clever indeed. How often was this going on? This had not just shifted from grassing when getting nicked. This was pre-planned grassing on a grand, organised scale. And the villains were being called clever shrewd.

Sitting in the Erdington sauna one afternoon, a bunch of guys walked in. They started yapping away, oblivious to me lying face down on the bench. Now I didn't know these fucking idiots, but I guessed they came from over Northfield way. They seemed to forget I was beside them, so they started throwing names up. Having got nicked and taken in for questioning, the one cop walked over to the one doing the yapping and showed him a photo of Johnny, the gangster. The yapper jumped back in shock. "No, no, no, never saw him before." Telling his mates only confirmed that this Johnny the gangster was the gangster with all the cops hot on his heels. I had difficulty hiding my amazement. It could have been obvious that that's exactly what the cops wanted them to think, thus protecting a prize asset. What kind of idiots was I associating with? Finally realising I was there, I could feel them nudging each other, stranger in the midst. As they walked out, I felt like saying I'll give Johnny the gangster your regards.

Even as I put these words down, I'm still partly in disbelief. Hinze is a mongrel. I know that I always have. If you've got a business, plenty of money and the space to do it like the Fewtrells or the Browns have, especially if you've got loyal blokes you can rely on, you can take all kinds of actions. But I had sweet fuck all. My dad just earned a nice living, as did my uncle Jeff. In truth, we were sitting targets. What baffled and stymied me even more, perplexed me no end, was that these guys were respected and liked by those same people, the Browns, Brady and Fewtrells, always being invited to parties, functions, etc. What does that say about all these people? Yet me and my brothers were being nicked, set up and sent down for basically sweet eff all, while these very same people were looking down on us as mugs for getting nicked in the first place. It's almost fucking funny. Not.

In the meantime, the Browns were growing from strength to strength. Well, Jean was, yes, she is a chip off the old man's block, alright, whilst David went on to buy and own a golf club over Earlswood. He went bankrupt for a while. When I say bankrupt, I don't actually mean skint, but he didn't have the big money Jean had. One day, a guy approached him with an opportunity. He knew of a ship that had sunk with a few hundred tons of steel in her hull; the saltwater had affected the steel, making it worthless, but Jean, clever as she was, knew of a way of treating it and re-establishing its value. David told the guy he didn't have the money, but his sister Jean did. Giving her a ring, he put the guy onto her, and she duly paid for the steel cargo to be lifted and brought back to her company for treatment and resale. She made an absolute fortune, millions. When David rang her up and asked for his due drink, she simply told him to fuck off.

Whether it was the competition between them or just that, natural sibling competitiveness doesn't matter. Still, as David's star declined, Jeans grew from strength to strength. With Brady's help and backing, they egged each other onwards and upwards. Brady had been a close family friend for years, first of David, then of Jean. Then, when a piece of land came up next to Jean's company on Chester Street, he and Larry Wills formed a little wire-straightening company. Simply put, with the contacts supplied by Jean, all they had to do was buy the wire in coils and then put it through a straightening machine before selling it on as steel rods. By an amazing coincidence, the company right next door also dealt in the same wire coils, hundreds of tons lying all over the yard, divided by a chain link fence.

If there was one thing Roy was not, that was slow; he wasn't called a Little Big Head for nothing. It didn't take them long, maybe all of ten minutes, to realise that all they had to do was carefully untwine one link in the six-foot fence to open it up. Each night, after most of the workers in both companies had gone home, Roy and his trusted little gang would set to work. They would remove a dozen or so coils, replace the link in the chain, go home, and then resume work on straightening the coils into steel rods the next day. They were making thousands of pounds a week whilst giving those trusted small groups of workers a drink on top of their regular wages. Everyone was happy. The company next door never sussed it out at all. If they ever did, dealing in so much, they would just assume it was natural sales and order more coils.

This type of scamming was always going on and was the most risk-aversive way of making money you could think of. Why go out putting yourself under pressure by robbing a security car for a few grand, putting yourself at great risk of spending time in clink when you can be legitimate, rob next door, and make thousands without the cops even looking in your direction? Brady was sharp, without a doubt. With his double act with Jean, they were a pair of monsters. Not many had that luck.

Yet another major positive was that Roy fell in love with May Brown, Jean's sister. Blonde with a nice figure to boot. When they got married, Roy's star ascended to the heavens. Now he was family; there was no stopping little fucking big head. He, together with Jean, was invincible. By contrast, Little Ernie Brady, Roy's brother, was completely different. Me and Ernie were mates. We boxed together at the Morris commercial and then Nechells. Ernie wasn't the best boxer in the world; he was steady, game, and completely different from his brother Ernie. He was modest and a nice guy. I would ring and wind him up, "Good afternoon, European steels?"

"Yes."

"Is that Mr Brady? This is Inspector Postons here, Mr O, Grady, and you are not giving us any bodies."

"Fuck off."

Yes, Ernie was a nice guy, genuine, modest. One day, while working in the yard, he got crushed from the waist down by one of the forklift drivers. The forklift driver was only a young kid, but Roy was furious. Ernie was rushed up to the general, and I went to see him. It was fucking tragic. Drugged up to the eyeballs with morphine to reduce the pain, Ernie was half in half out of the world. Suddenly, and without any warning, Ernie sat up in bed swinging his fists in boxing mode before laying back down and dying, his last stand.

Ernie's dad, Vince, still lived in his council house up Cooksey Lane. Paying my respects, I could see Vince was broken. Besides calling Roy Little Big Head, I guessed he had a soft spot for Ernie. The driver of the forklift truck disappeared off the face of the earth. Whatever happened to him, no one knows. Whether he was put in the acid bath or simply done away with it was never mentioned again.

By now, Little Big Head was living up to his nickname, sharp and clever. He and Jean lived up to their names and the reputation spreading around Birmingham, the Mafia. In contrast, Jean had always been competitive with her brother David. Now, with Roy, there were no limits. I guess it was a constant competition to think of ways to fuck people to enhance their reputations. They had a small, loyal army of workers who worked within the company and amongst the other regular workers who hadn't a clue as to what was going on. In the main, these lads were not only loyal, but they were also tight knit. All from around the immediate Aston area knew each other and were all prepared to stand with each other. If you were to explain that they were being used, they would laugh you out of the yard. It only dawned on Lawler years later when we talked about it that Colin admitted to being used. Sadly, through the drugs, he was dying and knew it. He kept to himself any regrets he had.

It was a fever that fed and grew off itself. With a decent wage plus extra financial perks, recruits were easy enough to find, loyalty and keeping your gob shut were paramount, and more importantly, you became part of a growing and powerful group, with the power lying with Jean and Roy. Everyone likes to attach themselves to success, and Jean was certainly successful, and so was Roy. Success breeds success, and Jean was one of the richest women in England. She revelled in her nickname of the Midlands 'Queen of Steel'.

By now me and Bet had bought our first house in Sutton, and we were over the moon, but for some reason, people started to cut themselves off from us. Was it our imagination? Was I getting paranoid? I don't know, but we felt cut off. Maybe it was because we all had to find our way in the world with the responsibilities that came with it. Certainly, Susan Kirby asked if we thought we were getting above ourselves, "Why don't you buy nearby, Tommy, in Marston Green?" Marston Green was just up the road from us in Kitts Green. No, thank you. Besides, it seemed I was putting myself on offer every time I walked out the door. My sister-in-law, Teresa, had the most venomous tongue in Kitts Green whilst thinking she was better than anyone else. June, the other one, was a complete fucking nut case, bouncing up and down Kitts Green's shoulders set like the proverbial pit bull, spitting blood and venom. She would confront anyone she had a mind to, rolling her sleeves up before threatening to do them in. Most women were terrified of her, the blokes also knowing they couldn't give her a smack. June was fucking certifiable. Certainly, my brother had married a major but exaggerated version of our mom, the other one not far off either.

Besides, I felt the world closing in on me in Kitts Green. Raymond would think nothing of popping across with a load of gear. "Store this for us, Tom, old son." Oh yes, if I get nicked, it's good old Tommy. I got up one morning ready to go to work in my fledgling haulage business, and I got a knock on the door. "Mr Lewin? Police, where were you earlier this morning?"

"I've just got out of fucking bed."

"The post office in Marston Green was held up this morning with people waving shotguns." Oh, so I'm on the fucking list for a wake-up call then. It so happened that whilst in a famous Irish nightclub a few months earlier, the owner, a 'friend', who had bought many a case of spirits off my brother, asked me about a recent fit-up. I just happened to mention that if I had a shotgun, I would like to shoot the bastards. It was one of those things you say in the moment. I never said it to anyone else. So, when the cops said, "We heard you had been asking around the town for a shotgun," I knew exactly who it was. As a family, we were well-known in Birmingham. I was also beginning to realise that several people either didn't like us or had no respect for us. So many people seemed to be looking after their own necks, protecting themselves to such a degree that they would throw anyone in to throw suspicion off themselves. Maybe I was getting paranoid. I obviously was not clever enough to navigate the minefield of villainy and grassing I lived amongst. No, we had to get out of the area, and Sutton struck us as a nice place to live. Like the fucking Nesbit's, we loaded all our worldly goods onto one of my lorries and set off on our merry way.

From that moment on, we were cut off. No one rang us up, no one asked to come over or visit us, and my brother Billy would only pop over to bring us a load of gear to store from his many little dealings. Billy wasn't a thief or a villain. But he would think nothing of bringing a load of dodgy gear over and expecting me to store it without even getting a drink, so he's putting 300 brand-new TVs in boxes in our garage and treating my house like his little warehouse, rent-free. For two years, except for my work, we never even left the house, between feeding the kids and paying the fucking mortgage we couldn't afford to. The only way I came across anyone was through the business, and in truth, I had started to realise that these people who I had thought were my friends were not my friends at all. One day, Caesar rang me up and asked me if I was interested in a job at the steel firm down Rocky Lane. I was gasping at the bit for all the work I could get, so I was down there like a shot.

By now, you never dealt with Jean herself or Roy. Dealing with anyone outside the office was a definite no for either of them. There is a chain of command, like royalty. As I pulled up, I was met by Caesar and Larry Wills, who were both nice guys. I had quoted them a tenner to move a lorry load of rubbish. Pulling up next to the pile, Larry and Caesar pulled in another couple of the lads and set to with the shovels. I was fucking grateful. Within twenty minutes, they had my lorry loaded. The competitiveness even extended from Roy and Jean down to her lads, who set to with gusto, trying to outdo each other on the shovels. Now, seeing the lorry was well overloaded, I asked Larry to ask Jean for an extra two quid, making twelve quid for the job, which was not a lot and something she could afford. Looking embarrassed, Larry trundled off only to come straight back even more embarrassed with a tenner, "That's all she'll pay, Tom." Grabbing it, I got in my lorry and pissed off. I was tempted to tip it straight back up in front of Jean's door, but I realised that would put her lads in a really difficult position.

Knowing what I found out afterwards, I considered myself lucky. Her and Roy were fucking people left, right and centre. The only ones who got paid were the utilities, HMRC, the tax man, and

British Steel. All the rest were fucked with some excuse, or another found to refuse to pay. Wanting her offices refurbished on Rupert Street, many of the lads asked my pal Reg Baldwin to put them up for the work. Reg told them to forget it, knowing they would never get paid. In the end, she employed a small company to carry out the refurbishment work. True to form, she found fault with the workmanship and refused to pay. It came to thousands of pounds, and the company went bankrupt. By now, her reputation was so fearsome that few dared to take her on. Between robbing banks and security vans, Reg and a few others were also working for Jean down the yard in Aston.

In between blags or other financial goals, a job with Jean at least kept the wolves from the door and saved them from putting their necks on the line out of desperation. The golden plus for Jean and Roy was that they both had a team of loyal and ready Rottweilers at their command. All they needed to do was dress up in the right gear, and you would think they were in their own little 18th-century feudal fiefdom. Jean lauding it from her little fortress palace, and Roy gagging at the mouth to carry out her commands.

One day, knowing Reg's brother, Henry, was a decorator, she asked Reg if Henry would be interested in painting her garage doors at home. The decorators she had used to decorate the house and never got paid had left the garage doors unfinished. Knowing the strength, Reg was naturally a little bit hesitant. "I'll ask him, Jean, so long as you pay him."

"Yes, OK, Reg."

Reg duly puts his brother in for the job, Henry goes to collect his money, and Jean gives him a cheque and pays him. A week later, Henry goes steaming into the yard, screaming his fucking head off at Reg. Jean had bounced his cheque. Trying to calm his brother down, Reg went into the office, "Jean, you've bounced Henry's cheque."

"Well, yes, Reg. After I had paid him, I went to look at the garage doors, but they hadn't been done properly."

Reg was no mug. The office went deathly quiet. After a bit of a standoff, Henry was paid, with Reg offering to double-check the garage doors. This treatment, to one of her trusted lieutenants, a pal? This kind of behaviour steps outside the boundaries. For the sake of a few quid, she and Roy are prepared to push the wrong people and create a war. Reg had tangled with mad Frankie Frazer, the Richardson brothers. Reluctant as he was, Reg nor his brother would be fucked about.

Another time, I got a call from Caesar and was again met at the factory down Rocky Lane. Handing the plans to me, Cesar pointed out that Jean wanted her garden landscaped in Earlswood. This was a big money job involving a lot of work and thousands of pounds; it was a big garden, and I needed the work. I was struggling, but if she didn't pay, I would be in deep shit street. Jean didn't even deign to come out to see me or talk to me herself. Oh no, there is now a hierarchy that has to be followed. Like the queen, it goes down through her minions.

"What's involved, Caesar?"

"Dead straightforward, Tom. Jean's getting a quote from three firms. The cheapest one gets the job."

"The cheapest one? That's it, Caesar. Tell her to fuck off, I'm not interested." I don't know if it was my imagination that I felt a sense of approval from him or maybe a sigh of relief. Desperate as I was, I couldn't take that risk. So, she gets firm in with the cheapest quote, examines the work, pulls it to pieces, and then refuses to pay. Great ay? At that stage, I didn't know how bad things had gotten or how ruthless they were, even with simple tradesmen. Just as well, really.

Not long after, I clocked big headlines in the Birmingham Mail. Jean, or rather Roy, had employed a carpenter to do some work for her, amounting to a couple of grand. She played her usual little stunt, found fault with the work, and wouldn't pay him. A word is often put in the tradesman's lug hole, and he decides to cut his losses, take it on the chin and disappear. This chippy wouldn't, he put it in the county court. The Birmingham Mail, by now becoming fully aware of Jean, her reputation and stroke pulling, saw the opportunity to expose her. Boy, did she and Roy shit themselves. Like a bullet from a gun, Roy Brady was up that court like a shot to pay the bill, minutes to the deadline. That must have been some humiliation.

But it didn't stop them. She was a multi-millionaire, for Christ's sake, one of the richest women in the country. Yet, she has to resort to fucking minor tradesmen for a few hundred quid. I know you have to be ruthless to be in business, but this takes the biscuit. Each lunchtime, a small fleet of black Rolls Royce's would be lined up outside the offices in Rocky Lane where she and her trusted little Rottweiler's would pile in to have lunch, all on the company one or two doing a line of coke each. Black Rollers, of all things. Very gangster.

I only came across Roy on the odd occasion, mostly funerals. Still, he would look down his nose at me like I was the mug each time. One time at his dad Vince's funeral, I was sorely tempted to stick one on his fucking chin but felt it would be very disrespectful to Vince, who was a nice guy, besides you can't smack someone at a funeral. Turning to Colin Lawler, who by now had gone tits up in his business and was working for Jean and Roy to keep his head above water, I said, "How come Little fucking Big Head is so arrogant? I mean, he ain't a hard case, is he?"

"It's the drugs, Tom, the coke. After a few lines of that, you start to feel invincible." Well, for Christ's sake, that explains it then. Now I know why so many idiots are strutting around the town and country on cloud nine, wanting to fight, stab and shoot everyone. But it wasn't just the drugs, surely. A few little cliques were growing around the city, little noses going up in the air now they belonged to the little gangster set they were in. They didn't have the brains to realise that, through my family and Summer Lane acquaintances, I had seen it all before. Self-important legends in their heads till they started getting a little bit of porridge. Age started creeping up, and the nice tickles started disappearing together with their bottle.

One or two I felt I could have joined and done business with, but when they were on top, they looked down on everyone else. When they did wake up or wanted to do business, it was too late. I had realised why their circumstances had changed, and they were now skint. In Colin's case, he was just mentally knackered with the drugs, the last one to do business with.

In business, you have to give and rely on credit. It was one of the burdens I had to deal with. Fortunately, in my case, it was only for small amounts, and it was spread amongst different companies. If one went bankrupt, I could still survive, difficult as it would be. Some people were into companies for thousands, and if they went bankrupt, it would send the other bankrupt. In Jean's case, it was even worse. She had money owing running into hundreds of thousands of pounds, and if they couldn't afford to pay her, she would be out of pocket by millions, literally millions. She had an answer for it. Well, several answers. She would set her Rottweiler's onto them. She had a ready-made team of gangsters, hard cases, thugs and henchmen, all willing and capable of carrying out her instructions, and there were a lot of them.

The team would go out loaded with pickaxe handles and sawn-off shotguns and head to the first debtor on the list, bursting into the office and bouncing pickaxe handles off the desks. Most shit themselves and paid up. These lads were very formidable, all very fit, strong and capable. They were good lads in the main, but in a team with the right ingredients, they presented the perfect storm. Some debtors would be invited to the offices to discuss the debt and find a way to resolve it. Before they knew it, they were bundled and tied up, dragged into the factory and hoisted by a crane above the vat of acid. If they didn't shit themselves first, they made the effort to pay up. No one wanted to disappear into that little tank. When Colin Lawler, who was not afraid to mix it, tells you in all sombre seriousness that it got very heavy, you have to believe it got very heavy.

One such debtor was a nice guy named Derek, who had a company called Quality Steels. He went bankrupt, owing Jean a couple of million quid. Known for being one of the best steelmen in the business, they came to a deal where Derek would work for Jean and clear the debt. After a couple of years, he had made her a couple of million quid plus a couple of million on top. When his wife contracted cancer and died, Jean never even sent a card, trying to foreclose on the house on the day of the funeral, after all they had done for her. Yes, that Jean had steel running through her veins alright.

Her ready-made gang of Rottweilers would be bunged a few quid on top of their regular wages for their extra-curricular endeavours and the added privilege of accompanying her around the nightclubs, all expenses paid, followed by a nice curry. I doubt it ever occurred to them that they were also her minders. If it did, they would wear the badge with pride. There were other little perks as well as the millions she and Brady were making from the business. Steel sheets, coils and rolls are worthless to anyone outside the business. Wait outside any steel stockholding business, and you will see artic lorries loaded up with thousands of pounds worth of steel waiting for delivery the next day or ready for delivery.

If a lorry load disappeared and the artic found dumped somewhere a few days later, the directors would just scratch their heads and wonder. If they reported it stolen, the cops would do the obligatory round of scrap yards, assuming that's where it would be headed. Who would assume another fellow steel stockholder would be having it nicked? Jean had contacts within the steel industry around the country. Lorry loads of steel were disappearing from steel stockholders from north to south. Countless fifteen to twenty-ton lorries loaded with thousands of tons of steel just waiting to be nicked. One such arctic was found in Jean's yard one morning before it could be unloaded. Someone had obviously squealed. The cops were desperate to nick her, but as she explained, many of her yard staff had a key. It could have been any one of them. So, she's the director of the company, who else is there to gain by having a lorry load of steel in her yard? Unbelievable, assuming no one is taking a big backhander, of course. The cops must have been fucking steaming with frustration. They couldn't bring in Pip the Planter or his equally bent colleagues. She was far too formidable. Besides, she had no criminal record, and Pip could only work his magic if you had form, but eventually, it did come on top for Jean and in the most spectacular way.

As a note, the above incident is on record. As are many other little incidents I have described throughout this book, so please don't get calling me a grass.

One or two of the steel company directors, terrified out of their fucking wits, decided to go squealing to the cops. Quite right, too. You can't have mobs going around threatening people with acid baths like it was Al Capone's Chicago in the forties. Trembling with excitement, the cops went steaming into the yard and arrested Jean and a dozen or so of her henchmen. Unless they squealed on the others, their usual tricks of threatening the lads didn't work. Being a grass under those circumstances was a definite no, no. Besides, Jean made sure they all had the best legal teams at their disposal. There is no legal aid here, matey. Being a bit of a new experience for the cops and not fully knowing the strength, they couldn't just fit them up either. This wasn't your average villain situation caught out on suspicion of robbing a payroll wagon. Oh no.

Before the trial could proceed, Jean developed Hodgkinson's lymphoma, claiming she was dying of cancer, with the necessary doctors notes confirming the fact the attorney general controversially passed a nolle prosequi order, which meant the case against the woman known as the midlands steel queen, a title she revelled in could not proceed because she was close to death, she even had a separate glass office built within her office with a bed put in whilst she could conduct her business. It was later discovered that relevant and secret documents had been destroyed or disappeared. Whilst the nolle prosequi was an abandonment, not an acquittal, the ruling did not bar any future prosecutions if she recovered. But without the papers, the possibility of any further future actions was impossible. What a nice touch. How convenient, indeed. For all the expertise and knowledge that the court and police had at their disposal, no one seemed to be familiar enough to realise that Hodgkinson lymphoma has a very high recovery rate. Some very heavy money passed over there, perhaps. We will never know.

Whilst these nolle prosequi's are only made on the grounds of serious ill health and can be considered permanent, eleven of her co-accused were accused of a variety of offences. Although several were acquitted on appeal, the judge was not happy, telling the co-accused he didn't feel happy about sentencing them when he knew they were and had been used as pawns. Jean's family claimed for years that she had been confined to bed, dying. It was only later discovered that not only had Jean made a full recovery but that eighty-five per cent of people who suffer from Hodgkinson's disease make a full recovery. When you're at that kind of level in business, without a doubt, you're bound to build up a lot of contacts and have the best legal brains at your disposal. The kind of money Jean had also gives you a lot of clout. With those three factors added to the fact she was as bent as a nine-bob note with a steel rod running through her spine, it wouldn't take a lot to rustle up a bent private doctor, and we already know there are plenty of bent cops in the force to help manoeuvre things along. Lost documents, indeed. Even a million quid to Jean would have been negligible if only Charlie Richardson had thought of that. He ended up doing a twenty stretch with no acid baths. If you wanted a more convincing example of how corrupt the system is in Birmingham, look no further than that. First, a let off for cancer that few die of, then serious legal documents mysteriously disappear into the heather.

Having fully recovered, Jean enjoyed her love of horse racing, buying three horses wearing the claret and blue of her favourite football team, Aston Villa and having winners at the Cheltenham Cup races. Jean continued to enjoy a nice life before it was discovered that she did get cancer to end her final days, according to rumour, in some pain. Maybe poetic justice. Being tough with competitors goes with the territory. It all passes down the chain. Try refusing to pay a fine simply for doing ten miles over the speed limit and see how ruthless the government can be. You will be thrown in the slammer quicker than you can say, 'innocent guv'. So don't feed me that moral high horse; it's illegal nonsense. It's only illegal when you get caught.

No, what most people objected to and what I despised, if you were on Jean's side, everything was fine and hunky dory. It became perfectly acceptable to fuck anyone to enhance your reputation. So, you are worth circa 50 million quid, but it looks great to fuck a hardworking tradesman out of a couple of grand. You just don't mess with Summer Laners, pal. What surprised me even more was why so many followed her like the Pied Piper. Even Colin Lawler, which staggered me. The eldest son of a respected liberal MP resorting to heavily armed tactics such as going into competitor's offices with pickaxe handles and guns, even being party to holding them over a bath with the odd one disappearing forever. It's amazing how much money brings out people's loyalty. You only have to look at Trump in America. He must have that many politicians in his pocket. You can see them shiting themselves in his presence. I saw it with the Browns. David's wife was known and revered as a princess. He wasn't the best-looking bloke in Aston, but being a millionaire makes up for that. Jean was as big as a barn door.

MONGRELS AND TOE RAGS

For years, I had been confused and bewildered by what was happening around me. My dad was never a mug, so when he told me something, I took it on board. When he mentioned that old Jack Brown used to pop down to The Barrell every Sunday lunchtime to have a drink while sitting in his Mercedes outside, a friendly smile on his face, I took it at face value as he put it to me. Only as time went on did I look at things with a different slant.

Was old Jack popping down to Summer Lane not to have a drink with his old mates? Because he wasn't having a drink with his old mates, was he? He was sitting outside in the comfort of his nice Merc, thanking his lucky fucking stars he was out of it and living in a nice, detached house in Walmley. I don't blame him, but it puts a nice twist on things. His son David used to do the same little thing as well. On rare occasions, he would pop in pubs like The Grosvenor, The Vine, or The Prince. He very rarely spoke to anyone, maybe just the odd nod of acknowledgement here and there. But on his way out, he would hand over a hundred quid to the landlord and buy everyone a drink after he'd left, like the benevolent uncle.

The landlord would be taken aback at this generous offer. No one in Nechells did that. OK, you bought your mate one. That was to be expected, and then they would buy you one back, but you didn't buy the whole fucking pub a drink. "OK, lads, everyone, David's just left you all a drink or two on him." The punters would jump up with excitement, "What a sound geezer that David Brown is." David's reputation would be enhanced all the more. "Do you know David bought the whole boozer a drink last night in The Mitre? What a nice guy." Well, the pub only held twenty fucking people and a hundred quid to him was nothing. In later years, as things picked up, I felt like trying the little move myself, but by then, the pubs around the green were well and truly dying off.

My dad also used to paint me a rosy picture of how life was in the lane back in the day when everyone stood on, one for all, all for one, like the fucking musketeers. But shrewd and almost cunning as my dad was, I realised he was quite naïve. He just didn't want to see bad in anyone except the cops, of course. Yes, pissed up in the pubs; if it went off, they would all stand together shoulder to shoulder like a band of brothers till one upset you. But sober, in the cold light of day, when the reality of life hit them, how loyal were they then? If you've only got a nicker in your pocket, it's not hard to buy your pal a pint for sixpence, even lend them ten bob, but when you've got a hundred quid in your pocket, it's a bit of a different ball game.

I grew up watching the villains come into our house on Friday and Saturday nights, full of joy, good spirits, genuine, sound, and a good heart. But did those same guys with those same standards pass them on to their kids? Raj Pot Kirby warned his son, my mate, Micky, that if you ever grass on anyone, you will never come back inside this house. Well, Micky took that lesson right down to the bone; he never committed a criminal offence to make sure. But what happened to the next generation? My generation.

For a time, until I got away from it all, I was finding it a fucking nightmare, a bloody minefield of grassing and stroke pulling. It felt like everyone was at it, even to the smallest of minor things. I put a lorry up for sale once from our house in Kitts Green, and I got a few calls before selling it. It was a sound ten-ton tipper. One caller was Henry Taroni. "Hello, about your tipper?" And with that tone of self-importance, you must know my name. "This is Henry Taroni here. Can I come and see it?"

"I'll tell you what, Henry, I'll bring it over to you." That shook him to the fucking core, "Who's this?"

"It's Tommy Lewin, Henry."

"Oh, OK."

Before I got to his yard, he didn't want it. Shrewd as Henry was, he didn't want to risk being turned over by Tommy Lewin and made a laughing stock.

One of the other callers was Pat Roach, the boxer, wrestler and actor. Pat was a nice, unassuming bloke, but he wasn't the sharpest tool in the box. What did he do to save face? He told everyone, including Henry, that I was touting the lorry all over Birmingham. Well, I was if he called putting it in the Birmingham Mail touting it all over the place. I wanted to fucking sell it, but it was a nice lorry. This gave more gist to the mill and added to my ill-deserved reputation. Watch out for that, Tommy Lewin. It wouldn't have been so bad if they had at least turned up to see it. Pat Roach only made a phone call. On that basis, he spread a lie. In Henry's case, he sent a lackey to tell me, and that was after giving me his record, a little publicity stunt called, I'm Henry the 8th, I am.

These were people I had grown up with. I'd worked for Henry and his brothers, except for Joe. They had all tried to jip me. They jipped anyone. I was already growing increasingly disappointed and unhappy with the people I grew up with, and thought were pals. Sunna would fuck anyone for a nicker. He admitted it and did it to me, even his own family. You can nick of your own family all day without getting nicked; how easy and clever. What member of your own family is going to squeal on you? No, they would just fuck each other back. Fortunately, even his missus had had enough and booted him out. His brother-in-law, Mick, wasn't far off. He blamed Sunna for nicking my radio, and Sunna blamed him. Years later, Micky had a nice tickle and brought a little scrap yard down Aston and became almost respectable, his past quietly being buried, and fair play to him, he was a pal, and considering he couldn't read nor write, he did very well. If someone rang up whilst I was in the yard, he would tell me to take the call. He couldn't jot down the name or address. He would pick up a paper and pretend to read it. Mick, the fucking papers upside down, but how do you judge success?

His brother-in-law, by marriage, was another little treasure. David was a different kettle of fish altogether, cunning like a little sheeny. David had been a mate of mine since we were kids. He was just a happy-go-lucky, ready-to-laugh normal guy. From kids, we progressed to the clubs, having a laugh and a bit of fun. It was all part of the fun if we had the odd little tickle along the way. When he got married, it slowly but surely all changed.

I called to say hello to him when he had a little shop on Stockland Green. His missus ran the shop while David wheeled and dealed. The first thing David did was ask me if I wanted a nice little car. Standing there, shoulders stooped, hands outstretched like a little sheeny, a smile on his face, a gleam in his eye. I thought, this is a fucking mate, and he's trying to have me in. He was by now living in Streetly, having bought his first house. I got the impression from Mick that some of his police neighbours were giving him and his kids some stick, which I thought was disgusting. The guy was trying to have a knock. Was this resentment or jealousy? The next thing I knew, he had moved and bought a nice bungalow on Monmouth Drive, Millionaire's Row, as it was known. Also, villains drive. Mind, that might be because of the villa players who lived there.

Fair play to him as well, I thought, although I was a bit pissed that he had got there before me. I didn't realise David had a little trick up his sleeve. The Social Security and Benefits office was very generous at the time. Still, the Asians soon caught on and started milking the system. In effect, you could go to the dole, sign on as unemployed, and the system would pay your mortgage. This was a regular little trick played by a surprising number of people. People would set up company directorships, on ex amount of a year's wage, go bankrupt, then go on the dole. The amount of money they had earned and the cost of their mortgage made it almost impossible to get another job with an adequate salary. They could claim all the benefits till the cows came home. Today, the Asians have caught onto it. They ain't slow either, when it comes to seeing a chink.

Two well-known brothers and family friends had a nice scrap metal and skip-hire business. Shrewdly, they put the business and all its dealings in the one brother's name with his daughter. They were strutting around Brum for years, buying drinks all around the nightclubs. We all thought how shrewd they were. What no one realised was that they had been signing on for years. It only came on top when two of the brothers died. The daughter put herself in charge and told the other to fuck off.

It only stopped when a businessman down south hit the headlines. His company went bankrupt, forcing him to sign on as unemployed. After some months of signing on, someone in the dole office decided to bring it to the attention of the newspapers, who put it right up there on the front pages. The guy screamed that he couldn't help it if his company had gone bankrupt. When the average house was about 150 grand, he had bought a luxury detached house in the stockbroker belt for circa 800k. There was no way the bloke could ever be offered a job paying that mortgage. Those in the dole office could only look on and bite their tongues.

Slowly, and eventually, the government, having looked at all the figures, started to stop it and put a ceiling on the amount you could claim. It took a few further years before they closed the gates almost completely. You're told to sell the house if you're unfortunate enough to lose your job now while having a mortgage.

That didn't affect the rental side, though, now that was a different kettle of fish. The government still paid the market rent for a property. The Asians, particularly, caught onto that little sweety. I had some of that experience when I first got into the hotel and property rental market down in Devon. Here in Birmingham, the Asians opened my eyes up. On selling a refurbished house once, I had a little tribe of Asians knock on the door the next day after putting it on the market. Led by a young Asian guy, they came in, looked around and left. An offer for the full asking price was put in the next day, but I couldn't get my fucking hat off.

I was used to seeing all kinds of scams regularly. My dad, Uncle Jimmy Pussyfoot and George Fruity Tuit Fewtrell had shown me a few little moves, most of which I thought perfectly acceptable, but this was a new ball game. The agent told me after I had accepted the price that the Asian community couldn't work out the difference in valuations on the same house on different roads. What I wondered was if he understood the other reason some of these Asians maybe didn't care. I only found out weeks later when the young Asian guy was strutting up and down the street smoking a fag like he hadn't got a worry in the world.

I winkled it out of him after a bit of prodding. While the house was his and his mom's, he hadn't bought it. His cousin bought it (these Asians think differently from us). Having brought it, he then rented it to this guy and his mom, who then claimed the rent from the government, who were happy if not pleased to pay it, which covered the mortgage and left him with a nice little sum on top of about one hundred quid—no wonder he was strutting about without a worry in the world. "You, white people, need to understand that when we Asians get off the plane into your country, we are met by an army of officials who tell us exactly what we are entitled to, having to survive for centuries on nothing. We know every trick in the book."

Well, knock me over with a fucking feather, they had a house rent, rates and mortgage free, for life, and rising, there's in all but name, well, same name, just different people, both cousins with the same name. His cousin would benefit in a number of other ways as well, which is very sensible. The Greeks had a similar mentality. Now I realised why the auction houses were full of Asians buying all the houses. This was teamwork, one for all, all for one. One day, someone might do all the sums. Oh, sorry, no. One doesn't want to be accused of racism. Now we have Asians risking their lives to get into the country by rubber dinghy, mobile phones at the ready with a whole list of phone numbers off friends dotted around the country, all with rooms and accommodation to rent, the government scratching their little barnets wondering why. As an added bonus, house prices went through the roof due to demand.

All this, of course, was fucking semi-legitimate. If you pulled someone, what could they do? What's the offence? Here I had my friends, well acquaintances, sweating their little nuts off planning a cash machine or armoured car robbery, talking in excited voices about there being 50 or maybe a hundred grand, giving them ten or twenty grand each but risking a ten stretch in the nick. Here, we were making twenty grand just by renting a property and letting the dole pay the mortgage for twelve months. I put it to one or two people, even my brother Billy, but it looked that simple people thought it was too good to be true.

According to gossip, David was a millionaire, with a chunk of land adjoining his bungalow. He started building a beautiful, big, detached house. It was magnificent, but then, unfortunately, the proverbial shit hit the fan. He sold the bungalow to his son, who also got a mortgage with ease. For some reason, David refused to pay the roofers, who returned mob-handed to remove the roof. They were met by David's little mob, causing a stand-off; the roofers left, dejected and defeated. By now, David's star was sinking as fast as it had arisen. Both houses were snatched of David and his son, causing massive humiliation. Sold at auction for circa one hundred grand each, I had just missed out, not having the cash to jump in. Someone grabbed a very nice deal. With all his millions, no one could understand why David didn't get someone to simply buy it, passing them the money. Problem solved.

David had got into the mortgage and rental business. At the time, the banks were bending over backwards to lend money and give mortgages on the rising property market. All you had to do was come up with the right figures, which was dead easy with a bent solicitor, estate agent, and valuer. I was buying houses to refurbish, making 25% gross profit, and David was just getting the agent to put 25% on. Well, the way things were going, the properties would be worth 25% more within a few months, and everyone knew that. Shrewd move, unfortunately, the market crashed. Whilst David and his partners owned a few million pounds worth of houses, they couldn't afford to pay the increased mortgage costs. It all came tumbling down, the banks moving in to snatch the lot back, and the mortgage fraud was exposed.

For his little enterprises, David ended up getting a little seven stretch. When he was released, he had to make the right few moves to get his 'millions' back, ensuring his reputation was enhanced even further for stroke-pulling and fucking people all over the place. None but the hardiest would dare deal with him for fear of being fucked. Even worse, he was being hounded all over the place by inland revenue, customs, and excise. As soon as he moved up Chester Road, they chased him and foreclosed on his house, forcing him to spend more and more time in Spain, no doubt where he is still being watched very closely and looking older than his years. Whilst in Spain, someone put a match to the house, ensuring the HMRC didn't get full whack. Quite right, too.

Yet another star on the wane were the Fewtrells like us from the back streets of Aston. Eddie lifted his brothers up by their belts and braces, giving them a fantastic opportunity. First, having made the Bermuda Club successful, he bought Cedar Club. At that stage, he started putting his brothers in. First, Donald by offering him the job of running the club. Donald hardly had time to put his wig on before hot-footing it from his job on the line at the Peugeot Coventry car factory. Wearing dinner suits to welcome the customers, his brothers were in their oil tots, earning a nice wage and having the opportunity to buy themselves a nice house, together with the prestige and position that went with it.

Soon, Eddie and his family were flying, eventually ending up with eight clubs and everyone having full respect. Still, Donald, having had fuck all, started to get greedy, as one does. He wanted a full partnership in the clubs, thinking he was indispensable and the oldest, so he put his demand on Eddie. Eddie, in turn, after a few arguments, sent him a formal notice to quit. Being the shrewdest and the most loyal brother, Eddie was no mug. Donald was out on his ear. Getting someone to put the money up, Don went into partnership, opening up one club before moving on to another, then another. The problem was that Don never had the flair or brains his brother had; while Eddie was very well-liked and respected, his brothers were not. His clubs just ticked over. Eventually, Don sold his club, Pollyanna's, and moved to Spain with his little Greek bird, big tits Nina.

After settling up with his wife by giving her fifty grand, she immediately gave it to her son, who, believing in the magic of his name, opened a club in the black country not known outside Birmingham. The club failed spectacularly. The fifty grand went in five months. Don told me he was not too happy that he just about had enough for a little apartment in Denia. Sadly, whilst he was a name in Birmingham, in Denia, he was just another old man with a syrup. As his son had found out, outside Birmingham, the Fewtrell name meant nothing. Plus, the golden era had disappeared, and the opportunities were gone. After the war years and entering the 50s, Birmingham was like the Wild West, just as in the early and late 1800s. There were gangs galore. It was bedlam. Whereas the fights in the early days were carried out by desperate thugs gangs on the street, today, they are more widespread. It focused on gangs trying to establish and assert themselves in a new era. Now, young studs were starting to make money, wearing nice suits, and the gangster image was being brought to the fore. As the clubs and pubs blossomed, so did the trouble and the fighting. This is where the Fewtrells had established themselves. There had been money flowing from robberies and wheeler-dealing galore. Now, the reality was setting in. Many big spending villains were getting nicked, the wheeler-dealers pulling back. With money running out and nothing coming in, big tits Nina persuaded Don to open a little restaurant. Having started as a cleaner in his club, Nina was not a cook. Very quickly, the restaurant started to fail. Showing me photos of his restaurant, counters laden with piles of rich food, Don was quite dejected that no one had turned up for his Christmas party.

At that point, Nina persuaded Donald to go back to Birmingham and throw himself at the mercy of Birmingham City Council, who gave him a top thirteenth-floor flat in Sparkbrook. Having been accused more than once in the papers of being racist, it must have been humiliating for Don with the place being full of Asians and smelling of curry and piss in both lifts and on every floor. Certainly, it was humiliating for Eddie, who was confronted with the story in the Birmingham Mercury. Don was that skint he sold his story for a few quid, not realising the implications. In the meantime, Nina was sitting back in the apartment in Denia, which coincidentally happened to be in her name. Every three months, Don would fly over, pick up his pension money and send it back to Nina to prop up the restaurant.

Coming over to visit him, she found a packet of condoms in a drawer. "Who the fuck are these?" Desperate, he blamed me. "They're Tommy Lewins." The prat never realised that Nina would go through his phone book and ring my number, putting the boot into my wife, Betty. The fact that I had never slept at his flat was irrelevant. It was all the excuse that Nina needed. She already had suspicions that Don was doing a bit of naughty stuff with his bouncer, Kelly, who had boasted in his younger days of bending over to earn a few quid. With a huff and a puff, she sacked Donald and returned to her nice little apartment in Denia. Shortly afterwards, palling up with a Spanish guy, Donald could never see how he had been outwitted and outmanoeuvred. "Well, it's only fair that she has the flat, Tom."

Eddie ended up selling the clubs following a mental breakdown. In the papers, it was reportedly ten million quid. Donald, who together with his brother Chris was now skint and pot less as well as being bitter, told me it was for far less. By now, they were both dejected and pissed off, blaming Eddie for all their woes. While refurbishing a house one day in Erdington, Don brought Chris down, who had tried to put the bite on me for twenty grand. Far from the cocky and arrogant Chris, I remember from my youth; his shoulders were slumped. He couldn't look me in the eye. His car sales pitch on the Stratford Road had gone bust. One of his brothers had fucked him for twenty grand. Why twenty grand? To restock the pitch. Being polite and showing interest, he then upped it to forty grand, "Won't Eddie help you?"

"Oh no," he spit out, "He wouldn't help."

"Why the extra twenty grand?"

"Well, for backup money." Thinking I might have security in the freehold, Chris pointed out it was a leasehold. It was only at that stage I had great difficulty not laughing.

Had they really sunk that far that they would try to fuck anyone or have them in the net, or was that the story of their lives? With his boxing promotions, Chris was already trying to latch onto Pat Cowdell, the boxer. Now, he was trying to have me in the net for forty grand after his brother had allegedly gypped him for twenty grand. It was only shortly after this that Don told me Chris was dying of cancer. Had he tried to have me in the net with this being his backup money? How many people did they have in the net like this over the years? What comeback would I have had once Chris had kicked the bucket? They had already bit Eddie to pay for a cruise around the Mediterranean. I guessed Don was well and truly on the floor when he handed me his jewellery and asked me to sell it.

As time passed, I was constantly surprised by the stories and what I heard about these people. Don's dad, Fruity Tuit, was a partner and a close pal of my dad, yet he'd think nothing of trying to turn me over. All's fair in love or war, ay? We used to meet up once or twice a week at The Actress and Bishop for a drink, and I was surprised to realise that no one wanted to speak to him. By now, his star was surely fading, and he was looking sadder by the week. Poor Don ended up topping himself in his bedroom wardrobe. Also using The Actress and Bishop was Pat Manning. Pat was a legend in his own mind, and his brother Alan owned the Midland Wheel in Birmingham. Living off his brother's reputation, Pat was a regular sight around the clubs in his dinner suit and bow tie. He looked the part, and I could never figure out where he got his money. Was he into the big stuff or just living off his brother somehow? If he was scratching and trying to grab a few quid like most of us were, he had sold some jewellery to a mate of mine nicknamed Banger from his boxing days.

Banger was a nice guy, but for some unknown reason, he didn't want to pay Pat, so fucked him, another regular pastime. If you need money fucking someone is par for the course as long as there is no comeback. Pat decided he wasn't having any of that, so, he was wound up by scouser Mark Bennet, who told him Banger was in the Strathallan Hotel on the Hagley Road. Pat waited outside with a claw hammer. Mark gave him the hammer.

When Banger walked out half pissed, Pat was waiting for him, giving Banger a right banging. He was left disabled and brain-damaged. Who squealed? I don't know, but Pat ended up in court and got a seven stretch. Pat never lost his swagger while doing his porridge with a bunch of cockneys. With cockneys, you can't swagger. Only cockneys can shout their gob off and give it the swagger. After upsetting Reg Kray, he did no more than catch Pat on the landing and cut his face up a bit, requiring lots of stitches and leaving him looking like New Street Station. True to the code, Pat kept his mouth shut and never squealed. For this, Reg Kray took Pat under his wing, protecting him. For that, Pat became devoted to Reg up to his dying day. At Reg's funeral, Pat duly turned up in his black Crombie and struck a sad figure as he was caught on television walking alone at the end of the procession. Now, Pat was resigned to eking out his miserly pension and poncing off anyone who would buy him a drink in The Elbow Room or anywhere else. Boosted up with the reputation that crept around Birmingham, he was a friend of the notorious Krays and Fewtrells.

One night in The Actress, Pat asked me if I could give him a lift home as he had the book he wanted to give me. I guessed it was for the lift home and not the book he wanted to give me. Whilst I had Pat's phone number, I had never been to his flat. On the twelfth floor, like Don, Pat lived on Park Street in Hockley. His flat was painted in all weird blacks and blues, which would have reflected his mind. Ray Mills was an old friend of the Krays and was in the flat in London with his brother when Reg Kray killed Jack 'The Hat' Mcvity. When it started to come on top, Ray shot up to Birmingham and, being a big bloke, got a job at the door of my Uncle Jeff Elliot's club, The Fleur De Leys. Ray was a nice bloke and soon opened a car valeting pitch in Small Heath. Unfortunately, the Old Bill were watching him, having palled up with Johnny, the gangster. It wasn't long before Ray got nicked and ended up doing a seven stretch for some jewellery robbery. When he came out, he skipped back down to London, only coming back up to spend a couple of days visiting Don, Pat or Big Albert in The Elbow Room, where he was treated with respect. Here, they would reminisce about the good old days, now long gone, when they were legends, missing out on the minor, unimportant bits like being skint and living in top-floor council flats paid for by the treacle.

Of course, a great advantage was the ability to reinvent yourself. Coming from Nechells, you might be living in a little shit hole back-to-back; well, in truth, they were all mostly shit holes back-to-back, but as soon as you got on that bus and out of town, you could reinvent yourself as someone else entirely. With your Hepworth's tailor-made suit, you could wash off your background and be anyone you wanted to be: a car dealer, a wide boy, a gangster; no one would know if you lived in a little council house or owned a nice big house. No one delved too deeply or asked personal questions. There were a lot of wide boys and gangsters around town. Everyone who felt they were anyone was trying to make their mark. Brian Cartwright was the ex-British flyweight champion, and when he retired, he had very little money but a big ego, together with his father-in-law, Johnny Mann. Another well-known ex-boxer and trainer/manager would get on the bus in their little suits and far away from Nechells. When I last saw Brian, he was driving a thirty-hundredweight pick up truck into Ray Corbett's yard. I'm not knocking Brian; he's earning an honest living, fair play to him, but picking up scrap as a tatter and then trying to be someone you are not is a bit of a contradiction.

Reggie Kray's brother Charlie also used to come up for a visit now and again, shoulders slumped. Shortly after his last visit to The Actress and Bishop, we all went to the Albert room, Pat, Don, and me tagging along like a stray dog. Shortly afterwards, Charlie got nicked for dealing drugs, getting another ten stretch. I think that finished Charlie off for good. He just disappeared never to be seen again. This was the problem. Certain people would grow up, shine brightly for a few years in our own little universes, then fizzle out, dropping to the ground like a damp squib. I had seen it so many times before. One minute, a well-respected gangster or villain strutting around the town, money to burn; the next, they just disappear, gone, off the face of the earth, never to be seen again, no one mentioning their name. I suspected quite a few ended up in paupers' graves. One such pal was Big John McCoy.

John was a nice bloke. Well, I thought. Standing at over six feet, it was rumoured that Big John had played professional football. Certainly, his brother had been a professional player for the Celtics. John was a very quiet bloke who never said more than two words put together if he could get away with one, all the while with a shy, steady smile on his face like he was holding some secret in his mind. John was a villain and a thief. He was also known to have done the odd murder for various gangs for a few quid. I never knew exactly what he did or got up to, but he worked for one or two teams around the town. I only found out when, one day, he asked me if I was interested in a little caper. In his usual quite shy way, John told me out the side of his mouth that he knew of a garage owner who lived in a bungalow in Castle Bromwich and kept twenty grand in his home. When prodded further, he suggested that we had to go in at night, threaten the bloke with a gun and make him spill the beans where the money was.

Just the mere mention of something like that made my bottle go. I'll never know why he asked me, but I made some excuse, and he never asked me again. Mugging a fucking bloke in his home with a gun? The next time I saw John was when he turned up at the warehouse, I was trying to get off the ground in Victoria Road Aston. He wanted to borrow my one-ton van, and in return, he would lend me his black 1950s car. Not wishing to refuse a friend, I agreed. Two weeks later, I got nicked for having a stolen car. I told my solicitor it wasn't nicked and that I had borrowed it from John McCoy, who was by now being held in Winson Green nick for the murder of Jock Lowe and the beating up of another family friend Johnny Kirby. He then came back, telling me that McCoy's barrister would not let him appear as a witness or give a statement in my defence.

Mccoy's barrister was none other than Judge Argyle, the most notorious fucking judge on the circuit. Getting to court, I was bullied into pleading guilty and getting a three-month suspended sentence, or not guilty and getting two years if found guilty. My choice was very limited. Getting into the dock, head bowed and dejected, who was the fucking presiding judge but no other than Judge Argyle. What a fucking fit-up. This is another problem I discovered too late in Birmingham. If you have form or are associated with any villain, innocent or not, the powers that be will bend over backwards either to find you guilty or force you to plead guilty. Oh, OK, a three-month bender is fuck all. Plead guilty and get it over and done with till the next time you get nicked. Then even more pressure is applied, plus you get to do the three months suspended. What a thick prat you are, old son.

Listening to my dad, I grew up thinking all the Summer Laners were sound people and the Browns were sound, genuine people. To me, being sound and genuine meant you were pals to your fellow brothers with a willingness to help each other out. Of course, that only applied when we were all skint and on the floor, sharing a doorstep chunk of bread. We had fuck all else to give. Silly billy, I never realised that when you get a foot on the ladder, it's fuck everyone else, booting them back down as you scramble like a rat up a drainpipe to climb up yourself. My youth had been spent watching and admiring these people, these villains, for the loyalty, values and integrity they held. In my twenties, I had to carry an umbrella and a steel plate on my back to protect me from all the stroke pullers, back stabbers and others who abounded. I thought it was the fucking norm. Honour amongst thieves, don't make me laugh.

Having run Sid Hobdays yard for a very few short weeks before getting my collar felt and feeling really sorry for myself, I turned to Inspector Sword Edge, so nicknamed because his name was the same as a well-known razor blade and asked him why I was being constantly picked on. Nonchalantly and without concern, he said, "Look, young Lewin, you could have earned a nice little 300 quid a week out of that yard. All you had to do was give us the odd body. (Don't forget the bung) I said I couldn't do that. He said, "Well, get out of town then because you will always be under the radar." I could see how some people could be tempted. The average wage was about £30 a week. Throwing the odd body in would allow me to buy a nice house in Sutton and be up there with the shrewdest and wide boys. Fuck it, never.

WAKE UP TIME

Bernard Hunt had been my dad's pal back in the day down Summer Lane. Now, his son Bernard had a scrap yard, and his brother Norman was into all manner of things, running the Kings nightclub in Hampstead at one stage. One day, Norman asked me to meet some bloke on a street corner. Now, Norman was a bit vague. "Just tell him I couldn't meet him but to let you drive the lorry loaded up with scrap metal back to me, and you would return with the money." Well, thick as I am, I went along with it, puzzled. Surely, he isn't going to fuck the bloke? Explaining to the bloke, he was hesitant, "Well, I don't know, son. I don't think I should be letting my lorry go." I didn't feel inclined to disagree with him. Going back to Norman, I could see he wasn't entirely surprised. He had intended to fuck him.

Bernard had a scrap yard and lived over Polesworth. Oh, he's a shrewd one, Bernard. He's loaded, with his private plate on his Mercedes. Bernard revelled in his reputation. I saw him years later after we had made an offer for our first hotel in Devon. Bernard had sold his scrap yard and now owned a combined pub and ten-bedroom hotel. It had a first-floor timber patio and dining area looming out over the seafront like the bow of a ship. It was a flipping gold mine, which is what I would have expected of such a sharp and clever character. Only he wasn't. His missus wouldn't be taken for such a mug as to put herself out for the punters. If they want tea in their room, they can come and fetch it. They never came back again.

One day, standing in his bar, he told me he had got it sussed, well, rather, his customers. "We've got it worked out, Tom. Between me and Ricky," his son-in-law, "We watch 'em. If they come in and order a pint, we watch them till they are left with the last bit in their glass. We give them exactly five minutes, and if they don't come up to order a pint, we go over, put our hands on the glass, having another, sir? They either say yes, or we grab the glass, and they soon piss off, Tom." I can't get my breath. Bernard had a potentially great business, a dining out experience looking out over the sea, and ten bedrooms. Instead of just putting a DJ on and bringing in all the customers, he expected to put an extra ten pence on a pint. If they nursed it, he pushed them out. He and his missus were adopting the back street methods of the scrap yard, and worse, they were blatantly trying to steal our guests. It didn't work. Within five years, they had to sell the pub, and Bernard and his missus ended up living in a mobile home overlooking the sea.

Jean Brown could have done so much to enhance the Brown reputation in a good way, leaving a lasting legacy but instead chose to make their reputation by fucking as many people as they could. Worse, it was mostly ordinary decent people as well. Instead of enhancing the reputation and inheritance of Summer Lane, they simply highlighted the worst aspects of it. I'm not talking about charity in the sense of bunging to charities but in other direct ways. Instead, perversely, she set out to compete with her brother David to become the biggest gangster in town. With millions behind you, backed up by a group of fit game loyal lads willing and eager to do your bidding.

David backed the Birmingham group, the Raymond Frogget band. Froggy had a contract with Micky most, but it was weighted in Mickey's favour, which resulted in Froggy doing fewer gigs. David was supposed to have bought Froggy out of his contract, but it was debatable whether it did him any good in the long term. But that was only through self-interest, like many. If he went to a charity function and items were put up for auction, he would outbid the others simply to gain that bit of glory. I witnessed it so many times.

For all the good Eddie Fewtrell achieved, his brothers did a fair job in trying to destroy it with their treatment and attitude towards customers. It didn't bother him at the time because whatever they did was only enhancing their reputation as gangsters; with a small army of bouncers at the ready, it wasn't too hard to achieve.

Not many hard cases go to a nightclub mob-handed, and if they do, they are stopped at the door. With six or more beefy bouncers on the door, not many people will argue. Big Albert had been a bouncer for years. A true heavyweight, he could fight. Before buying and taking over The Elbow Room, with only a couple of bouncers to back him up, there was a fight almost every night. By the time he eventually sold it years later, Big Albert was looking the worst for wear. But Birmingham was not London; times were changing, and slowly, attitudes were changing. Brendan could and did employ plenty of bouncers on the door of the Garryowen, but he simply liked laying it out on people.

When Eddie eventually retired, he brought a smallholding in Ross on Wye in Hereford. It was about the same time Bet and I had bought a pub and campsite in Hereford. Hereford, for its size, was renowned for its gossip. If you farted in the centre of town, people twelve miles away knew about it before you had finished. I had people coming into my bar, knowing I was from Birmingham, asking if I knew about the gangster who had moved in just down the road. Twenty miles away was just down the road to Hereford people. It must have started to affect Eddie as well, as he tried all ways to dismantle the reputation he and his brothers had built up for years. Now, here in Hereford, no one was impressed. It meant nothing. Hereford had their SAS in Credenhill just half a mile from our pub. When his daughter and her husband tried to capitalise on the reputation by writing a book, Eddie disowned her, denying he was ever a gangster. But he had fed her the stories in the first place, filling her head with how he had battles with the Krays everyone knew were nonsense.

Eddie's daughter had turned up Skint with her husband. Eddie put them up in a small cottage on his smallholding rent-free, where they picked his brains on his battles with the Krays and other gangster stories. Her husband saw the opportunity for a best-selling book/film on par with some London gangster books. We can only imagine Eddie slightly embarrassed at this exposure, knowing it was all cobblers. After twelve months, poor Eddie kicked them out. He rang the Birmingham Mail, giving them a scoop whilst disowning his daughter and denying ever being anything other than a respectable businessman.

Contrast that with Bernard Haywood, the exhaust specialist who achieved great things in Birmingham from modest beginnings, even helping others. Bernard was a great bloke. He set up with an old mutual pal named Harry Walker. Harry was a great mate, loud and cocky but likeable with it. Bernard set him up with his own exhaust fitting business, which he called B.E.E. Birmingham Exhaust Equipment, with a picture of a big bee above the caption. I thought it was brilliant, and Harry was clearly going places. Within months, Harry had opened another fitting yard, and just as he was on his second hurdle, Tubes Investments came along and offered him ten grand for the business. They only wanted the name. At the time, ten grand was a lot of money; it would buy three nice houses in Sutton Coldfield, but he had a growing business worth a lot more. Regrettably, he sold it. The ten grand went within months, and Harry disappeared off the face of the earth owing Bernard a right few quid. Some say Bernard had helped him disappear for good. This was a terrible shame and indicative of the mindset that we grew up in. I had seen it in close family and friends. It won't last forever, so grab it quickly whilst you can. Harry had a great, growing business, yet at the first sign of a lump sum, his nerve went, and greed took over.

So, these were the next generation. The next generation of the Peaky Blinders, no honour, no integrity, fucking each other for a few quid at every turn, doing deals with the police, squealing like the trapped rats they were. I was glad to get out and away from them. The general public, driven no doubt by the newspapers, will just shrug their shoulders. If the police have to resort to such methods to catch the crooks and put them away, so be it. But remember and realise it is not clearing or eliminating the problem, merely shifting it from one side of the room to another. Helping the police with their enquiries, i.e., throwing my dad and me in after fitting us up, all it did was release Charlie Hinze to do other little jobs, which enabled him to set up in business. It was the same with scrap dealers. For everybody they threw in, they could buy another ten loads of bent metal, which was very clever indeed. Many of the major villains I know are now dealing in drugs, and this filters down the chain to the smallest drug dealer. Now, we have one of the highest percentages of drug taking in the world. Its evil tentacles spread far and wide across the country. Hundreds of little towns and villages, the new forest, seemingly beautiful little towns, and the pubs ravaged by drug taking. Very clever.

Taking or dealing drugs is a crime, right? Yet we give knighthoods to known drug takers because they pay a lot in tax and are pop stars. So that's OK then. We allow the likes of poor Amy Winehouse to walk around drugged up to the eyeballs, blood coming out of her toes, yet bugger all is done about it, and now the poor talented girl is dead. Well, if Mick, Paul or Amy can take drugs, why can't we? Drugs ravage towns, cities and villages with the cops fighting an uphill battle, yet celebrities are boasting about getting their heads on coke daily. Upmarket celebrity parties are notorious for having silver trays overflowing with coke, and the cops know about it, and the judges know about it. With their colleagues, they more than likely have a little snifter themselves. It's recreational, you see. They can handle it. It's the lower orders, the riffraff, that create the problem. So, you can admit to taking drugs, which I thought was a criminal offence, yet nothing is done about it. No doubt, because so many politicians and the legal profession like a little snort (just on social occasions, mind). We are going to hell in a hand cart, and everyone is turning a blind eye. The cops go out nicking the weakest, the most vulnerable just as they did, and still do, nick the petty crooks and villains around the country, all looking good and filling the quotas. Whilst a hidden army is climbing and spreading throughout the country like a leaky colander, even prisons are awash with drugs.

Yet the answer is simple: in law, the offence of receiving is considered the most serious offence of all. Without the receiver, there wouldn't be any crime, right? My dad was fitted up and given a heavy sentence for buying a small amount of jewellery. As was my uncle Jeff Elliot. Yet the country is awash with people receiving and taking illegal drugs. Sir, Mick Jagger and Sir Paul McCartney, along with most pop stars and major celebrities, boast, have admitted, and, in many cases, been caught puffing on the old ganga, sometimes mixed with a bit of coke or crystal.

We all know and see it, yet none of us says anything. It's the norm. Johnny Depp openly walks around in a drug-induced coma, whilst the old ones are more discreet. The young ones have now taken over, forming the new line of rebellion, actors, singers, models, fucking great, ay? Yet what would have happened if the full weight of the law had cracked down on McCartney and Jagger back in the 60s when they were first known to be doing the drugs? How many young people would have been influenced by what they saw? "Ay, man, let's have a bit of Ganga." I was there, I saw it, and I experienced the mindset. When you see our leaders, our prime ministers, people like Tony Blair who aspired to and were almost besotted with the superstardom, even admitting to smoking a bit of Ganga, street cred, see. Big money. Pop stars, actors, let's not upset the boat guys, fuck the integrity.

All judges, solicitors, barristers, pop stars, celebrities and politicians should be tested weekly. That would shake the barrel up. Even better, bring in Pip the Planter and a few of his pals and resurrect them from Lloyd House. If they can't find a bit of coke, then plant some. A nudge here, a bit of verbal, would have soon stopped it, notwithstanding any bungs going in. Never forget, shit slides downhill.

EPILOGUE

The world today is different from the one I grew up in, where everything was in black and white. There was no colour, and houses were decayed and dismal, with the front door leading off the street or courtyard. If people around Aston or Nechells had a back garden with grass growing, they kept it a secret. Dust hung in the air from the bomb pecks constantly, and the only trees I ever saw were in the cemetery, unappreciated by its residents. In winter, the streets were covered in a dark, dismal fog, referred to as a peasouper because that's what it was like pea soup. We thought it was normal, not realising it was caused by the thousands of coal fires supplying the only form of heating to the houses in the city, getting into our pores and lungs. When you caught a cough or the inevitable chest infection, the go-to cure was a chunk of fresh, warm tar tied around your neck. If you didn't die of the common cold or bronchitis, you could likely die of sucking in the fumes from the tar.

Then you had the smells. Within a hundred yards, your nostrils could be assailed with the smell of the wood yard, fumes from Frank Grounds lorries, the coke from the local gas works, then the hops from Ansell's brewery. Sometimes, it is mixed with the overpowering smell of the HP sauces in Aston and elsewhere, but the smell carried for miles. If I was up early enough, which was rare, I would see my neighbours and my friends' fathers going off to work. A knapsack on their back and shoulders slumped as they dragged their feet along without a smile on their faces to the building sites or factories where they slaved away for a pittance. During the day, I saw the wives shuffling across to the shops for daily food bought on the slate, put in the book Mabel. Then I would see them dodging the rent man who called every Monday, or Blundell's, the debt collector who came for his weekly money, their daughter's school uniform or a pair of work boots for their husband. By the time he got paid on Friday night, there was barely enough to pay the never-ending bills or maybe a couple of pints down the boozer. The only people I saw with money were my dad or the villains that were about and at it.

Today, it's different. The sun shines even in winter, the air is clear and fresh, most houses have a front garden and a back lawn, and many trees give oxygen to the air. The schools treat the kids differently than we were treated. It was made clear to us from nursery school that we were factory fodder, and by the time we reached the seniors, it was made even clearer. Today, any kid leaving school can go on to college or university. Any girl can look up and reach for the stars. There are opportunities for everyone. My nephew, John, became a successful accountant from humble beginnings.

Now, we have the minimum wage. It's not riches, but it allows everyone to enjoy a better quality of life, even two or three foreign holidays a year, far more than we could ever have dreamed of. We are one of the largest homeownership countries in the world. Once you own property, you have money. You're also tied to the yolk. Today, only mugs go out thieving. What has taken its place is drug dealing, and for every ten MPs who want to crack down hard, another one will beg leniency and make it legal, most likely because they indulge themselves. I know of or suspect at least a dozen of my ex-acquaintances who are now dealing drugs on a major scale. Multiply that throughout the country; I've half concluded that the government thinks it's a convenient way to help keep us in check. This, together with mass immigration, is a sure way to keep us and our wages down. While those at the very top grow ever richer. It's called the Kalergy Coudenhove conspiracy.

I hope if anyone is kind enough to buy and read my book, I will leave you to decide the truth of what I say. Certainly, my paternal granddad on my dad's side was a peaky blinder. My maternal great-granddad was Henry Lark Pratt, the famous artist. My grandmother, that poor lady who left Derby as a trained teacher, the proud daughter of a respected painter and ended up dying at an early age in poverty, three kids having to go into an orphanage. No wonder my mom fell for my dad, married him and led the life she did, backing him 100%. They both knew and experienced the reality of poverty and hardship.

It took me years to realise how uneducated I was on leaving school. Sometimes, it might be only days or weeks after an event occurred before I realised, stopped and thought how stupidly I had reacted to a situation. But in mitigation, I have mixed with all kinds of people, customers in hotels and various businesses, and over the years, I have never failed to be amazed at how ignorant or uneducated so many people are—even educated people. Thankfully, my real education began after I left school.

The teacher, David, and his wife lived next door to us in Sutton in the four-bedroom house they could ill afford. Still, it didn't stop them from putting an act on and trying to be something they were not. All posh on the surface, we would hear him effing and blinding his kids when he thought no one could overhear him, but we did. Hundreds like him and his wife live in Sutton to this day. The businessman, 'the company director,' engaged me in building a brick wall in his garden. His wife had a cleaning job to help pay the bills, yet her hands would be blue and cold as she made us a cup of tea. So fearful was she of putting the heating on, he would ask me to take things from his company to dump that were worth hundreds of pounds, simply because it was beneath him to try selling them, and he called himself a businessman. It was all about putting an act on.

I've come across quite a few police officers who have treated me and my friends like shit because they had the uniform on, and we came from the slums. The detective sergeant from Handsworth police station, an attractive woman, to be fair, got shot at one night by one of the black Handsworth burgher boys. The bullet brushed her cheek, frightening the crap out of her and her two colleagues, which enabled the shooter to get away. Back at the station, whilst filling out the report, the inspector walked in, saw it and tore it up. If they had completed and filed the forms, they would have been open for any journalist to inspect. That was the last thing the inspector wanted. They were terrified of being accused of racism.

By that one little act, the idiots created more problems when dozens of the very same gang held the Barton Arms pub in Aston hostage, shooting at the police and police helicopters that responded. Having gotten away, the cops had to resort to fitting them up to ensure they got a result. You can't have cops being shot at on British television. Those blacks knew the fear they were exuding, the power that being mob-handed gave them.

The sergeant resigned from the force on the spot, coming close to death and having kids she didn't want to continue. She divorced her husband and moved to Spain for a few years to get over it. When I met her, she wanted me to move her from her daughters to a little flat she had managed to rent with her few basic belongings. She didn't know me and never thought about who I was. I moved her again twice after that, this time from one little house to another, with a new long-haired, bearded boyfriend she had managed to tag on to. Their furniture was so cheap and tatty that I'm amazed they had the nerve to use it, obviously having begged it, but sometimes, that's what people are like. We live in our little nests, each hiding the truth from our neighbour and each other. But the cops hide the biggest truth of all.

Sutton opened my eyes to many things about life and how it can be so discriminatory, well, how the judicial system can be so discriminatory. We all know that there is one law for the poor and another for the rich, right? After all, we see examples of it regularly, and I know the government is trying to address it. No one is above the law, and justice is blind, blah, blah. Cobblers. I saw police corruption from an early age. Still, without any real yardsticks to go by, you just accept it as the norm. Bribes, fitting up, planting stuff on people suspected of crimes, whether guilty or not, trust me, the cops nor the solicitors or judges give a shit. They have goals to maintain numbers to tick off.

Consideration doesn't come into it. In Aston, Nechells, when all the rebuilding was going on, all the houses were being demolished or bombed out after the war, and the bomb pecks were our playground. At ten years of age, nothing was illegal about climbing into and over empty houses awaiting demolition. If it wasn't for it to be scrumping, which we knew was wrong because it was someone's garden, we were climbing over, but everyone did it. People would boast about how they would go scrumping as kids. If you didn't go scrumping, you hadn't lived and weren't normal. Even cops will admit if they are honest enough, that they did a bit of scrumping as kids; most won't because it's breaking the law. It was and still is human nature, so where do you draw the line?

The only problem was we couldn't figure out what we had done wrong. It was just a game. It wasn't until many years later, when my wife and I stuck our neck out and bought our first house in Sutton Coldfield, that we saw the difference in attitude. I don't know why we bought our house in Sutton; it wasn't through snobbery, though I was accused. The schoolteacher Ruth Smith, who used to encourage me to visit her house and do garden work, inadvertently encouraged me to want to live in Sutton. She had a beautiful house with a long garden rising in tiers, and it soon dawned on me that I wanted something nice like that. I didn't want to live in a council area, too much jealousy back stabbing and gossiping. Simply put, Sutton was and still is a nice area. For the extra few grand or so, it was a move I didn't regret, but it was an eye-opener in more ways than one. We purchased the house on Friday and decided to move in the following day, Saturday. Still, we went over to measure up for curtains, etc., and I first noticed the neighbours walking out of our garden carrying a lump of rockery and a clothes prop. I was fucking incensed, nicking out of our garden, we never spoke to them again. The next shock was seeing the vendors strip the house bare and light shades, shelves, the lot. I said to Bet, "What the fucking hell kind of people have we moved amongst?" I thought we had left the villains behind in Kitts Green.

But no, this was just the foretaste of things to come that were to open my eyes ever wider and daily. The very people who we had caught nicking so blatantly out of our garden were the very ones who would sneer at the likes of me and my friends for doing, as ten-year-olds, no worse than they were doing. Sutton, even today, is well known for its thieving by the Sutton school kids. When I say well known, I mean only well known by the Sutton people, mainly the police and the shopkeepers, it's not broadcast aloud to anyone outside. Oh no. But when the school leaving time arrives, Aldi, the other supermarkets, and the local pound shop go into overdrive. You can see the panic as they all gather en mass; the staff watch them like hawks as they swoop around the store, laughing and giggling. The cops won't want to know; many of the parents are very well off and have the resources to employ good solicitors and will insist on their little angels not being thieves but just young children having fun and doing what all children do. One lady, who had befriended my wife, lived on Monmouth Drive (Millionaires Row as it was once called) with a successful businessman husband and had a thirty-foot yacht on their drive.

Their two young sons had been caught bang to rights, nicking from the shops in Boldmere. Again, the cops were called, and they then called the parents. The wife admonished the police, who acted suitably humble, "Oh, for goodness sake, they were just children having fun, in high spirits. They were not stealing," of course, the boys were not arrested or charged. The shopkeepers later told my wife they were sick to death of them. "They're in here everyday thieving, and the cops do bugger all." Of course, all this was in the early days. We were to see more and more as time went on.

My daughter came in one day quite upset. A group of four of her friends had had a serious crash on Thornhill Road. Three died instantly, and the fourth, a friend of my daughter, survived but with serious injuries. It affected him so badly that he was later admitted to a mental institution due to the tragedy playing on his mind so much. One of them had nicked their parent's car and taken it for a joyride, as kids can do, of course, but they were all high on drugs as well. Thankfully, one of them was the son of the local police inspector who ensured that no mention was made of the drugs, only that they had borrowed the one car. That's fine, and yes, as it should be, it was just reported as a tragedy, but when it happens to some young kid from Aston, it's a different matter. The police highlight it to emphasise and explain the crash, "Ah, the little toe rags were on drugs." I found that many businesspeople were bent or inclined to larceny. They wouldn't go out and steal something; no, that is way too obvious. Only those with no brains and who are uneducated will do that. No, they nick it differently. They nick it legally. It's still nicking, but it's different if you see what I mean.

Richard Branson, the billionaire, was caught bang to rights defrauding customs and excise by illegally claiming VAT payments. He was given two choices: be charged and get done, hence a criminal record, or pay a fine of some twenty thousand pounds. This was some years ago when twenty grand was a lot of money. Fortunately, coming from a well-off middle-class family, Richard could put the bite on his dad, who coughed up the twenty grand and left Richard free to go on and make his millions. I like and admire Richard Branson, so I speak not from resentment or bitterness. Still, it was interesting that I read that a few years later, having established himself as an adventurer and businessman, he was hosting a big party and Bruce Reynolds, one of the great train robbers, crashed it and when Richard was made aware of him gave the guy a filthy look. He left shortly afterwards. To me, it begs the question, what makes him so different, and if he had come from the same background and had the same opportunity, would he have tried robbing the train? Make no mistake, he would nick just as much as anyone else. But as I was to find, nicking or defrauding the tax man or customs was legitimate.

My brother Reg came to see me one day, in awe of Sutton and its perceived reputation. When I told him, "Reg, trust me, there are more crooks around here than there ever were in Aston," he was shocked. But that's the rub, see. Living in Sutton woke me right up, and being in business woke me right up. The more time I spent in business, hotels, pubs or shops, the more corrupt I became. I became corrupt like the judges, politicians, and the other businessmen I've met. I learned that the only big difference between business and businessmen is that you have to understand the ground rules of business. The aim is to make money and make a profit. You are not the best pals. You might be friendly or friends, but you are in business.

In truth, the working class are their own worst enemy. The upper class, the ten per cent, and the bosses know this and rely on it to their advantage. Put three thousand men in a car factory, everyone is secretive about their wages, furtively hiding the contents from their colleagues as they shuffle through their wage slips, but they are all on the same fucking money. I grew up thinking backbiting, gossiping, and stabbing my fellow man or neighbour in the back was the norm. We are encouraged to inform on our neighbours of the slightest misdemeanour. Had half a pint too many? Ring the police. If we see anything suspicious, ring the police. We have become a nation of police informers; such is the norm and acceptance. It's now rippling through all classes, even into government, thankfully.

What better way to destroy someone than to inform and get them sacked? A throwback to Nazi Germany. Now the cops are running around like headless chickens trying to cherry-pick which complaints to look into; so many are there, we need more police, goes out the cry. No, we don't, we need fewer fucking complaints.

In return, we are given positions of importance and job titles commensurate with our standing in the community. There are over 12,000 job titles to describe every job held in the country, from the waste technician, i.e. Dustman, to the director, which sounds great but can mean very little. In the car factories, we now have line assemblers. Working at the Rover company many years ago, my job description was semi-skilled line technician. I was pushing grommets into the underbody of the car. A monkey could have done it. I lasted three weeks.

I will never know if it was like this in my dad's or granddad's days. I like to think it wasn't. Certainly, my dad tells me it wasn't. Back in his day, everyone was in the same boat. No one could put an act on as none of them had fuck all. We were all skint and trying to survive. If people argued, they did it face to face, got it off their chest, and then forgot it. Now, people go on and yearn for the good old days. Well, loosen up guys. The good old days are here, even better. The problem is, as people, we have changed for the worse. We are the next generation.

ABOUT THE AUTHOR

Tom Lewin is a successful semi-retired property developer and landlord, having had various businesses, including hotels, pubs, and campsites, with his beloved wife, Betty. He now spends much of his time touring Europe, visiting medieval towns, villages, and other places of interest, and writing books. This is his sixth book. His other books include:

Against the Odds, from the Slums of Summer Lane
The Climb Up and Away from the Slums of Summer Lane.
Touring Europe on a budget, and a wing and a prayer.
Happy camping around Europe
Meandering around England in a motorhome.

Please buy at least one to help keep him in the comfort he has become accustomed to. He can be found on TikTok and Instagram.

www.ingramcontent.com/pod-product-compliance
Lightning Source LLC
Chambersburg PA
CBHW030330200626
46816CB00006BA/1995